the
betrayal

the
betrayal

Laura Elliot

Bookouture

Published by Bookouture

An imprint of StoryFire Ltd.
23 Sussex Road, Ickenham, UB10 8PN
United Kingdom

www.bookouture.com

ISBN: 978-1-910751-34-3
eBook ISBN: 978-1-910751-33-6

Also by Laura Elliot

FRAGILE LIES
STOLEN CHILD
THE PRODIGAL SISTER

ACKNOWLEDGEMENTS

I'd like to acknowledge the many people who helped me with advice and encouragement throughout the writing of *The Betrayal*. First off, special thanks must go to my husband Sean who showed infinite patience throughout this process. He was always willing to read and comment on the latest draft and keep the coffee coming. To my family, Tony, who broke my day with his regular phone calls, Ciara for her thoughtful analysis of my story, and Michelle, who talked me down every time I insisted I was taking up bungee jumping as a less stressful hobby option to that of writing fiction. Thanks also to their spouses and partner, Roddy, Louise and Harry – and to my grandchildren, Romy and Ava who have brought such joy, laugher and love into my life.

I'd like to extend my appreciation to Sinead Mullally for her willingness to discuss the mysteries of the comatose state. To Patricia O'Reilly who regularly took time off from her busy writing career to meet and talk about *The Betrayal*.

Thank you to Oliver Rhodes and the team at Bookouture, my editor Claire Bord for her sensitive editing, Kim Nash for her enthusiastic promotional expertise and Lacey Decker for her eagle-eyed scrutiny of my finished manuscript. It has been a pleasure working with you.

My extended family, those close to home and those separated by continents, your steadfast support throughout my writing career has been invaluable. You've kept a firm hand on my back and your wise counsel has been much valued.

To my friends, too many to name, but always ready to phone and insist it's time to switch off the computer and meet for a catch-up chat and meal ...thank you for always being there.

Also, thanks to Faith O'Grady, my agent with whom I've worked closely over the years.

Finally, to my readers – the engine of every writer's career – thank you one and all for your loyalty, your letters, reviews and social media interaction. It is always a pleasure to hear from you.

DEDICATION

To Pauline, Louise and Ronan in Vancouver – oceans apart but always close.

Also dedicated to the memory of my much-loved brother-in-law, Don.

Part One

CHAPTER ONE

Nadine

A glimpse. That's all it takes. One glimpse as she steps from the taxi and I'm back there again, on the edge of a blade, waiting for the relief of another searing cut. I watch her go, her confident stride in tune with the sway of her pert behind. Karin Moylan is more beautiful that I remember, still the petite, hourglass figure, the dainty Cinderella feet. A scar from my teens opening on the turn of a heel. No time for hesitation. I ease back into my car and take refuge. What a coward I am. To hide from my past instead of confronting it with a nonchalant nod, a casual greeting, a polite enquiry about her mother's health... no... that's not possible. I watch as she enters the airport. The automatic doors open and close behind her. Able to breathe again, I turn my face towards Jake when he taps on the window to say goodbye. I slide the glass down. He leans forward to kiss me. His lips touch mine, a fleeting caress.

'Ring you when I get to New York,' he says.

'Have a safe flight.' My hands tighten on the steering wheel, my foot impatient on the accelerator as an authoritative voice on the public address system warns about the penalties of lingering overlong in the drop-off zone.

Jake grips his overnight case, his briefcase in his other hand. Years of experience have taught him to travel light. He follows in her footsteps and turns to wave at the entrance to Departures.

It's been raining all morning and the windscreen wipers swish briskly as I drive towards the Eastside Business Quarter. Did she see me when her taxi veered past my car and parked further along the drop-off zone? Her scarf fluttered like wings over her shoulders. I'd forgotten how she always favoured blue plumage. Would Jake notice her among the crowd of passengers surging through Departures? Would he recognise her if he did? I fight back panic, shake my head. Too many years have passed since that summer in Monsheelagh and their time together was fleeting.

I could ring Jenny when I reach the office but she's probably asleep. The eight-hour time difference between here and Vancouver spoils any chance of an impulsive conversation. I'll ring her later this evening when I'm calmer.

Shock recedes. It has no place else to go as my day gathers momentum. With Jake away we're one down in Tōnality, the company we run together, and most of my morning is spent tracking a lost consignment of mandolins that was supposed to be en route to us from China. The lost mandolins are traced and rerouted back to us via Rotterdam. I work throughout the afternoon on a new marketing strategy for the STRUM brand. The business park is empty by the time I set the security alarm and close the shutters. No one hangs around here in the evenings. It's too soulless, too uniform with its cube-like buildings and parallel roads. Jake calls it a battery coop, a place to labour and leave when the day is done.

The silence of the empty house bears down on me when I open the front door. I should eat something; rustle up a pasta, grill a steak. In the end I scramble eggs and toast bread. The kitchen glistens, chrome and granite, honey-toned wood. Four years ago, when we moved here from our modest three-bedroom house on Oakdale Terrace, I joked with Jake that we'd need a skateboard to work this kitchen. I've become accustomed to my spacious surroundings but now, with everyone gone, the atmosphere feels different, filled with unresolved issues. The weight of lives lived separately within its walls.

My footsteps seem unnaturally loud as I walk across the marble tiles. A pair of shoes that Jake decided against bringing to New York lie in the hall. I carry them upstairs to our bedroom and place them on the shoe rack. The bed is as tossed as we left it this morning, our pillows still dented. I kick off my high heels and lace up my trainers, change into a track suit. A run will pound her out of my head.

Could I have imagined her? I've done so in the past, glimpsed a swirl of blonde hair and found myself staring into the blank, blue gaze of a stranger. This woman's hair was short, sculpted to her scalp. Perhaps I was mistaken, hassled by traffic jams and having to drop Jake off at the airport. But why that sudden shocked recognition? My skin lifting as if electrified by memory? No, I was not mistaken.

The gates of Bartizan Downs slowly slide apart. I turn right and drive towards Malahide. The village is quiet, apart from a trickle of people emerging from the railway station and a few smokers standing outside Duffy's pub. I turn down Old Street and head towards the estuary shore where strollers, joggers and dog walkers come in the evening to close off their day. I love this place, with its shrieking seagulls and stately swans. The rain has stopped but the clouds are heavy with the threat of more to follow. It will be dark soon. Already, Sea Aster is invisible on the opposite shore. I lived there with Jake when we were first married. Gentle Rosanna with her camera and binoculars gave us succour when we were desperate. Does her ghost hover over the old house, trapped by the threads of memory? Three months since her death. All that wonderful bird knowledge ebbing away on her last breath. It was her time to go but I still feel the raw grief of her passing. The house belongs to Eleanor now but she will never love it as her mother did.

I'm tired by the time I return to Bartizan Downs. Lights blaze from neighbouring windows. We don't draw our curtains here. We're gated and protected, fortified against each other and from the world outside by high walls. I shower and slip on my pyjamas.

Jenny is at her desk when I ring Vancouver, her printer clattering beside her. She listens without interruption while I tell her about this chance sighting.

'Are you sure it was Karin?' she asks when I pause for breath.

'I'm almost positive. Her hair's short now but she still has that cut-glass profile.'

A second phone keeps ringing and interrupting our conversation. 'Hold on, Nadine. I'd better take this.' She sounds distracted.

'You're busy. I'll go. I just wanted to tell you about her.'

'No, *wait*.' She speaks briefly to someone than comes back to me. 'I can't believe she still has the power to upset you so much.'

'Neither can I.' Once again I experience that breathless jolt of recognition.

'It's so long ago,' Jenny says. 'What happened was not your fault. You've worked through it. You've moved on. Don't let her get to you again. She's not, and never was, important.'

'I'm sorry I interrupted you.'

'You didn't interrupt me.' Her voice sharpens. 'Are you listening to me, Nadine?'

'Yes... yes.'

'Ring me anytime you want to talk some more about this. Promise.'

'I will. How's work?'

'We're wrapping up the documentary. It's always manic at this stage. Is everything okay in Tōnality?'

'Business could be better,' I admit. 'This recession is getting worse.'

'I keep reading the financial reports. It sounds grim.' The second phone rings again. 'Hold on a minute. I'll switch this off.'

'No, take it Jenny. You've obviously up to your eyes. I'll be in touch soon. Love you.'

'Love you, too.'

Then she's gone, back to her world of ozone layers and climate change and melting icecaps. Her documentaries are more scary than a zombie movie. She's my best friend, wise and sensitive–and has had her heart severely broken on two occasions. When she gives advice I listen.

Karin Moylan Never Was Important.

CHAPTER TWO

Jake

Some people play with worry beads when they are stressed, others attend a shrink. Jake Saunders used music. As an escape route it never failed him and now, with an hour to kill before he boarded his flight to New York, he opened his laptop and plugged in his earphones. He replayed the last recording he had made. A melody with potential, he decided, but the lyrics were weak. Hackneyed lines that made him wince. He needed to hack down to the heart of the song. A long goodbye to a love affair. The relationship over but the dependency on togetherness too ingrained to allow for separation. Art reflecting life; it was a thought too close for comfort.

Nadine's abrupt departure at the airport bothered him. Her expression had been so distant as she stared at him through the car window that, for an instant, he thought she was going to drive away without saying goodbye. Her mood changed so easily these days. The pressure of running Tōnality was taking its toll on both of them. The impact of an empty house, their parenting done. This should be their time to wind down. Instead, they were locked into a recession and a debt that was balanced like a rock on their shoulders.

The boarding area gradually filled up. Jake bent lower over his laptop and tried to ignore the pungent garlic fumes emanating from the man sitting beside him. He should be working on the spreadsheet for Ed Jaworski instead of wasting time on a song that was certain to remain unsung. He had a drawer full of such songs. Half-finished ideas that inevitably fizzled out when some new emergency at work took over.

His neighbour stood up and stretched, strode towards the toilets. His seat was immediately taken by a woman. Her perfume battled against the garlic fumes and won. Jake breathed deeply. The perfume Nadine used was light and floral but this was heavy and curiously intimate, as if the scent had been blended in a moist, exotic jungle. She opened a magazine, flicked pages, crossed her legs: small, slender feet, blue shoes, sheer tights. He stole a sideways glance at her. Mid-thirties, maybe older, he guessed. There was a maturity about her full, glossy mouth, and her blonde hair, short and brushed back from her forehead in a quiff would only be worn by a woman confident enough to know she could carry off such a chiselled image and still look beautiful.

Earlier, he had noticed her when he was going through security. Something about the tilt of her head as she spoke to an official looked familiar. The impression was so vague that she had passed through the security gates and out of his mind until now.

A collective groan arose from the passengers when an announcement informed them that their flight to New York would be delayed. She closed her magazine, tapped her fingers against the cover. Her nails, perfect ovals, were painted an iridescent blue. He switched off his laptop. Impossible to concentrate. He hated airports. The ruthless security routine, the slumped wait in the boarding area and the eventual slow shuffle aboard after unexplained delays. He accidentally jogged her elbow as he removed his earphones.

'Sorry.' He rubbed the back of his neck in frustration. 'I wonder what's caused the delay?'

'Some technical hitch, I guess.' She stood up and buttoned her jacket. 'I'm going for a coffee. Can I bring something back for you?'

'Why don't I go with you?' He put the laptop in his overnight case and zipped it. 'Stretch my legs. We'll be sitting long enough when we finally get on board.'

He slowed his stride as they walked towards the coffee bar. The women in his life were tall and long-limbed, his wife and mother, his two daughters. Everything about this woman was petite, from the crown of her head to the toes of her high-heeled shoes. He insisted on paying for cappuccinos and two Danishes, which he carried to a nearby table.

'Will the delay affect you?' she asked when they were seated. She sounded Irish but her accent, with its slight drag on the vowels, suggested she had been living for some time in New York.

'I've to attend a business meeting but it's not until tomorrow,' he replied. 'What about you? Business or pleasure?'

'I live in New York.' She removed her jacket and hung it from the back of the chair. Her dress was sleeveless with a low V in front, the hem resting primly on her knees.

He stretched out his hand. 'I'm Jake.'

'I know who you are.' She shook his hand and tilted her head, a half-smile tugging at her lips. 'You're *the* Jake Saunders from Shard.'

He felt a once-familiar and long-forgotten buzz of recognition.

'I'm flattered that you remember.'

'Oh, I *do* remember.' She held out her arm, the inside exposed, and ran her fingers along the pale skin. 'This is where you once signed your autograph.'

'I'm sorry…' He struggled for a name, an occasion, a place to remember her by. How many autographs had he signed? Thousands, probably, writing his name with a flourish for the young women who called out to him as they waited outside the pubs and clubs, their arms and autograph books an extension of their thrusting, nubile bodies. 'I'm afraid you'll have to enlighten me.'

'I'm Karin Moylan.' She spoke with the certainty of someone who knew her name would bring instant recollection.

'Karin Moylan… I don't believe it.' The memory came back to him in disjointed flashes. The holiday, the music, and Karin, a waifish shadow against the glow of Nadine with her blaze of red hair and long, coltish legs. 'I'd never have recognised you. No… that's not true. Now that you say it…' He stopped, embarrassed as he attempted to join the fragments of that holiday together. What was the name of the place where they stayed? Somewhere in West Clare, he remembered. Fishing boats and a cliff, a golden beach and long sunshine days. A ramshackle house where he, along with the lads who made up the band, had stayed for a month to work on their first album.

'Monsheelagh,' she said, as if picking up his thoughts. 'I was on holiday with my parents.' Her eyes, slightly too large for her small, heart-shaped face, had a disconcerting directness when she added, 'Nadine was staying with us.'

'Yes,' he said. 'I remember.'

'How is she? It's been so long since I've seen her.'

'She's good. Busy, as we all are these days.'

'I was studying in London when I heard about your marriage. You were both so young.' Her voice dropped a tone, donating pity. 'I hope everything worked out for you.'

'Yes, it did.' He resented her pity and rushed defensively to banish it. 'We've a good life and four terrific kids.'

'I never meant to lose touch with her but you know the way it is.' Her scarf rippled when she shrugged, the material so light and gauzy it seemed as if a deep breath would float it from her shoulders. 'Our lives veered off in different directions but I've never forgotten her.'

'These things happen,' he agreed.

'I still imagined you with long hair and those wild tiger streaks.'

'The streaks went a long time ago,' he admitted. 'So did the wildness. These days I'm one of society's staunchest pillars.'

'Oh, I don't know about that.' She tilted her head again, a finger pressed to her cheek. 'You still have that look… you know… slightly edgy, alternative.'

It was pathetic to be flattered so easily. His black hair was slightly longer than the norm, his style of dressing more casual, and he still had the rangy physique of his youth but, in truth, Jake felt indistinguishable from the other grey-suited business-men swarming from the business park every evening with their laptops, briefcases and mortgages.

'What about you?' he asked. 'What have you been doing with yourself?'

'I run a graphic design agency in New York,' she replied. 'But I'm considering moving back to Dublin after Christmas. My mother has some health issues and I'm an only child.'

'Nothing too serious, I hope?'

'She'll be fine. She always is.' Her sigh was almost inaudible but Jake understood the depths of frustration it carried.

A voice boomed over the loudspeaker and drowned his reply. Their flight was ready for boarding.

'We'd better go.' She stood up and brushed imaginary crumbs from her dress, buttoned her jacket, adjusted her scarf.

'See you in New York,' she said when they boarded the plane and made their way to their allocated seats.

'Enjoy the flight.' He continued down the aisle and settled into a seat four rows behind her on the opposite side. What a strange coincidence to bump into each other after all that time. Her profile was visible as she removed her jacket. She was unable to reach the baggage hold above her and the man beside her stowed her jacket away. He was young and heavy-set, his square face framed by a mop of black curls and a startlingly long beard. Earphones the size of saucers rested on his shoulders.

When the last of the passengers were seated and the cabin crew had closed the overhead lockers, she slanted her legs to one side and allowed him to leave his seat. He hurried down the aisle and hunkered beside Jake.

'Your friend's asked me to swap places,' he whispered. 'It's no problem, mate. She's shit scared of flying and to be honest, no offence, but it's a long flight. If she's gonna use that sick bag I'd prefer it to be on your time, not mine.'

'No problem.' Jake almost laughed out loud at Karin's woebegone expression when she turned to look back at him.

'I hope I haven't been presumptuous,' she said when he sat beside her and clicked the safety belt. 'The thought of interacting with that beard for the entire flight was more than I could handle.'

'I can imagine.' He was conscious of her bare arm on the armrest between them, the heady waft of perfume. The engines growled and the cabin staff began to outline the safety instructions.

'Inflating your life jacket as the plane goes down must be the most ineffective way of spending your last moments on earth,' she said as the plane taxied down the runway.

'How would you spend them?' he asked.

She look thoughtful, as if visualising the downward plunge, and replied, 'hopefully, in the arms of my lover.'

He wondered whose arms would hold her if the plane plummeted from the skies. It seemed too blatant a question to ask. Enquiries about a wife and family were okay. Pallid information. But a lover…how could that be phrased? Is your lover married? Are *you* married and having an affair? Is your lover a he or a she? Jake took nothing for granted.

Tiny blue gemstones sparkled on her ring as she stretched upwards to adjust the air conditioning.

'Allow me,' he said.

The jolt of pleasure was instantaneous when their hands touched. No wedding ring, he noted as the cool air flowed over their faces.

'Are you going to New York for business or pleasure?' she asked.

'Purely business,' he said. 'I'm only staying two nights.'

'Do you go there often?'

'About four times a year. Trade shows, business meetings, that sort of thing.'

'Are they always flying visits?'

'Not always. We usually manage a show or two while we're there.'

The 'we' slipped out like an unintended hiccup.

'We?' She quizzed him.

'Nadine runs the company with me.'

'Business and marriage,' she mused. 'Is that a difficult combination to manage?'

'Not really. We've been doing it for a long time.'

'I don't think I could work with someone that close to me. It would be claustrophobic. I need my own space.' The swell of her bottom lip suggested there was turbulence behind her smiling demeanour.

'Except when you're on a plunging plane and need your lover's arms around you.' The conversation had come full circle and Jake was pleased at his adroitness.

'I'll have to find one first. Unlike you and Nadine, I haven't been so lucky in love. No husband, no children... not even a lover.'

'I refuse to believe you. Any guy would...' He hesitated, suddenly uncertain if he wanted to continue the conversation.

'Would what?' she prompted softly.

'Consider himself the luckiest guy in the world.' He could no longer pretend he was not flirting with her. What harm? A mild flirtation always alleviated the boredom of a long flight.

'When you find him, package him and send him on to me by first class mail.' Like her perfume, her laughter had a tantalising intimacy, as if everything outside the space they shared was of no importance.

'I'll need an address first.'

She opened her handbag and handed her business card to him. Kingfisher Graphics. The logo was a kingfisher, glossy blue feathers that matched her eyes.

'Tonality.' She glanced at the business card he slipped from his wallet. 'That's an unusual name. What kind of business do you run?'

'We supply musical instruments. From mouth organs to church organs and everything in between for sale or hire. If you ever need anything....'

'All I can play is the tambourine.'

He glanced quickly at her and away again. Was that a throwaway remark or one loaded with significance? Impossible to tell by her expression. This was the moment to say something meaningful about that holiday but would they be the right words? And would she want to hear them after… how long? Twenty-four, twenty-five years?

'Nadine wanted to be an artist,' she said. 'What a pity it didn't work out for her. She was good. I couldn't draw a straight line yet I ended up becoming a graphic designer.'

'Do you specialise in a specific area of graphic design?' He took his lead from her. Let the past rest in peace.

'It varies from commission to commission,' she replied. 'My latest contract is with a film company.'

'That sounds exciting.'

'It can be, especially when it's a historical film, as this one is. I'm researching the props we need from that period, signage, calligraphy, portraits. I could go on and on. It's fascinating to dip in and out of the past, don't you think?'

He leaned his head against the headrest, content to listen to her. Clouds lay below them, gossamer mountains rimmed with gold.

When the plane landed at JFK he waited with her while she reclaimed her luggage. She lived in the East Village. A fire escape on the outside of her apartment and a view of the city to die for, she said. Should he ask to view it with her? Suggest meeting for an evening meal? A stroll in Central Park? Hot dogs on Coney Island? Usually the women he met on such flights occupied his thoughts for a day or so until they became an amalgamation of all the other flights he had taken, the similar conversations he had enjoyed, the ignited spark that was always extinguished once he landed on terra firma. But Karin Moylan was not a stranger. She came with a past and its potency had grown during their journey together.

'Perhaps when you return to Dublin we could get together…?' He allowed his words to trail into a question.

'It would be nice to see Nadine again.' Their gaze locked for a fraction longer than politeness demanded. 'If that is what you have in mind?'

'I'm sure that could be arranged,' he replied. 'If that's what *you* have in mind.'

She fanned his business card before her face and smiled. 'I'll ring you when I come back,' she said. 'Perhaps we'll have decided by then.'

CHAPTER THREE

Nadine

Twilight is settling over Broadmeadow Estuary as I drive along Mallard Cove. Coots, oyster catchers and greenshanks forage between the mottled green islets of the bird sanctuary and the swans, noticing my car, waddle ashore seeking bread. The wind is brisk and the windsurfers, curving into its power, glide across the water. Eleanor is already parked outside Sea Aster. A glance at her watch rebukes me for being ten minutes late. I don't react. I've learned to save my energy for the big battles. This is my first time to return to Sea Aster since Rosanna suffered the massive stroke that confined her to a nursing home. The ivy that once burnished the walls in a coppery glow throughout the autumn has been removed and Sea Aster looks almost indecently naked with its stark, grey exterior, the sharp apexes and curved bay window.

When it was obvious Rosanna would never again return to her home, Eleanor had the house renovated into two apartments, one up, one down, two separate entrances. She sounded nervous when she rang Tōnality earlier today. She had hoped Jake would meet her here this evening. He's still in New York so I offered to come in his stead. My mother-in-law does not normally display signs of nervousness. Rushing headlong into confrontation is more her style but the tenant who rented Sea

Aster, and has now left, proved to be a match for her. The battle to evict her when her lease expired was prolonged and bitter. Eleanor received some threatening phone calls so she's right to be cautious. Sea Aster is isolated and cries for help would only be heard by swans.

'When did the ivy go?' I ask as we walk towards the front door.

'I had it removed during the conversion,' Eleanor replies. 'It was too unruly.'

Unruliness. A cardinal sin in her book.

When she opens the front door I'm dismayed to see how the hall's once-elegant dimensions have been divided by a crude plasterboard wall. My dismay turns to shock as we climb the stairs to Apartment 1. Strips of wallpaper have been torn from the walls and graffiti sprayed on the ceiling. Flies swarm against the windows. A hole has been kicked in one of the doors. The smell of overflowing ashtrays competes against the stink of cat urine. In the living room we draw back in disgust when we discover cat turds on the carpet. Containers carrying the congealed remains of four-cheese pizzas litter the table and floor.

'I'm photographing everything.' Eleanor's rage grows as she surveys her inheritance. 'This is what happens when promiscuity and anti-social behaviour are allowed to run riot.'

I offer to organise a swat team of fumigators, cleaners, and a vermin death squad. The mouse droppings in the kitchen suggest that the tenant's cats was useless at anything except dumping its load behind the living-room sofa.

'That won't be necessary.' She waves my offer aside. 'The whole interior will be gutted.'

'There's no need to gut the house,' I protest. 'This is disgusting but it's only superficial damage. The ceilings… those carvings. The graffiti can be removed without damaging them.'

'Gutted,' Eleanor repeats. 'It's the only way to make a fresh start.'

She has no feelings for Sea Aster. It wasn't her childhood home and she never understood why her mother, a passionate bird-watcher and amateur photographer, decided to leave her comfortable bungalow in suburbia when her husband died and move here. She's particularly fixated on a pair of black lacy stockings tied to a bedpost in one of the bedrooms. Six potted cannabis plants wilt on the dressing table. Jake and I once slept in this bedroom. Now, it's defiled, revolting. Eleanor continues taking photographs. She will do a Powerpoint presentation with those images. The members of First Affiliation will love them. They are the standard bearers for family values, a fringe political party that believes society will fall apart if their members, led by Eleanor, don't keep a strict and watchful eye on the moral status quo. She plans to convert the old house into their headquarters. Their current premises has damp issues and a lease that's due to expire soon.

We leave the odorous atmosphere behind and walk around to the back of the house. To Eleanor's relief, Apartment 2 on the ground floor has been left in pristine condition. She shakes her head when I invite her back to Bartizan Downs for something to eat. She has a meeting to attend and a speech to write before she goes to bed tonight. Work on converting the house will begin as soon as she receives planning permission to change its use from residential to First Affiliation's headquarters.

I drive towards the gates of Sea Aster and pass the old stone barn where Tonality first began. Darkness fell while we were inside, and the windsurfers have folded up their sails. Swans are clustered close to shore and a heron stands impassive and still in the shallows.

Rosanna wanted her ashes to float across this estuary on a slow, eddying tide. Eleanor refused point blank to even discuss the possibility of a cremation. An ad hoc scattering of ashes would be an undignified and messy ending to her mother's long, active life, she insisted when I argued that it was Rosanna's dying wish. She had her way in the end and Rosanna is buried with her husband, a boring man who, she once told me, had defined his identity by the club crest on his blazer and made love to her in the missionary position every Saturday night. At least on this occasion Rosanna is on top. *Stop...* I resist the urge to laugh out loud and swallow, suddenly close to tears as I apologise to Rosanna for being unable to organise the simple ceremony she desired. Will the members of First Affiliation appreciate their new headquarters? Or will they be too busy plotting strategies to notice the rugged beauty surrounding them? I suspect the latter.

An arts programme plays on the car radio as I drive along Mallard Cove. A female poet describes how her latest bout of depression inspired her new collection of poetry. You and me both, I think. But I'm not depressed. Just... what? 'Flat' is the only word that comes to mind. Seeing life in a pale, predictive palette sounds more descriptive. The depressed poet would forgive the alliteration and approve.

Jake insists I'm suffering from empty nest syndrome. Four children leaving home in the space of two years does take some adjusting yet I'm glad for all of them. Proud that they're following their dreams. That's X-Factor-speak, but it's true. Last year we said goodbye to Ali, our eldest, as she headed to London and a career on the stage. A month later Brian dropped out of art college and moved to the Dingle peninsula where he lives in the shadow of a mountain and crafts beautiful shapes. Then we said goodbye to our twins Sam and Samantha when they left for Silver Ridge University. The fact that we produced not one, but two elite athletes is a never-ending source of amazement to us. We were aware of their speed from the first time they stood upright and tottered forward on long, sturdy legs. Now, the years of training have paid off and they've started a four-year athletic scholarship in California.

The heron dips its beak and the water flurries as an unfortunate fish is snapped from life. Triumphantly, its supper assured, the heron lifts its broad wings and flies away. Herons have no need for monogamy. Jenny made a nature documentary about them once. They mate to breed, good and dutiful parents, sharing incubation and feeding. But when their chicks are independent, ready to take their own paths through life, the parents return to their solitary vigils. To their solitary freedom.

The radio presenter introduces a travel writer who has just launched a book about his travels in Papua New Guinea. Instantly, Karin Moylan comes to mind… again. Ants on my skin, heart lurching. Is this what sufferers of post-traumatic stress experience when the past whizzes like a bullet through their memory?

I meet her mother occasionally, and always by accident. Joan Moylan is polite and sober yet I still visualise her stretched on a sofa or in bed, the duvet drawn tight, her gaze unfocused, the smell of stale alcohol on her breath. Sometimes, when it's impossible to avoid speaking, we hold brief conversations about the weather and the price of groceries and how the cost of property has gone beyond ridiculous. We never talk about that summer in Monsheelagh, yet it's moving in slow motion in front of our eyes. No wonder we hurry from each other in mutual relief.

I ring Jake when I return home but he's not picking up. New York time means he's probably still in meetings with Ed Jaworski.

I detest Ed, with his phallic cigars and New York abrasiveness, but he's the reason Tōnality changed from being a moderately successful supplier of musical instruments into the European distributors for STRUM. It's a far cry from the early days when Jake worked from the barn in Sea Aster and Tōnality just consisted of a few guitars and drums for sale or hire. His brief fame with Shard — the band that almost made it internationally — had given him a certain cachet within the music industry, especially among the up-and-coming young bands who hoped to go one step further and actually make it. Within a few years he was able to move to Ormond Quay in the heart of the city. Tōnality became the place for young musicians to hang out, to check the guitars, have a roll on the drums, a tinkle on the piano. I joined him when the twins started school and took over the marketing side of the business. We set up a coffee bar and held open mic nights, impromptu music sessions. And that's how we would have continued if we hadn't met Ed Jaworski at a trade fair and took on the STRUM brand of saxophones, recorders, trumpets, ukuleles and mandolins. We expanded from our cramped city premises to the Eastside Business Quarter with its brash, modern offices and spacious warehouse. I can park here and move without fear of bumping into guitars but I still miss the sway of the Liffey outside the window, the footsteps of passing pedestrians stirring the heartbeat of the city.

Tonight I eat well. A steak and salad, two glasses of wine. I enter my home office and wait for Jake to ring. I switch on my laptop and bring up the new marketing plan for STRUM. The demarcation line between home and work has become increasingly blurred these days and this office is as cluttered as the one in Tōnality.

It's after eleven and there's still no word from Jake. I shower and slip on my pyjamas, apply night cream. The lines around my eyes look deeper, more ingrained. Laugh lines, as they're euphemistically called. I see nothing funny about them. They're chipping away at my youth when I still have to discover what it's like to be young and carefree. Why hasn't he rung? He knows how anxious I am about his meeting with Ed. This recession is relentless and Ed will be disappointed with the latest STRUM figures. They are within the agreed growth margin but Ed expects more. The concept of squeezing blood from a stone is not something he understands.

My phone is out of charge. No wonder Jake hasn't been able to get through. I ring him on the landline. Evening time in New York and he's heading out for a meal. He sounds rushed, his phone on speaker. His echoing tone fills me with alarm.

'What's wrong, Jake?'

'I've been trying to ring you all afternoon,' he says. 'Where were you?'

I explain about Sea Aster and my phone being out of charge but I sense he's not listening.

'How did the meeting with Ed go?' I ask.

'I'll tell you about it when I'm home,' he replies.

'Tell me now,' I demand. 'What's happened?'

'I'd rather not discuss it over the phone.'

'Have we lost the STRUM account?'

His silence confirms my worst fears. My mind goes into overdrive, calculating lost business, lost reputation, lost everything we've struggled so hard to achieve.

'But why, Jake? Our sales figures are bang on target.'

'He's pulling out of our contract in case this recession affects the brand. He says it's nothing personal.'

'But that's ridiculous. He can't break our contract because he *thinks* there could be a slowdown in business.'

'We'll fight this all the way.' Jake sounds too hearty, too confident.

'You know what that will entail. We can't afford a long, drawn-out legal battle.'

'Look, Nadine, I'm heading out for a bite to eat and I'm exhausted. STRUM is not the be all and end all of our company. We've other equally strong brands and we'll acquire more. Right now, all I want to do is wind down for a few hours and get my head together. We'll talk about everything tomorrow when I'm home. Try not to worry. With or without STRUM, we'll get through this crisis.'

He's closing down the conversation and there's nothing I can do except agree that we'll cope, as we always do, and survive. 'Enjoy your meal, Jake. I'll pick you up at the airport tomorrow.'

Distance helps us to pretend. We're unable to look into the whites of each other's eyes and see our panic reflected there. But there's something else on his mind. I sense his hesitation before he says goodbye. I can always tell. We're capable of simultaneous thoughts, which we often speak aloud in the same instant or exclaim, 'That's *exactly* what I was going to say.' The twins also have the same capacity for synchronised expression, but that's to do with a split zygote whereas Jake and I have simply developed a hybrid mentality.

CHAPTER FOUR

Jake

He arrived before her and took a seat at the bar adjoining the restaurant. A pianist in an embossed, velvet jacket played softly on a grand piano. A candelabra blazed on top of the piano and orchids in a moon-shaped vase emitted a faint scent of vanilla. Karin Moylan entered shortly afterwards, aware but indifferent to the eyes that followed her as she walked towards him. Shrine was her favourite restaurant in New York, she told him as they sipped an aperitif. Her dress was black and figure-hugging, accessorised by an elaborately coiled blue necklace.

The waiter led them to a table for two in a secluded alcove at the back of the restaurant. Lights shimmered on the ceiling and picture windows overlooked a leafy view of Central Park. Over lemon sole and wood-fired tiger prawns, she told him about the cities where she had lived and worked: London, Paris, Milan, New York. She kept him amused between courses with gossipy, witty anecdotes about the celebrities she had met on various film sets. Jake suspected she had told the same stories many times but he was content to listen and be entertained by her. The relief of not talking about business was overwhelming. Reality was outside, clawing to get back in but for these few hours he would keep it at bay.

Earlier today, shell-shocked and furious, he had gone straight from STRUM's headquarters to his hotel and tried to ring Nadine. Only she would understand the enormity of what had occurred. Her mobile phone had been switched off. Tōnality was closed for the night and the house phone remained unanswered. He had ordered a whiskey at the hotel bar when his mobile bleeped and a text arrived. He checked the ID screen, expecting to see Nadine's name but only a number was displayed, an unfamiliar one with a New York prefix.

You were a blast from the past, Jake Saunders, he read. *Good to see you again. Hope all went well at your business meeting today. Best for now, Karin.*

He had forgotten her in the turmoil of the day but her text nudged him briefly from his misery.

Difficult meeting, he replied. *But it was worth the trip to see you again.*

He could have stopped it there and then. Instead, he added a question that sought an answer. *How are you?*

I'm good, she texted back. *But you sound like you're having a rough time. New York can be a bruising bitch. Anything I can do to help? K.*

The decision to ask her out for a meal was the easiest one he had made all day. The alternative was to find a bar with photos of faded movie stars on the walls and spend the night drinking himself into oblivion. It was the thing to do in New York... to do anywhere… when a momentous decision was delivered with a one-punch knock-out body blow.

He was getting ready to meet her when Nadine finally contacted him. Her worried intake of breath, the pitch of her voice crashed him back to earth. He resisted the urge to hang up. To shut down the worry and the guilt and sink, instead, into amnesia, even if only for a few hours. He should have mentioned meeting Karin. They were best friends once yet Nadine never spoke about their friendship, never mentioned her name. Throughout that holiday in Monsheelagh they had seemed inseparable but, two years later, when he and Nadine exchanged sultry glances of recognition through the slash of lasers and dazzling strobes, she told him their friendship was over. She had gone backstage with Jenny to see him after the gig and made it clear that she had no intention of discussing Karin Moylan.

'But I thought the two of you were best mates,' he said. 'What happened?'

'I don't want to talk about her.' Her voice had been clipped and hard. 'Not now, not *ever.*'

Over the years that followed she remained true to her word, which was hardly surprising when he thought about how their holiday ended. The memory would be indelible, especially for Karin, but throughout the meal she never once referred to Nadine or that summer.

'Do you ever regret leaving Shard?' she asked when they returned to the bar for an after dinner drink. 'You were going stratosphere in those days. What was it the media called you? Ireland's answer to… Metallica?'

'It was actually Guns n' Roses,' he admitted, modestly. He admired the perfect curves of her knees as she crossed her legs.

Was she wearing tights or stockings with lace tops, he wondered. Was there a smooth, silken gap of skin between her thighs and the line of her panties? He was familiar with female underwear, the frippery and the functional, hanging on clotheslines, drying over radiators, knickers, thongs, tights and bras tumbling from the hot press when he was searching for socks in the mornings. But this was an alluring fantasy and very different from the detritus of family living.

'Of course it was,' she said. 'Guns n' Roses… my goodness. How life changes. Selling musical instruments instead of playing them must have been quite a difficult transition for you.'

Was she mocking him? He flattened his anger. These days it lay dangerously close to the surface.

Nadine had asked him once, soon after Shard broke up in a storm of recriminations and accusations, if the band had seen her as a Yoko Ono, responsible for causing friction between them. It was a grandiose comparison yet, in her own way, she had upset the agreement that parents or girlfriends should not interfere with Shard's upward projection and ambitions. He had assured her she was not to blame. Ultimately, it all came down to his inept use of a condom. Such inattention to detail altered everything.

'Circumstances change,' he said.

'Sacrifices. We all make them sooner or later.' Karin lifted a tiny umbrella from her cocktail glass and twirled it between her thumb and index finger. 'Do you ever think about reforming the band?'

'Occasionally.' He shrugged. 'But then I think about walking on the moon. We all have our dreams.'

'But why is it a dream? Bands are always making comebacks these days. Shard had a brilliant reputation.'

'You're talking a long time ago. Who do you think remembers us now?'

'You'd be surprised. It's a new era. Social media. Facebook. YouTube. You could get the message out quickly enough.'

He shook his head. 'If only it was so easy. Tōnality takes all my time these days.'

'You'd another life before Tōnality.'

'I never had a chance to have another life.' It came out unintentionally, the resentment he usually managed to hide and Karin, aware that she had touched a nerve, drew back slightly.

'Sorry. I'm being intrusive.'

'It's okay. It's just… it's a while since I've talked to anyone about Shard.'

'Are you still in touch with the band?'

'I meet Daryl occasionally, but I haven't seen the others for years. Reedy is the only one still professionally involved in music. Twenty-five years is a long time to keep a dream going but he's managed it.'

'Twenty-five years?'

'Since we did our first gig.'

'You should do a reunion gig.' She twirled the cocktail umbrella one last time and placed it back in the glass, signalled to the barman for a refill. 'Think how wonderful that would be. All those fans dying for an excuse to organise babysitters and relive their youth. You owe it to them.'

He shook his head. 'It's a wonderful idea but impossible. I've more than enough going on in my life at the moment.'

'Be warned, Jake Saunders. To squander our creativity is to displease the gods. Nothing is impossible if we decide otherwise.' She trailed her middle finger lightly along the back of his hand. 'Will you tell Nadine we met tonight?'

'I suspect not…'

'Don't you think she'd understand? Two old friends catching up on the past.'

'Is that what tonight is?' His skin tingled at her touch, the slow, deliberate stroke that was almost an itch and the urge to draw her hand downwards, not to tease but to hold him, the hard width of him, aroused and wanting, blinded him to everything that was going on around them.

'It's whatever you want it to be,' she said. 'Like that night in Barney's Bar. Do you remember?' She paused and waited for him to fill the silence.

'Yes, I remember.' The shock of that memory jolted him from his fantasy. 'It must have been a heartbreaking time for you.'

'I'm talking about *us*, Jake,' she interrupted him, her voice quickening. 'Just the two of us together in that little snug. Things could have been so different, if only…' Her features tautened as if she, like him, was picturing the small harbour bar in Monsheelagh, its whitewashed walls and black wooden beams. Noisy, smoky, crowded with jostling young people who had come from the holiday homes and caravans to hear the band. He had signed his name on her honey-tanned skin and she had kissed him for good luck in the tiny, old-fashioned snug before the gig began. Later, she had stepped onto the makeshift stage and lifted a tambourine from one of the amplifiers. Nothing waifish about her then as she raised it above her head, her slight body swaying, the swing of her long, blonde hair…and afterwards when everything fell apart, the panic she must she have felt as the storm raged around her.

He stared at their empty cocktail glasses, a smear of lipstick on hers. She had been drinking that night too. She was only fifteen then. Reedy, who was the eldest of the five band members, had ordered a vodka at her insistence and smuggled it into the snug. It was probably her first time drinking. No wonder she was so frenzied when she climbed onto the stage.

'A last one for the road?' He nodded towards their glasses but she shook her head.

'Don't let your dreams die, Jake,' she whispered into his ear. 'It can happen so easily. We have to fight to walk our own path. Think about that reunion gig. A Shard retrospective.' She draped her pashmina over her shoulders. The deep blue weave matched the colour of her eyes and the trimming of silver thread glinted under the overhanging chandeliers. 'But we've talked enough for one night. It's time you took me home.'

Outside the restaurant she hailed a cab. They were silent on the short ride to her apartment. It was as she had described, brownstone, high steps, a fire escape jutting over the entrance. She opened her bag and removed a key. Her pashmina slipped from one shoulder, exposing the depth of her cleavage, the smooth length of her arm.

'I'd invite you up for a nightcap but this is not the right time,' she said. 'You've a lot on your mind and an early flight to catch in the morning.'

'You're very astute,' he said. 'Work's tough at the moment. I'm sorry it showed.'

'It didn't.' She stretched upwards and kissed his cheek. 'Thank you for a wonderful night, Jake.'

He took the cab back to his hotel and allowed the fantasies that had teased him throughout the night to fade. He was relieved rather than disappointed by her decision. He tried to understand this relief. Was it caused by fear or fidelity? Despite occasional torrid fantasies that always petered out under the pressures of work and family Jake had been a faithful husband.

Was it uncertainty that scared him off? Fear of failing in the bedroom? No, remembering her alluring eyes, the seductive swell of her bottom lip, he knew such fears were unfounded. But, now, away from her dizzying presence, his brief bout of amnesia, fuelled by alcohol and anticipation, was over. He was chilled by the reality of his situation and the future of the company that he and Nadine had worked so hard to build.

CHAPTER FIVE

Nadine

A Shard retrospective. Our business is falling apart and Jake talks about offering fans a chance to relive their youth. At night when he's not rehearsing he closes the door of his music room while I try and catch up on the backlog of work. We could be facing bankruptcy but his eyes glaze when I try to discuss this terrifying possibility. Ed Jaworski's decision fell upon us like the sword of Damocles and we're still reeling. We can take legal action, of course. Spend a fortune and face a team a STRUM lawyers across a courtroom. They will beggar us, rubbish our reputation, break us down before the first hearing has concluded.

Tonight, when he returned from band practice, he stood outside the door of my office. I heard his footsteps stop then move on. I heard the door of his music room close. We live in a house with many rooms, spacious and stylishly furnished, yet the two smallest rooms are the ones we use most frequently. Our refuge from a marriage we tolerate for everyone's sake but our own.

We don't fight anymore. Not the way we did in the early years, hurling insults without caring where they landed and forgiving each other in bed with the same pent-up ferocity. Now, we use evasion, a polite chilliness, reasoned discussions that respect each other's point of view, even when it doesn't tally with our own. I remember these youthful rows with a certain indulgent nostalgia. We were so aware of each other then, conscious of tinder boxes and the danger of a hapless remark. One particular row when I was expecting the twins stands out in my mind. It began as a casual discussion about what we would be doing if we were still free and single. I was lying on the sofa in the breakfast room in Sea Aster, heavily pregnant and Ali and Brian, still babies, were sleeping upstairs. My wish list included art college, living in flatland with Jenny, a gap year in Australia, Euro-railing through Europe; aspirations vague enough not to offend Jake. He was more specific. Recreational drugs and eventual rehab, all night parties, riding a Harley Davidson on Route 66, the rise and rise of Shard, and an occasional threesome. The latter was meant to be a joke, he insisted afterwards, but by then it was too late.

'What a pity we didn't make it a threesome at the time,' I snapped. 'Then, maybe, the other girl would have become pregnant instead of me.'

'Just my luck,' he retorted. 'Think how wonderful my life would be if she'd been blonde, beautiful and sexy, instead of always moaning about her fucked-up marriage.'

'Whose fucked-up marriage are we discussing?' My anger heaved with resentment and the twins kicked frantically at my drum-stretched stomach. 'You're the one who feels trapped. You're the one who can't wait to take off on your Harley Davidson. If you'd known how to use a condom…'

'Oh, here we go again.' He hinged his arm exaggeratedly and studied his watch. 'Now it's time to bring up the subject of the defective condom— '

'It wasn't the condom that was defective….'

On and on we went, one word borrowing another until it seemed as if our bitterness was beyond healing. But it did heal and that night, before we slept, we promised each other that if we still felt trapped when the twins were eighteen and independent we'd give each other the freedom to pursue the life we would have led if we had not been so heedless.

I wonder if Jake ever remembers that hurt-filled night. I doubt it. Each row is a fresh one to him, unencumbered by the past whereas mine are weighted with history and etched on my memory cells. This is a female trait, he believes, rather like premenstrual tension or the ability to carry hot objects to the table without scalding my hands.

We left our twins at the airport last month. They never looked back. No last, lingering glances, their eyes eloquent with gratitude for eighteen years of nurturing and unconditional love. Instead, they looked ahead to their futures, unaware that their departure would snap the last fragile link holding their parent's marriage together. I've poked at this truth, worried it like a dentist prodding a tooth nerve. I've waited for a reaction, the jerk of reality that signals pain. Nothing. Our marriage has a serene surface, a veneer that has taken us to the point where Jake seeks solitude in his music room rather than opening my door to say goodnight to me.

Ed Jaworski's brutal decision has proved that a contract is not worth the paper it's written on. Vows can be broken and the sky does not fall down. What I feel for Jake is affection and gratitude for the years we've shared. I remember what it was like in the beginning but that flame has cooled into ash. Only an odd spark reminds us of what we've lost… and how it all began.

❋   ❋   ❋

I danced with Jenny, handbags at our feet, short skirts swirling over leggings, stonewashed denim jackets. We were seventeen years of age and dizzy with the wonder of it. The mirror ball spun a kaleidoscope of colour across our upturned faces. Moonflowers exploded, strobes pulsated, and I danced harder, my eyes swallowing the sight of him. His black hair streaked with blond, skin-tight jeans, leather vest — rangy and sexy and ready. Two years since we'd met in Monsheelagh but all that was behind me and I was living in the thrilling, exhilarating now of a new beginning.

Alone at last, away from the sweat and the noise and the crush of heaving bodies, he unhooked my bra. My body glowed with a hot, shivery excitement, as dangerous as it was demanding. His tongue caressed my nipples, strummed my pleasure, darts of fire low in my stomach. He'd borrowed his mother's car for the night. We laughed over the First Affiliation posters in the back seat. Something about a Divorce Referendum. Eleanor's smiling mouth and watchful eyes staring at us. We shoved the posters to the floor and came together again. My legs trembled, opened under the pressure of his hand, his slow deliberate journey between my thighs, delicately stroking upwards and he, sensing my nervousness, waited until I relaxed and the smear of desire glistened his fingers.

Fate was waiting in the wings, sly smiling, as I pulled down his jeans, touched him, held him, guided him in. We were meant to be together, one flesh, one beat. Our future was shaping but the present was all that mattered as we lay there, pressed limb to limb, mouth to mouth, ready to be engulfed, engorged, ravished. How was it that such a moment would so easily be forgotten in the dread that followed?

My mother was the first to guess. Dismay in Sara's eyes as she stood outside the bathroom door listening to the retching sounds from within. Morning sickness in all its misery consumed me for the first three months. I emerged eventually, goose pimples on my skin, eyes streaming, and stood facing her in my school uniform, unable any longer to hide the truth.

I met Jake's mother for the first time and was terrified by this impeccably groomed woman, who summed me up in a glance as 'trouble' then set about resolving the problem as swiftly as possible. Her contacts were excellent in the mother and baby home where I'd stay throughout my 'crisis pregnancy.' Every time Eleanor said 'crisis pregnancy', and she said it often, I felt like a statistic to be shunted out of sight, out of mind. Everyone agreed that we were too young to be parents. Jake was nineteen and I would have just turned eighteen when our baby was born.

Sara remained implacably opposed to adoption but my father, not being a man to disguise his feelings, was on Eleanor's side. My untimely pregnancy was interfering with his Big Plan, as he called it. My parent's house was sold and we were moving to Australia. I'd argued, wept and fiercely resisted this decision but Eighties Ireland was in recession and Eoin was determined to make a new beginning.

In the weeks that followed there were meetings, discussions, angry scenes and decisions made. Jake and I were in the eye of the storm, right at its heart where we belonged, but no one was listening to us.

My parents were arguing when we entered the house one night, unaware that we could overhear every bitter word.

'I'm not letting her hold us back.' Eoin's voice was flinty with determination. 'She was careless enough to get herself knocked up by some guy she hardly knew and now we're supposed to deal with the consequences.'

'She's our only child, Eoin.' Sara sounded distraught. 'We need to be here to support her. Otherwise, she'll be bullied by that dreadful woman and our grandchild will be adopted.'

'Adoption is the best solution,' my father shouted. 'At this stage in my life, I'm not prepared to cope with a baby. And neither are you. As for Nadine, what does she know about parenting? Zilch, that's what!'

I heard the snap of his fingers, a pistol shot in the immediate silence that followed this statement.

'But that's why she needs our support.' Sara's anger spilled over into sobs. 'I want to be with her when her baby is born.'

'Where are you supposed to live? Our house is sold. In six week's time we're supposed to be flying to Australia. Nadine comes with us. I'm not delaying our departure date.'

'She wants to be with Jake. This is also his child.'

'And he'll walk out on her the first chance he gets. If she won't have the baby adopted and she won't come with us then she can make her own bed and lie in it. You and I go together as planned or I go alone. Make up your mind, Sara. We've come too far to allow this mess to change our plans.'

Unable to listen any longer, I gripped Jake's hand. We left the house as silently as we'd entered it.

This argument changed everything. It strengthened our resolve. Instead of seeing a problem that needed a solution we were able to visualise a baby. Our baby. We became fiercely protective of this life we'd so wantonly created. This gave us the courage to stand up to Eleanor. No adoption. She insisted on a quiet, swift wedding. Ali moved in my womb as I exchanged wedding vows with Jake, a butterfly patter, almost imagined. New life kicking into action while my old life disappeared.

A week later my father left for Australia where a job in construction was waiting for him. Sara would stay with me until her first grandchild was born. Gentle Rosanna took care of us all in Sea Aster. Ali was two months old when I embraced my mother for the last time. The farewell at the airport. The sense of unreality as I watched her disappear through the departure gates. I waved goodbye and held Ali high in my arms for her to see. Then she was gone, heading towards a new life that was extinguished eighteen months later when she was killed in a road accident.

I flew with Jake to Australia, travelled through day and night when I received that shattering phone call from my father. Sara was on life support. Dark bruises on her forehead and hands were the only external marks I could see but, internally, all was lost. Hearing, said the hospital chaplain, was the last sense to go. I'd time to whisper in her ear, caress her hands, kiss her repeatedly before Jake led me away.

'She looks so peaceful,' my father kept saying, as if this would give me some consolation. 'She never knew what hit her.'

Jake held me upright when her life support was switched off. He supported me from her graveside and back home to our children. To the life we were slowly building together.

CHAPTER SIX

Jake

At first, Jake believed the seed Karin planted in his mind had fallen on barren soil. But it kept growing shoots. Fierce, demanding shoots that made him question why he had to rise at six in the morning to beat the rush hour traffic. Why the workload he brought home at weekends kept growing. Why so many people were breathing down his neck. His bank manager, who, in the heady days of easy borrowing, had insisted the boom times were here to stay but now looked askance when Jake mentioned a loan extension. The VAT officer who arrived without an appointment to inspect Tōnality's VAT records and gave Jake a dead fish stare when he asked if everything was in order. Tōnality's biggest customer who had declared himself bankrupt and ended any hope of settling his account. If it wasn't for Shard he would go crazy. Thanks to Karin Moylan, he now had an escape route.

He never intended losing touch with the band but after the twins were born and the lads were still talking about hangovers, garage raves and one-night stands, he could no longer pretend to have anything in common with them. Apart from Daryl Farrell who formed Shard with him when they were fourth-year students in St Fabian's College, Jake had not seen the others for years.

Soon after his return from New York they met in a bar on Grafton Street to discuss the possibility of a Shard reunion. The old camaraderie was still there and they spent the night reminiscing about the past. Reedy, the bass guitarist, looked older than the others, a lived-in face with premature crevices. Too much touring and weed, he confided to Jake. Hart, who used to stumble drunk on stage and play his rhythm guitar flawlessly, was now the owner of a yoga centre called Hartland to Health. Something to do with shoulder stands and a third eye. It all sounded very mysterious to Jake who, was astonished to see Hart drinking soda water with a slice of lemon instead of knocking back shots of tequila. Daryl, Shard's one-time lead guitarist, had recently become a first-time father. He spoke about breastfeeding with the confidence of a wet nurse and swiped his finger over his iPhone to show them photographs of his baby daughter crying, smiling, kicking her legs in the air. He made Jake feel old, his role as a parent just beginning whereas any one of Jake's four adult children were capable of turning him into a grandfather. Barry, the drummer, once known as Bad Boy Barry Balfe, had made a fortune laying bricks during the boom. Unemployed since the collapse of the construction industry, he was examining his options. The reunion gig was manna from heaven.

They would perform the songs that made them famous and introduce Jake's newer songs, dust them off and bring them to life. Reedy claimed they would need a boot camp to kick them into shape if they were to appear in public again and they now rehearsed three nights a week in the basement of a recording studio. Now, two months in, they had formed into a tight, cohesive unit. The rehearsals were chaotic, argumentative and fun. Jake had forgotten what it was like to have fun. Forgotten what it was like to be the singer in a band.

Tonight, before he left for band practice, Nadine made a comment about fiddling while Rome burned. She said it tersely, pointedly. He hoped she would be in bed when he returned. Band practice had gone on longer than anticipated and he had wanted to spend an hour in his music room before calling it a night. Reedy, whose musical opinion he respected, liked 'The Long Goodbye' but believed the arrangement needed further development. He was walking towards his music room when he noticed a light under the door of Nadine's home office. He had hesitated outside. He should go in and say goodnight, face her accusatory gaze, her acerbic comments. But the composition was inside his head, guitars strumming, drums drumming, a keyboard adding depth to the arrangement. He needed to pin it down before it evaporated under the harsh reality of talking about Tōnality, which was all he and Nadine ever did these days.

His phone bleeped when he was in his music room. A text from Karin with an attached photo. She was on a film set, sitting on the steps of a trailer while people in Regency costumes walked past her. *Busy day on the set,* she texted. *How did band practice go?*

He heard a door slam, Nadine's footsteps on the stairs. He should have mentioned Karin as soon as he returned from New York. It would have been so easy when she picked him up at the airport. Guess who I met on the flight... an old friend... Karin Moylan sends her best. But he said nothing and now it was impossible to drop her name casually into their conversation. She was his secret and her importance was growing in proportion to the clandestine nature of their texts.

Her texts came every day, usually accompanied by whimsical photographs of New York, an opera she had attended, a flash concert in a shopping centre, skyscrapers lit at night on Fifth Avenue, an image of her jogging in Central Park, her skin glowing, her nipples straining against her sweat top. She never mentioned Nadine, nor did he. But what pithy, witty response could he text in return? Cash flow problems and an irate bank manager? The kiss of death, Jake reckoned. His own responses were equally bland and light-hearted.

New York was his coded word for her.

Is New York awake yet?

What's happening in New York right now?

Raining here, pining for some New York sunshine.

Wish I was in New York and could stay there forever.

He had deleted that last text, its double entendre too blatant for anyone's eyes but his own. She had become his buffer zone, his cloud nine, his fantasy against his daily grind of cancelled orders and lies about the cheque being in the post. He should buy a new phone with a secret number. The thought that he was becoming a cliché appalled him. Nadine would never check his phone and what harm if she did? The texts were harmless, mildly flirtatious and, like Shard, a welcome distraction from running his troubled company.

Nadine was in bed and awake when he lay down beside her. She was still annoyed with him. He could tell by her eyes. The chill factor.

'Sorry I was so late getting back from band practice,' he said.

'I thought you might come into the office and acknowledge my existence.'

'I didn't want to disturb you.'

'Of course you didn't.'

'What's that supposed to mean?'

'Analyse the meaning yourself.' She turned away from him and pressed her face into the pillow. 'It's late and I'm tired. Goodnight.'

CHAPTER SEVEN

Nadine

Smart Art's is crowded tonight but Art has kept our usual table for us. Friday night is our wind down time, pizzas and beer on our way home from work. We made a rule when we started this weekly ritual that we would not discuss Tōnality. We keep to this decision, even though it's uppermost in our minds. We talk about the children, although we both agree we must stop calling them 'children.' They're adults, eligible to vote, eligible to marry, eligible to die for their country, if called upon to do so. But what do we call them instead? We give up on that one and talk about Ali's disappointment when she didn't receive a phone call after her last audition. I read out a text from Samantha informing us that Sam had beaten his personal best and we discuss Brian's new pottery collection. It's noisier than usual in the pizzeria. I ask Jake if we can break the taboo and discuss Tōnality. He sighs, shrugs.

'If you must.'

A man at the next table starts singing 'When I'm Sixty-Four'. He's too drunk to remember the words and Jake rubs his hand across the back of his neck.

'This recession could ruin us.' I raise my voice as Jake leans forward to hear me. 'We should sell Tōnality while it's still viable. Let's take a look again at those offers we received last year and seriously consider the best one.' I look away as his eyes widen, their greyness exaggerated by the flickering nightlight on the table.

'What's brought this on?' His astonishment is not surprising. I've leaped in at the deep end without testing the shallows first but I feel reckless tonight.

'Think of it, Jake. We sell the company to Paul Rowan or Susanna Cox. Both offers were good. Then we sell the house.'

'Sell the house?' His eyelids flicker. 'How many beers have you had?'

'Just the one.'

'I'd hate if you'd had more. You're talking absolute nonsense.'

'Just hear me out. If we sell them both we can pay off our debts and you'll be free to do what really matters…like Shard.'

'Is this about the reunion gig?' He's instantly on the defensive. 'I know you resent the time…'

'I don't resent it at all.' I cut across him. 'I've always felt responsible for the band's breakup. I'm glad you're seeing the lads again.'

'What is it, then?' he asks. 'We're managing to keep our heads above water and you love that house.'

'Not any more. It's like a mausoleum since the kids left.'

'But they'll come back to live there,' he says. 'At least the twins will when they finish college. And Ali and Brian will come home for holidays.'

'The twins won't be back here for another four years. We've no idea where they'll decide to live. Ali and Brian have never settled in Bartizan Downs. Where they stay for their holidays is not going to bother them.'

He knows I'm right. When we first moved into Bartizan Downs they were thrilled with their spacious bedrooms, the fully equipped gym in the basement, the home cinema and games room. Such giddy excitement until the novelty wore off and they returned to a sprawled position in front of the television. They demanded a yearly subscription to the Oakdale Leisure Centre where they could link up with their friends. When it was time to leave, they did so without regret. Like Eleanor and Sea Aster, they've never considered it their family home.

'I've been thinking a lot lately about our... our....'

This is the moment to say it. Our marriage is over. We should buy two separate houses. A mews for Jake. Somewhere close to the city with space at the back to open the record studio he often talks about. I'd like something in the country, an old, converted schoolhouse, perhaps, or a cottage with a river running through my back garden.

'Our what? Jake is waiting for me to continue. 'Have you found something else you want to sell?' He smiles grimly at his own joke but his gaze is wary.

Art stops at our table and interrupts what I was going to say. He plans to buy a guitar for his son's thirteenth birthday and wants our advice. Jake makes a few suggestions and tells him to call in to see us in Tōnality.

'You were saying?' He leans his elbows on the table when Art leaves.

'Forget it. It was just a thought.'

'You don't throw something like that at me without thinking it through,' he says. 'You've obviously seriously considered selling Tōnality and the house.' This is not an accusation, more like a consideration, as if I've opened his mind to other possibilities. 'Is there something else you want to tell me?'

I can't do it. Marriages usually end after hate rants and havoc, accusations, revelations, confessions, vows of vengeance, tears, blood and sweat. What excuse do I have? How can I destroy twenty-three years of togetherness simply because I'm stressed and overworked, not thinking rationally?

'Nothing that can't be discussed another time,' I reply.

'Are you sure?'

'Absolutely.'

Art returns with the bill and places it discreetly on the table. A business card falls from Jake's wallet when he removes his credit card. I notice the logo as I hand it back to him. A bird, vivid blue head, russet chest. Kingfisher Graphics is written in blue below the logo. I turn the card over and see her name. The letters rise towards me then dissolve into mist. My eyes sting.

'Where did you get this?' I hold the card out to him.

The pause that follows is insignificant. In fact, it's hardly noticeable, yet I'm acutely aware of his breathing, how it shortens before he clears his throat.

'Probably at some trade fair.'

'Which trade fair?'

'How do I know?' He shrugs, spreads his hands outwards, as if shoving the question away then his face clears. 'No, that's wrong. I remember now. We met on a flight to New York.'

'You never told me.'

'I meant to… then it slipped my mind.'

'It *slipped* your mind?'

He takes the card from me and glances at the logo. 'She's a graphic designer.'

'I know what she is.'

'She gave me her card in case we ever need her services.'

'Why should we need a graphic designer?'

'We don't need most of the services offered on the business cards that people give us,' he replies. 'Have you ever looked at your desk? It's littered with them.'

The heat from the pizza ovens blasts over me. I press the beer glass to my cheeks. My forehead is hot, suddenly sweaty. 'Yes. They're on my desk, not in my wallet.'

'I'd forgotten it was there. Why are you getting so uptight?'

'Did she mention me?'

'I can't remember. We were only together for a short while. It took me ages to even remember who she was.' Nothing in his voice or expression suggests he's lying but there's a tremor running through this conversation. It makes me nervous.

'You never told me why you fell out with each other,' he says. 'I know what happened that summer was dreadful but I don't understand why it destroyed your friendship.'

'I've no intention of raking all that up again.' I hate the hard snap in my voice but it's better than a quiver. Karin Moylan will never make me quiver again. Why is Jake asking? Is it idle curiosity or did she say something? They must have talked about Monsheelagh. How could they not?

'But you obviously haven't forgotten,' he says.

'I said I don't want…'

'Okay… okay.' He rips the card in two and flings the pieces on the table. 'Let's get out of here. The noise is doing my head in.'

I remember the kingfisher in Odd Bods. Why I should suddenly think about a jumble shop in Gracehills Village where my mother loved to potter on Saturday afternoons is surprising but my mind darts like a silverfish towards the memory. Two months had passed since my return from Monsheelagh and I was with Sara when she discovered the stuffed kingfisher in a glass case, almost hidden behind a set of occasional tables.

'What do you think, Nadine?' She pulled it free and held it towards me. 'How would this look on the hall table?'

I backed away from the bird's iridescent plumage, its savage gaze.

'It's too gaudy,' I said. 'I hate it.'

'If you feel that strongly about it…' She shrugged and replaced it back behind the tables. It was sold the next time we returned to Odd Bods.

Karin Moylan's name has been ripped in two but the king-fisher is still recognisable: its long dagger beak and pitiless eyes.

The high, black gates with their sharply-pointed tips open and admit us to Bartizan Downs. The round, ornate bartizans are jutting like medieval turrets from the gate posts but the houses with their lush rolling lawns are in darkness. Only the smooth growl of our car suggests that lives are lived within this gated community.

We go our separate ways when we enter the house. Jake closes the door of his music room with unnecessary firmness. I go into my home office. After a short search I find a photo album in a bottom drawer of my desk. My mother was conscientious when it came to dating photographs. The albums she filled tell the story of my childhood. I've been tempted over the years to remove the photographs of Karin Moylan but that would break the link of who I am today. And, so, she stays in her allotted slot.

One of the photographs is larger than the others. A day in summer. Rocks and coarse golden sand, a gouged cliff face where kittiwakes fly high above us, swirling and scattered as black flakes of ash. Four weeks of blistering sunshine and frayed tempers. I'm wearing a pink bikini and leaning back on my hands, my face raised to the sun. My hair is tangled, my shoulders sunburned. Karin, in a blue bikini, sits between me and her father. She hugs her knees, taut shoulder blades raised like slender wings. He's wearing swimming trunks, his long legs sprawled before him. Someone else must have taken the photograph because Joan Moylan is also in it. Maybe it was Jake who snapped us. Unlike the rest of us, Joan is fully dressed in jeans and a flowery blouse, a sunhat shading her face.

Fifteen years of age was a time for dreaming, and, oh, how I dreamed those days away. I walked that long, curving beach in a lovesick haze, imagining a future that was never going to happen. The tide was far out, stretched to its limits before it turned and flowed back over the hot sands, obliterating my footprints in one fluid swell.

Jenny is wrong. The past does matter. That's the trouble with it. Like elastic, it can only be stretched so far before it recoils and slaps one in the face. *Twack.*

Part Two

CHAPTER EIGHT

Gracehills – twenty-seven years earlier.

I fell in love with Karin Moylan when I was thirteen. This was a platonic love. I was not about to enter or emerge from any closet and my love for her was akin to that reserved for a precious item like a treasured doll or a delicate piece of jewellery. And even if I had loved her in that way, the physical differences between us could well have been a deterrent. She was small-boned and dainty. I was tall and angular, awkward elbows, knees as gangly as a colt, cheekbones too pronounced for my long, thin face. As for my hair, those unruly curls. I felt like a scarecrow who'd been left out for far too long in the rain.

We met in the fitting room of a department store. A summer heatwave had arrived and Dublin sweltered beneath it. I, too, was hot and surly, stooped with self-pity as I stood in the fitting room and tried on my new school uniform. The skirt was too long, the jumper too wide and the sleeves of the blazer hung over my hands. A smaller size would have been perfect but my mother believed I'd grow out of it within months. The fact that she was right added to my misery. In those days, I had the growing momentum of a beanstalk. The colours, maroon, cream and charcoal grey, drained my complexion and I was convinced I'd look like a corpse for the next six years. I twisted the lobes of my ears and stuck my tongue out at my reflection… in out… in

out… in out. My five-year-old self came effortlessly to the surface on certain occasions and this was one of them. The fitting
room curtains opened slightly and Karin's reflection appeared
behind me in the long mirror.

'Can I try on my uniform when you've finished admiring
your tongue?' she asked.

I snapped my mouth closed as she pressed her fist against
her lips to stifle a giggle. Her heart-shaped face in the mirror,
her blue eyes bright with laughter; this was a frozen moment,
never forgotten.

'I'm sorry…' Colour flushed across my cheeks, spread down
my neck.

'I'm sorry too,' she said. 'I thought the fitting room was
empty.' She shook out the school uniform she'd draped over her
arm. 'God! It's hideous, isn't it?'

'Hideous.' I should have faced her but, somehow, talking to
her reflection felt less embarrassing. 'It's far too big for me and
I *hate* the colours.'

Her lips puckered. I thought she was going to laugh again
but, instead, she said, 'I hate them too. I'll look *so* disgustingly
fat in this skirt.'

'No, you won't.' I turned around and spoke directly to her.
'It'll look lovely on you.'

'Tell me what you think.' Before I could move, she wriggled
out of her t-shirt and jeans. She was wearing a bra, a flimsy white
piece of lace that pushed two swelling buds upwards and outwards. Mine barely existed. It seemed unfair that someone so
small should have such beautiful breasts. She buttoned the blouse
and fastened the skirt. The hem of her skirt rested neatly on her
knees and the cream blouse enhanced the colour of her skin.

'It's dire on both of us,' she said, almost apologetically. 'I
suppose we'll just have to get used to looking awful.'

'No, it looks really nice on you.' I felt no envy towards her as we stood together and observed our reflections.

'Are you nervous about starting in St Agatha's?' she asked.

'Sort of,' I admitted. 'I know some of the girls from primary so that will help.'

'I won't know anyone,' she said. 'I hope we're in the same stream. My name's Karin Moylan. What's yours?'

'Nadine Keogh.'

'Do you think we'll be bullied?' she asked.

The same fears had been running through my own mind. I'd heard of wedgies and heads being pushed down toilets but that seemed like boy torture. With girls it was different. I imagined being excluded from groups, whispered about, picked on, the victim of vicious lies.

'Why should you be bullied?' I couldn't imagine such treatment being meted out to her.

'People will pick on me because I'm small.' She looked up at me, her eyes filled with dread. 'I can't sleep thinking about it. But you'll be all right. You're so big they'll think you're a fourth-year.'

I immediately stooped my shoulders, a habit I'd developed the previous year when I became the tallest girl in my class.

The curtains opened again and my mother said, 'What's keeping you, Nadine?' She stopped when she saw Karin. 'Oh, I didn't realise you were with a friend. Come on out so that I can take a proper look at the pair of you.'

We emerged from the fitting room. Karin was composed as she twirled around but I stood self-consciously in the open space, aware of my large feet and gangling arms, convinced the customers passing by were comparing my lankiness to her petite frame.

Her parents were sitting on a sofa in the waiting area. Max Moylan had the resigned expression that men acquire in an all-female shopping environment. The sofa was a two-seater but, even then, I sensed the distance between him and his wife. Joan had her daughter's small-boned physique but her hair, split in the centre, was long and black, a fringe almost covering her eyes. Max stood up when he saw us and whistled. Karin had inherited his fair complexion and his wide-eyed embracing gaze. I'd never known a father who wore a ponytail. It seemed incredibly cool and daring.

'You look very elegant, young lady,' he said to me. 'I reckon you'll be a famous model someday. Mark my words, you'll knock them for six on the catwalk.'

Karin tilted her head. Her gaze sharpened, as if she was viewing me with fresh eyes. She smiled and said, 'Wouldn't that be *absolutely* brilliant.'

When our uniforms were purchased, we headed towards the exit. Our mothers exchanged a few words before they parted. The natural light emphasised the artificial blue-black sheen of Joan's hair, the colour too stark for her pale face. Later, my mother would claim that Joan was freeze-framed in the sixties. Karin walked ahead with her father, her arm linked in his, and I knew she'd already forgotten me.

On the first day of term I saw her in the assembly hall with Sheila Giles. Sheila, who'd been in my class in primary school, suffered from acne. Her face looked painfully inflamed against Karin's creamy complexion. I waved across at them. Sheila waved back but Karin's expression was puzzled, as if she was trying to remember where we'd met. From that day on they ignored me. They ate together in the school canteen and walked home arm-in-arm in the evenings.

I hung around with the girls I knew from primary school. In our intimidating new environment we were drawn to each other by familiar ties. When Lisa Maye turned fourteen we were the only girls in St Agatha's invited to her birthday party. Sheila arrived with her older brother Theo and some of his friends. The atmosphere changed soon afterwards. The older boys hung out in the garden where the trees were slung with fairy lights and a gazebo had been erected. They grew more boisterous as the night wore on. Lisa's father – who organised the teenage discos in the tennis club and was no slouch when it came to sniffing out underage drinkers – ordered them to leave after he discovered their secret stash of vodka in his garden shed. Sheila had been drinking with them. She was incoherent by the time her mother collected her. She collapsed as she tried to walk to the car and was immediately driven to hospital. There were rumours of a stomach pump being used but Sheila, when she returned to school, kept her head down and refused to speak to anyone about that night.

Her friendship with Karin was over. They sat at opposite ends of the canteen and Sheila walked home from school alone. She was crying in a cubicle when I entered the school toilets one morning. We were the only two pupils in the toilets and the sound stopped when I asked if she was okay.

'Mind your own business,' she snapped.

I recognised her voice, though it sounded thick, phlegmy. She must have been crying for a long time. She blew her nose and cleared her throat. 'Buzz off and leave me alone.' This command ended on a hiccupping sob.

That evening I stayed behind to speak to Miss Knowles, my art teacher. She believed my drawings had a maturity not normally found in the work of a first-year student. Her praise excited me, removed me a step further from my own self-absorption.

Most of the pupils had left by the time I reached the bicycle shed. I was about to wheel my bike out when I heard a boy shouting behind the shed wall.

A girl screamed but the sound stopped so abruptly I knew a hand had been pressed to her mouth.

'Shut up, you fucking bitch.' The boy's voice was deep and guttural. Probably a third or fourth year student. 'If you slag her off again about her face I'll fucking kill you. You weren't invited to that stupid party so stop taking it out on her.'

I grabbed the pump from my bike and ran around to the back of the shed. Theo Giles had pushed Karin against the wall and had, as I suspected, gagged her with his hand.

'Leave her alone,' I shrieked.

He glared back at me but kept his hand over her mouth. 'Fuck off, stupid ginge,' he yelled. 'Me and this bitch have agro to sort out.'

I struck him across the back of his head with the pump. He was so surprised that he released Karin immediately and spun around. Like Sheila, he suffered from acne. His face was mottled, his expression murderous as he lunged towards me. Karin screamed again. The sound ricocheted across the empty schoolyard. A flock of crows perched on a rubbish bin shot into the air. Her eyes were gleaming with what I believed was terror but would later realise was fury. I flailed wildly at Theo with the pump but he wrenched it easily from me.

'Run, Nadine,' Karin yelled and grabbed my hand. She was fast, her small feet drumming the ground. We'd lost him by the time we reached Gracehills Park, a shortcut home from school. We cut across the grass towards the tennis courts and into the shady passageway leading towards the park gates. Bare branches tangled overhead. The wintery sun glanced off our faces then cast us into shadow again.

'What was all that about?' I asked.

'He's a freak,' Karin linked my arm and shuddered. 'All that acne...*disgusting*. I felt sorry for his sister and that's the thanks I get for being her friend.'

'Did you have a row with her about the party?'

'What party?'

'Lisa Maye's. He said—'

'He's a liar.' She flicked her blonde hair over her shoulders. 'I was honest with Sheila about her acne. I didn't want to hurt her feelings but sometimes the truth has to be told. Did you know it's contagious?'

'I don't think it is.'

'You're wrong.' She was emphatic. 'It's a filthy disease and it's contagious. See that spot on my forehead?' She pushed her hair back. The smooth skin between her eyebrows was marred by two tiny pimples, barely visible. 'That's how it begins,' she said. 'I've been to the doctor and he's treating me with a special ointment so that it doesn't spread. But I can't risk being infected again.'

I wanted to reassure her that she was wrong. I knew all about acne. It was one of my dreads. So far I was pimple-free. I'd read medical articles that claimed it was not contagious but to contradict Karin would suggest she was lying when, clearly, it was the doctor who'd made a mistake.

'Where's your bike?' My mother asked when I arrived home.

'I decided to walk home with Karin instead.'

'Karin?'

'The girl we met when we bought my school uniform.'

'Of course. I remember her. Will your bike be safe?' She looked worried. ' You know how expensive it was.'

My parents had presented it to me on my twelfth birthday, a sturdy racing bike that I loved. The following day I'd find the tyres slashed. The handlebars were twisted and the pump broken. All repairable and a small price to pay for my friendship with Karin.

I was her bodyguard, strong, tough, and protective. She relied on me to keep her safe from Theo Giles and his boot boy friends who, for a while after the incident in the bicycle shed, waylaid us with water bombs, eggs and globs of spittle on our way home from school. I spoke to Miss Knowles, showed her the egg stains on the sleeves of my blazer. The bullying stopped shortly afterwards.

I no longer hung around with the girls from primary school. My friendship with Karin was intense and exclusive. We couldn't let an evening go by without phoning each other to report on a row with a parent, a rant about a teacher, a glance from a boy. We sat cross-legged on my bed and sang Adam Ant songs at the top of our voices, a streak of white across our cheekbones, strands of hair braided with bows, jangling earrings.

We both lived in Gracehills but her house was larger than mine, detached and with an extension built on the side. This was where her father wrote books when he was home from his travels. Max Moylan was a travel writer. His books, translated into many languages, lined the bookshelves in his study. I never felt awkward or too tall when I was with him. Even if I had been taller, he would have made me feel petite with a few complimentary words. But Joan reminded me of a ghost, her footsteps too light, her gaze so vague I felt as if she was looking through me. She ran a flower shop in the village. I'd see her through the window as she made up bouquets and chatted to customers. She looked so different then, brisk and busy compared to the woman who became so maudlin and whiny whenever I stayed overnight in their house. Her voice would slur in protest when Max removed the bottle of wine from the table. He would coax her to eat a little and regale us with stories about his travels. Handsome Max Moylan, intrepid traveller and raconteur. We never grew tired of listening to him.

I was fifteen when the Corcoran family moved next door: mother, father, three sons and a daughter called Jenny. It was impossible not to like Jenny Corcoran. She was my age and mad about hip-hop. She introduced me to groups like Deadly Fish, Combustion EX and Middle-Sized Boyz. I liked the hard, urgent beat of their music and stopped listening to my favourite glam bands unless I was with Karin.

Jenny broke through our closed friendship. We were now a threesome but in the evenings my phone conversations with Karin were no longer artless and rambling. They were focused on Jenny. On the things she had said and done that day to offend Karin. The incidents she described, the insults Jenny was supposed to have inflicted on her were so different to what I'd witnessed that I wondered if we were living in parallel universes. When I tried to calm her down she accused me of taking sides. If I remained silent, unwilling to agree with her tirades, her resentment grew. We'd been friends for two years, she said, and I was allowing someone I barely knew to break up that friendship. Was that what I wanted? I had to choose.

Life without Karin, I couldn't imagine it. When Jenny called in the mornings I made excuses about not being ready for school. After a few mornings she stopped calling. Soon, she had created her own circle of friends. Watching them in the school canteen, their table crammed with chairs — the arrangements as to who sat where changing constantly but the group never losing its shape — I began to question why my friendship with Karin was so closed-off, so intensely concentrated on each other.

My body was smoothing out. It seemed to happen overnight. A metamorphoses that vanished my awkward angles or, perhaps, they just began to work for me. I lifted my hair and studied my cheekbones, the length of my neck, the smooth roundness of my chin, and did not flinch from my reflection. I stood tall, aware of unfamiliar sensations swooping low in my stomach when boys turned to stare. I hitched my skirt higher to show off my legs, rucked the hated school socks over my ankles, wore my tie at a rakish angle. Karin never had to grow into herself. She still had those same doll-like curves. We rowed more easily now. Trivial arguments could flare without warning. When I was convinced our friendship was over, and I'd be cast aside like Sheila, I was conscious of relief rather than regret. But she always rang, repentant, anxious to make up. And that was how things remained between us until that summer in Monsheelagh Bay when we tore each other apart.

CHAPTER NINE

Monsheelagh – twenty-five years earlier

I'd heard so much from Karin about Cowrie Cottage that I believed it couldn't possibly live up to its reputation. I was wrong. The cottage where she spent a month every summer with her parents was as perfect as she claimed. Perched on a cliff overlooking the Atlantic, it had a thatched roof and windows framed with cowrie shells. My bedroom was tiny, a bed and a tallboy for my clothes. The low growl of the ocean lulled me to sleep at night and I awoke each morning to the call of kittiwakes swirling against the cliff face. A gate at the end of the back garden opened onto two paths. One ran along the top of the cliff and ended with stone steps leading down to Monsheelagh Bay. We used the steps when we needed to carry picnic baskets, windbreakers and the various bits and pieces necessary for a day on the beach. The second path was a shortcut forged through heather, descending in a steep, direct line to the cove. Jagged rocks bordered the base of the cliff and Joan constantly warned us to be careful when using the second path. Not that we paid any attention to her warnings. We had the agility of mountain goats and could reach the beach by this route within minutes of leaving the cottage.

The front garden overlooked the road leading to Monsheelagh Village. A couple of pubs, a bingo hall and a summer carni-

val offered the only entertainment at night but that didn't bother us. The weather was glorious and, after a day on the beach,
we were happy to stay home at night playing board games, listening to music and talking about Shard. Five of them, Jake,
Daryl, Reedy, Hart and Barry, had arrived in a ramshackle van
driven by Reedy and they were staying in an old house at the
other side of the village. They came to Monsheelagh Bay every
day. Its sheltering cliff walls trapped the sun and the cove was
a smooth, sandy strand, perfect for volleyball. Jake Saunders
stood out from the others as he scooped and dived and ran rings
round them, his tanned, muscular body glistening with oil. We
planned strategies to attract his attention but walking past in our
bikinis or scampering in pretended terror from the approaching waves had no effect on him. He already had a girlfriend, a
big-bottomed girl from Galway, who was staying in the cara-
van park. We watched the two of them strolling hand-in-hand
by the water's edge and sneered enviously over the provocative
sway of her bottom in her skimpy polka dot bikini. Sometimes,
instead of playing volleyball or French cricket, they'd disappear
behind the rocks and later emerge hand-in-hand with reddened
blemishes on their necks.

'Love bites,' Karin would hiss. 'She's *such* a whore.'

Daryl flopped down on the sand beside us one afternoon
and asked if we'd like to join the volleyball team. From then
on we were part of Shard's gang. The Galway girl went home
but not before she had bleached Jake's long black hair with yellow streaks. He reminded us of a tiger and we growled at him,
our hands arched like claws. Sometimes the lads would arrive
with guitars and an impromptu music session would begin. We
raced into the waves, our screams echoing across the cove as we
splashed each other before diving headlong into the cold Atlantic swell. Jake would lift Karin up in his arms and fling her back

into the water. She was as sleek as a fish, a blonde mermaid with streeling golden hair. Jake never attempted to lift me, afraid, I guessed, that it would not be such an easy task to lightly toss me into the waves.

Max Moylan was abroad for that first fortnight. Somewhere in India, working on another travel book, Joan said in her vague way that made everything outside her range of vision seem irrelevant. She was not drinking and she seemed to enjoy bringing us horse riding through Monsheelagh Forest, playing crazy golf and barbecuing for us in the evenings. One night she brought us to the pub on the sea front where musicians played fiddles and accordions. She drank iced water with a slice of lemon and set-danced around the floor with a local fisherman in a woolly hat, their feet flying in intricate steps too fast to follow.

'It won't last,' Karin said in a voice loaded with knowledge. 'She keeps the misery for Dad.'

On Monsheelagh Bay she retreated behind her floppy sun-hat and read her book while Karin and I competed for Jake's attention. I was the fastest swimmer in the group, thanks to my father. Eoin believed I could become a champion swimmer. The training programme he devised for me after I won some local championship medals meant rising three mornings a week before school to do lengths in the Gracehills Leisure Centre. I knew my own abilities better than Eoin. I'd never rise above the regional championships but I could outswim the others. Karin nicknamed me Moby Dick. The inference was obvious. I asked her to stop referring to me as a whale. She laughed and demanded to know when I'd lost my sense of humour. We were no longer prepared to swoon together over Jake Saunders. Karin was determined to have him. And so was I.

Joan roasted a leg of lamb and sprinkled it with sprigs of rosemary on the day Max Moylan was due to join us. Karin painted a *Welcome Home Dad* poster and hung it over the front door. We blew up balloons and tied them to the front gate. The hour of his arrival came and went. The pungent scent of rosemary evaporated from the kitchen and the lamb cooled on its platter. Karin kept going to the gate to check for his car. Darkness settled slowly during those summer evenings and Joan grew increasingly edgier when the lights were switched on. I avoided looking at the locked press where she kept an unopened bottle of vodka. Would she break the seal on it and pour a measure? Karin sulked in her room and played her music too loudly.

'Get lost, Moby,' she shrieked and flung a book at me when I entered without knocking. The warning signs were obvious. Karin and her father, when he finally arrived, would side against Joan, who would drink too much, laugh, talk and cry too much. I'd be invisible to them all, except when Karin reminded me that I'd the attributes of a whale.

Afraid of being overheard if I used the cottage phone I left the house without telling them. I rang Jenny from the phone kiosk on the harbour. Our ways had parted months previously and I hadn't told her I was going on holidays with Karin.

'Are you having a good time?' she asked, her life too busy for grudges.

'It's okay,' I said. 'I wish you were here with us.'

'It wouldn't work,' she said. 'Two's company, three's a crowd. Karin doesn't like me.'

'Oh, that's not true.' I wasn't sure who I was trying to convince. 'She just finds it hard to make new friends.'

'I know that. When are you coming back?'

'Not for another fortnight, more's the pity. Have you ever heard of a band called Shard?'

'Don't think so. Why?'

'They're here on holiday. We both fancy the singer.'

'Is that why you're fighting with Karin?'

'I didn't say we were fighting.'

'One boy. Two girls. Of course you're fighting.'

'Very funny.'

'Who's winning?'

'Neither of us…so far. She calls me Moby Dick.'

'If she can't treat her best friend with respect that's her problem, not yours. Don't let her get to you.'

'What are you doing?'

'There's disgusting raw sewage flowing into the sea at Dollymount. I'm making a video.'

'*Jenny!*'

'Stinky work but someone has to do it. Dad bought me this brilliant handicam for my birthday.'

'If I was home I'd go with you.'

'Would you?'

'Yes.'

'Good luck with the singer.'

As if her words had materialised him from the ether Jake suddenly appeared outside the phone kiosk. It was the first time I'd seen him without the others from the band. He grinned when he noticed me and pressed his face against the glass, flattening his features and clawing at the kiosk with his nails.

'Oh, my God, he's outside.' I whispered. 'I'd better go. I'll call into see you as soon as I get home.'

'Best of luck until then.'

I pushed against the door of the phone kiosk and Jake pushed back.

'Back off, Godzilla,' I yelled in mock terror and he staggered backwards in an equally exaggerated stumble.

We sat on the harbour wall, our legs dangling over the water. I smoked my first cigarette. He told me the band had taken the summer house to write songs and firm up their act in preparation for the international fame that awaited them. Their manager Mik Abel believed they were Ireland's answer to Guns n' Roses. So far, they'd only played a few venues and Barney, the owner of the harbour pub where Joan had danced with the fisherman, had offered them a gig in a fortnight's time.

I wondered if he would kiss me. Our heads were so close together. Would our breath be heavy with smoke? Should I allow him to put his tongue into my mouth? Would his lips be hard like the rim of a jam jar which was how Dean Redmond kissed? Dean was the only boy I'd ever kissed and the experience had fallen far short of the swooning sensation I'd anticipated. Jake lit another cigarette and talked some more about Shard.

'Will you and Karin still be here when we play Barney's?' he asked.

'I guess.' I stood up and tugged at the end of my shorts. I always seemed to be tugging at my clothes, as if, somehow, this would shrink my size. 'I'd better go back to the cottage. They'll be wondering where I am.'

He climbed up the steps behind me. I walked with him to the whitewashed pub where the others were waiting for him. The air was thick with smoke, densely packed with holiday makers. A piper played the pipes and a young girl stretched and pleated her concertina in a mournful wail.

'Call that music.' Jake threw his eyes upwards. 'They won't know what hit them when they hear Shard. See you tomorrow on the beach.'

The main road leading from Monsheelagh Village was bright with street lamps and a blaze of light from the late night pubs. I left Jake at the door of Barney's and walked towards the winding road leading back to Cowrie Cottage. There was no footpath, just a hedgerow and tall river reeds. The darkness would have been impenetrable except for my torch. The beam wavered before me as something swift and pattering darted across the road. I walked faster, aware that river rats were probably crouched between the stalky reeds. A car approached, the headlights swerving around a corner. I moved into the grass, hoping my feet wouldn't slip into the ditch below. The car stopped. A light flared inside when the driver opened the door. I froze, afraid to move forward yet knowing I'd never escape if I ran. Why had I been so stupid? Joan had forbidden us to walk this narrow road alone at night. She had feared a road accident but had not mentioned the possibility of being attacked by a murderer or a rapist. My fears disappeared when I recognised Max Moylan.

'In you get, young lady,' he said. 'Walking a country road at night is dangerous. You could easily have been knocked down. I'm surprised Joan allowed you out on your own at this hour.'

'She doesn't know I'm out.'

'Does Karin?'

'No.'

'Did you have a row?'

'Sort of.' I climbed into the passenger seat. 'They were expecting you earlier.'

'Sounds like I'm in the dog house again.' Max sighed and slapped his hand to his forehead. 'Oh well, it's not the first time and it won't be the last.' He smiled across at me, a gash of white teeth against his tanned skin. 'Should I duck when I enter?'

I nodded, remembering the book Karin had flung at me with such venom. I was annoyed with him for spoiling the day. He would breeze into the cottage as if nothing was wrong and Karin would forget her disappointment, forget the hours she'd spent watching out for him. Joan would pour one glass of wine after another and make us forget how lovely she looked when she danced in the pub with the fisherman.

It was as I expected. Max threw out excuses about a missed flight. He danced Joan around the kitchen when she demanded to know what *actually* kept him. Her feet tangled in his steps. It was obvious that she'd already opened the vodka bottle. She looked clumsy and cross when she pulled away from him and announced it was time to eat.

As we ate the cold lamb Max regaled us with stories about his travels. I imagined him in a turban and sarong, sitting cross-legged in villages, recording voices and taking photographs of withered old faces with life stories written between the wrinkles. Karin was enthralled, her hand resting on her chin, her eyes fixed on his handsome face. Joan rubbed her knuckles together when he talked about the elegance of Indian women in their luminous saris. She picked at her food, poured wine with a steady hand and drifted away from us. She lurched forward and fell when she rose to go to bed. The suddenness of her fall shocked Max into silence. For an instant no one stirred. I wondered if he would leave her there, sprawled inelegantly at his feet. Then we moved as one and bent to lift her. We laid her on the bed and Max pulled the duvet over her.

I saw him the following morning sitting on the rocks in Monsheelagh Bay. His hair was loose from the ponytail and looked as if he hadn't bothered combing it. I'd risen early to draw the kittiwakes and had my sketch pad under my arm. We exchanged a few words as I walked past. The sky was rosy, the sun just up. We were the only people in the cove. Even when I moved behind one of the rocks and began to draw I could see him in my mind's eye, sitting with his face turned to the sea. So still he could have been carved into the cliff face. He was still there when I came back. I remember making breakfast for him when we returned to the cottage. Later, Karin came into my room and accused me of monopolising him. It was impossible to argue with her. Her father was not to be shared. Her eyes flashed as she spoke, that glacial blue stare that could suddenly melt, like her mood, and draw me back once again into her toxic, all-encompassing friendship.

CHAPTER TEN

The sky was cloudless, the day balmy when I trekked through the shady trails of Monsheelagh Forest with Karin and her father. It was a tough, uphill climb and Monsheelagh was spread like a green patchwork quilt below us when we finally emerged from the trees. Max pointed to a white dot in the distance. Cowrie Cottage, he said. I pictured Joan sleeping in her rank-smelling bedroom. I hoped the windows were open to the healing breeze. She was supposed to come with us on the trek but she'd changed her mind that morning. We pretended not to notice the smudges of mascara around her bloodshot eyes, the stale smell of alcohol on her breath. Karin behaved as she always did on such occasions, scornful and untouchable.

We stopped to picnic by a river. After we had eaten Max rested his back against the trunk of a tree. Karin, her eyes closed, lay with her head resting on his thigh. He told us about the journey he would soon take through the Sahara Desert with a tribe of nomads. He'd ridden camels before but this would be a long journey over mountainous sands where buried cities would one day be excavated. The long grass tickled my cheek as I lay on my side, elbow propping my chin, his melodic voice lulling me into a light doze. A rustle of wings startled me and a bird flew so close I felt the wind in its wings. We watched it dive into the water and reappear. The shimmer of blue feathers, something silvery wriggling in its beak before it flew away.

'That was a kingfisher.' Max plucked a feather from the ground and ran his finger along the quivering barbs. He told us a story. A Greek legend about the lovers Alcyone and Ceyx, lost to each other through death. He spoke as he wrote, a mesmeric spinning of words into pictures that transformed the strippled rush of the river into a surging ocean and the twitter of birds into Alcyone's keening grief as she sought to be reunited with her drowned husband. I imagined the waves closing over her head, her body riding on the crest of a wave before it dragged her down into the dark nothingness. The gods, taking pity on the doomed lovers, transformed them into kingfishers. I saw them rise and reel above the waves. Their blue wings whirred as the thunderous waters fell calm and lapped tranquilly to shore so that Alcyone could lay her eggs on the sands. Those were the halcyon days, Max said. The calm before the storm.

'We've had our halcyon day,' he said when the story ended. 'It's time we were heading back to the cottage.'

Karin stood and stretched lazily, her hands raised in a salute to the sun. I knelt on the grass and gathered the wrappings from the picnic.

Max slipped the blue feather into my hair. 'Alcyone,' he whispered or, perhaps it was just his breath escaping fast as he rose to his feet.

Karin lowered her arms and stared into the river.

'Come on, lazybones,' he said to her. 'Time to move.'

'I don't want to go back,' she said.

'What do you want to do?' He chucked her under her chin. 'Live in the forest?'

'Take me to the Sahara with you?'

'We've been through this already, Karin,' he replied. 'You know that's not possible.'

'But you promised I could go with you when I was fifteen.'

'I made no such promise. You're still way too young for such an arduous trip.'

She faced him, eyes blazing, fists clenched by her sides. 'Liar! You did… you *did*.' Her mood change was sudden but I had become used to those unexpected outbursts.

I picked up apple and orange peelings, cheese wrappings, butter melting gold into the grass. Eighteen was the age she planned to leave with him. She spoke about it often enough.

'Why are you doing this?' Max asked. 'We've had a perfect day and you're spoiling it by making a scene.'

'I'm going with you,' she shrieked. 'You can't leave me alone again with *her*.'

'Don't refer to your mother as "her."' I thought he would lose his temper, as my own father would have done, but he never raised his voice. 'She loves you and has always taken care of you. Why are you pretending otherwise?'

'But you don't love me. If you did, you'd take me away. You never keep your word. It's all your fault that she's an alco – '

'Stop it at once.' This time I heard his anger and Karin paused, her mouth open on that ugly word.

I emptied out the dregs of tea and screwed the top back on the flask. The ripples the kingfisher had made were still visible in the flow of the river.

'Tell him, Nadine.' She dropped to her knees before me. 'You heard him promise. He said *fifteen*.'

I bent my head, afraid to look at her, and fastened the straps on my backpack. She leaned forward until I was forced to meet her eyes.

'Tell him to his face that he's a liar,' she said. 'I want you to say it.'

'You're the liar.' I straightened my shoulders, stared her down. 'He never said any such thing.'

She pushed me backwards with such force that I lost my balance. I think she would have pummelled me if Max had not pulled her away.

'Have you finished?' he demanded when she stopped struggling. 'If you're still determined to behave like a sulky puss then go into the forest and shout at the trees. We're going back to Cowrie Cottage. Whether or not you come with us is no concern of mine.'

He lifted his backpack and slung it over his shoulder. The leather was scuffed and covered in stickers from places he'd visited. Karin walked on ahead, almost running in her effort to get away from us. The breeze blew my hair before my eyes and the feather was tossed lightly on a current of air before settling on the water. I watched it flow downstream and out of sight. We returned in silence to Cowrie Cottage, each of us wrapped in our own private thoughts.

The remaining days slid together in a blur of sunshine and games on the beach. I played volleyball and swan until I was exhausted. The sun played over my body when I lay face down on the rug to recover my breath, an intoxicating drug that pressed my thighs hard against the yielding sand and filled me with unfamiliar stirrings. I was in thrall to the wonder, terror, bliss, achiness, illusions and splendidness of first love. At night I wrote love letters, secrets outpourings for my eyes only. I cut a slit in the lining of my anorak and hid them deep inside it. Soon it would be time to go home. We would be returning to Gracehills on the day after Shard's much publicised gig in Barney's pub. Like Karin, I was in the grip of mood swings, wanting the holiday to end, longing for it to last forever.

CHAPTER ELEVEN

On the morning of the gig we met Reedy and Daryl in the small village supermarket. They were stocking up on beer for a party after the gig and the trolley was filled with six-packs, crisps and frozen pizzas.

Karin had begged her parents to let us go to the party. Joan refused to even consider it. We could go to Barneys to hear the band but we were returning with her and Max to Cowrie Cottage afterwards. He agreed with her. Subject closed. We were too young... always too young for everything, Karin raged. Joan was an 'alco–' she almost spat the word at me, and had no moral authority to refuse permission. The abbreviated word sounded harsh. I imagined Joan ending her life as a bag lady, sitting in doorways, a bottle hidden in a brown paper bag. We seethed together, united in our sense of injustice but things had changed between us that morning. Karin hadn't spoken to me at breakfast, nor did she speak to me as we walked through the supermarket where the locals were pretending not to stare at Daryl's dreadlocks or Reedy's jeans with the slits across the backside. Joan was pale but sober, her lipstick a red gash against her pale skin, her long, black hair matted. Her dress was torn under one arm, not deliberately, like Reedy's jeans, but uncaringly, as if how she looked no longer mattered. She reminded me of a Goth, not glamorous or exotic, just defeated.

Karin grabbed Daryl's dreadlocks and shrieked laughing when he lifted her and pretended to throw her into the shopping trolley. But once she left the supermarket she became quiet again and went immediately to her room.

The hot spell of weather had broken. Sullen clouds covered the sky and the tide rode on a grey swell. I spent the afternoon in Monsheelagh Bay, sheltered from the wind by the rocks. I'd knocked on Karin's door and asked if she wanted to come with me but she'd shouted at me to go away. I'd packed my clothes. We had an early start in the morning. I tried to concentrate on the book I'd brought with me but I was unable to think of anything except the reality of leaving Monsheelagh. How would I cope? What had been a magical time would end as soon as we drove from the cottage. Small children ran naked into the wind and fathers struggled determinedly into the water. I watched out for Jake but no one from Shard appeared. I figured they were probably rehearsing for tonight.

By evening the rain had started to fall. The smell of roast chicken wafted from the kitchen. Joan was peeling potatoes at the sink. She peered at me through her tangled fringe and I knew immediately she'd been drinking. Max was on the phone in the little parlour. I could hear his voice but not what he was saying. Lynette, his editor, rang every day to talk about the nomad book.

'Where's Karin?' I asked Joan.

'Sulking in her room,' she said. 'She's still annoyed about the party. Do you understand why I won't let you go?'

'You're afraid we'll get drunk.' Like you, I almost added then felt ashamed as I hurried from her into the privacy of my bedroom.

She called us for dinner. Max put a record on the old-fashioned record player. Dubussy, he said. 'Clair de lune'. French for 'moonlight'. He looked towards the window. 'No stars tonight.'

We helped with the washing up then went to our rooms to get ready for Shard. I heard a sudden crash, as if something fragile had been shattered against a wall. I moved quietly past Karin's room and along the corridor to the parlour. Max and Joan were arguing. Their voices slid under the door and brought me to a standstill. Joan's high-pitched voice was hardly recognisable. She didn't believe Max was going to the desert. He'd make it up like he always did, she said. Spin a yarn from a few encounters. Oh, he had a way with words all right. And his way with women. I ran back to my room and locked the door. I wanted to hide somewhere deep and safe. I opened my journal and tore out a page. The words I wrote made no sense. Unable to concentrate I pulled my anorak from the hook on the door and shoved the crumpled sheet of paper into the lining. My fingers probed deeper into the torn slit. All I felt was an empty space. I tore at the lining, the material ripping as I turned it inside out. My letters were missing. I broke out in goosebumps and pressed my face into the anorak in case I screamed out loud. Only one person could have taken them. Karin must have searched my room while I was on the beach in the afternoon. How could I ever face her again? The lash of shame, I've never forgotten it. As if someone had taken a blade and sliced into my heart, exposing its secret for all to see.

They were still shouting. Karin must also be able to hear but she stayed in her room. A door banged. Max was leaving. Joan shrieked something after him. I huddled under the duvet. Rain struck the walls in flurries and the wind whistled against the thatch. I thought about the three little pigs and the house of straw but the roof held strong. Only the furious rattle of the window frames disturbed the silence that settled over Cowrie Cottage. I knew we would not be going to the Shard gig tonight. I couldn't wait for morning, to be on the road and in the warm circle of my mother's arms.

An hour passed. I knocked on Karin's door. She refused to answer. I knocked harder, called her name. When she didn't come out I went into the parlour where Joan was curled in an armchair, a rug pulled over her shoulders. Broken glass covered the floor beside the back wall. Her face was red and blotchy, her eyes slitted from crying. The bottle of vodka on a small table beside her was half empty. She was drinking it neat. The room stank of alcohol. She was incoherent when I persuaded her to go to bed. I helped her into their bedroom. She was so light I could have carried her. I thought of deadwood, ready to snap. The bed was unmade, the indent of two heads still visible on the pillows, the sheets tangled. She tripped over Max's mountain boots – the ones he'd worn when we did our trek through Monsheelagh Forest – and sprawled forward onto the bed.

I pulled the duvet over her and listened, really listened, to the gale outside. It reminded me of an orchestra, shrill musicians without a composer to keep them in tune. Joan's hair covered her face. Her eyes, when I pulled the fringed aside, were closed. I wasn't sure if she was asleep or unconscious.

I waited for Max to return. Another hour passed. Was it the front door he'd slammed behind him? If so, he'd probably gone to the village. If it was the back door and he was on the cliff he should be wearing his boots. I banged again on Karin's door. Still no answer. I turned the handle. The door was locked.

I shook Joan awake. 'Where's Max?' I kept shouting into her face. 'Where has he gone?'

'Gone to hell… to hell,' she muttered. Her head lolled to one side, her clavicle a taut outline against her throat.

I checked the kitchen press where the torches were kept for walking home at night from Barney's pub. One was missing.

I took the red one I always used and zipped up my anorak. I walked along the top path. I was drenched in minutes, my feet sodden from the long grass. The steps were slick with rain. I held tightly to the railings as I descended and was almost swept off my feet when I shone the torch on the dark ocean below. The tide was full in, higher than I'd ever seen it. Savage white horses dashing against the cliff. I called Max's name repeatedly but the wind buffeted my voice and pitched it into the waves. Spume moistened the air, salted my lips as I clung to the railing and made my way back to the path.

I was frantic when I reached the gate leading to the cottage. Could Max have taken the steep path to the cove? My trainers skidded on the mud when I tried to find the trail. I sat down heavily, grasping heather and bracken to stop my fall. Lightening flailed like a whip in the pitch black sky. I huddled into my knees as the thunder roared. He would never have taken this path. Nor would he have used the steps. He must be in the village, drying off in Barney's pub.

I crawled back to safety and returned to the cottage. Somehow, Joan had pulled herself together. She'd showered and wrapped her hair in a towel, smeared on lipstick and made black coffee.

'I can't find Max.' I was sobbing, terrified by fears I was unable to utter aloud.

'He'll be back.' Her voice was still slurred but I could make out what she was saying. 'He always comes back… like a rolling stone he'll roll back to me. A bad… bad rolling stone… he'll roll back to me and lay all his moss at my feet.' She rocked back in the chair, a mug of coffee between her hands, and laughed. Her amusement only added to the wretchedness of her sad, clown face.

'He's been gone nearly two hours.' I tried to make her understand. 'What if he's on the cliff?'

'He can walk it blindfold,' she said but she slopped coffee on the table when she put the mug down.

Water dripped from my anorak and pooled at my feet. I sat on the edge of the bed and peeled off my wet jeans. When I'd changed into track suit bottoms I pressed my ear against the wall. The silence from Karin's room was absolute.

'Your father is missing,' I shouted. 'I'm afraid he's on the cliff.'

Still no answer. There was only one explanation. She must have gone out earlier. Maybe she was with Max. They could be in the village listening to Shard, relieved that they had escaped Joan's drunken tantrum. Was she showing him my letters, laughing at me for my foolishness?

'The phone's dead.' Joan stood on the threshold of my room, the towel wrapped like a turban around her head. 'I'm going to the village to ring the guards.'

'Maybe that's where he is,' I said. 'Karin's not in her room. She must have gone with him.'

She was scared at last and sobering fast as she walked unsteadily towards the front door. I ran after her. The wind gusted through the hall and slammed the door from her hand. She swayed against the door jamb then straightened and stumbled into the night. The towel loosened from its turban and flapped like the wings of a demented bird as it was blown away.

Her driving was erratic. I covered my eyes as she swerved wildly around corners but, thankfully, there was no traffic coming towards us. The waves were dashing so hard against the harbour wall it was impossible to park near it. She found a spot in the next road and held onto my arm as we ran towards the pub. My first time to hear Shard. Loud, raucous rock, so very different to the usual traditional music played in Barneys. The pub was packed.

We pushed our way through the crowd surrounding the bar and into the back where Shard were crowded onto a small stage. The walls vibrated with the energy of their music. Karin was on the stage beside Jake, her hands raised about her head as she slapped a tambourine. She had tied her hair in a ponytail and her resemblance to Max was clear in her sharp profile and the slant of her determined chin. Jake hugged her when the music stopped.

'Let's hear it for Karin,' he roared into the microphone and the crowd roared back. I looked around. Max was not there. Otherwise, he would have been in front of the stage cheering her on. My knees gave way. I grabbed the back of a chair and steadied myself. Joan's lips were puckered, as if frozen on words she was afraid to speak.

She pulled my arm, drawing me down to her level. 'I have to phone the guards,' she shouted in my ear. 'It's too noisy here. I'll ring them from the harbour phone. Get Karin down. We've got to get back to the cottage.'

The exultant glow in Karin's eyes darkened when she saw me. She blinked, as if the effort of looking at me required too much effort. She ignored me when I gestured at her to come down. The band was about to start a new number. I stepped onto the stage and grabbed her arm. Jake had signed his name on her skin. She jerked away from me and smacked the tambourine against my face. The crowd howled, their laughter thick with anticipation.

'Fight… fight,' someone roared and the cry was taken up.

Jake came between us. My lip was bleeding where one of the metal zils had cut the skin. I wiped the blood with the back of my hand, hardly aware of what I was doing.

'Whatever's going on, take it elsewhere,' Jake shouted. 'This is our night. Don't fuck it up.'

'Where's your father?' I yelled at Karin when she followed me from the stage. 'I thought he was here with you. Your mother's ringing the guards.'

'What's she doing that for?' She took a packet of cigarettes from her pocket and lit one. It was the first time I'd ever seen her smoking.

'He's been gone over two hours.' I had to make her understand. 'If he's on the cliff he could have had an accident.'

'Don't be so stupid,' she shouted. 'He'll be back soon. He always is.' The crowd pressed against us as Jake began to sing. She held the cigarette upright between her fingers and blew smoke into my eyes. 'Go back to the cottage with her. I'm staying with Jake. I showed your letters to my mother and I'll show them to him. Then he'll know what you're really like... you lying *cunt*.' She pressed her knuckles to her mouth, as if she was as shocked by the word as I was.

'I've been searching for him – '

'Filthy prostitute... that's what you are.'

Her words glanced off me. A terrible certainty had taken over and I was beyond being offended.

'What if he doesn't come back? Don't you care? He's *missing*. I went down to the beach searching for him but the tide's in over the sand. What if he's fallen from the cliff?'

For the first time she seemed to hear me. She shoved through the crowd, beating at them with her fists when they refused to move. It was still raining as we ran towards the harbour. Joan was talking to a man outside the phone kiosk. I recognised Charlie, the old fisherman who had danced with her all those week ago. She handed her car keys to him and he drove us back to the cottage.

'He'll be waiting for us,' Karin said. 'He'll be mad at us for going without him.' She shivered, drenched, as I was, from our run to the car.

'Of course he'll be there,' said Charlie. 'He's a man who knows his way around there parts, right enough.'

The cottage was as we'd left it. The sodden towel lay on the path and the front door banged open and closed. A squad car arrived shortly afterwards. The night was long and loaded with dread. Guards came and went. Searchlights illuminated the cliff. The coast guard and a mountain rescue team joined in the search. We sat up all night and convinced ourselves he'd run away. Karin said he'd come back for her. She repeated this like a mantra. I longed to cover my ears but I listened and agreed.

His body was found the next day, washed in on the tide. We knew he was gone by then. We'd seen where he'd fallen. The scrub broken and uprooted had been unable to stop his fall as he pitched forward into the night. He would have died as soon as he hit the rocks, dead before he was washed out to sea. Karin and her mother were assured of this fact many times, as if, somehow, this was a balm to be applied over their grief.

We both knew our friendship could never be rekindled. How could it? We only had to glance across at each other to remember the waiting hours and the dread of what the morning would bring. I wrote to her after her father's funeral and asked if we could meet and talk. The envelope came back to me by return of post. My note was inside, shredded.

Part Three

CHAPTER TWELVE

Jake

Jake took the Gibson from its stand and sat down on the straight-backed chair he always used when playing his guitar. He turned the tuning peg and checked the B string. Still too sharp. When the guitar was in tune he began to strum 'The Long Goodbye'. He needed to calm down. Music usually provided the perfect antidote but not tonight. He had needed a slap back to reality and that was what he received when the Kingfisher Graphics business card fell from his wallet. The shock on Nadine's face. Such unguarded hurt in her eyes. What had she been remembering when she picked it up? She had been silent of the journey home and had gone straight into her office. Had she believed him? He needed to delete those texts and photographs, stop behaving like a lovesick schoolboy and bid goodbye to a fantasy that was never going to become a reality.

She crossed the hall and entered his music room without knocking. They had an unwritten rule to respect each other's privacy and his uneasiness grew when she sat down on the edge of the tatty, old sofa, the only piece of furniture they had brought with them from Oakdale Terrace. His fingers pressed nervously on the fret as he strummed lightly, nervously.

'I want to talk about our marriage.' Her back was ramrod straight, her cheeks flushed.

'What about our marriage?'

'We both know it isn't working anymore.' She twirled a hank of hair around her middle finger, a habit she had never outgrown when she was upset. 'I'm sorry for blurting it out like this. I've been trying to think of a right way to say this… but the right way doesn't exist.'

'Not working? Since when has our marriage stopped working?' He automatically tightened the D string then twanged it so violently it snapped and cut his finger.

She flinched at the discordant sound. 'You're bleeding. I'll get a bandage.'

'It's okay… okay.' He pulled tissues from a box and wrapped them around the cut. 'I'm confused. Are you saying you want to leave me?'

Her eyes filled with tears. 'No, Jake. I want us to leave each other. I want us to be free to do the things we've always wanted to do.' Her stance, the rigid set of her shoulders added to the tension in the room.

He stood up and rummaged in the media unit where he kept the spare sets of strings. 'Let me get this straight. First of all you want to sell Tōnality. Then the house. Now you want to end our marriage. Am I leaving anything out? Would you like to disown our children, perhaps? *Pretend* they never existed?'

'Are *you* going to pretend you still love me?'

'Of course I love you.' His hands shook as he tried to restring his guitar. He gave up and replaced it carefully on its stand.

'Like a brother loves a sister,' she said. 'Like friends. That's us, Jake. How often do we make love? We're too tired, that's what we say. We both know that's not true. We never wanted this marriage but we knuckled down and made the best of it.'

'We did more than that, Nadine. We worked at it.'

'We've worked it to the bone. It's made us old before our time. I won't be forty for another six months but I feel as if we've lived the full circle of life when, really, there's still so much more we can experience. I need more from my life and so do you.'

'Stop telling me what *I* need,' he shouted. 'You're willing to risk our marriage, our family, our home, our company on some harebrained notion that life should offer you more. I *can't* believe what I'm hearing.'

'You know I'm right. It's time we stopped pretending.'

'I'm not pretending.' He sat beside her on the sofa, the space of a cushion between them. He grasped her shoulders, pulled her close to him. 'What are you trying to do to us?'

'I'm giving you back your freedom.'

The word throbbed into the open and a new energy, apprehension, tumultuous fear – Jake was unable to define it – vibrated between them.

'I can't talk about this anymore tonight,' he said. 'I don't know what to think... what to say....'

She swayed suddenly and moved closer to him, flushed, eager, her hands held outwards, pleading with him to embrace a vision only she could see. 'We can make this work, Jake. You'll thank me in the end. Once the children understand that nothing fundamental is going to change in their lives, they'll accept our decision. It's our time now.'

He felt her heat, the tremor of her breath when they kissed. Her lips opened under the pressure of his tongue. To his surprise, and, probably Nadine's, they made love on the old sofa, as they used to do when the children were in bed and they lived in a small house where even a hiccup could be heard through the walls. No wonder the sofa sagged in the middle.

They did not bother removing their clothes. No foreplay to delay the inevitable clash of pleasure. No awkwardness as they unzipped, unhooked, unbuttoned, undid each other's resolve to pretend that this was anything other than a familiar ritual. She was moist and ready, sweet and juicy as the apple she had so temptingly held before him. Her desire matched his own, their cries buried in each other's shoulders as they shuddered into relief. When she moaned he was unsure if the muffled sound was carried on pleasure or pain.

The sofa was uncomfortable, broken springs pressing into their hips, legs cramping as they untangled themselves, the aftertaste of sex on their lips. A slight embarrassment as she fastened her bra, her face averted from him.

In bed, she fell into an exhausted sleep. He tried to imagine waking up beside a different face, a different form — Karin Moylan sauntered into view – but the leap was too great for his imagination. Nadine turned, still sleeping, and slid her arm across his hip. A practiced gesture, as established as his regular breathing when he finally drifted asleep. Her words were out there now, asteroids in space, already spinning off in directions neither of them could foresee.

CHAPTER THIRTEEN

Three weeks had passed since that night. Sometimes, in the throes of work, Jake wondered if he had imagined their entire conversation. Freedom. The word had dangerous connotations and Nadine had teased them out in front of him. Was she crazy? Was he crazy not to listen to her? She had not mentioned their discussion since, nor had he, but ignoring something did not mean it would go away. She was waiting for him to make up his mind. When they were together he was aware of her every movement, each change of expression, the undercurrent of tension behind her words. Had he ever known what went on beneath that storm of red hair?

Small but significant changes were taking place between them. They had not made love since that night. The desire that flamed so swiftly had burned itself out and, now, they lay chastely apart, apologising, almost embarrassed, if they made contact. They avoided intimate actions like walking naked from the shower or dressing in front of each other. They tapped on their office doors before entering and no longer checked each other's work diaries, something they used to do without a second thought. And the texts he had intended on deleting remained on his phone. New ones arrived from Karin but they no longer lifted his spirits or sank him into a reverie. He was focused on only one thing. The decision he must make. He had the unsettling sensation that a tamed animal might feel when faced with the challenge of an open cage door.

Then Darina Moylan died. Five years in the grip of Alzheimer's, Darina passed gently away and Karin flew home from for her grandmother's funeral. It was literally a 'flying' visit, she emphasised to Jake in her text. She would spend two days in Dublin where she would attend her grandmother's funeral and view the apartment she hoped to buy.

They met in the Clarion Hotel beside Dublin Airport for an hour before she flew back to New York. She was waiting for him when he arrived, still dressed in funeral black, the brim of a hat low over her eyes. Darina had outlived her contemporaries and her funeral had been a quiet ceremony, Karin told him when he expressed his condolences. She was pleased with the apartment and had decided to buy it. He knew the location. One of the flashy Celtic Tiger developments built on the once derelict docklands overlooking the Liffey.

'How's the Shard reunion coming along?' she asked after he had viewed photos of the apartment on her mobile.

'We've had to postpone,' he admitted.

Her eyes narrowed with disappointment when he explained that Reedy had been offered a contract with a band whose guitarist went into rehab just as they were about to tour the States.

'We've still four months to go before we're officially over the twenty-five year mark,' he said. 'So, it will happen before March.'

'I'll be living back here by then,' she said. 'Will you invite me?'

'It's an open concert. Anyone can come.'

'I'll look forward to it.' She stirred her cappuccino and licked the froth from the curve of the spoon. 'How's Nadine?'

'Busy.'

'That's all you ever say.'

'What do you want me to say?'

'The truth. Is she happy with you? Are you happy with her? And, if so, why are you here with me?'

'That's a lot of questions, Karin.'

'Are you going to answer them?'

'It's complicated.'

'That's not an answer.' She was challenging him, her head tilted at that now familiar angle.

'I'll tackle the last one first,' he said. 'I'm here with you because I can't get you out of my head. You're a torment and a pleasure. I keep thinking about New York. About what could have happened if you'd invited me into your apartment.'

'I've thought about that too,' she said softly. 'But I'm not sure what we're going to do about it.'

He had forgotten the power of her gaze. The smouldering promise carried on the sweep of eyelashes.

'When are you moving back here?' he asked.

'Why?'

'You shouldn't have to ask.'

'Oh, but I do. Dublin isn't New York, Jake. It's like a village with its ear to the ground. What about Nadine? If we do see each other… what are you offering me? An affair? I've been down that road before. It doesn't lead anywhere.'

He was tempted to throw caution to the wind and tell her everything. Instinct warned him it was too soon. He was standing on the edge of a crevice, his toes braced against the fall.

'I'm not offering you an affair, Karin.'

'What then?'

'A relationship… if that's what you also want. But…'

She smiled ruefully. 'Married men always have a 'but.' What's yours?'

'I've some important decisions to make. I can't say more than that for now. Can you trust me to have everything sorted out when I see you again?'

'Are you a rarity, Jake Saunders? An honest married man? Or are you teasing me? Promising something you can't possibly deliver? Where's Nadine in all of this?'

'Nadine wants what I want.'

'Really?' She checked her watch and stood up. 'You two seem to share everything, including the desire to end your marriage. It's time to catch my flight.'

'Is something wrong?' He was startled by her abrupt comment but she had bent to pick up her overnight case. A slit at the back of her dress opened to reveal a trim of kingfisher blue. He admired the way she used her signature colour, flamboyantly draping it over her shoulders or discreetly revealing it in the bend of a pleat. She was smiling again when she straightened.

'Why should anything be wrong?' she asked as they walked towards the exit. 'I want you, Jake. I always have… ever since that summer. But I don't share. That's something you have to accept or this relationship you've promised won't work. Is that a commitment you're prepared to make?'

'Yes.'

At the top of the steps she stretched on her toes to kiss him. No longer eye-to-eye, mouth-to-mouth. A new configuration, his tall frame against her diminutive figure. Would their conversation have moved so swiftly from a light flirtation into something more demanding if Nadine had not dangled such alluring possibilities before him? She had kicked the supports of their marriage from under him and he was adrift on anticipation. On the newness of discovery. Addictive, mind-blowing emotions.

'You were right about everything,' he told Nadine when they were in bed that night. 'Thank you for having the courage to take that first step.'

She looked exhausted, dark shadows under her eyes. Was she regretting her decision already? Too late now. His resolve was as fixed as the markings on a new coin.

'It won't be easy,' she said. 'Eleanor will be furious.'

'I'll deal with her. What we've decided to do is none of her business.'

'We'll tell the children when they're all together at Christmas?'

'We will.' A claw sharpened with guilt scraped against his chest.

'Do you think we'll have phantom pains when we separate?' she asked. 'You in your mews. Me in my cottage.'

'Phantom pains are possible,' he replied. 'For a while, anyway… until we get used to being apart.'

'I hope we don't end up hating each other.'

'Impossible,' he reassured her. 'I'll always love you.'

'And I'll love you.'

Declarations of love… what a way to end a marriage. They loved each other once with passion. Now they loved with affection. A world of difference existed between loving someone and *being* in love, overwhelmed, besotted, crazed with yearning, giddy, and delirious.

❄ ❄ ❄

The trees lining the pavements of Bartizan Downs were bare now and the black branches had the clenched arthritic look of winter. It was dark when he and Nadine left for Tōnality in the mornings and dark when they returned in the evenings.

Ravens crouched like a menacing army on the rooftops. Beady eyes and cruel beaks, their feathers sleek as oil as they rose in black, clamorous flight, heading to roost in distant trees in the Malahide Demesne.

Poverty and the downfall of a family, Rosanna used to say. Harbingers of doom, that's ravens for you.

CHAPTER FOURTEEN

Nadine

The twins, their peachy skin bleached by the chill of an Irish winter, are the first to arrive home. They radiate energy and purposefulness in their tight jeans and runners, ribbed tops showing off their flat, muscular stomachs. Ali, wrapped in faux furs and Uggs, follows a day later. Brian arrives late on Christmas Eve. He's grown a beard and his hands feel abrasive, as if clay has lodged deep in the pores.

Our house emerges from its tomblike silence. It's filled with voices, laughter, music, the clatter of footsteps, phones ringing. My family are happy to be together again. They seem possessed of a manic but joyous energy as they wrap presents and dash in and out from each other's rooms to borrow wrapping paper, gift tags and glitter bobbins. They play CD's of Christmas carols and outdo each other in their choice of gaudy festive jumpers. How will they react when we tell them? How have they not picked up on the nervousness between myself and Jake? When they were younger they could sense a shift in our moods by holding a finger in the air. These days, I suspect, we'd need to attack each other with axes before they'd notice.

For years the seating arrangement around our table on Christmas Day never changed. Four generations gathered together, the six of us joined by Eleanor, Rosanna and my uncles,

Donal and Stuart. This year Donal, my father's brother, is the only one of the older generation to join us. Stuart, my mother's brother, is remaining in London. Six months ago he was diagnosed with cancer. He's positive and upbeat, convinced of a good outcome, but his chemo has been tough so he's staying close to home with friends. We'll miss our beloved Rosanna and Eleanor – who always endured rather than enjoyed this noisy and often boisterous family meal – is spending Christmas in Wicklow with friends from First Affiliation. I tried not to look relieved when she told us. The dreaded moment postponed.

Presents are exchanged on Christmas morning. No squabbles, sulks or disappointed silences. Each gift is judged to be the perfect one. Brian gives us pieces of pottery. I receive a decorative ceramic box from his new Willow Passion collection. It's shaped like a heart, the lid split down the middle in a gentle curve. Can he possibly suspect… but, no. His eyes are guileless as he waits for me to comment on it. The glaze is subtle. Weeping willows hazed in mist, two figures glimpsed within the pale-green fronds. The position of their bodies hint at secret dalliances, stolen moments, but the image is so delicately drawn that it adds to rather than diminishes their sexual vigour.

Their happy mood continues throughout the day. I've never known them to be so civilised, pleasant and entertaining. They burst into applause when the turkey is carried to the table and Jake brandishes the carving knife. They heap their plates and talk about their childhood with the bittersweet nostalgia of octogenarians. Flash bulb memories, all of them zooming in on their old house in Oakdale Terrace. Jake demands to know if they're talking about the house where they constantly complained about swallowing each other's air? The house where warfare broke out over who should enter the bathroom first in the morning? They laugh and insist it was all part of its charm.

'A toast to the best parents in the world,' Ali's brown eyes shine with appreciation.

Donal raises his glass in a salute and says, as he always does,'*Is féidir linn a bheith go léir le chéile ag an am seo an bhliain seo chugainn,*'

'I agree.' Samantha leans towards him and clinks glasses. 'May we all be together at this time next year.'

'Cool,' agrees Sam.

'What's all this about?' Jake clasps his chest and pretends to topple from his chair. 'No one's getting an increase in their living allowance and that's that.'

'Oh, Dad, stop being such a cynic.' Samantha slaps his hand and cries out, 'Merry Christmas to one and all.'

What will next Christmas bring? Is there a protocol for separated couples? Where will we gather to feast and be merry? Jake's mews? My place? I keep changing my mind about where I want to live. A cottage or a small, terraced townhouse, mellowed with memories? A smart city centre apartment with a balcony and good light for painting?

We wave Donal off in a taxi and settle down to play Scrabble. Jake takes out his guitar and we sing the same Christmas songs we've sung since they were children. He plays some of his own songs, something he's never done before. They listen appreciatively then Ali says, 'they're brilliant, Dad. Now play 'Frosty the Snowman.''

Jake is first into the kitchen this morning. He cooks a fry-up for breakfast and they come to the table without having to be coaxed from their beds. They're fully dressed, instead of slouching, dead-eyed and baleful in onesies or pyjamas. They epitomise the perfect family as they tuck into rashers and sausages, pass toast and various bottles of ketchup to each other. My heart fails me when I look around the table at their happy faces. I want them to turn savage, to rain insults on each other as they once did without the slightest provocation. Anything to ease my guilt. But they continue to laugh at each other's jokes, listen to each other's opinions and discuss the planned hill-walking expedition we will take later in the week, weather permitting.

It's late evening and they're lolling in armchairs, eating cold turkey and chocolates, when Jake switches off the television. Now that the moment has arrived I'm consumed by panic. This is a dreadful mistake. How have I allowed my desire for a different life to obscure the value of the one I have? Why do I have this urge to strike out on my own and discover the person I could have been if things had worked out differently? It's such a puny, selfish reason. I could have controlled it...would have controlled it if that business card had not fallen from his wallet. He met her on that flight and never thought to mention her to me. His casual indifference astonished me. And with it came the anger. But I'm calmer now... surely it's not too late to pull back from the brink? I gaze across at Jake. He'll read my mind and understand that we must stop this madness now. His eyes meet mine, fixed, grey, steely.

'We've something important to discuss with you,' he says.

The gravity of his tone silences them. Samantha moves closer on the sofa to Sam. Brian stops searching for the box of Trivial Pursuit and sits back on his heels.

'We want... we're going to....' Jake's carefully rehearsed words falter before their expectant faces.

I press my hands against my stomach and lean forward. Jake, aware of my panic, pats my shoulder.

'Oh my God, Mum!' A horrified expression sweeps across Ali's face. 'You're going to have a baby!'

My breath explodes outwards. 'How can I be pregnant when your father has had – '

Jake coughs warningly. His vasectomy is something he never intends discussing with his children.

'No, Ali, I'm not pregnant,' I reply in what I hope is a reassuring tone. 'We want to talk to you about some… some important changes we intend to make.'

'Like what?' Brian looks from Jake to me.

'We're going to sell the house.' Jake finds his voice again. 'It's too big for us, now that you've all left home.'

'It was always too big for us,' Samantha agrees. 'We should never have left Oakdale. Do you remember the time – '

'Selling it is an excellent idea.' Ali cuts short another trip down memory lane. 'You said *changes*. What else?'

'We're also selling Tōnality.' Jake examines his thumb then folds it into a fist. 'We've decided to do something different with our lives.'

'*Different?*' Samantha sounds astonished.

'I'm hoping to enrol as a mature student and study art,' I reply.

'I'm looking at options,' says Jake. 'I'm thinking of setting up a recording studio and reforming Shard.'

'Cool,' Sam exclaims through a mouthful of Ferrero Rocher but Ali looks equally horrified by this possibility.

'Reforming Shard at your age, Dad? That's *so* embarrassing.' She gazes sternly at us. 'This is serious mid-life crisis stuff. Are you going through the change, Mum?'

'First I'm pregnant and now I'm menopausal.' It's important to remain calm. 'Make up your mind, Ali.'

'I'm *sorry*,' she shrugs. 'I just figured… you're at that age.'

'At *our* age we still have lives to lead and that's why we've decided…' Jake falters once again before continuing, 'We've come to an agreement… we've decided to separate.'

'Separate what?' asks Samantha.

'Separate from each other,' he replies.

'You're leaving Mum?' Brian stares disbelievingly at his father.

'*Dad*,' Ali shrills. 'You *can't*! This is *too* awful.'

Samantha and Sam fix accusatory eyes on Jake.

'After everything she's done for you?' says Samantha. 'Is that all the thanks she gets? It's not fair, Dad. It just *isn't*.' She dashes to my chair and flings her arms around me.

'Too right,' Sam agrees.

I prise my head loose from Samantha's fierce embrace and speak with as much composure as possible. 'Your father and I came to a mutual decision. We're going to lead our own lives but that won't make any difference whatsoever to *your* lives. We'll have family days together, celebrations, Christmas. Whatever comes up we'll be together to share it with you. This will be a perfect divorce.'

'A *perfect* divorce.' Brian snorts in disbelief. 'That's a paradox if ever I heard one.'

'You'll end up hating each other.' Ali's voice shakes dangerously. 'That's how it always works out.'

'No, you're wrong,' says Jake. 'This doesn't mean we stop liking each other or anything ridiculous like that. But we're still young enough – '

'*Young?*' The twins, speaking in unison, appear stunned by this notion.

Brian shoves the box of Trivial Pursuits back into the press and Ali shrills, 'Thanks, folks, for making this the *jolliest* Christmas ever.'

They go to bed early, close their doors quietly. The atmosphere in the house has changed. The lights on the Christmas tree are too bright, the bedecked garlands mocking this season of good cheer.

My earlier panic has eased now that we've told them the truth. I shake my head when Jake asks if I'd like a drink. I don't want to talk about what we've done. He pours a measure of whiskey but leaves it sitting on the arm of his chair. He, too, seems reluctant to talk. What is left to say?

The following day my children treat me with an eggshell caution, convinced I'll crack and splatter them with my grief.

'I'll talk to Dad,' Ali says when we're alone in the kitchen. 'He always listens to me. I can't bear to think of you being left on your own.'

'This is what I want, Ali. It's a mutual decision.'

'So you keep saying. But you're allowed to be upset. Leave the stiff upper lip to the Brits.'

Samantha offers a muscular shoulder for me to cry on. 'I've never seen Dad as the marrying kind,' she says. 'He's so… you know…?' She taps her bottom lip as she searches for the right word. 'So cool. Those posters of Shard are *really* retro. He could have made it big, gone international. Maybe he'll do it this time… now that he's free to follow his dream.'

I ask if I'm the marrying kind and Samantha, oblivious to the chill in my voice, shrugs. 'Can't say I've ever thought about it. I mean, you're my mum.'

My father doesn't pretend to be surprised when I ring him in Australia. 'I always knew he'd pull up stakes and leave you sooner or later,' he says. 'You've got to put your foot down and demand that he pays you proper alimony.'

Why does everyone automatically assume it's Jake who wants out of our marriage? It implies that he's the most dissatisfied, most disillusioned, most eager to escape. I'm filled with a childish desire to yell, 'It was me! *My* decision. Mine alone!' Instead, I inquire about the weather. What degree is it in Sydney when they are dining al fresco. Eoin has never lost the Irish compulsion to discuss climatic changes. When we've exhausted that topic he hands the phone to Lilian who's polite, as always. I've never accepted her as my stepmother and our conversation is always an exchange of information about furniture and health. She must have overheard the discussion with my father, but our roles are too defined to tackle emotional issues. She tells me about her gall stone operation and the new suite of furniture she bought last week in a Harvey Norman sale. Just before we say goodbye she whispers, 'Grab life by the balls, Nadine. Don't let go, even when it shrieks.'

'I will,' I promise and we wish each other a happy New Year.

CHAPTER FIFTEEN

The wind is brisk this morning, the sky clear with a sharp, wintery blueness when they set off on their hill-walking expedition to the Dublin Mountains. I won't join them this year. Some traditions have to break and I can't endure their pity for another day. It's good to have the house to myself. I tidy the living room and am about to stack the dishwasher when the front doorbell rings three times in quick succession. My heart sinks. Only Eleanor can make chimes sound imperious.

She's pale but composed as she sweeps past me into the kitchen and places her handbag on the table.

'Where's Jake?' she asks. 'He's not answering his mobile.'

'He must have turned it off when he went out.' I switch on the kettle. 'Something to eat, Eleanor? A mince pie, perhaps? Some Christmas cake?'

'No, thank you. I'm too upset to eat anything.' She gazes reproachfully at me for ruining her appetite. 'I would have preferred to speak to you and Jake together but, perhaps, that's just as well. Woman to woman we can sort this out. I've had a most distressing phone call from your father.'

My jaw clenches. Trust Eoin. He could never keep his mouth shut.

'Tell me he's mistaken,' Eleanor makes it sound like a demand. 'Jake has his failings, like all men, but he'd never walk out on his wife and family.'

'He's hillwalking with his family right now.'

'Don't be facetious, Nadine. You know what I mean.'

'We intended telling you ourselves. Eoin had no right to ring you.'

'So, it's true? He's leaving you?'

'It's a mutual decision.' Is my voice developing a sing-song incantation, rather like a Buddhist chant? 'And the children have accepted – '

'I'm glad you mentioned your children.' Years of battling on the airwaves have perfected Eleanor's interruptive skills. 'Have you any idea of the trauma you're going to cause them if you go ahead with this rash decision? The statistics on broken marriages that First Affiliation have compiled would make your hair stand on end.'

'Why should they be unhinged by our divorce?' I demand. 'We're not going to play games with their emotions. The truth is that Jake and I have outgrown each other and – '

'Do you think marriage is a growth hormone, Nadine?' She arches her eyebrows. Over the years, as her hair greyed and was dyed to a steely blonde, her eyebrows have remained black, as finely curved and expressive as calligraphy. 'You don't outgrow it like a pair of shoes. What do you think would happen to marriage if couples were to separate because they were *bored* with each other?'

'I guess it would become one of those quaint customs from the past, like sacrificing virgins or foot binding.'

'Sarcasm is the lowest form of wit, my dear,' she snaps. 'You must realise how such a reckless decision will affect my reputation.'

At last she's reached the nub of the matter.

'You can't be held responsible for our decision,' I argue. 'It's not as if we're going to broadcast – '

She delves into her handbag and slides a leaflet across the table towards me. 'This woman is a highly qualified marriage counsellor. I want you and Jake to make an appointment with her. You can begin to sort out your problems by sitting down and discussing them with her.'

'I've no intention of seeing a marriage counsellor, nor has Jake. This is all about perception. That's all you've ever cared about. Your precious reputation.'

In a radio interview shortly after the twins were born Eleanor spoke about the joys of being a grandmother. She described myself and Jake as a shining example of a young couple devoted to each other and their family. Sleepless with the demands of four children under three years of age and aware that she had never once offered to babysit, I tore the paper in shreds before ringing her and forbidding her ever again to use her grandchildren as propaganda. That was the first time I ever confronted her. Eleanor was used to tougher combatants than her hysterical daughter-in-law and she took the attack in her stride. But I never forgot my exhilaration as I slammed the phone down, dizzying in its mix of anger and elation. The sensation I now feel is similar.

'Yes, my dear, I care about perception and make no apologies for doing so,' she says. 'It's often a more potent force for change than truth.' She pauses, swallows audibly, the veins in her neck tightening. 'You and Jake have no right to ruin the lives of your children with your selfish recklessness.'

I long to slap her inflexible face. The feel of flesh on flesh, the sting of satisfaction. 'You must respect our wishes, Eleanor. Jake and I are getting divorced. You have to stop interfering in our lives.'

'And you must stop trying to ruin mine.' She closes her handbag, pulls on her driving gloves. 'This counsellor is experienced and discreet. I'll tell her to expect your call.'

It's dark now. They'll be home soon. I carve the last of the turkey. Jake will be relieved to eat something spicy. He detests turkey but any time he suggests a succulent roast lamb or a cracking belly of pork instead of the traditional Christmas dinner, our family rise up in protest. The tyranny of tradition. I slice deeply into the white flesh and add it to the simmering curry sauce. My eyes sting from the piquant spices. I set the table, six places once again.

A text comes through, the sharp bleep startling me. I reach into the corner unit for the phone and have clicked into the message before I realise it's Jake's mobile I'm holding.

*Xmas over at last. Homeward bound soon. It's up to you…
New York… New York!*

The front door opens. They're glowing from the outdoors, crumpled anoraks, muddy hiking pants and boots, beanies pulled low over their foreheads.

'Smells delicious!' Jake sniffs the air and makes a beeline for the cooker. 'Alleluia! It's the end of the turkey.'

'I opened one of your texts by mistake,' I tell him when the others have gone upstairs to shower.

'Oh… what was the message?'

'Something about New York. Your phone's over there if you want to read it.' I gesture towards the corner unit.

'I wondered where I'd left it.' He glances across at the phone but makes no effort to pick it up. 'It's probably Reedy.'

'Reedy?'

'He's gigging there at the moment.' He lifts the saucepan lid and inspects the contents. 'This looks *so* good.'

'Eleanor was here. She knows.'

He meets my eyes for the first time. 'Who told her?'

'Eoin.'

'That figures. Was she dreadful?'

'There were no thumb screws involved but, otherwise, yes, she was her normal bullying, egocentric self.'

'I'm sorry I wasn't here. I'll talk to her tomorrow. Make her understand.'

'You're an atheist, Jake. You don't believe in miracles.'

'She can't stop us doing what we want.'

'That's true.' I strain the rice. 'You'd better scrub up. Dinner's almost ready.'

'Okay then.' He removes his phone from the shelf and slips it into his pocket. 'I'll have a quick shower. Be down in five.'

I remember Reedy. Basset hound eyes and stick legs in skinny jeans. I see his name on album credits, always as a session musician. 'Have bass guitar will travel'.

When dinner is over, the twins, Ali and Brian head off to meet their friends from Oakdale.

'Peace at last.' Jake switches on the television and settles down to watch the box set he received as a present from the twins.

'Why does everyone believe you're the unhappy spouse?' I ask him.

'You know the kids.' He shrugs, unconcerned, and presses the remote. 'Once they get a notion into their heads, that's it.'

'I'm sick of fending off their pity.'

'I wouldn't let it bother me.'

'Well, it does.'

'It shouldn't. Anyway, what's unhappiness got to do with it? You never mentioned that word until now.'

'But you must have been unhappy or you wouldn't have agreed so readily when I asked for the divorce.'

'*Readily*. Give me a break, Nadine.'

'Would you have asked for one if I hadn't suggested it first?'

'That's a hypothetical question. And I wasn't aware we were involved in a competition to see who dumped who first.'

This is a ridiculous conversation. I'm behaving like a sulky child. But something's wrong. I sense it, like nails scratching against my forehead, and I'm edgy, not knowing what it is.

'I'm sorry, Jake.' This is not the time for a row. 'It's been one of those days – '

'Forget it.' He flaps his hand in my direction. 'You're probably due your period.'

'Oh, here we go again!' My anger explodes. 'Nadine's asking awkward questions so she must be due her period. Nadine's in a bad mood so she must be due her period. Nadine tore my head off for being a prick so she must be due her period! Why do you always do that?'

'Sounds like it's due tomorrow.' He remains unruffled.

'That's it!' It's years since I've shrieked like this at him. 'I'm moving into the spare bedroom.'

'Go ahead,' he replies. 'It's what you've wanted to do for months.'

'Correction… it's what *you've* wanted me to do for months.'

The following morning we make up our row. Stress, we both agree. Who can blame us? We agree on this also. We're perched high on the stress pyramid. An impending divorce, selling our house and business, a bank manager with the heart of a rock, adult children who need constant financial support until they're ready to make their own way in the world. And Eleanor. I'm unsure where she should rank on the pyramid. The apex, probably. I refuse to allow her that vaulted position. My mother-in-law can and will be handled.

When Jake visits her I remove my clothes from our bedroom, clear my make-up and jewellery box from the dressing table.

'What did she say?' I ask when he returns.

He throws his eyes upwards. 'Three guesses. But there's nothing she can do to change our minds.'

'I've moved my stuff into the other room. It's more honest, don't you think?'

'I would have moved – '

'It's done, Jake.'

I acknowledge the dragging pain in my back. He's right, damn him. My period will have arrived by tonight. I can never decide if being premenstrual means I'm overreacting to situations or staring at the truth with a hard, unflinching gaze.

CHAPTER SIXTEEN

Jake

The New Year began as the old one ended. Recession... austerity... downturn... crash. Such words invaded his dreams and dominated his waking hours. He had married Nadine in the eighties on the cusp of a recession and now they were divorcing on the cusp of another one.

Paul Rowan from Brass & Strings, who had been trying to buy Tōnality for years, was no longer interested. He had invested everything in property and had a dead-man-walking expression when he met Jake for lunch. Flushed cheeks and red veins on his nose, an ominous sign. Susanna Cox from HiNotes Music Academy had also changed her mind. Contraction, not expansion was the only way to survive the recession, she said. Her offer to buy Tōnality was off the table. A third buyer – who had once made a derisory offer for Tōnality – was approached. This derisory offer would now be welcomed with open arms but since Tōnality lost the STRUM contract the buyer was looking elsewhere to expand.

Jake contacted an estate agent, a smooth-talking young woman, who convinced him their house would sell easily. Nine couples came to the first showing. After poking into corners and inspecting the presses, not one of them expressed any further interest. Jake suspected they were sightseers, voyeurs who, in centuries past, would have brought their knitting and watched the guillotine coming down. The estate agent was now talking about making 'realistic market adjustments.' This meant only one thing: drop the price.

He kept waking in the small hours. Unable to go back to sleep he would toss restlessly until it was time to get up. The bed was too big for one person but Nadine showed no inclination to share it with him again. Working together used to be easy but nowadays they snapped at each other over little things, tempers flaring when they were both exhausted.

'You and Nadine should be sitting tight on your assets and riding out the recession together,' said Daryl when Jake confided in him.

'How long will that take?' Jake asked.

'Five years… six max.'

'Are you kidding?'

'I wish I was.'

Daryl worked in investment finance and had been claiming for years that the banks were in a bubble. When Jake had argued that the economic experts claimed there would be 'a soft landing' Daryl had snorted and said, 'We're talking about the economy, stupid, not a bouncy castle.'

Politicians had called him and his ilk 'prophets of doom.' Now it turned out that they were simply 'prophets.'

'If you and Nadine are serious about splitting up, you should talk to my sister,' Daryl said. 'Divorce is Carol's area of expertise.'

Jake hesitated, nervous about taking such a huge step forward. 'Isn't it too soon to involve solicitors?'

'I'm just suggesting an informal meeting with Carol,' Daryl replied. 'Find out exactly what's involved. I'll ring her if you like, let her know you'll be in touch.'

'No harm, I suppose,' he said. 'I'll check with Nadine.'

Jake had known Carol Farrell since she was pumping iron in a baby bouncer. She threw up over his first pair of Converse and could beat him and Daryl at arm wrestling by the time she was six. Now she had a brass nameplate outside her office and was known in family law circles as The Avenger.

'I have to admit that this is the most civilised divorce I've ever come across,' Carol said when she heard their details. 'Normally, on a first meeting I'm dodging verbal bullets across my desk.'

'This is a mutual decision,' said Nadine with unnecessary firmness. 'We're both in agreement that we want a fifty-fifty split and no animosity.'

'I'm glad there's no animosity.' Carol checked the documents they had brought with them. 'But if you decide to go through the courts I can't work for both of you. One of you will have to be represented by a different solicitor.'

'You belong to me,' said Jake, half-joking, wholly serious. 'You still owe me for a pair of Converse.'

'Marion Norman is a good friend of mine and very competent.' She glanced across her desk at Nadine, who nodded in agreement.

'This seems perfectly straightforward,' said Carol. 'All your details appear to be in order. When there's an equal division of assets I don't foresee any problems. If you remain living apart for four years you'll automatically be granted your divorce.'

'Four years!' Jack was unable to hide his shock. 'Why does it take so long? This is a no-faults divorce.'

'Under Irish law that's the timespan.' Carol pressed the documents together until the edges were aligned. Her nails were white-tipped, squared off, efficient. 'If your mother and her merry band of zealots had had their way, you wouldn't have a snowball's chance in hell of getting a divorce.'

'Don't remind me,' said Jake. 'I still remember the arguments you used to have with her.'

'The best days of my life.' Carol's eyes sparkled. 'Eleanor trained me to be a cage fighter.' She handed two information booklets to them. 'Everything is explained here. Consider your options and get back to me when you've decided how you want to proceed.'

She shook their hands and escorted them to the front door. They walked in silence towards the gates of St. Stephen's Green. It was a mild January day and the park was busy with people on their lunch break, some relaxing on benches, others strolling along the paths with cartons of coffee and baguettes.

'Four years!' Jake sighed when they reached the duck pond and sat down on a bench. 'I'll probably have a brood of grandchildren by then.'

Nadine laughed shortly and leaned her head back, her hand screening her eyes. 'Do you think we'll ever emerge from this mess?' she asked.

'I wouldn't call our marriage a mess,' he protested.

'I'm talking about Tōnality. Losing STRUM is really affecting us. We're in a lot of trouble, Jake.'

'I know. But we'll manage. It'll just take a little longer than we expected.'

Who was he trying to convince? Not Nadine, if her expression was anything to go by. He watched the ducks waddling towards a small, chubby boy in a peaked cap. The boy held out a crust of bread but let it fall before the ducks reached him. He scampered back to his mother, who lifted him up in her arms. Sunday afternoons when the children were small, this was where they came. The scene never changed, only the ducks and the children moved on.

A woman dressed in a blue coat emerged from the shadow of trees. Blonde and slim, confident stride, Jake saw her everywhere, a flash, an illusion, as this one probably was.

The hill-walking expedition had been ruined when he realised his phone was at home. He had been consumed with dread that a text would arrive from Karin and be read by Nadine. The fact that that was exactly what happened had horrified him. No more muddied thoughts, half-baked fantasies, ridiculous texts. Text sex… his kids would coil up and die with shame if they knew. As for Nadine… how would she have reacted if she had searched his phone, discovered Karin's photographs, read her pithy, witty comments? That night, before he could change his mind, he deleted every text and photograph he had received from or sent to her by phone. Then he emailed her.

Dear Karin,

You asked if I was a rare thing, an honest married man. When you read this email you may think your suspicions that such a species doesn't exist are well-founded. I want to see you again… but I'm still married to Nadine. Lying to her doesn't sit easy with me. We plan to begin divorce proceedings as soon as possible but we also have a business and a house to sell before we can move forward. Everything will be different once that's done.

Can you wait until then before we contact each other again? I need a clear head for the moment and you fill my thoughts far too much. I understand if you're not prepared to wait but I hope you'll give me this time to sort out my life. I'll be in touch as soon as I can offer you something more than empty promises.

In anticipation of better times,

Jake

She responded with a brief text.

New York is waiting for your call.

That too had been deleted.

Nadine straightened and tucked her hands under her arms as a sudden flurry of wind tossed her hair. She checked her watch and stood. 'We'd better go back to work.'

'Are you okay?' he asked.

She nodded, and shoved her bag over her shoulder. "It's just… meeting Carol and all that… it's so real now.'

The ducks bobbed their heads under the water, tail feathers fluttering. The woman, far too tall to be Karin Moylan, crossed the bridge above the pond and disappeared from view.

On Grafton Street the buskers were out in force: guitarists, artists in goggles, violinists, fire eaters, a threesome of cellists. A young woman worked two sticks and created enormous, elongated bubbles. A bubble floated towards them. An instant of luminosity. Rainbow hues shimmering, its distended belly almost touching the pavement before it disappeared with an inaudible plop. How could such a delicate transporter of air be responsible for killing the rip-roaring Celtic Tiger?

CHAPTER SEVENTEEN

His mother had already arrived when Jake drove into Bartizan Downs. The blinds were open and he had a clear view of her silhouette, the high sweep of hair, her imperious head. She was in a dangerous mood. He could read her body language, the subtle signals she gave out, the merest pressure of her lips, the lift of her eloquent eyebrows. He had no interest in being inside her head. Understanding one's mother was almost as unhealthy as having an Oedipus complex. He squared his shoulders and hurried towards the front door.

She had rung him earlier in work and invited herself to dinner, insisted she had something of the utmost importance to discuss with him and Nadine.

'If she mentions another word about marriage counselling I'll strangle her with my bare hands,' Nadine threatened before leaving the office early to shop and prepare an evening meal.

'I'll help you hide the body,' he had promised.

He entered the drawing room and air-brushed Eleanor's cheek before heading to the kitchen where Nadine was removing a roast chicken from the oven. She looked composed but she was moving around the kitchen in a controlled frenzy.

'Eleanor's got something up her sleeve,' she whispered. 'I know the signs.'

'She can't make us do anything we don't want,' he whispered back. Why were they whispering? Their kitchen was almost the size of a football stadium.

He carved the chicken while Nadine mashed potatoes and strained green beans. Years of co-ordinated practice had welded them into an efficient team when it came to bringing a meal to the table.

'Any word on the house?' Eleanor asked as soon as they were seated.

'Nothing definite as yet,' Nadine replied. 'We're had a lot of interest and we're confident we'll close the deal soon.'

'How long has it been on the market?'

'Not long,' Jake said.

'Just long enough for the *For Sale* sign to grow roots and sprout branches in the spring.' Eleanor's short bark of laughter set his teeth on edge.

'And Tōnality?' she asked.

'Almost there.' Nadine passed the green beans to her. 'We have a buyer who's seriously interested in making us an offer.'

When had his wife become such an accomplished liar?

'Are you still going ahead with this ridiculous separation?' Eleanor ladled the beans onto her plate and added chicken from the platter.

'With our divorce, yes,' said Nadine and Jake nodded in agreement.

'Then listen to what I have to say.' Her voice softened to a persuasive pitch he instinctively mistrusted. 'I want to help.'

'We've not having a repeat discussion,' Nadine said. 'No marriage counselling. That subject is closed.'

'This is not a discussion, it's purely a suggestion. You and Jake are lying through your teeth. Putting food on the table in the middle of a recession is a more immediate priority for families than buying grand pianos.'

'We don't just sell grand – '

'Property prices have collapsed,' Eleanor cut through his interruption with scythe-like determination. 'Just listen to this evening's news if you need a reality check. I passed two other *For Sale* signs on this estate and your house, if you do manage to find a buyer, will sell at a considerable loss. The same applies to your company.'

'This is none of your business, Eleanor.' Nadine's knuckles tightened as she sliced into her chicken.

'You're my family and that makes it my business,' said Eleanor. 'A house of cards doesn't fall slowly. All it takes is a finger flick and the whole edifice collapses. You and Jake borrowed heavily to set up in that business park. You've lost STRUM, your customers aren't paying their bills and it'll be impossible to move your unsold stock while this recession lasts. No one is interested in buying Tōnality. Your most sensible option is to agree a quick sale on your house and use the money to pay off your bank loan.'

'How dare you make such assumptions about us!' Nadine's hair swept forward and hid her face.

'I'm a pragmatist, Nadine. Essential in politics. I've changed my mind about Sea Aster. A number of planning difficulties have made it difficult to proceed with the renovations. First Affiliation can wait a while longer for its new headquarters. In the meantime – '

'I can see where this discussion is going, Eleanor,' Jake interrupted her before Nadine could do so. 'You can stop right – '

'You want your freedom, don't you? Well, freedom comes at a price. I'm willing to give you Sea Aster. No rent in lieu of maintaining the house and grounds for me. Two apartments, two entrances. Do what you like within its confines but, outwardly, to the world, you remain a married couple.'

'That's a preposterous suggestion.' Nadine laid her cutlery beside her plate and abandoned all pretence at eating. 'We've no intention of accepting it.'

Eleanor dabbed her lips then placed the serviette back on her knees. 'Consider my suggestion, that's all I'm asking.'

'Why would you do this, Eleanor?' Nadine asked. 'Why does our marriage matter so much to you?'

'It matters because I love you both. I don't want to see you making a dreadful mistake.'

Jake laughed, an abrupt bark that hid his anger. If only he could leave the table and retreat to his music room. But those days were gone. He no longer had the urge to write down a catchy line, or record a riff with potential. He was sleepless, stressed, helpless. And his mother believed maternal love was the answer to his problems.

'When did this flowering of love occur?' he asked 'Was it sudden or was it your best kept secret?'

'Don't be cruel, Jake,' she said. 'Repetition diminishes meaning which is why I don't often express my feelings for you and Nadine. And my grandchildren, let's not forget them in this scenario. I want them to have a base when they come home, some place where we can all be together. Sea Aster will be there when you need it.'

Undaunted by their refusal to consider her offer, she left shortly afterwards.

'We'll pretend this conversation never happened.' Nadine rose from the table and gathered the plates and serving dishes, unwilling or unable to discuss the crisis they were facing.

They were living on borrowed time. Soon it would run out of control. Jake opened his laptop and clicked into the Kingfisher website. Karin Moylan stared back at him from the homepage. The longing to contact her was constant but nothing had changed since he emailed her. He was stuck in the same rut. Soon he would have to meet his bank manager and plead with him once again for an extension of his loan. The domino effect of recession. Jake felt a chill ring of perspiration around his neck, a noose tightening.

❊ ❊ ❊

Gerard Lyons tapped on his computer screen and repeated words like 'insolvency' and 'repossession.' Jake hoped desperately that he misunderstood what they were being told but one look at Nadine's stricken face told him otherwise. Their house now belonged to the bank. They had offered it as collateral when they borrowed to expend Tōnality. There would be no extension on their loan. They should go quietly, their bank manager advised. No sense making a scene in front of their neighbours. Missed VAT repayments had been uncovered. An examiner was being appointed to run Tōnality and they were not allowed to set foot inside the premises.

The air seemed different when Jake emerged from the bank, stultifying and thick as soup. The ground tilted beneath him, at least that was how it seemed, and he was forced to hold onto the wall for support. Vertigo, it had happened to him on a few occasions and always at times of intense stress. As he staggered towards his car the trees lining the centre of the road appeared to move, the branches to embark on a mad can-can dance. He swallowed bile, forced himself to focus on the car parked in front of him. If he concentrated hard enough on that one spot the nausea would pass. Slowly the branches stopped swooping and his surroundings came into balance again.

'Be careful what you wish for — you might just get it.' His lips felt chapped, his mouth dry. 'You have it now, Nadine.' His voice was so hoarse that she had to lean towards him to hear. 'No house. No company. No marriage. Everything we've achieved… all gone in a puff of smoke.'

Like a butterfly flapping its wings in a distant jungle, the re-verberations of her decision had caused chaos. He knew he was being illogical but logical thought was impossible as he came face-to-face with his failure. She sat stiffly beside him, glassy tears sliding down her cheeks, and made no reply. A house of cards doesn't fall slowly, Eleanor had said. Jake wondered why there was no sound, no crash or clatter as their lives collapsed around them.

CHAPTER EIGHTEEN

Nadine

Sea Aster is my salvation and my jail. No bars to keep me here but they exist, tough as steel and as unyielding. Having lost everything, we're still in the palm of Eleanor's hand, crushed tight by her determination, her will. But I can't blame her for our recklessness, our over-borrowing, our pursuit of freedom. We did that all by ourselves.

The debts we built up were an amorphous blob until Gerard Lyons pulled the rug from under us. I'm horrified by the scale of what we owed – and how little we actually owned. Our cars have been repossessed and the only income we have is the in-heritance Rosanna left us. It's a small off-shore account but it will keep us going until we find our feet again.

We would be homeless except for Eleanor's largess. I should be grateful. On my knees thanking her. She had the grace not to say, 'I told you so' but that doesn't make any difference to how I feel.

We tossed a coin when we moved into Sea Aster to see who would occupy Apartment 2 on the ground floor. We both want-ed it, particularly the breakfast room with its curving bay win-dow overlooking the garden.

I lost the toss and climbed the stairs to Apartment 1 where the previous tenant wore black lace tights and kept cats with bowel problems. I'm convinced I can still smell them. Jake insists it's my imagination. The apartment has been scoured, bleached and buffed, painted, redecorated, and a new bed installed. All traces of cats have been expunged and he shows no inclination to switch with me. Eleanor, having handed over the keys, has left us to our own devices. She has First Affiliation to run and it's up to us to pick up the pieces of our shattered lives.

I awaken every morning with good intentions. Today I'll sort out the attic where, on our arrival, we dumped the possessions we still actually owned. I'll cut the grass, weed the flowerbeds, stamp some of my personality on my apartment. Instead, I sit at the window and stare for hours at the shifting moods of the estuary. When the spring tide overflows the shore, the swans swim with regal indifference along Mallard Cove. I envy their unconcern, their indifference to their sudden change of address. If only I could adjust so easily. I've come to believe I'm suffering from chronic fatigue.

'You're still in shock,' Jenny reassures me every time we speak. 'So much has happened so fast. You need time to absorb the changes. Find a job. It'll keep you sane until you can move from Sea Aster and buy your cottage. Or is it a town house you want?'

'What does it matter?' I fight back the urge to weep. 'I can't afford a shoebox, let alone a cottage.'

'Then rent,' she advises me. 'It's no big deal. Do anything except stare at swans. Scrub floors, toss burgers. Otherwise, you're going to sink into depression.'

'I've sunk into it already.'

'No, you haven't. You've sunk into self-pity because things haven't worked out the way you planned. Big difference. You and Jake are young enough to begin over. You have to get back on your feet and gain control over your life again.'

I blink back tears, wretched tears that make no difference no matter how many I shed. 'All I can think about is how we're still together but not… and all we've lost. Jenny, you've no idea what it's like to lose everything.'

'But you *haven't* lost everything. You've lost possessions. You still have your family, your friends. Everything else can be regained in time or, maybe, you never needed all those possession in the first place.'

'It's the failure — '

'Failure, my foot. That's an Irish concept. Over here we look upon failure as a learning curve. Onwards and upwards to the next stage.'

'Tossing burgers?'

'If it gives you a leg up, yes.' For the first time my friend sounds impatient. I suspected a slight lack of sympathy when I told her the reason for ending our marriage. Jenny can understand adultery, violence, mental cruelty, alcohol and substance abuse. Even boredom, she admits, is grounds for such a sundering but she can't get her head around the notion of 'freedom.' She makes it sound like a bauble with too much sparkle and I know she's remembering her ex-partner Christopher, who stuck a farewell note about regaining his freedom to their fridge door with an *I Love Vancouver* magnet on the day before her thirty-eighth birthday. Timing was never Christopher's strongest point.

'How's Jake?' she asks.

'Coping much better than I am. He's clearing out the old barn and reforming Shard. They had some idea about playing a reunion gig but that bit the dust, along with everything else. Now he's talking about a come-back launch for the band.'

'Has Daryl still got the dreadlocks?'

'A distant dream, Jenny. His baby daughter has more hair than he has.'

She fancied Daryl in those early Shard days. For a while I thought, maybe, but after Jake and I married she moved to Vancouver to study film.

'And Hart?' she asks.

'He teaches yoga.'

'*Hart*… you've got to be kidding.' She laughs away her astonishment and says, 'I thought he'd be pixilated in alcohol by now.'

'He lives on alfalfa sprouts and bottled water.'

'What about Bad Boy Barry?'

'Bricklaying in Saskatchewan.'

'I'm nearly afraid to ask about Reedy.'

'He's still the same.'

I asked him how his New York gig went when he came to Sea Aster to inspect the barn.

'It was Boston,' he replied. 'Haven't been to New York in years, more's the pity. It's a brilliant place to gig.'

I consider telling Jenny about that conversation. The fact that Jake lied about New York. But, maybe, he didn't. Reedy gigs all over the place. Hard to keep tabs. Downstairs, Jake is hammering something. I never realised how much noise he makes. When we lived together his music was contained in a soundproofed room and the noises he made outside it were indistinguishable from the hubbub of our family. After they left, there was so much space in the house that our individual sounds lost their way back to us. Now, all I hear is him. Doors banging, his stereo blasting, footsteps stamping, chairs scraping, phone ringing. If I listen hard enough I'll hear him turning in his sleep. His energy invades my space and is a constant affront to my lethargy. I've bought a cheap second-hand car but he spends most of his time working on a clapped-out band van he picked up on DoneDeal. It looks as if its next journey should be to the scrap yard but he's intent on restoring it.

Susanna Cox from HiNotes rings one afternoon and shakes me back to life. I'm surprised to hear from her. None of our ex-business acquaintances have been in contact in the month since we lost Tōnality. I guess they're afraid our bad luck will rub off on them.

'I wanted to ring after I heard what happened but I wasn't sure you'd appreciate a call,' Susanna sounds uncertain. 'How are you?'

'Keeping busy.' Just as well we're not on Skype. At three in the afternoon I'm still in my dressing gown and the panda slippers Ali bought me for Christmas. 'How are things in HiNotes?'

'Just holding our heads above water,' she admits. 'Wanker bankers… but I don't have to tell you that. Thankfully, parents still want their darlings to become music virtuosos so that keeps our doors open. Are you working again?'

'Not yet. My CV is with a recruitment agency. I'm expecting to hear from them soon.'

Why tell the truth when a little white lie makes conversation that bit easier? The young woman in the recruitment agency looked appalled when she checked the educational qualifications on my CV. No degrees, not even a teeny weeny certificate? Years of experience with Tōnality were dismissed with a shrug of her shoulder pads. My earlier confidence drained away as she explained why a degree, and preferably, a masters or PhD, were *de rigueur* these days in her high-powered business world.

'I thought about you last night when I was having dinner with a friend of mine,' Susanna says. 'Jessica Walls. You may have heard of her?'

Who hasn't heard of Jessica Walls? Those living in caves, perhaps, but, even there, word would filter down through the limestone cracks.

'She's looking for an advertising manager,' Susanna continues. 'I mentioned your name.'

I feel my chin lifting, my mind growing still.

'Are you interested?' she asks when I don't reply.

I clear my throat and try to keep my voice from wobbling. 'Does it matter that I don't have a business degree?'

'Jessica had zilch degrees to her name when she launched her first magazine,' Susanna replies. 'School of life, just like you. Go and meet her. I've filled her in on your background. She trusts my judgement.'

'Does she know about Tōnality?'

'She knows and understands how it can happen. She's folded twice and picked herself up again. Each time she grew bigger. Now she has *Lustrous* as her flagship magazine. Selling advertising will be your main responsibility, although you'll probably be involved in other aspects of the magazine. Jessica works her staff hard but you won't be bored. What do you think?'

'Sounds like Tōnality. I was Jill of all trades there.' I force myself to sound confident. As Eleanor would say, perception is everything. 'Thanks, Susanna. I appreciate your help.'

'One other thing,' she says. 'Tell Jake to ring me if he's interested in some part-time teaching. One of my guitar teachers is heading for Australia next month. Sign of the times, I'm afraid.'

His jeans, ripped at the knees, are covered in oil, his khaki t-shirt damp with sweat when he emerges from under the chassis of his band van.

He agrees to ring Susanna about the guitar classes.

'Things are looking up, then,' I say.

'I guess.' He slaps his hand off the van and the side window slides down.

There's a streak of dust on his cheek. I instinctively lean forward to wipe it away then pull back. He bends and picks up a wrench.

'Good luck at the interview,' he says. 'I know you can do it.'

CHAPTER NINETEEN

Jake

Pale walls, a light wooden floor, a table set for two, glass doors opening onto the balcony. Dublin city lay below him, spires, rooftops, bridges, luminous glass pyramids, and Liberty Hall jutting like an amputated thumb into the skyline.

'What do you think of my view?' Karin joined him on the balcony.

They leaned over the rail to stare down at the ant-sized pedestrians and the stream of traffic flowing along the quays. Life pulsed here, unlike Sea Aster with its secluded entrance and quietly lapping estuary.

'Beautiful.' Jake gazed into her eyes. 'Quite perfect and as beautiful as I remembered.'

Her lips opened. The hot, hard dart of her tongue aroused him instantly. She moaned softly in response but was the first to draw away.

'I've spent all afternoon preparing a meal for you,' she said. 'Let's sit down and eat before it's cold.'

She had cooked medallions of lamb with a port jus, gratin potatoes and asparagus with roasted peppers. They steered away from dangerous topics throughout the meal. Nadine's name was never mentioned. He heard about the design commissions she had received since returning home. He told her about Shard and clearing out the barn, and how he was restoring the band van. Reedy had organised occasional session work for him in the Raison D'être studios, which paid well, if irregularly, and Reedy also intended to find a new drummer.

Was he speaking too fast, laying breathless facts before her? These days he found it impossible to slow down. Being busy was the answer, the only way to cope. And it worked. Mind over matter. Rise in the morning instead of lying in bed and letting his thoughts scurry like ants deprived of their sheltering stone.

Dessert was simple and delicious, fresh raspberries and homemade ice cream, served in blue-rimmed bowls. When it was finished she poured brandy into goblets and carried them to the sofa. Her dress, a buttery shade of yellow, settled in folds around her knees when she sat beside him.

'Tell me what happened?' she said. 'From your email I got the impression you and Nadine had gone through a bereavement, rather than a separation.'

'A bereavement?' He pondered the word. It seemed appropriate, if inaccurate. Music played softly in the background. Clair de Lune, Jake recognised the expressive sway and sweep of Dubussy, the rhythmic notes challenging yet soothing. 'I wanted to contact you,' he said. 'I lost count of the times I stopped myself from ringing. Nothing was working out as planned and I didn't want to burden you with my problems.'

'Would you have got in touch if I hadn't made the first move?' she asked.

He hesitated. Since the collapse of Tōnality she had become a wishful thought, an almost forgotten allurement, and that's where she would have stayed if she had not emailed him to ask when he intended keeping his promise.

'I promised to contact you when I'd sorted out my life,' he said. 'But how could I come back to you and tell you I was still living with Nadine, even though we'd separated.'

She listened without interruption while he described the tumbling apart that had left him and Nadine still together.

'Upstairs… downstairs,' she said. 'That's close.'

'It may seem that way but I assure you – '

She touched his lip with her fingers and silenced him. 'Space doesn't matter, Jake. It's your emotions that will determine the distance between the two of you. How close are you to Nadine… here?' He saw a flash of blue below her cleavage as she leaned towards him. She lifted his hand and pressed it to her chest. He felt the steady thud of her heart against his palm and when she moved, almost imperceptibly, his hand curved on the swell of her breasts. 'And here,' she whispered. 'How close… how close… Jake?'

'My marriage is over, Karin. This is what I want…' His voice rasped as his fingers slid under the V of her neckline. He glimpsed the edge of lace and his breath, harsher now, stirred the blonde, feathery strands framing her face.

'Show me how much it's over.' She was still whispering as her dress pooled on the floor. The sight of her breasts, so pert and perfect in their kingfisher blue cups and slender straps, almost undid him. He was afraid it would be over before it began and he stopped, allowed the rush of desire to abate before he continued unhooking her, hoping he would not fumble and ruin the moment. When her breasts were free she held his face in her hands, forced him to look into the deep blue irises, her gaze unblinking, her whispering words commanding him to show her… show her… show her. He tore his gaze away and bent to trace his tongue over her dusty-pink nipples, to sink his lips into unfamiliar contours and crevices.

Her hands eased his trousers over his hips and he kicked them from him, uncaring now, her pliant body astride him, feather-light as he had known she would be, her blue thong eased aside and he was inside her, sliding in deep and easy, hearing her twittering cries as she arched back, their bodies moving together in a primal yet always familiar rhythm.

Afterwards, she collapsed against him, the sheen of perspiration on her forehead, her hair damp and spiky from the fervour of passion. She curled into his lap, her eyes half-closed, her breathing calm again, and his breath also quietened into the drowsy aftermath of spent desire.

'My Jake.' She murmured his name and raised both arms to his neck. He kissed the top of her head, nibbled the lobe of her ear. The musky scent of their love-making trailed from their fingers, rose in an intimate plume when she stirred. He watched her walking from the room, intoxicated by her nakedness, the sway of her slight frame with its surprisingly rounded curves. When she returned she was swamped in a bulky towelling bathrobe, a second one across her arm. He slid his arms into the sleeves and followed her to the bathroom. The water was running in the bath, and the air was scented with lavender as they sank together into the eddying waves of pleasure. He was cutting through the strings of his marriage and letting himself fall. A clean-shaven Rip Van Winkle returning to the world after an absence of twenty-three years.

CHAPTER TWENTY

Nadine

The view from my office overlooks Merrion Square Park. Sometimes, when the windows are open, the voices of children reach above the traffic and rise towards me. The first weeks were terrifying, so many meetings, new faces, responsibilities. Now, two months later, the newness has worn off and the skills I took with me from Tōnality have come to the fore.

Lustrous is the most prestigious of Jessica's eight magazines and is my responsibility. It's devoted to celebrity culture, glamour and escapism, scandal and the red carpet. Her other magazines are equally targeted, weddings, businesses, interior design and then there's *Core*, a muck-raking tabloid at the other end of the spectrum from *Lustrous*. Both magazines are edited by Liam Brett.

I don't usually dislike people on a first impression but Liam has proved the exception to the rule. He addresses the female staff as 'Babe'; a useful moniker that prevents him having to remember our names. I suspect he enjoys building up the celebrities who feature in *Lustrous* so that he can crash land them later with an exposé in *Core*.

Susanna was right when she said there would be blurred demarcation lines on the magazine. When one of the editorial team on *Lustrous* resigns after a row with Liam I offer to write her copy until she's replaced. This involves writing features about celebrities who have done something to damage their image and need a sympathetic revamp on their reputations – or wannabes who are seeking any reputation, damaged or otherwise. Jessica makes excuses when the weeks pass with no sign of a new copywriter being appointed.

'I don't know how I ever managed without you, Nadine,' she says. Compliments are her ammunition against protests. 'You're so multi-faceted.'

We used to laugh at *Lustrous*, Jake and I. All those celebrities posturing and pouting. He nicknamed it *Ludicrous*. My only fear is that I'll do the same at a staff meeting.

I awaken on a Saturday morning filled with determination. No lying on in bed. The time has come to make a start on the attic. My life plan has changed but there's no reason why I can't turn the attic into a studio. Over the years I've enrolled in night-time art classes but I seldom finished a term. Nothing to stop me now.

The attic is chaotic, filled with clutter that needs to be sorted out. Dire warnings have come from California, London and the Dingle peninsula. Nothing belonging to Ali, Brian and the twins is to be thrown out until they've had a chance to decide what should be kept.

They too are feeling the effects of change. We can no longer afford to finance Ali as she waits to be discovered. When I reminded her that waitressing is the apprenticeship for an acting career, she sounded as if I'd asked her to stand on the block at a hiring fair. The twins were equally appalled by the idea of working part-time while they train for gold.

I'll organise containers in a storage warehouse for the 'must-not-throw-outs' and the rest can be divided between Oxfam, the local recycling plant, the junk yard and Ebay. I look at my paintings stacked against the eaves, some finished, others abandoned at the halfway stage. Amateurish. They'll make a fine bonfire.

I want Jake to help but his van, now roadworthy, is missing from the previous night. He arrives as I'm packing the boot with boxes for Oxfam. His hair is shaggier than it used to be and the strain he's carried on his face for months has disappeared. He looks ten years younger whereas I'm only beginning, literally, to lift my head from the debris that was once our lives. He's spent the night with someone. I know this to be true, not just by his crumpled shirt and sated eyes but by an aura surrounding him, something I can only sense: elation, suppressed excitement.

We've discussed this possibility… probability… actuality. If the law forces us to wait four years to finalise our divorce then we have the right to decide how it should end emotionally. Circumstances interfered with our plans but if we're to survive this living together, yet apart, we will practice discretion. That means never bringing anyone with whom we have a relationship back to Sea Aster. We made this pact calmly, purposefully but I hadn't reckoned on the shock of sensing… no, knowing… that he is moving on. I feel nauseous as an image of his naked body above a faceless woman flashes through my mind. I swallow and steady my breathing.

'Looks like you've decided on a major clear out,' he says. 'Why didn't you tell me? I'd have given you a hand.'

'You weren't around.' My legs buckle under the weight of a box. A brash new Shard sign has been painted on the side of his van. Splintering icy-blue slivers with a reddish-orange glow give the impression that the ice is blazing. SHARD is stencilled in a three-dimensional font. Each word looks as if it was hacked around the edges with a finely honed chisel.

'I'll help you now.' He steps forward and tries to take the box from me.

'No need. I'm managing fine.' My voice is sharper than I intend and he draws back, his expression wary.

'What's the matter? You seem tense. Are you…?'

If he tells me I'm pre-menstrual I'll take a brick to his head.

'Finding it difficult?' he waves his hand towards the boxes. 'All the memories – '

'They need to be faced,' I reply. 'Better sooner rather than later. And I'm not tense. Just busy de-cluttering. It displaces negative energy, I'm told. What's happening in your life?'

'Same old … same old.' He answers too fast, too glibly. 'How's *Ludicrous*?'

'*Stop* calling it that.' I point to the sign on the van. 'Very dramatic.'

'It was a band decision.' He bends and lifts another box. 'We're practicing this afternoon otherwise I'd take this lot to the charity shop in the van.'

'Don't worry. I'll manage.'

'We should arrange to get together some evening and do a major clear out.'

'Sure… let me know when you're free.'

He stands back as I start the car. I glance in the rear-view mirror before I turn around the curve on the driveway. He's already disappeared.

In Malahide Village I carry the boxes into Oxfam. I imagine our discarded bric-a-brac taking up space in other peoples' houses, the paintings hanging from different walls, the lamps glowing in new corners, the glass displayed on stranger's shelves.

On a whim I drive from the village towards Bartizan Downs. The gates are closed and I no longer possess the means to enter.

The trees are beginning to green, a shivery growth that partly hides these fortified houses with their sweeping lawns and quiet air of luxury. The gates slide apart and a woman glares suspiciously at me from her towering jeep. Cars do not loiter outside Bartizan Down without attracting attention. There's so much to plunder and rob behind those coded gates with their ridiculous bartizans. What possessed us to buy such an ostentatious house? Why did we allow ourselves to be lured there by the purple prose of property supplements and the Judas kiss of a banker? I know the answer. Bartizan Downs was a statement. Its brash opulence proving to the world that Jake and Nadine Saunders, against all the odds, had made it.

The silver rush of the Broadmeadow River spills into the estuary as I drive back to Sea Aster. Saturday is a day for families and cars are parked under the trees. The swans are out of the water, intent on snatching bread from the fingers of excited children. They're thuggish when they emerge onto dry land and grudgingly waddle from my path.

Music hits like a hand on my chest when I step from the car. A white van with *Feral Childe Drummer* painted on it is parked outside my apartment. Three other cars are parked on the grass. Cables run from the window of the breakfast room into the barn and the walls seem to vibrate with amplified energy. I peer through the open barn window, reluctant to be seen but unable to resist the temptation to see the band in action. Amplifiers are arranged on a makeshift stage and the retro Shard posters are pinned to the walls. Jake has installed the old sofa from Oakdale, as well as some bean bags for lounging. He has created a man shed and a boy's den all rolled into one.

Hart moves with a sinuous grace that makes him unrecognisable from the shambling rhythm guitarist I used to know. Reedy plays with that same world-weary impassivity. Feral Childe, the new drummer Reedy recruited, has tumbleweed yellow hair, jeans with strategic rips and the figure of a teenage boy. I recognise the tune pulsing through the barn. One of Jake's earlier songs. It's different now, a slower beat with more depth, more melodic. Daryl juts his guitar into the air and Jake, his body already leaning into the music, begins to sing, his growly voice still sexy.

I was part of that circle once. Summer days in the garden, myself and Jenny sprawled in deckchairs, Rosanna carrying out jugs of lemonade and packets of Hobnobs. I clench my fists then determinedly unclench them. Throughout the afternoon I'm conscious of Shard. Not so much the pounding beat, just the reverberations of the past. When the rehearsal ends, Daryl climbs the stairs to my apartment. His eyes are shadowed. Another sleepless night, he confesses. Teething problems, flushed baby cheeks, nappies oozing an indescribable odour. He shows me a video of Jasmine spitting a blob of pureed carrot with ferocious determination at the camera.

I ask how Feral Childe is slotting into the band.

'She's cool,' says Daryl. 'Jake's delighted with her. We all are.'

'Feral can't be her real name.'

'May Smith,' he says. 'She changed it by deed poll on her sixteenth birthday.' He swipes his iPhone again.

'What's her background?'

'She was with Collective of Calm. Ever heard of them?'

'No.'

'They were based in New York and were anything but calm, from what I've heard. Feral came back home when they split.'

'When was that?'

'Early this year. Did I show you this video of Jasmine eating spaghetti? It's a hoot.'

'You showed it to me last week.'

'Sorry, Nadine.' He grimaces and slips his phone back into his pocket. 'I used to hate baby bores like me.'

He looks relieved when I tell him it's an addiction that will pass when Jasmine enters her teens.

Soon only the white van remains outside Sea Aster. Jake is cooking in the kitchen. Spicy, mouth-watering smells drift upwards. I hear Feral laughing, cutlery clinking, chairs being dragged to the table.

He knocks on my door shortly afterwards.

'I can't find a corkscrew. Do you have the one with the fancy lever?' he asks.

'I'll get it for you.'

'You can come down and join us if you like,' he says. I don't detect the slightest hint of enthusiasm in his voice. 'It's just a lamb tagine, nothing fancy.'

'No, thanks.' I hand him the opener. 'I've things to do tonight. Enjoy your meal.'

I hear the dishes being cleared from the table and the hum of the dishwasher. Jake begins to play his guitar. Feral accompanies him on the bongos. At least they're not in bed. I shy away from the image of her tumbleweed hair on the pillows, her boyish figure straddling him. Moving with the same pulsing force as she exercises over her drums.

They're still making music when I ring Jenny.

'Did I tell you Shard's new drummer is female?'

'Yes. You've mentioned it on a number of occasions. Why? Is that an issue?'

'She's downstairs playing the bongos. Can you hear her?'

'Are you jealous?'

'Absolutely not.'

'Then why should I listen to her playing the bongos?'

'I think Jake's having a thing with her. Remember that New York text.'

'What about it?'

'I'm sure she sent it.'

'Do you care?'

'Not at all.'

'So….' Jenny pauses, coughs meaningfully. 'Why are we discussing her?'

'I'm not… it's just… I can *hear* them.'

'Doing what? Shagging?'

'*Jenny.*'

'Okay…making love by the silvery moon…is that what we're discussing here?'

'No. Sea Aster is off limits for *that.*'

'An eminently sensible decision. Did I tell you I'm seeing someone?'

'As in serious?'

'Could be.' She utters a most un-Jenny-like giggle.

'Tell me everything,' I demand.

And she does.

Downstairs Feral has changed from the bongos to a mouth organ. The melancholic strains writhe like an eel though the floorboards of Sea Aster. It's after midnight before I hear Jake's apartment door opening. I watch from the window as Feral walks with him towards her van. The outside light has switched on. I've a clear view as they stop beside the van and hug each other. This is not a brief hug. It's spontaneous, filled with vigour and promise. Does it matter? Of course not. He's free. I'm free. I need to escape from here. Watching Jake play out his new life in front of me is torture. At last they separate. Feral drives away, the wheels spraying pebbles. Jake stands in the pool of light until the rear lights disappear around the side of Sea Aster.

CHAPTER TWENTY-ONE

Jake

The sense of déjà vu startled him when Karin drove into Grace-hills and they passed Nadine's old house. Karin stared straight ahead and made no reference to it. She must have spent time there, stayed overnight, sat on the garden wall, walked to and from school with Nadine through Gracehills Park. A different front door and windows, the front garden paved, it was hardly recognisable but Jenny Corcoran's house was unchanged. The same neatly-trimmed privet hedge, the rose bushes beginning to bloom. Her parents still lived there. Last year she had arrived home for Dan Corcoran's seventieth birthday. At his party she and Nadine sang a rap song they had composed for the occasion to thunderous applause.

Today, Joan Moylan was celebrating her birthday. A white box on the back seat of Karin's car contained a cake with her name and birthday wishes inscribed on the icing. Jake had only the vaguest memory of meeting Joan during that summer in Monsheelagh. Her face was usually shaded by a floppy sunhat and sunglasses. Her hair was drenched that night when she entered the harbour pub where Shard were playing and Jake only caught a fleeting glimpse of her distraught expression before she disappeared into the storm.

She had made lasagne and a salad for the birthday meal. Broken thread veins and the lines on her face suggested battles lost and won. The conversation around the dining table was strained. Joan spoke about a book she had read and a televised crime drama she enjoyed watching. Jake found himself filling in the silences that inevitably fell once a topic had been exhausted.

Karin carried the birthday cake to the table. Two waxen numbers six and eight were stuck like miniature plump ladies in the centre. When Joan had blown out the candles Karin sliced the cake and poured tea. No champagne. Her mother was a recovering alcoholic, she had told Jake on the way to the house. Joan could never be trusted, even after twenty-five years. When Jake said that twenty-five years without touching alcohol suggested she was a fully recovered alcoholic Karin shook her head.

'There's no such thing,' she said. 'The temptation is always there. That's why I find it so difficult to be around her, especially on days like today.'

She brought Jake into her father's study to show him Max Moylan's books. It reminded Jake of a shrine. A museum filled with mementoes of his writing career. One wall was lined with his hardbacks: Max Moylan in Africa, Vietnam, Japan, China, Nepal. His desk was cluttered with pens and notebooks. photographs casually lying at the side of his typewriter created the impression that he had stepped outside for a breath of air before choosing the ones what would go into his latest work in progress. The air was musty, a blind halfway down on a window that Joan Moylan must never open. Flowers wilted in a vase. Karin replaced them with the fresh bouquet she had brought with her. She stabbed each flower precisely into place and stood back to admire the effect. Uneasy in the fusty atmosphere, he sat on the edge of the desk and watched her at work. Something blue on top of the filing cabinet caught his eye. A stuffed bird in a glass case, wings spread as if it was about to land on a bed of river reeds. One glittering eye was visible, the feathers gleaming.

'Do you know the legend of the kingfisher?' Karin asked.

'I wasn't aware there was one.'

She lifted the case down and ran a cloth over the dust on the glass. 'They're called the halcyon birds.'

'This one doesn't look very calm,' he said.

'It's an ancient Greek legend.' She rubbed harder on the metal base. 'I'm surprised Nadine never told you about it.'

'Why should she?' He tensed at the mention of her name. Living below Nadine was proving more problematic than he had anticipated.

'Try to keep the noise down,' she had said when he returned the corkscrew he borrowed the night Feral stayed on after band practice.

'What noise?' He had been genuinely surprised. 'I never hear you.'

'That's because I respect your right to a peaceful existence,' she said in the clipped voice she used when trying to hold on to her temper. 'You're no longer playing your guitar in a sound-proof room. You must be aware of how sound travels through this house.'

'I'd no idea you were monitoring my life by sound effects,' he replied with the same chilling politeness. 'Don't worry. It won't happen again.'

Since then, he returned from Karin's apartment after Nadine had left for work. Her initial efforts to clear out the attic had stalled and she had not taken him up on his offer to help.

The metal base was shining when Karin replaced the glass case on the filing cabinet. She walked to the bookshelves and pushed one book that was out of alignment into position. 'Nadine was with us that day,' she said. 'We were hiking in Monsheelagh Forest. Would you like to hear the legend that inspired the name of my agency?'

'Another time. We should go back to your mother.'

'Don't worry,' she said. 'Joan likes her own company best.'

Karin's voice had an almost compelling intensity as she related the legend to him. Lovers transformed into kingfishers so that they could be together in death.

'I understand that kind of love,' she said when she finished the story. 'Do you have any sense of its compulsion?'

What exactly was she asking him? He did not understand a love that drew a woman under the waves to join the man she loved. It was a typical Greek tragedy, too dramatic for his taste. He remembered Karin's words on the plane. She would choose her lover's arms rather than a life jacket if the plane was plunging downwards.

'I've never wanted to be a kingfisher that badly enough,' he joked. 'We really should go back – '

'He promised to bring me with him on his next trip,' she said. 'We were going to the Sahara to live with nomads. He had it all worked out. How we would tell my mother, persuade her to let me go. I was only fifteen – '

'I remember.'

'I know you do.' A red telephone on the desk had an old-fashioned rotary dial. She dialled a number, watched the dial rotate and settle again, dialled another. 'Nadine said I was too young. She sided with my mother. I found that hard to forgive. Have you been talking to her recently?'

The question was so unexpected that he hesitated before replying.

'Have you?' she repeated.

'I spoke to her this morning. She was flying to London. Something to do with *Ludicrous*…I mean *Lustrous*. Why?'

The repetitive whirr of the telephone dial was beginning to irritate him. As if sensing his irritation she sat down in the swivel chair behind the desk and slowly spun it from side to side.

'She threatens me. I don't mean physically. Just the memory of her… all those years you had together. How can you stay away from each other?'

'I've explained our situation,' he said. 'Neither of us can change anything at the moment. The debts…'

'How do I know you're telling me the truth?'

'What do you mean?'

'Married men are programmed to lie. It's an inevitable consequence of cheating on their wives.'

'I'm not cheating on Nadine. We made a decision – '

'Then maybe you're cheating on me.'

'That's a ridiculous accusation. You've no reason to be jealous of Nadine. She's determined to leave Sea Aster as soon as she can afford to rent her own place. I intend to do the same. We just need time to get our lives together again.'

'Why don't you bring me to Sea Aster? Let me see exactly what's involved in this 'under the one roof' arrangement.' She waggled a finger on each hand to suggest quotation marks.

'That's never going to happen, Karin.' His irritation snapped into anger. 'Not as long as Nadine is living there. I made a pact with her. It's the only way we can handle this arrangement. I'm not prepared to break it. I don't know why we're having this *stupid* argument.'

'Don't you?' She steadied the chair and parted her legs, trapped him between them. 'It really turns me on when you get angry.'

'I'm not angry. I'm trying to explain...' The tense clasp of her thighs, her skirt sliding upwards, the glimpse of a blue thong nestling like a feather in the nest of blonde hair, he wanted her with an urgency that made him forget the quiet presence of Joan Moylan in a nearby room.

'You're hard and I'm wet... so wet,' she murmured. 'I want you inside me right now... right now, Jake.'

He lifted her onto the desk and steadied her as she unzipped him. Her tongue flicked against his ear and all was forgotten as she pulled him under the same riptide of passion that had swept a Greek goddess to her death. It was over in an instant, a pulsating collapse into relief, his hand over her mouth to stop her crying out.

He was flushed, still breathless when they returned to the living room. Joan was watching the evening news. The same stories, austerity, repossession, despair. Jake knew all about halcyon days. The calm before the storm. He sat down on an armchair and stared unseeingly at the screen.

'We have to go now,' Karin said.

'Be a pet and make me a cup of tea first,' Joan said.

She lowered the volume on the remote when Karin was in the kitchen and turned to Jake. 'How long have you been seeing each other?' she asked.

'Three months,' he replied.

'You and Nadine...I have to assume your marriage is over?'

'Yes.'

'I'm sorry.' Her eyelids sagged heavily over her eyes but she had the same disconcerting stare as her daughter. 'How is Nadine?'

'She's fine. We've had an amicable separation.'

'You're one of the lucky ones then. An amicable separation is not an easy thing to achieve.'

Did he imagine a dart of pity in her expression before she turned back to the screen?

'We are where we are.' The politician being interviewed on the evening news had the haunted look of a man clinging to a cliché. 'Burning the bond holders is not in our best interests.'

Jake disagreed. He wanted a pyre. He wanted to strike the match, smell roasting flesh, hear the sizzle of gristle, the splatter of muscle. He wanted a walk of shame, bankers, politicians, developers, speculators, all in handcuffs, in the stocks, being pelted with eggs and rotten fruit. But all he heard was empty rhetoric. We are where we are. How blindingly obvious was that?

CHAPTER TWENTY-TWO

Nadine

Plus Beauty Expo is, as its name suggests, all about beauty. From lip gloss to collagen, contour creams to liposuction, face masks to face lifts, we can have it all as we battle with free radicals and the unrelenting grind of time. I'd hoped to meet Ali while I'm in London but she's in Manchester for the weekend at a Stanislavski workshop. At least I'll have a chance to see Stuart. The last time we met he was about to undergo his chemo and I feel guilty that I haven't been back since. He sounded strong and positive when I rang to tell him I'd be in London. He's making an excellent recovery and has finished all his treatments.

Jessica and Liam work with me on the *Lustrous* stand. I distribute free copies of the magazine and speak to potential customers about the advantages of advertising with us. By the end of two days walking the long halls and talking about *Lustrous* it's a relief to take a taxi to Canary Wharf where Stuart is waiting for me. I glide smoothly upwards in a tower of glass and steel to the seventh floor.

Stuart holds my hands in a hard clasp of welcome. I'm conscious of their structure, of sharp bones beneath the flesh. He's always carried weight, solid flesh not flab, but he's thinner now and it suits him. He's my godfather, my only link with my mother and I always feel a startling jolt of recognition when I see his angular cheekbones, the gap between his two front teeth, his warm, welcoming smile.

'Tell me about everything.' He opens a bottle of wine and pours a glass, hands it to me. A pot of lamb ragú simmers on the cooker. 'I'm still trying to get used to the idea of you and Jake separating. Of all the couples I know who are on the verge of divorce and, believe me, I know many, you two are the last couple I expected to break up. I always thought you were joined at the hip.'

'At least we're young enough not to need hip replacements,' I joke and he smiles warily.

'How are you managing under the circumstances?' he asks. 'Is it difficult living under the same roof with Jake? A clean break would be that much easier.'

I agree it's not an ideal solution. I don't want to think about the nights I wait for Jake to come home or the envy I feel but must control because that was never part of the deal we made.

'What about you?' I steer the conversation towards Stuart. His hair has thinned and turned completely grey since we last met. His face, I realise, is thin, not lean, and the skin under his neck sags, as if unable to cope with a sudden weight loss. 'Have you finished all your treatment?'

'All done and dusted,' he says. 'I'm heading to Alaska in August.'

He specialises in industrial photography and I assume this is another commission, an oil refinery, perhaps, or a coal mine.

'Not this time,' he says. 'I've retired. This is all about ice.'

Photographing ice is Stuart's hobby. Icicles hanging from eaves, ice cubes clinking in a glass, glaciers, icebergs, frozen cobwebs suspended between the stems of flowers. Ice has brought him to the summit of mountains, the Arctic Circle and up close to garden hedges. Now, he's chartered a boat for August and intends to sail along the Southeast coast of Alaska.

'How long will you be away?' I ask.

'I haven't booked my return flight. It all depends…'

'On what?'

He swerves away from the question and finds a map, spreads it over the table. He runs his finger along the Alaskan coast line, touching Juneau, Skagway, Sitka, Glacier Bay. He names inlets, coves, islands, bays, straits.

'The owner of the boat will come with me,' he says. 'Daveth Carew has been conducting tours since he was a teenager. He knows the coast like the back of his hand.'

When the sailing is done Stuart will move inland to photograph the Juneau icefield. He needs someone to look after him. He never married. No woman would put up with his erratic lifestyle, he said when I asked him once. Always on the go, travelling here, there and everywhere. I think of Max Moylan. The same nomadic lifestyle and the toll it took on his marriage. But Max needed women, unlike Stuart who always found contentment in his own company.

'Would you consider coming with me?' he asks.

'*Me?*' For an instant I think he's joking but his expression tells me otherwise.

He laughs at my astonishment then stops abruptly, as if the sound has become unfamiliar. 'Don't look so astonished. I'm said I'm going to Alaska, not Mars. You've as much as admitted that you and Jake are living in an impossible situation.'

'But I know nothing about boats. I'd be a hindrance more than anything else on a trip like that.'

'I wouldn't ask you if that's what I thought,' he replies. 'This is a chance to do something different. Don't give me your answer until you've had time to seriously consider my proposal.'

'You could easily get someone with more experience.'

'I could,' he admits. 'But you're the closest I've ever come to having a child of my own.' For the first time I hear emotion in his voice, a quiver he's unable to disguise. 'Life is short, Nadine, and we allow so much of it to slip through our fingers. It would give us time to get to know each other a little better.'

I walk to the window and look down upon the city. Rooftops shimmer in the stillness of high places. It's still bright outside and sun is a translucent disc, barely visible in the hazed London air. He's offered me an escape route, but is sailing in treacherous seas with two men, one a stranger, the answer to my problems? Of course not… but what have I to lose? A domineering mother-in-law whose unbending attitude is never going to soften, a scattered family, a job that bores me and Jake… with his inscrutable gaze and secrets. The silence of vast empty spaces instead of the constant thud of music from his apartment when he's there. The pressure of unasked questions when he's not.

Stuart is knowledgeable and confident but there is a manic edge to his enthusiasm that worries me. Is he oblivious of the fact that gale force winds can whip without warning and change everything? The urge to ring Jake and discuss this preposterous proposal with him comes and goes. I'll make up my own mind. By the time the elevator stops at ground level I know the answer. Madness. No way will I even consider it.

CHAPTER TWENTY-THREE

Jake

Eleanor opened the front door to Apartment 2 with her own key. It annoyed Jake that she could enter his apartment without knocking but he could hardly object when Sea Aster was her property. He swivelled his shoulders to loosen them and laid his guitar aside. He had been so engrossed in his music that the morning had slipped by unnoticed and Eleanor's visit had been forgotten.

She entered the breakfast room and surveyed the beer bottles arranged in a semi-circle on the bay windowsill. Band practice had ended late last night. Afterwards, they had ordered pizzas and opened a few beers.

'That brings me back to your youth,' she said. 'I feel quite nostalgic looking at the chaos of your life.'

'I've been up since eight working on a new song,' Jake protested. It should not have sounded like an apology but it did.

'A *new* song.' Her eyebrows lifted. 'Wouldn't it be a better idea to look for a *new* job.'

'I have a job. I'm playing professionally as a session musician and teaching guitar in HiNotes.'

She impatiently swept his excuses aside. 'Did you follow up on that contact number I gave you?'

'I told you, I'm not interested in a retraining course. I'm reforming the band – '

She lowered herself into an armchair, her face settling into the obdurate lines he knew so well. 'For goodness sake, Jake! You're not a teenager any more, so stop behaving like one.'

'I'm *not* behaving – '

'Perhaps you've forgotten how I was pilloried by the media the last time you were in that band. I still shudder when I remember that dreadful publicity… the time you urinated on stage.'

'That was lime juice… a syringe… illusion.'

'And when you ended up in jail… those dreadful Satanic lyrics.'

He almost laughed out loud, remembering. '*When fucked about by Mum and Dad, Fuck them back and be as bad…*' The passion with which he sang those lyrics. A defiant pastiche on Philip Larkin's 'This Be The Verse', it caused a riot when the guards invaded the club where Shard were playing and arrested them under some obscure obscenity act. The media loved the story. Talk radio had lit up with parents protesting, demanding that Shard be banned from ever appearing in public again. Jake was back on stage the following week, the toned-down version rippling with subtle undertones that created even more impact among his fans. How could he have known that a year later he too would be struggling with the reality of being a parent?

'We've calmed down a lot since then,' he assured her. 'We're middle-aged, for goodness sake. Anyway, who's going to drag that up again?'

'The media have long knives and even longer memories.'

'I can't be responsible for your reputation.'

'But you can protect it by accepting my invitation to the conference.'

'What conference?'

'Didn't you read my email? I sent it to you last week.'

'I don't remember receiving it.'

'That's probably because you never checked. This conference is important. We've a number of influential guests from abroad speaking at it. When I deliver the keynote address, I want you and Nadine there supporting me.'

'In other words, you'd like us on our feet for the spontaneous ovation.'

'If a spontaneous ovation occurs then, yes.' Irony was lost on Eleanor.

'We won't be there. It's too hypocritical.'

She was on her feet before he finished, flushed and angrier than he had seen her for a long time. 'Is this how you thank me?' she demanded. 'I came to your assistance when you needed my help. I gave you and your wife a roof over your heads when you were homeless and broke. The least you can do is support me on one of the most important days of my life.' She pressed her hand against her heart and exhaled heavily. 'Have you any idea of the effect your decision has had on me? Sleepless nights, palpitations, anxiety. I'm terrified the members of the party will find out about you and Nadine. Our core values are based around the sacredness of the marriage vow.'

'They won't.'

'Please, Jake, I need my family around me. Be there for my speech, that's all I'm asking.'

'I'll talk to Nadine,' he promised.

'She's already responded to my email. I didn't like her tone. I'm sure you can persuade her to change her mind.'

No sense trying to work after she left. Her visit had drained his creativity. What was the catalyst that drove her to devote her life to a single issue? Why not take on the health service, bankers, political corruption, land speculators? Why not protect stray dogs, endangered snails, battery hens, exhausted foxes? Why the determination to impose her idealised view of family values on society?

He was convinced that early widowhood had left her with a romanticised belief that the bloom never faded from a marriage. Her years with Adam Saunders were the happiest of her life, she claimed. He died from a brain haemorrhage when Jake was eight. His strongest memory of that time was the hush that descended over the house when the music stopped. His father used to play the piano in the evenings when he came home from work and Jake's favourite memory was his manic imitation of Jerry Lee Lewis. Eleanor, unable to look at the piano without crying, sold it shortly after his death and joined First Affiliation. Jake had filled that silent space with his own music, distancing himself from her disapproval with small acts of rebellion that led eventually to Shard and all that post-punk aggression played out on stage.

He showered after she left and headed to HiNotes. Susanna kept increasing his classes and he was teaching guitar three afternoons a week. He dropped a note about the conference through Nadine's letterbox.

Karin had tickets for an outdoor film screening in Meeting House Square. HiNotes was only a short distance from the square and she was waiting for him when he arrived. After the screening, they walked through Temple Bar. They stopped to buy ice cream and listen to buskers. Her heels were high, treacherous on the cobblestones, he thought, but she walked gracefully, her arm lightly linked in his. He still found it difficult to be with her in public.

What if Nadine saw them together? She could be out with friends from the magazine, sitting by a restaurant window watching the crowds passing by. What would she say… do… should such an encounter occur? Would she feel betrayed? And, if so, why? Broken friendships happened all the time. Ali's childhood had been dominated by the drama of fallouts and make-ups. Karin had given him a glimpse of the fractures that had ended their friendship. A summer of discontent, spoiled by their infatuation with the singer in the band. He had laughed self-consciously when she hinted that he was the reason for the jealously that had pulsed between them. Was it that memory that had caused Nadine's face to flush with such unguarded animosity the night she discovered Karin's business card? Women. Jake shook his head. He would never understand the elephantine nature of their memory cells.

The following morning when he returned to Sea Aster Nadine had dropped her reply about Eleanor's conference through his letterbox. It consisted of two words, heavily underlined. _No way!_

CHAPTER TWENTY-FOUR

Nadine

It's after one in the morning when my mobile phone rings. The number is unfamiliar, the female voice clipped with authority. She's calling from Emergency in the Mater Hospital. Eleanor Saunders has been admitted by ambulance after suffering 'a sudden turn.' The nurse is unable to contact Jake and I'm second on the list of Eleanor's next of kin.

I've never know Eleanor to be ill. Her redoubtable nature is capable of scaring off the most persistent germs. What does 'a sudden turn' imply? And where is Jake? His van is missing…as usual. I leave a message on his mobile and drive to the hospital. Eleanor is still on a trolley in Emergency, ashen-faced, her voice muffled behind an oxygen mask.

'Such a fuss about nothing.' She pulls the mask aside and squints at me. Her lips are drained of colour. 'It's a total overreaction. Where's Jake?'

'I don't know. What happened to you?'

'A touch of indigestion. I called my doctor. Before I knew what he was doing there was an ambulance outside. I'm furious with him.'

'He wouldn't have called an ambulance unless he was worried about you. What are your symptoms – '

'Ah! At last you're here.' She looks beyond me and flaps her hands outwards, exasperated palms exposed. 'About time, too. Where were you until this hour?'

Jake's hair is ruffled, the collar of his shirt turned in on one side.

'I'm sorry,' he said. 'I came as soon as I got the message.'

'But *where* were you?' Eleanor repeats. 'Why didn't you answer your phone? I had to depend on Nadine to leave her bed to come here. With all the free time you have these days I thought I could depend on you to look after me.'

'I was with friends.' He's tight-lipped, embarrassed, avoiding my eyes.

He came from her bed. That much is clear. She might as well have scrawled her lipstick across his forehead, attached strands of tumbleweed hair to his jacket. Not my business… not my business… it's highly inappropriate to be wondering whose bed my husband occupied, and if it's still warm, when his mother could be dying in front of our eyes from 'a sudden turn.' But, unlike behaviour, our thoughts are not controlled by a moral code and I search for signs that will betray him. Nothing except a shirt collar turned in and the buttons out of kilter. He looks around for a doctor to consult. A nurse arrives and fixes Eleanor's oxygen mask back into position.

'Please don't touch this again, Eleanor,' she warns. 'This mask has a function and should not be treated like a snorkel.'

Eleanor heaves with impatience and Jake follows the nurse, who is hurrying towards an elderly man about to fall from his trolley.

'They're monitoring your blood pressure,' Jake says when he returns. 'It's on the high side but your ECG is okay. They're waiting for the results of blood tests.'

'How soon can I be discharged?'

'First they need to discover the reason you're here.'

Two hours later we're still waiting in Emergency. The ward fizzes with bad temper, exhaustion and lack of space. An elderly woman in the next cubicle yells 'Nurse… Nurse… *Nurse*' with agonising repetitiveness.

I find a coffee dispenser and return with two cartons for myself and Jake.

'Overcrowding in our hospitals. You should make that the main issue for debate at your party conference,' says Jake. '

Eleanor snatches the oxygen mask from her face. 'We're a one-issue party, Jake, as you very well know. Tell one of those children I want to be discharged immediately.' She points to a line of young doctors standing before a bank of computers. Steam hisses from the mask when she places it back into position.

'I certainly will not,' Jake replies. 'You heard the nurse. You must wait until your blood results come back.'

Eventually, when the results have been checked and Eleanor is on her feet again, we're called into a consulting room by a doctor with gritty eyes and the ashen pallor of an insomniac. He looks younger than Sam.

'I'm Doctor Noonan.' He waits until we're seated in front of his desk before continuing. 'All your tests are clear, Eleanor, except for your blood pressure, which is elevated. We're organising a blood pressure monitor over a twenty-four hour period. Have you been acutely worried about anything in the recent past?'

'Acute is an understatement, Doctor.'

'My mother is actively involved in politics,' Jake explains. 'That creates its own tensions.'

'Allow me to speak for myself, Jake.' Eleanor turns back to the doctor. 'Politics is child's play compared to my family life but that is neither here nor there. What exactly is the matter with me?'

'We intend booking you in for some further tests but it seems clear that you're displaying classic symptoms of panic and anxiety. Do you have a previous history of stress?'

'She thrives on stress,' says Jake, before Eleanor can reply. 'It's embedded in her psyche.'

'The dangers of stress cannot be undermined.' Dr Noonan frowns at Jake's flippancy. 'I'm aware of your political background, Eleanor. You've reached an age when it's advisable to take things easier…' He falters when he sees my mother-in-law's expression. 'I'm thinking of your health, Eleanor.'

'*Mrs* Saunders, if you don't mind. I'd appreciate some gravitas if you insist on discussing my advancing years.'

'*Mrs* Saunders, I urge you not to ignore my advice.' He glances nervously at his notes and draws courage from the written word. 'I'm going to prescribe blood pressure tablets and a mild sedative to alleviate your immediate symptoms. This is just a short-term measure but the overriding issue that brought about this episode needs to be addressed. Otherwise, you'll be prone to another attack and that could have more serious consequences.'

'Thank you for your advice, Doctor.' She glances from Jake to me and nods. 'I'm sure my son and his wife will do everything in their power to ensure that my life, political and personal, is kept free from stress from now on.'

CHAPTER TWENTY-FIVE

Jake

Protecting Marriage in a Dysfunctional Society was written in red on a banner above the stage in the Orbit Hotel. Cora Reynolds, whom Jake had known since he was a boy, escorted him and Nadine to the front row.

'This weekend has been amazing,' she whispered as she removed two Reserved signs. 'We've had wonderful speeches from our international guests and the workshops have been so energising. We're zapped up and ready to rock.'

'You always were a rocker,' said Jake. He liked Cora, who used to bring him sweets whenever she came to his house for First Affiliation meetings. She was different to the other activists, the women with sanctified faces and intractable hearts and the colourless men in dark suits that draw any remaining vitality deep into the seams. Did she know the truth about his marriage? If so, she was the only member of the party who did.

'I'm so glad you could both make it.' Cora continued her furtive whispering. 'Eleanor has prepared an inspiring speech. She's going to knock the socks off that lot.' She rolled her eyes towards a group of smartly dressed younger members seated a few rows back.

These days First Affiliation had a new dynamic. He had noticed it at Rosanna's funeral where the younger members formed a separate group from the older ones still surrounding Eleanor. Their leader-in-waiting, Lorna Mason, with her swinging pelmet of brown hair and modulated tones, would project a softer, more media-friendly image than his mother's usual combative approach.

'Are they giving her a hard time?' Jake whispered back.

Cora nodded. 'Let's just say Eleanor knows how to keep them in their place.'

'What does she use?' he asked. 'Rubber bullets or water cannon?'

'Oh, Jake, you *are* a scream.' Cora stifled a short, sharp giggle. 'Sit down there now and enjoy the rest of the evening.'

The conference room filled with anticipation as the audience waited for their leader to deliver her keynote address. Eleanor's appearance roused them to a standing ovation. She allowed the applause to reach a certain momentum before silencing them with a graceful wave.

'Thank you… thank you… my dear friends,' she said. 'I'm sure you'll all agree that the weekend has been an inspiring and stimulating experience for each and every one of us.' The applause that greeted this statement was again silenced after a suitable interval. 'Our distinguished panel of speakers left us with much to consider as we go forward into the next stage of our action campaign. But it is your attendance here, all of you united in our common core values, that has made this conference such an extraordinary success. From the bottom of my heart, I thank you. I also want to thank my family, my son Jake and his beloved wife, Nadine, for their unwavering support over the years and for the years to come.'

'Cunning, conniving, controlling cow,' muttered Nadine from the side of her mouth.

Working in *Lustrous* was honing her alliterative skills, Jake thought. Her feet, slender in red shoes, tapped so rapidly against the floor that he feared she was going to stand and walk out.

He placed his arm across the back of her chair and hissed, 'Calm down. We agreed to go through the motions but this is the last time… the *last* time…' He looked towards the stage and found himself face-to-face with a television camera. Instinctively, he and Nadine smiled as the camera swamped them in its lens then moved on.

'We believe that the edifice of marriage is supported by the two sturdy pillars of husband and wife.' Eleanor's voice rang with conviction. 'Marital love is the foundation upon which our edifice stands, but that love brings responsibilities. Outside forces will try to convince us that marriage, in all its beautiful manifestations, is an old-fashioned custom, quaint and outdated, like foot binding, for instance.'

Nadine stiffened. 'She's stealing my lines.' She sounded more astonished than angry.

'Shush,' hissed a voice from behind.

'Civil partnership or gay marriage – should such a law be introduced – will undermine the core principals of our party,' Eleanor continued. 'I don't have to spell out the consequences that will result from such liaisons. The demands these people will make on our already fractured, dysfunctional society. '

'Bring it on!' A female voice yelled from the centre of the hall.

'Bring it on!' echoed a second voice, male this time.

More voices joined in, each chanting the same slogan. Eleanor's mouth opened and closed, her words inaudible in the growing tumult.

'Is a beloved union between wife and wife not equally blessed in the sight of God?' This voice had a familiar ring and Jake swallowed convulsively when he recognised it.

Nadine, who had turned to stare at the protestors, swung her head towards Jake. 'That's Feral Childe,' she gasped. 'What's she doing here?'

'She probably came with her wife.'

'*What?*'

'Her wife,' he repeated. 'Didn't I tell you Feral was married?'

'You certainly did not! Which one is her wife?'

'Sit down.' He pulled her arm until she collapsed back into the chair. 'I don't want her to see me. Her wife's the leader of a gay rights activist group.'

'Do they know Eleanor is your mother?'

'What do you think? It's not something I'm inclined to boast about. '

The members of First Affiliation were on their feet, booing at the group of men and women holding banners that proclaimed *Marriage Equality is Our Right! and God Does Not Differentiate!*

The protest group was unceremoniously escorted from the hall by four heavy-set security men. Eventually, when the door slammed behind them, Eleanor continued her speech. She had lost her audience, who whispered among themselves, their impatience obvious as they waited for her to finish.

'Let's go,' said Nadine as soon as the short standing ovation ended and the audience surged from their seats.

The gay rights activists were continuing to protest outside the hotel. Journalists shoved microphones towards Feral's wife. Doyle and demanded to know how she and Feral, as a married couple, felt about being denied the right to participate in the conference. Without waiting to hear her reply Jake sprinted towards Nadine's car. He had been ordered by Eleanor not to bring his band van to the conference. Once inside the car they stared at each other.

'Don't you dare make me laugh,' Nadine warned.

'As if I would.'

'My mascara will run.'

'Not as fast as I'll run if Eleanor discovers one of the chief hecklers is the drummer in my band.'

'Oh, Jake… Eleanor's face…' Nadine bent over the steering wheel, her shoulders heaving. 'I shouldn't be laughing… I shouldn't,' she gasped. 'And neither should you. It's cruel.'

'You're right about the mascara,' he said.

'I'm like a panda.' She pulled down the front mirror and dabbed at her eyes with a tissue. 'I actually thought you and Feral were… you know…'

'You *what*? Are you mad? She's a married woman.' It was good to laugh with her again. 'Fancy going for a drink?' he asked. 'I need one after that shemozzle.'

In The Boot Inn he ordered two glasses of wine and listened, astonished, when she told him about Stuart's extraordinary invitation. The conference had banished the tension between them and it was almost like old times when they talked about the children. Ali had joined a drama group and was waiting tables three afternoons a week in a tapas bar. The twins, according to Samantha, were cleaning out the student vomitorium. Roughly translated, this meant tending the student bar in Silver Ridge University. Jake admitted to his frustration with the slow progress of the band. Reedy and Feral were professional musicians with other commitments and the date had passed for the come-back launch. Hart was worried about falling membership at Hartland to Health and Daryl – who once offered to sell his soul to Satan if it helped him play his guitar better than The Edge – had a full-time job and a baby daughter who was turning into a terrorist. They looked upon the band as a hobby, a light relief from the stresses of the day. To place Shard in the same category as wood-whittling or plane-spotting was insulting but Jake understood their reluctance to give more time to it.

Nadine had lost weight. Not a lot but enough to give her figure an added sleekness.

'Stress is the new liposuction,' she joked when he commented.

Was she seeing someone? To imagine her in another man's bed, her hair riotous on his pillows... those sea-green eyes deepening to the lambent glow of desire. It was an uncomfortable image, unsettling. His phone rang. He checked his watch, surprised at how quickly the time had passed. He was due in Karin's apartment in an hour.

'Why not answer it?' Nadine said. 'I won't eavesdrop.'

'I'll take it later.' He cut the call but the lightness had gone from their conversation. Nadine, appreciating that the mood had changed, finished her wine and pulled on her jacket.

Outside Sea Aster they hesitated, awkward at parting.

'See you round,' she said. 'You should ring Eleanor and see if she's okay. This won't have helped her stress levels.'

'Stress levels, my foot. That was a con job if ever I saw one.'

'She wasn't faking, Jake. Keep in touch with her.'

He stopped for petrol on the way to Karin's apartment and, on impulse, plucked a bouquet of roses from a bucket beside the pay station. Every traffic light seemed set at red to deliberately thwart him. He eyed the roses lying on the passenger seat and recalled a conversation on talk radio in which a women claimed she broke off her relationship with her partner when he presented her with a bouquet of garage roses. Too tawdry and cheap, she said. A lazy, thoughtless gift that reflected his view of their relationship. Afterwards, the phone lines zinged with women who claimed they would have welcomed roses, no matter where they originated, as a sign that their husbands thought about them, even for those brief moments when they filled their cars with petrol. Should he dump the roses in a refuse bin and arrive empty-handed? Better keep going. Karin was ignoring his apologetic texts and he was already forty-five minutes late.

He heard a dog barking when he stepped from the elevator. High yelps that belonged indoors, probably a small dog with scurrying legs and a puffed-up sense of its own importance. The yelps rose to a crescendo as he hurried towards Karin's apartment.

'You've arrived.' She made this terse, self-evident statement when she opened the door. 'Thank you for taking the trouble to show up.'

'Sorry I'm late. It's mayhem out there tonight. You should have seen the traffic on the Eastlink. There's a concert on the – '

'Why didn't you answer your phone when I rang earlier?' She faced him, arms folded. Her pouting bottom lip, glossily purple, told him roses would not appease her. She strode ahead of him into the kitchen. Tonight she had promised to cook her special signature dish. He had no idea what it was but he had expected the kitchen to be redolent with spices, steamy and warm. Instead, the chrome fittings glittered coldly and the hob was empty, not a saucepan in sight. She had been cooking earlier. The faint smell of turmeric and cumin still lingered, despite the low, determined purr of the air extractor above the hob.

'I was driving.' He laid the roses on the counter. They looked even more wilted now, the petals turning brown on the edges. 'Didn't you get my texts telling you I'd been delayed?'

'If you'd taken my call it would have saved you the trouble of texting. I rang to tell you tonight was cancelled.'

'What's wrong?'

'You're a liar,' she stated. 'That's what's wrong.'

'Don't make that accusation again, Karin.' The dog was still barking, its high-pitched yaps adding to Jake's unease. He was unsure if it was the persistent yapping or her shrill certainty that fanned his anger. 'You'd better tell me what's bothering you or I'm leaving right now.'

The dog, as if exhausted or muffled, fell silent.

'You should see this before you leave.' Karin flounced from the kitchen, her high heels sparking against the tiled floor and stood in front of the television in her living room. She pressed the record button. 'How do you explain this?'

His heart sank when he saw the banner *Protecting Marriage in a Dysfunctional Society* draped above his mother's head. The conference had featured on the six o'clock news and Karin had recorded it. He listened to Eleanor's forceful voice declaring, 'I also want to thank my family, my son Jake and his beloved wife, Nadine, for their unwavering support over the years and for the years to come.'

The camera swept over him and Nadine. Why was his arm around her? They looked like besotted teenagers staring into it. Why on earth were they smiling? He remembered the moment. Their anger at Eleanor's duplicity. The invasive lens. The news item then cut to the protest and an interview with Eleanor when she emerged from the conference room.

'You told me you were getting a divorce.' Karin's eyes glittered. 'Now I discover that you're living happy ever after together.'

'We *are* getting a divorce…' He gestured towards the television. 'That's not what it seems – '

'Oh, *really*.'

'We did it for my mother's sake. She's been unwell.'

'More lies.' Her voice quickened. 'I was foolish enough to believe you. You're just the same as the others. Every word from your mouth was a lie… what a fool I've been… you're just another lying, deceitful bastard…'

He tried to grasp what she was saying but she spoke too fast. He caught some words – abusive, manipulative, controlling – and tried to recognise himself in the verbal storm flaring around him. He grasped her shoulders. The fine blades tensed at his touch. Her head jerked back as if avoiding the smack of his hand. In the midst of his confusion he understood that he was no longer the target of her anger.

She had told him about her relationships with other men. Relationships that had left her scarred and suspicious. A thug called Hal who cut up her clothes one night and flung them from the window of their New York apartment when she went clubbing with her friends. Malcolm, an alcoholic, Cody, a control freak, Jason, married but desperately pretending otherwise when he placed an engagement ring on her finger, and Carl, so physically abusive that she needed two years of therapy before she had the strength of will to leave him. She wore her scars lightly or so he had believed until tonight. Now, the veneer was stripped aside, her hurt fully exposed.

'Listen to me, Karin,' he pleaded. 'Today meant nothing. Do you understand, *nothing*. Nadine agreed to do it for my mother's sake. We're worried about her health. Otherwise we'd never – '

'We… we… *we*. You're supposed to be single. How can you be apart when you're still living under the one roof?'

'Believe me, it's possible. I'd leave Sea Aster tomorrow if I could. So would Nadine.' He brought her hand to his chest, allowed her to feel his heartbeat, the pumping rhythm, part shock, part exhilaration. 'You told me that space doesn't matter. It's how close we are here that counts.'

He watched the anger drain slowly from her face, ease from her shoulders. She undid the buttons on his shirt and pressed her ear to his chest.

'My God, your heart is thumping. I've really upset you… I'm sorry… so sorry.'

'It doesn't matter.'

'But it does. If we don't have trust between us, we have nothing except deceit and disloyalty.' Her voice was muffled against his skin. 'Does Nadine know about us?'

'No.'

'Why won't you tell her?'

'I will… when the time is right.'

'There is no right time. If we're serious about each other she needs to know the truth.'

'She will… soon.'

'I love you, Jake.'

She was waiting, poised to fly if he hesitated too long. She had saved his sanity, stopped the onslaught of depression when the structures in his life collapsed around him.

'I love you, too,' he said and hoped she could not hear the hesitant crack in his voice.

The row was over, their passion heightened by the ferocity of her anger. She marked him with her teeth, drew blood with her nails. Astride him, under him; her body arched and hollowed as a cat at play, she allowed him no rest that night.

'You and I belong together,' she murmured when they were finally sated, exhausted. With the tip of her finger she gently pressed the mouth she had kissed so violently, sliding it between his lips to touch his tongue once more. 'Don't ever lie to me, Jake.'

CHAPTER TWENTY-SIX

Nadine

Tomorrow morning I fly to London with Liam Brett to attend a jewellery trade fair. The idea of spending an overnight trip with Liam is off-putting but he's made it clear that, outside of business hours, we'll go our separate ways. I've arranged to meet Stuart in the evening to say goodbye before he leaves for Alaska. I'll see Ali on Sunday before I fly home. I need time with my daughter. She tells me so little about her life, the auditions that end in dashed hopes, the struggle to keep believing in herself, the new drama group she's joined.

I stop outside Brown Thomas. It's late July and the colours on display in the department store windows are becoming more subdued. I need to buy something new for the London trip and have thirty minutes to spare before I'm due back at *Lustrous*. The magazine is being redesigned and updated. A graphic designer has not yet been appointed and interviews are being held this afternoon. Jessica has asked me to join her and Liam on the interview panel.

I take the escalator to the fashion floor. The dress I choose is moss-coloured and slim fitting. I've become aware of my body in a new way. The glance I used to cast at my reflection has become a lingering examination, critical and objective. I enjoy the sleek feel of my stomach, the easy glide of a zip over my waist. And I'm beginning to notice looks from men. Have I been blind to the signals in the past or am I exuding a primal spoor, pheromones, the subtle scent of freedom, availability, desire? Occasionally, I go to pubs with Gina from Admin. Three men have invited me to their beds. It's a direct invitation. Time is precious these days so why waste it on irrelevant conversation? I refuse politely and wonder if it was that brutal with Jake? Memories gather a softer skin over the years… but, no, we made love yet we also talked. We confided slights and hurts, perceived or otherwise, to each other and breathed secrets with promises never to tell. But that's also untrue. Some secrets lie quiescent until something, a song, a casual meeting, a face that looks familiar but belongs to someone else cause memories to rise in a clamour.

I see her as I emerge from the department store with my carrier bag. She moves, vanishes. My forehead feels clammy, the crowd too dense, pushing, shoving as I walk towards the top of Grafton Street. Did I imagine her? Or is she once again in my space, stealing my oxygen?

The afternoon passes quickly. We interview four graphic designers. None of their presentations excite me. Jessica and Liam feel the same way. I'm about to close my file when Liam says, 'There's someone else we should interview. She came late to me with her portfolio. Said she didn't realise we were looking for a designer until the submission date had passed. She's worth a look.'

He passes a CV to Jessica who scans it and hands it to me. Saliva fills my mouth when I see her name.

Jessica glances across at me when she hears my intake of breath. 'Do you know her?'

I nod and press my hands flat on the table to keep them still.

'Did you tell her to submit her portfolio to us?'

'No. I haven't seen her for years.' I sound unruffled. How strange. I touch my wrist and scars, faint as silvery skeins, seem to ripple the surface of my skin.

Jessica's eyes skim over the pages of Karin Moylan's CV. 'Liam's right. She certainly has an interesting track record. Bring her in.' She nods at Liam and leans back in her chair.

They rise to greet her. I force myself to stand with them and lean across the table to shake her hand. She still has the ability to render me once again in a gauche, shambling teenager but I've learned poise and pretence in the years since. My grip on her hand is firm. If she's surprised to see me she hides it well. Her smile is as white as I remember.

'It's nice to meet you again, Nadine.' She's dressed city-smart, a charcoal-grey skirt and jacket, the waist emphasised by a wide blue belt.

'I didn't realise you were back in Ireland.' I concentrate on sitting down rather than collapsing back into my chair and as Jessica waves Karin to a seat.

'I returned some months ago,' she replies. 'I wanted to be close to my mother. She's not getting any younger.'

'But she's well, I hope.'

'She is indeed, thank you.'

'So, how do you two know each other?' Jessica asks.

'Oh, we go way back,' I reply.

'We certainly do.' Karin addresses her directly. 'Nadine was my best friend in secondary school. We haven't seen each other for years. How long do you reckon that is, Nadine?'

'Twenty-five… could be twenty-six years,' I reply. 'You haven't changed at all, Karin. I'd have recognised you anywhere.'

'Thank you. I'll take that as a compliment and return it to you. You're looking wonderful.'

Are we really fooling the others with this civilized exchange? From their polite expressions as they glance at her application letter it would seem so.

I glimpsed her at the airport and she gave voice to a discontent I'd barely acknowledged. A discontent that could be ignored because I was afraid to squander my marriage with notions of freedom. Then her card fell from Jake's wallet. I stared into the kingfisher's chilling gaze and stopped pretending to be satisfied with the predictability of the life Jake and I had moulded from our rough beginnings.

I turn away, unable to look at her and stare at the wallpaper. An abstract swirl in lurid colours. The room feels as if it's shifting on its own accord. The effect is nauseating and brings me back to the journey home from Monsheelagh in the back seat of my father's car. Eoin drove too fast around the bends on the cliff road and my stomach churned as I lowered the window, seeking fresh air too late to prevent me from throwing up.

Karin had a new friend when we returned to St Agatha's in September. Vonnie Draper was thrilled by the secrets she confided to her. A whispering campaign began soon afterwards and grew implacably. Each day brought new distortions, new lies, all making their way back to me by those who believed I should 'know' what was being said behind my back. I smelled, according to Vonnie: bad breath, body odour, sweaty feet. I had 'lesbo' tendencies and always tried to kiss Karin whenever I slept over in her house.

I cleaned my teeth until my gums bled, stood under scalding water in the shower and refused to walk to school with Jenny in case this gave rise to new rumours. I sat alone in the school canteen and lived in dread that Karin would tell Vonnie about the letters I'd written during our holiday. Love letters that she had stolen from me.

Jessica's brisk voice snaps me to attention. 'Liam was very interested in the ideas you submitted with your CV, Karin.' She makes a steeple with her fingertips and taps them together. 'Could you begin by telling us how your specific design skills could benefit *Lustrous*.'

Karin swivels her chair slightly to the side and opens her portfolio case.

'I've developed my skills through years of experience from working abroad,' she says. 'I've worked mainly in New York but also in other major cities. However, my most important attribute is my creative talent, which, I believe will be of enormous benefit to *Lustrous*.'

'Can you elaborate on those talents?' Liam asks. He's more animated than I've seen him all afternoon. Before the interviews began we worked out the specific questions we would ask each interviewee. I hesitate when my turn comes. Jessica inclines her head towards me as the pause lengthens.

I clear my throat and ask Karin to tell us what she knows about *Lustrous* and its readership. She answers without hesitation, trots out circulation figures, statistics, history. She quotes headlines from the first issue of *Lustrous*, mentions some spectacular photographic shoots that have featured in the magazine over the years. Jessica is warming to her. She and Liam lean forward expectantly when Karin removes mock-up drawings from her case and hands them around. She switches on her laptop and does a Powerpoint presentation. She's worked on other magazines, a film company, some banks and corporations.

Her designs reflect the latest graphic trends from New York. She demonstrates how the fonts from *Vanity Fair* and *Hello* would look on *Lustrous* and suggests various alternatives. One of the fonts catches my attention when it flashes on the screen. It's gone before I can figure out why it looks familiar.

Liam's eyes glide over Karin as she speaks. I can almost hear the smack of his lips. No chance he'll ever call her 'Babe.' She shows the magazine pages on the screen from different angles and is obviously used to presenting her ideas to a panel.

'Nadine, would you like to give us your opinion on what we've just seen?' Jessica waits expectantly for my reply. I scrabble around for something constructive to add to the discussion. I know that she and Liam have already made up their minds.

'I like the overall design.' I'm amazed at my self-control, the conviction I convey as I explain why the pages should be less crowded with content. More white space would make them easier on the eye for the average *Lustrous* reader, whose attention span could be compared to that of a gnat. I keep the latter opinion to myself. Jessica takes her role as her celebrities' chronologist quite seriously.

'I have to leave now.' Liam stands and shakes Karin's hand, speaks directly to her. 'There's someone waiting to see me in my office but I'm interested in discussing your ideas in more detail, especially in the context of *Core*, my other magazine. Call in on me before you leave and we'll talk some more.'

Jessica's mobile phone rings. She checks the screen. 'Apologies, I need to take this.' She moves towards the window and out of earshot.

Karin sits, legs crossed, poised. I hoped desperately that she would do a bad interview but she hasn't put a foot wrong. The bows on her shoes, the buttons on her white blouse, the brooch on her jacket are the same blue as her belt. Each co-ordinating detail trails attention over her body.

'I've often thought about you, Nadine, and wondered how your life worked out,' she says.

'As you can see, I'm getting on very well.'

'Do you have family?'

'Four children. And you?'

'Unlike you, I've been unlucky in love.' She tosses this comment towards me with a wry smile.

She lies. Beautiful people like Karin make their own luck. She must be remembering, as I am, how she turned me into fodder for the school grapevine. When nothing was said about my letters, no breathless comments from Vonnie making their way back to me, I comforted myself with the belief that Karin hadn't shown them to her. Otherwise, even under threat of torture, Vonnie would have been unable to keep their content a secret.

'Hopefully, you're still happily married,' she asks.

'Jake and I are still together,' I reply. 'Some things never change. He told me you met on a flight to New York.'

Her eyelids flutter. She tilts her head. I remember that birdlike gesture, the darting glance, and those eyes, so compelling. 'A chance encounter,' she says. 'I hardly recognised him but years of domesticity do that to a man.'

'Apologies… *apologies*.' Jessica returns and interrupts this brittle exchange. She ends the interview shortly afterwards with a promise to be in touch with Karin as soon as a decision is made.

'She's definitely tuned into our wavelength,' Jessica says when the door closes behind her. 'I'm more than happy to go with Kingfisher Graphics.'

Karin Moylan is exactly the right person to redesign *Lustrous* magazine. To smarten it up so that more and more readers can stare at our vacuous, airbrushed photographs and envy a world that doesn't exist.

'She's good,' I admit. 'I was also interested in our third interviewee. We should call him back for another interview.'

'He's not what we want.' Jessica has decided. 'You'll enjoy working with each other on this project. It makes such a difference when there's a good team spirit.'

I return to my office and stare out the window. I can't remain in this job. I'll toss burgers, clean offices, sweep the streets rather than sit facing her again. Her hands will be all over the magazine, the way they were all over the blackboard in our classroom when she drew my image for all to see.

I press my nails hard against my bottom lip as I recall in detail the morning I entered the classroom and saw a naked figure with small breasts, a grotesque penis and large feet drawn on the blackboard. No name was written underneath but the flaming red hair and exaggerated corkscrew curls were instantly recognisable. Unable to look at the pupils clustered around the blackboard I ran from the classroom to the toilets. I huddled in a cubicle until Jenny, who'd gone directly to the principal's office to report the drawing, coaxed me out.

The blackboard was wiped clean when we returned to the classroom. None of the students claimed to know who drew it. No one was held responsible, nor could it be proved that Karin had anything to do with it. But I saw the truth in her eyes when she pressed a finger to her cheek and tilted her head, appraisingly. Nothing has changed since then.

Liam taps on my office and enters. 'I reckon we've made our decision.' he says. 'As far as I'm concerned it's the last interviewee. I'm taking her out for coffee. I'll be back in half an hour.'

He taps on my computer and opens a *Core* file. 'Take a look at those shots and write some captions for them. Jimmy French is off sick today and I need them ready for production by five.'

'Sorry, Liam.' At last I can let my anger show. 'Do it yourself. *Core* is not my responsibility.'

He frowns, leans over my shoulder, overpowers me with his aftershave.

'In Wall Publications everyone mucks in. Otherwise Jessica throws a hissy fit and, believe me, that's something you don't want to experience.'

I stare at the screen after he leaves. It's typical *Core* material, the photographs taken outside a nightclub. A dead-eyed model hanging from the arm of a celebrity chef who does a weekly cookery programme on television with his chirpy, bright-eyed wife. How will she feel when she sees these photographs? I want to delete them but nothing can be hidden anymore. Hard drives, CCTV, mobile phones, paparazzi. This wife's fate is sealed and his too. As for the model – we'll feature her in *Lustrous* when she comes out of rehab.

Caked Out! I write and delete. *In the Stew* suffers the same fate. I close down the file and write a note to Liam. *Do it yourself and let me deal with Jessica's hissy fit!!!* I dig my pen viciously into the paper.

I enter his office and leave the note on his desk. Karin has left her portfolio case against the wall. She must be coming back to pick it up. I hesitate then walk towards the door. The corridor is empty. Quickly, I return and place it on the desk. I unzip it and turn the pages. My hands begin to sweat. One of the plastic pages slips from my grip with a heavy flap. I lift it again and stare at an image. Jagged shards of ice, blazing. The letters SHARD chiselled as finely as pinheads. The pages slap loudly as I close the leather case. The zip jams on the corner. I lean my hands on the desk to steady my breathing. It's almost four o'clock. They're due back any moment. I pull the zip back then ease it gently around the corner before returning the case to its original position.

Unable to face the stifling atmosphere of my office, I run outside and stand on the steps. I remember the unnecessary force Jake used when he ripped the Kingfisher Graphics business card in two. I remember the text... New York... New York... homeward bound...

Children's voices ring from the park across the square. The tall Georgian houses sway towards me. I grip the railings. Rage tears at my throat. It pulses in my wrists and in the serrated scars I believed had healed. New York... New York calling... Frank Sinatra sings in my ear. An ear worm. I've always disliked that song, the inevitable circle swaying backwards and forwards at the end of a wedding, drunken legs kicking outwards.

CHAPTER TWENTY-SEVEN

Jake

Their first harrowing row marked a change in their relationship. Now, Jake heard steel in Karin's voice when she spoke about give and take. Essential elements in a shared relationship, she said. Sooner or later Nadine had to know the truth. So, too, had his children and Eleanor. When would that be? She put these nightmarish questions to him calmly, argued rationally that she should not be expected to hide indefinitely in the shadows of his family life.

Tonight, in an Italian bistro overlooking the Liffey, she asked him to bring her to Sea Aster. She cut him short when he mentioned his pact with Nadine.

'Did she tell you we met?' She drew back from him, her face shadowed in the glow of candles.

'What are you talking about?'

'In *Lustrous* on Friday. I've been commissioned to revamp the magazine.'

'You never mentioned.'

'I figured she'd tell you.'

'How? I spent the night with you. She'd left for London when I returned so I wasn't talking to her.'

The waiter came to the table to offer them a dessert menu. They both declined and waited in silence while he removed their dishes.

'What did she say to you?' Jake asked when they were along again.

'That her marriage is in perfect working order.'

'I don't believe you.'

'She told me you're still together. Some things never change, that's how she phrased it. I can take that two ways. You're together under one roof or together in the same bed. Which one is true?'

'You know exactly what she meant. I haven't lied to you about our living arrangements.'

'Then why don't we spend tonight in your apartment?'

'I told you – '

'She's in London with Liam Brett. They're not due back until tomorrow.'

'That doesn't matter. We have an agreement.'

'Who am I supposed to believe? You? Her? She knows we met on that flight. You claim you didn't discuss it with her. She has no reason to lie. You, on the other hand, have every reason to deceive me. You promised me a future yet you won't even allow me to see your apartment.' She pouted warningly. 'We spend all our time in my space. Tonight, I want to spend some time in yours. Otherwise, this just becomes another one-sided relationship.'

The silence when they entered Apartment 2 was eerie, almost oppressive. Jake switched on lights, turned up the music, opened wine. Nothing could banish his unease.

'Stop worrying.' Karin watched in amusement as he gathered unwashed dishes from the coffee table and carried them to the kitchen. 'You're making me nervous. Sit down and relax.'

'Just give me a moment.' He headed to the bathroom, unable to remember the last time he splashed Harpic around the rim of the toilet bowl. In the bedroom he picked up his clothes from the floor and shoved them into a laundry basket. Thankfully, he had changed the sheets the previous day.

He was smoothing out the duvet when she entered the bedroom. Her glance flickered around the room, checking for the feminine touch, the spill of powder on the dressing table, necklaces hanging from black, ornamental fingers, perfume, a silk scarf draped over the back of a chair. Satisfied that this was an all-male environment, she stood before the full-length chervil mirror. Slowly, teasingly, she opened her blouse, her gaze sultry yet playful as she undid each button. Her breasts rose, plump and firm, from the cleavage of her bra. She waved the blouse over her head before tossing it across the room then unzipped her skirt, kicked off her high heels, rolled down the lacy tops of her stockings. The urge to take her in that instant, to plunge in deep and hard, to hear her sharp little cries and feel her nails digging deep into his shoulders almost overpowered him. Her eyes – reflecting back at him in the mirror – commanded him not to touch her. She unhooked her bra, tantalisingly removed her thong. Only then did she turn to face him, her body as smooth and flawless as a doll. The air was musky with her scent, her sense of anticipation as he lifted her in his arms and lowered her onto the bed. He kicked off his shoes as she unbuckled his belt, her fingers nimbly unzipping him, freeing him. She laughed at his urgency as he pulled off his shirt then traced his lips from her throat to her breasts, moved downwards over her taut stomach. She opened to him, her legs rampantly splayed as his tongue probed deeper, tasting her, hearing her whimpering cries, the rush of her breathing.

Nadine's presence hovered above him like a reproachful shadow. He forced her away. The unknown could not hurt her but in that pause, that instant of guilt, remorse, shame, he had no idea what to call it, he became aware of sounds from Apartment 1.

He tensed as he heard the clatter of wheels. Nadine was dragging her overnight case up the stairs. He tightened his hands on Karin's wrists, forced her to be still.

'That's Nadine. You said she wasn't due back until tomorrow.'

'That's what Liam Brett told me. Monday, he said. Not Sunday.'

'Then she must have come back early.'

'It doesn't matter. She won't know I'm here.' He felt her resistance, the strength of her thighs as she arched towards him.

'We should leave. I can't… not with Nadine upstairs.'

'Poor Jake, you're really spooked.' She laughed softly and ran her finger over his lips. 'Just relax.'

He heard music, a door slamming, a phone ringing. Nadine was right about sound carrying. It was a cacophony. She crossed her bedroom floor. He imagined the high arch of her foot when she kicked off her shoe, then the second one. He listened to the pull of wood against wood as she opened drawers, hinges whining, a chair being dragged closer to the kitchen table, the rumble of pipes as the taps ran. Why had he not been conscious of those sounds before now? Had she moved so silently that the only indication of her presence was the occasional blare of the radio? No, he thought, this evening was no different to any other. It was guilt that honed his awareness. Lies. That was the difference. Submerged in lies… submerged in desire… submerged yet afloat. The words contradicted each other and mired him in deceit. The wood squeaked as Nadine climbed down the stairs. That would be the seventh step. It had creaked even when he was a boy. He heard the front door open and close. His doorbell rang.

'Does she usually come to your apartment at this time of night?' Karin whispered.

'No, never... not at night.'

'Don't answer it.'

'Something must be wrong.' He pulled on a pair of boxers, grabbed his fleece top from a chair and padded bare-footed towards the front door.

'We need to talk.' Nadine had changed into trainers and a tracksuit but there was nothing casual about her expression.

He stepped outside, eased the door closed behind him. 'What's wrong? Has something happened to Ali?'

'Ali's fine.'

'Stuart?'

'He's good. Are you going to ask me in or do we have to conduct this conversation on your doorstep?'

Light flared from the breakfast room. Nadine turned, startled and walked to the bay window. He watched, too shocked to move, as she stopped and raised her hands to cover her eyes. Karin, unaware that she could be seen, was standing in the curve of glass. She was wearing one of his shirts. Not just any shirt. His favourite one, pale blue twill, a present from Nadine. She had bunched it loosely over her bare shoulders, her hands clutching the two edges protectively over her breasts. The gesture made her nakedness underneath even more provocative. Suddenly, aware that she was visible, she pulled the curtains across but it was too late. The enormity of his betrayal washed over him when Nadine dropped her hands and he saw her stricken expression. She opened her mouth to speak but no words came out. The only sound to break the silence was the slap of her hand against his cheek. Its force sent him staggering backwards. By the time he recovered she was running towards her car. He followed her but he knew that no matter how fast he ran he would never be able to catch her.

CHAPTER TWENTY-EIGHT

Nadine

The moon is full and racing behind trees as I drive from Sea Aster. I slow at the gates. The turn onto Mallard Cove is sharp and dangerous. Not that there's likely to be anyone driving past at this time of night but good habits persist even in the midst of trauma. Once onto the road I accelerate again. The hedge-rows whip against the car as it judders over the uneven surface. Broadmeadow Estuary is a glaze of midnight blue and the heron stands stoic and alone at the water's edge. The road still bends but the surface is smoother, the view clearer. I drive past lone bungalows, past housing estates, Seabury, Chalfont, slumbering suburbs. Private lives sleeping behind closed blinds. The railway bridge looms before me. This arched space allows only one car to pass through at the same time. I should slow down. I must slow down… too late I realise that an oncoming car is about to enter the arch.

I'm driving too fast to brake and the oncoming car pulls sharply against the wall before the bridge entrance. The driver blares a warning until I'm out of earshot. I turn up New Street. The restaurants are closing for the night, the pubs still doing business. Traffic lights turn red when I reach The Diamond crossroads. My hands tremble on the steering wheel as I wait for the green signal.

Headlights blink in my rear-view mirror. I recognise the silvery sheen of Jake's van, the sleek, hearse-like lines, the icy heat of its signage. The thought of them planning it together adds to my fury. I swear at the lights until they change then I veer left towards the coast. The sea is rough tonight. Slanting waves heave with froth and rush silently ashore. Coast Road twists along the shore. Accidents have occurred here in the past, cars plunging over the embankment onto the rocks below. I press the brake when I reach another bend but my car swerves dangerously.

I must stop, must concentrate. I pull into a deep curve where cars park during the day. I switch off the headlights and rest my head on the steering wheel. Jake has not yet reached the bend. His survival instincts must be stronger than mine. A minute passes before his headlights swamp the darkness and pass on. I lower the window and allow the night air to cool my cheeks. A plane flies overhead, followed by another, their lights winking towards the slow descent into Dublin airport. There's something hypnotic about watching the lights emerge from the dark horizon and fly across my line of vision. Only an hour ago I was up there, planning what I would say to Jake, my head pounding as the time for confrontation drew nearer.

The overnight trip had been a non-stop series of business meetings, interspersed with my visit to Stuart and lunch with Ali. No one seemed aware of my inner turmoil, the furious, imaginary conversations with Jake broiling in my mind. Now, huddled in darkness, I want to throw a tantrum, fists and heels pummelling, as Sam used to do when he was small and Samantha, the calmer of the two, would work herself into the same frenzy in solidarity with her twin.

Shale, washed with waves, gleams in the moonlight. That summer in Cowrie Cottage… no… I don't want to go there…

but they come like wraiths, those memories, black cloaks flapping.

Headlights approach from the opposite side of the road. Before I can duck out of sight they dazzle and swerve in a U-turn. I stare ahead and ignore Jake when he raps on the window. He continues banging, the sound more frantic, louder.

'Go away and leave me alone.' I lower the window and shriek at him. 'If you don't I'll ram your van onto the rocks below.'

'For God's sake, Nadine – '

'You don't believe in God so shut up and leave me alone.'

'I want to explain – '

'What's there to explain? Go back to her and finish what you were doing when I interrupted you.'

'I intended on telling you about her.'

'You had your opportunity. Why couldn't you have told me the truth?'

'I knew you had a history with her – '

'A *history*? Is that the new name for coping with a paranoid bully?'

'See what I mean?'

The only thing you see is her *cunt*. I want to scream the word at him, batter him with obscenities.

'How long have you been together?' I don't want an answer yet I have to know.

'Not long.'

'That's not an answer. Tell me the truth.'

'Let me into the car and we'll talk.'

'*No*. I want the truth. Were you seeing her when I found her business card?'

'Not then. Later. After we moved into Sea Aster.'

'How often has she been there?'

'Tonight was the first time. Honestly, Nadine, I never meant to hurt – '

'I don't believe you.' The thought of them together is unendurable. 'Go away from me... *go* away.' I fumble for the automatic window switch and he draws his hands back as the glass slides upwards.

When I start the engine he runs to the front of my car. Our clashing headlights distort his features. His lips move but the sound can't reach me. When he thumps the bonnet, demanding that I listen, I keep my hand on the horn and rev the engine. I want to reduce him to pulp, to traces of DNA, nothing less.

I don't notice the squad car until it pulls in behind me. Doors open. Two guards in uniform and hi-vis jackets approach. One of the guards speaks to Jake. The second one knocks sharply on my window.

'Are you the owner of this vehicle?' she asks.

My mouth is dry, my throat ticklish. She waits impassively while I cough and try to gain some control over my breathing.

'Yes, Guard. It's my car.' Finally, I'm able to speak.

'Were you the sole occupant tonight?'

'Yes.'

I can't stop staring at the wart on her chin. A fine clump of hairs grow from its centre. Has she never heard of electrolysis? Doesn't she care that potential criminals will *stare*? I've a wild desire to laugh. It's safer than keening. I avert my eyes from the offending wart and concentrate on her face. She has a thin, straight mouth that suggests a low level of tolerance for demented drivers. I display my driving licence and her torch forms an arc as it sweeps over the tax disc. The registration plate is checked, as are the tyres and exhaust. If she asks me to walk a straight line I'll stagger and probably have to be breathalysed.

'A car answering this description almost caused an accident under the back estuary bridge.' She returns to the window. 'We also had a report about a similar car driving in an erratic manner along Coast Road.' She turns the pages of her notebook and squints at her handwriting. 'And, just now, you blatantly disturbed the peace by blowing your horn after hours.'

'I'm sorry, Guard. I'd no idea I was breaking the speed limit.'

'What *is* the speed limit through Malahide Village?'

'Fifty kilometres, I think.'

'You shouldn't think. You should know.' She removes a breathalyser kit from the squad car and orders me to blow into it.

'Zero.' She sounds dubious as she checks the reading for the second time

Jake is receiving the same grilling from the other guard. How ridiculous he looks in his boxer shorts. His feet are bare. I hope the pebbles cut his flesh to the bone.

The guard can't find anything wrong with my car. She delivers a lecture on dangerous driving that could not only end my life but those who are unfortunate enough to be in the wrong place at the wrong time.

Like my mother, innocently driving home from the supermarket and finding herself face-to-face with that truck driver. My tears blind me. She removes a box of tissues from the squad car and hands it to me, waits until I blow my nose before continuing to lecture me.

'You've disturbed the peace, broken the speed limit and driven dangerously through a bridge that only allows one-way traffic. You'll be hearing from us again, Nadine.'

How dare she call me by my first name? I understand why Eleanor berated that young doctor for patronising her. But what should this guard call me? Mrs *Saunders?* No, never again will I use that name.

Jake is free to go, no charges pending, no breathalyser. My hope that he drank at least a bottle of wine tonight and is put away for life is thwarted. This is a domestic incident and the police are already losing interest.

'You're in an extremely distressed state.' The guard's voice softens a little. 'I suggest you lock your car and allow your husband to drive you home.'

'I have no home.' I grind out the words. 'It's been violated. I'd prefer to spend the night in handcuffs than go back there again.'

'We can do that if you insist,' she snaps. I must have imagined the softening. 'But an easier option would be to take a taxi to your intended destination. Do not under any circumstances attempt to drive this vehicle tonight.'

I lock my car and hail an approaching taxi. The driver, seeing the squad car, indicates and brakes.

'Where to?' he asks when I collapse into the back seat.

'Stoneybatter.' I close my eyes and shut out the tableau, Jake, the two guards, my abandoned car, the last wrecked vestiges of my marriage.

'Were you driving over the limit?' The driver meets my gaze in the rear-view mirror. What must I look like, flushed, my hair wild, my face blotched from weeping?

'I was driving over the limit of my tolerance,' I reply. 'Not to be recommended.'

Donal, my kind, quiet uncle, is the most uncurious man I know. He doesn't question why his niece should phone him late at night and request a spare bed. He's waiting for me when I arrive in Stoneybatter, the fare ready for the taxi driver, a pot of tea brewing. He carries the tray into his small living room where two large porcelain dogs sit like sentinels on either side of the fireplace. When I stop shivering and the tea has cooled in my hands, he suggests I try to sleep.

Donal is a train enthusiast and his spare bedroom is a model railway concourse. He apologises for the lack of space as he leads me around the tracks and trains covering the floor. This room enchanted me when I was a child. I switch on the concourse and watch the trains chugging, hooting and whistling through junctions and level crossings. Their frenetic activity hypnotises me into a childlike trance and, eventually, when their journey is complete, I fall asleep.

CHAPTER TWENTY-NINE

Jake

What a scene that was. Worthy of their finest battles. It was a long time since he had heard Nadine shriek like that. Like she was riding into battle with a scream on her lips and the knowledge that the making up that followed would be memorable. Not this time, though. This time they knew there would be no reconciliation, no tumbled passion, no shocked, rueful apologies. He even feared, at one stage, that she would carry out her threat and run him over.

A taxi was emerging from the gates of Sea Aster when he returned. He pulled in sharply to let it pass. A glimpse of blonde, her head held erect and away from him.

Her note was pinned to the wooden rim of the chervil mirror.

> *Jake – I don't share. You've known that from the beginning yet you lied to me about your wife. You may be separated from her but you're the most married man I know. For that reason I'm ending our relationship.*
>
> *Don't contact me again.*

What else had he expected? Being with Karin Moylan was to play on thin ice, the chill and the thrill.

She had been holding the keys to his van when he ran back to the apartment to collect them and follow Nadine. He heard the crunch of gravel under the tyres as she drove away.

'Let her go,' Karin said, her face blazing. 'Your marriage is over… unless you've been lying to me from the start.'

'Give them to me.' He resisted the urge to lunge at her, wrench them from her grasp.

'What will you do if you catch up with her?' she demanded. 'Do you honestly think she's going to listen? Give her time to cool down. Then we'll explain.'

'*We?*' He had hated her in that instant, the plump swell of her lip, her accusatory blue stare. 'This is something I do by myself.'

She let the keys fall from her hand to the floor and walked away when he picked them up.

He parked the van and limped into the kitchen. His footprints left blood on the tiles. Gashed and grazed, his feet throbbed from the pebbles on Coast Road. The water turned red when he soaked them in the bath. He must have looked a sight in his bare feet and boxers. Not that anyone was laughing. He dried his feet and found bandages in the medicine cabinet.

The house stirred with night sounds, creaking floorboards, the gurgle of rusting pipes, and a flapping sound, as if a sail was snapping against its mast. Nadine had mentioned that her bedroom shutter was loose and he had promised to fix it. How long ago was that? A month, at least. When he could no longer stand the repetitive noise he walked around to her apartment. The lights were still on, the front door unlocked. He entered her bedroom and pushed up the window, reached towards the shutter and secured it against the wall. The clasp was loose, as Nadine had said, and would only hold for a while before it slipped again. Tomorrow he would fix it properly. Her over-night bag was open, clothes spilling across the bed. He picked up a paperback on the bedside locker. *Revolutionary Road* by Richard Yates.

Revolutionary Road was one of the last films they watched together. The tedium of the suburbs and April Wheeler's frantic efforts to escape it. Nadine loved it. He had been bored, just as April Wheeler had been bored by her tedious lifestyle. Death was a great solver of insolvable problems. Nadine could have been killed tonight. His skin crawled with delayed shock as he thought about her reckless drive along the estuary.

He had a sudden urge to check drawers, open presses and rummage through her clothes. Who was this woman who had turned his life upside down by demanding a perfect divorce? He thought her knew her, understood her impulses, her moods. She used to say they had formed into a hybrid. She was wrong and he was adrift on that mistake. He replaced the book on the bedside locker and left the room.

She did not return to Sea Aster until the following evening. An hour after she entered her apartment she rang and said she wanted to talk. They sat in her kitchen, no coffee, no wine – a formal meeting to decide their futures.

'I don't want to discuss what happened,' she said. 'Nor do I want excuses for the lies you've told me. It's in the past, like our marriage. I'm going to Alaska with Stuart. I made that decision when I realised the extent of your betrayal. That's why I called last night. I wanted to tell you I was leaving Sea Aster. You can contact me through email if you want to discuss the chil-dren. Contact me through my solicitor Marion Norman should any legal issues arise about the company or our divorce. I don't know what my future holds right now. My only certainty is that I'll never forgive you for bringing her here.'

'I never meant to hurt you – '

'Then don't insult me with platitudes.'

'Why won't you give me a chance to explain?'

'You'll just lie, as you've been doing all along.'

'Would you have understood if I told you? I wanted to… many times. You were her best friend once. But you've never talked about her. Why is that, Nadine? What did she do to you that was so awful… or was it something you did to her?'

'Why don't you ask her next time she's lying naked beside you?'

'There won't be a next time. It's over.'

'So are we, Jake.' Her bottom lip whitened as she tugged at it with her teeth.

'Why do you hate her?'

'I don't hate her. All I ever wanted to do was forget her.'

'Why?'

She lifted her shoulders and released a shuddery breath. 'She made my life hell. But she wasn't responsible for how I dealt with it. That was something I did all by myself.'

Part Four

CHAPTER THIRTY

Nadine

I'm cocooned in ice. That's how I feel when I stand on the deck of *Eyebright* and look outwards towards the glittering walls. They seem unbreakable until a deep fissure sends an icy shoulder cascading into the sea. At times I want to pinch myself. Is this really happening? Whales surfacing in a torrent of water? Sea lions basking on rocks? Magnificent white cruise liners reducing our boat to toy-like proportions?

Daveth Carew, the owner of *Eyebright*, is perfectly at ease among the shimmering ice sculptures. He looks older than his forty-five years, his skin tanned and seamed around the eyes from squinting at new horizons. He specialises in tours for small groups who prefer a more intimate cruise than the ones offered by those massive floating cities. *Eyebright* caters for eight people. It's spacious with just the three of us on board and easy to manoeuvre. My duties are light, the boat easy to maintain. I email and Skype the family when we dock at night. I've had no contact with Jake.

Eleanor rings one morning, nighttime at home, and asks why I ran away from my children? I suspect she's had a glass or more of wine.

'Jake won't tell me anything about you,' she says. 'I've absolutely no idea what you're doing.'

'What's there to tell?' I reply. 'One iceberg is much the same as another.'

'An interesting observation, Nadine, but quite untrue. Even snowflakes have unique characteristics. This man Daveth… you're not –'

'No. We're *not*. Goodbye Eleanor.'

Ali phones regularly and talks about Barnstormers, the drama group she joined. Cutting edge, she says. Avant garde and experimental. The artistic director is amazing. She mentions Mark Brewer too many times for objectivity and shrieks in denial when I ask if he has stolen her heart.

'It's nothing like that, Mum,' she insists. Mark Brewer is simply an inspirational director who understands the interior of her soul and how she must use it for dramatic effect.

They're definitely in a relationship.

'Dad sounds weird when he rings,' she says.

'Weird as in?' I ask.

'Like he's trying to walk through quicksand.'

'I can assure you that your father is on dry land and in no danger of sinking.' I resist the urge to add, more's the pity.

Brian rings to tell me that Shard have finally got their act together and have set a date for their comeback gig. He's curious but reluctant to probe too deeply as to why I'm staring at whales instead of selling double page spreads for *Lustrous*. The twins continue to run around tracks and concentrate on improving their personal best. They were born self-contained and focused. No reason for them to change simply because their mother has run away from home and their father is snatching back his dream. I'll visit them in California when my Alaskan adventure is over.

This evening we've anchored in a small, sheltered slip in Funter Bay. I serve dinner on deck. Daveth eats with relish, king crab legs and halibut but Stuart is unable to finish his meal. His complexion has a waxy sheen that worries me. I've been uneasy about his health since the trip started. Initially, I put his bouts of nausea down to seasickness. I, too, hung over the side of *Eyebright* on a few occasions before I found my sea legs. Any questions I ask about his health are batted away.

We're finishing our meal when the water surges off shore and a pod of whales surface. I grab my binoculars. Stuart steadies his camera. We watch their tails fanning the air before they sink again into the heaving sea. This sight invigorates him, as if he draws strength from the sheer bulk of these enormous mammals. His colour is better but he staggers when he stands to go to his cabin. He steadies himself and makes his way downstairs. I allow him time to undress then tap on his door. He's sitting up in bed, examining the photos in his viewfinder.

'How are you feeling?' I sit on the edge of his bunk and take his hand in mine. Without his bulky jumpers he looks so much thinner.

'I'm good,' he replies.

'Are you ill, Stuart?'

'Just a bit tired. Don't fuss, Nadine. I wouldn't have undertaken this trip if I couldn't cope with it.' He checks the viewfinder again and shows me the photographs he's taken since the trip started. I understand that it's his way of avoiding any further discussion about his health. I respect his decision and hold back on the anxious questions.

I make my way to the deck where Daveth is relaxing with a drink.

'Come and sit for a while.' He hands me a bottle of beer. 'I could do with some company.'

A boat pulls into a nearby slip. Figures stand motionless on deck, sculpted against the serried backdrop of pines. Like me,

Daveth is worried that Stuart is finding the trip too arduous. We've two more weeks at sea before we move into the lodge he's rented.

'Stuart says you've been doing these tours since you were a teenager,' I raise the bottle and take a tentative sip. The beer is gassy but not unpleasant.

'On and off,' he says. 'I worked initially for one of the ship builders. I built *Eyebright* after I married and have been organising these tours ever since.'

'Does your wife ever come with you?'

'Not anymore.' He remains silent for a while. I wait until he's ready to speak. Time seems slower here and silence is an easy companion. 'Olga died three years ago,' he eventually says.

'I'm so sorry, Daveth. I'd no idea.'

'Why should you?' He drains the bottle and rubs his hand across his mouth. 'I usually keep my personal and business life separate.'

'Thank you for telling me.' It's almost midnight and the sky is still bright. Boats clang and clatter together, like they're conversing port to starboard. I've seen her photograph in the galley and had assumed she was waiting at home for his return. A sprinkling of freckles, tanned skin, windblown brown hair, Olga Carew must have loved the outdoors.

'We knew our time together was limited,' he adds. 'That kind of knowledge concentrates the mind. We made every moment count.'

'You must have wonderful memories of her.'

The wind is stronger now and adds an unearthly keen as it blows through the riggings. I think about banshees, how they are supposed to haunt certain families at the time of death. Anything seems possible in this raddled, icy terrain. I wonder if he has children. I suspect not or I would have seen their photos somewhere on the boat.

'The blood disease she had was hereditary.' He picks up my thoughts. 'She didn't want to risk passing it on to another generation so we never had children.' He uncaps another beer and passes it me, shrugs aside the enormity of what he's revealed. 'Everyone has a story. What's yours?'

'One marriage on the rocks and four grown-up children.' It's possible, it seems, to condense my life story into a single sentence.

'You must have married young.'

'Seventeen.'

'That *is* young. What made you decide to end it?'

'What makes you think it was my decision?' I ask.

'I can't imagine it was the other way around.' He raises his bottle in a salute to me and waits in the stillness that settles between us. I feel mildly flattered by this assumption. But who did or did not end our marriage is no longer important. What matters is what followed. Lies of intent. Lies of omission.

Daveth's hands are blunt and strong. I imagine them on my body, trailing, stroking, probing, the glide of his lips between my breasts. This longing is sudden, shocking in its intensity, and gone just as fast.

I lean over the rail of *Eyebright* with its bright, fluttering bunting. There should be room here to lance my memories. To fling the past into the frozen depths so that it can never again reflect back at me.

Time passes. I feel the light touch of Daveth's hand on my back.

'It usually happens on a trip like this,' he says. 'Whatever we're running from catches up with us sooner or later.'

'You're right.' My eyes feel heavy, the skin puffed and red. I think of his wife, that vital force stubbed out so young. How did he cope with her death? Did he run towards the first woman who opened her arms to him, as my father did? I doubt it. He survives on the good memories whereas I've focused on the bad ones, used them as my defining touchstone.

'I'd better turn in,' I say. 'We've a long trip ahead of us tomorrow.'

'See you in the morning then.' He gathers the empty bottles into a refuse bag and allows the starless night to close around us. Float planes glide low over the harbour. The sky is too bright to view the northern lights. I'll have to wait until later if I want to see them. Will I still be here? The vastness of the scenery bears down on me. The rocky permanence seems eternal but time has a chisel that never stops chipping. I've no idea how my life is going to change, only that it must. It always does.

I can't sleep. There was a moment with Daveth when everything could have changed. He knows the preciousness of moments. He could have been my bridge over loneliness. Why did I let it go? My breath deepens as my hand slides downwards and comforts me in this narrow bunk. Relief is swift, sharp, unsatisfying. And Karin Moylan remains a mind flash… flash… flash… framed within glass. A tableau I can't banish. Jake's shirt draped like a wanton veil over her arms. The bloom of sex on her skin.

CHAPTER THIRTY-ONE

Jake

The Bare Pit was a popular place to hear new bands. Reedy and Feral had attracted a sizable number of fans, and there were fans from the young Shard days. Couples in their late thirties, early forties, babysitters organised for the night. The support act was concluding, the crowd swelling. Soon Shard would be on stage. Jake rocked on his toes, wiped sweat from his forehead. How could he have forgotten the fear before each performance? He read texts from Ali and the twins, wishing him luck, and spoke briefly to Brian, who had arrived with Peter Brennan, his one-time next door neighbour from Oakdale Terrace.

He thought about Nadine. Phantom pains. She asked him once if they would suffer from them. He had not heard from her since she left for Alaska but he had seen the photos on the *Eyebright* website. Three of them in short sleeves and sunglasses, standing on the deck of the *Eyebright*, bunting fluttering above them as they headed down the Gastineau Channel. Nadine's red hair was hidden under a bandana and Stuart, looking lean and fit, had his arm around her shoulders. The man on her other side was a forty-something with a sturdy, muscular frame and a ruddy, outdoors complexion. She was right about the phantom pains. They were bound to happen, especially on a night like this.

His nerves disappeared when he began to sing. It was like riding a bike, like sex, like everything that, once learned, brought instant recall. He was sweaty and hot, fevered with the thrill of playing before a live audience. Like the pre-performance nerves, he had also forgotten the magic of the adrenaline rush. He noticed Mik Abel among the crowd. He grinned widely and gave Jake a thumbs up. The odds of Mik remembering five strutting teenagers he once managed had been remote, or so Jake thought when he contacted him with Shard's demonstration disc of *Collapsing the Stone*. It turned out to be a wise move. Not only did Mik remember the band but he had produced the album.

The 'Collapsing the Stone' video flashed on the screen behind the band. Maggie Doyle-Childe. Feral's wife and a music video maker, had filmed Shard on a ghost-estate. The band looked grim and menacing as they stood among abandoned sewage pipes and cranes, the smashed windows of half-finished houses staring outwards like blank, reproachful eyes.

The audience stood around the stage or sat on high stools as the night club reverberated to the music of Shard. Karin Moylan, in black jeans, tight and satiny, moved from the midst of the crowd onto the dancefloor. Her see-through blouse had loose fluttery sleeves and the cropped-top she wore underneath moulded her breasts in a swirl of blue. As she moved in and out of the flashing laser beams she looked as if she was preparing to fly. A man joined her on the floor, his snake-like dance movements contrasting with her fast, almost frenetic steps. Each time the music stopped she rested her head against his shoulder. She seemed oblivious to Jake yet she was there as a taunt, each move designed to trigger memories of the hot, sex-drenched nights they once shared. Each gesture designed to show she had lost no time replacing him. He must focus on the music. Tonight, Shard was all that mattered.

The audience applauded, whistled, stamped their feet, roared for more. After three encores, when he was finally free to leave the stage, he ordered a drink at the bar. People slapped his back and congratulated him. Karin was nowhere to be seen. His mood slumped, the shock of her appearance finally hitting him. Brian and Peter told him the gig had been fantastic then hurried off to party elsewhere. Mik Abel sat beside him and discussed the tours he hoped to line up for the band.

The club was almost empty by the time Mik left. The other members of Shard had also gone home when Jake went backstage to collect his guitar.

'How are you, Jake?' She was waiting for him when he emerged from the storage room. The plume of perfume was instantly familiar, her voice hesitant and low. 'I couldn't leave without telling you how brilliant Shard was tonight.'

'I'm glad you enjoyed it.' He had kept busy since she left, forced himself to stop checking his phone in case there was a text, a missed call. What would he do if she contacted him? His mind had swung between one scenario where she rushed headlong into his arms and another where he resolutely turned his back on her. Now, standing before her, he had absolutely no idea how to react.

'You never contacted me,' she said.

'Did you really expect me to... after the note you left?'

'We both said hurtful things to each other that night.'

'That's true.'

'You accused me of deliberately causing trouble between you and Nadine.'

'You certainly did that.'

'But *not* deliberately. What happened was a dreadful accident. I'd switched on the light without thinking... and I'd never have asked to go back to your apartment if I'd thought for a minute that she'd be home so soon.'

'She didn't arrive too soon.'

'That was Liam's fault. He said Monday, not Sunday.'

'It doesn't matter now.'

'It matters to me. Nadine used to be my friend. Did you really believe I'd go out of my way to hurt her?'

'I didn't know what to believe.'

'I forced you to choose between us. I'd no right to do that…' She paused, touched his arm. 'That's why I'm here. To apologise for making such a ridiculous scene that night. I should have contacted you the following day but I didn't think you'd want to hear from me again.'

'You should have allowed me to be the judge of that.'

'You've no idea how much I've missed you, Jake. Can you forgive me?'

'That guy with you…'

'Liam. We're friends, nothing more than that. He told me Nadine is in Alaska. Was I responsible for her leaving?'

'No.' He shook his head vehemently. 'I'm responsible for driving her away. I didn't want to hurt her. But I did.'

'It's impossible to go through life without hurting someone,' she said. 'She hurt you when she decided to end your marriage. I hurt you when I left your apartment that night. You hurt me when you followed her. I could go on and on. Hurt's a thread that needs a sharp snap every now and then. Will you hang up on me if I ring you next week?'

'There's only one way you'll find out,' he said.

Was he mad to restart something with so many echoes, so many unasked questions? He knew the answer. He had written his name on her arm once but she was the one who had branded him.

CHAPTER THIRTY-TWO

Karin was still sleeping when he pulled on his tracksuit and moved silently from the bedroom. The front gates of Sea Aster screeched as he pushed them open. He must remember to oil them. The house and grounds needed constant attention, one chore leading to another and demanding more of his time each week.

He jogged along Mallard Cove. The air was filled with a sea-weedy smell, slightly rank but not unpleasant. The ducks were still sleeping, heads tucked under wings, and the swans formed ghostly silhouettes as they glided through the hazy air. He breathed evenly, his body moving to a relaxed rhythm. When he reached the remains of an old jetty he sat on the stone surface and recovered his breath.

Reactions to the gig had been amazing. Bookings were coming in and tours being planned into the future. Shard could become the poster band of the recession, Mik Abel believed. The 'Collapsing the Stone' video had received numerous hits and Jake's songs, chronicling the destruction of an economy, were being discussed in print, on radio and on music blogs. Everything was so immediate these days.

Karin was possessed by that same immediacy. This time it was all or nothing. Soon after the Shard gig she presented him with the key to her apartment, boxed and tied with a red bow.

She had watched, a half-smile playing around her lips, as he felt through the layers of tissue and his fingers closed over the cold metal. His first inclination was to hand the key back. It was too soon for such an exchange but he had promised her a relationship and this was her commitment to it. He used Eleanor's ownership of Sea Aster as an excuse for not being in a position to give her a key to his apartment. It was a weak excuse but she seemed willing to accept it for the time being. What she was not willing to do was hide in the shadows of his family life.

'It's the perfect opportunity to introduce us,' she said when Jake casually mentioned that he had booked a meal for two for Eleanor's birthday. Over the past fifteen years she had celebrated her birthday in Louisa's Loft with the family, Nadine and Rosanna, Ali, Brian and the twins, the eight of them sitting around the circular table in the centre of the restaurant. Gradually the numbers decreased and this year it would be just the two of them. He imagined Eleanor's eyebrows rising, her acerbic comments or, worse still, her chilling silence if he introduced Karin to her. The idea was unthinkable.

'It's too soon to meet,' he said. 'We have to take one step at a time.'

'What step is that?' Karin asked. 'As far as I can see we're not moving at all.'

The sun rose beyond the distant viaduct, a dazzling rim that streaked a crimson vertebrae across the sky. He had better return to Sea Aster. Karin was an early riser. In Alaska there was no dawn to watch, he thought, just a midnight sun to blood the opening of a new day.

'Where were you?' She was sitting up in bed, tousled and pouting, when he returned.

'On the estuary watching the dawn.'

'You should have woken me.'

'I didn't want to disturb you.'

'Was it beautiful?'

'As always.'

'We should have been watching it together.' She sounded wishful. 'That's what lovers do. But there'll be other dawns we can share.'

The stage was bare, their equipment packed. Reedy, Hart and Daryl had already left. This was the lonely moment, the dazzle stripped away, lasers, strobes and spotlights switched off, microphones silenced. The only musical note was the clink of glasses being cleared away.

Feral stopped packing her equipment and glanced curiously across at Jake. 'You and Karin watching the dawn together,' she said. 'I never realised you were such a romantic.' She zipped her main drum into its cover and headed for the exit.

'What do you mean?' Jake lifted an amplifier and followed her outside to the carpark where their two vans were parked.

'We bumped into each other on Grafton Street yesterday. She twisted my arm to have a coffee with her. She's really into you.'

'I guess.'

'What about you?'

'It's not that straightforward.'

Feral slammed the back door closed. 'As far as she's concerned, it is. She talked about you the whole time.' She grinned. 'I can't pretend it was the most fascinating conversation I've ever had in my life.'

'Why ever not?' He feigned indignation to hide his uneasiness. Why would Karin lie over such a trivial issue as a sunrise? 'What else did she tell you?'

'Oh, this and that. Woman talk.' Feral took out her keys and climbed into the van. 'She strikes me as a woman who gets what she wants. Just be sure you want the same thing.'

'That sounds like a warning.'

'You're a big boy, Jake. If you can't look after yourself by now it's too late to take cover.'

He watched her drive away. One night after band practice she had stayed behind in Sea Aster and played music with him. Unlike Maggie, who was a staunch gay rights activist, Feral was content to drum her way through life. She told him that night how they had met on a Greyhound bus that was bringing them from Boston to New York. As a love story it lacked excitement but sparks had flown and that was that. Their future sealed.

Two years after that summer in Monsheelagh he would look out from the stage and recognise Nadine instantly. She had waved from the crowd and smiled, he remembered it was a hesitant smile, as if she was uncertain he would remember her. He smiled back and held her gaze for the remainder of the song. He had sought her out as soon as the band stopped for a short interval. A moment of recognition, their future sealed.

A melancholic yearning for the early years of their marriage swept over him. The sleepless nights, the dazed periods of bliss when their children were asleep and they could finally collapse onto the old sofa, laughing as they reached for each other. But those years had a sepia tinge and he found it increasingly difficult to recognise himself as that young, hassled father, or the brittle husband who had moved to Bartizan Downs, smugly convinced that his future had a graph that could only rise.

CHAPTER THIRTY-THREE

The circular table in Louisa's Loft had been taken over by a noisy family group and Louisa, the plump, friendly proprietor, seated Jake and Eleanor at a table for two. She took their orders, removed the menus and placed a jug of iced water before them.

'It's sad when a family falls apart and there's only you and I left to celebrate my birthday.' Eleanor sighed heavily and gazed out the window at the view over Howth Harbour.

'We haven't fallen apart,' Jake protested. 'Children grow up. They leave home. Old people die. It's called life.'

'And wives leave their husbands,' she reminded him. 'Nadine sent me a book for my birthday. *Two Women in the Klondike*. I'll read it when I retire.'

'It's going to gather dust, then.' He attempted a joke but Eleanor's sense of humour had never tallied with his.

'Probably,' she replied. 'I'm far too busy to even think of retiring.'

'You should relax for a change and kick back your heels. Remember what the doctor – '

'Foals kick back their heels, Jake. Since when have I ever displayed the slightest equine tendencies?'

'All I'm saying is that it's time to let some of the younger members in First Affiliation do the heavy lifting for you. You're sixty-seven now.'

'What would you like me to do?' She tapped her fingers off the table. 'Dribble on my chin and shuffle into a nursing home on my Zimmer?'

'Of course not. I didn't mean…' A long night stretched ahead. He needed to bite down hard on his tongue. 'Any word on the planning permission for Sea Aster? It's taking forever.'

'Bureaucracy. Don't talk to me about it.' She was on her favourite hobby horse and Jake, relieved, filled their glasses with wine.

The restaurant door opened and a woman entered. Dainty feet in ankle boots, a slim-fitting leather jacket and a short skirt hugging her thighs. He sloshed the wine as he set the bottle back on the table. One step at a time, he had said. Karin had obviously decided to take that step on her own. Her mobile phone was pressed to her ear as she approached the reception desk. She ended her call and spoke to Louisa. Eleanor was still complaining about delays, ineptitude and the wastage of taxpayer's money. Her words scattered above his head as Karin followed Louisa towards a vacant table.

'I don't believe it.' She stopped beside him and raised her hands to her cheeks. 'Jake Saunders! It's been so long. My goodness… how many years?' Her voice lilted with astonishment. 'It's *so* good to see you again.'

'Karin… what a surprise.' He almost knocked over his chair as he rose to greet her. 'You're the last person I expected to meet here. How are you?'

'Being stood up, I'm afraid.' She waggled her mobile at him. 'I was supposed to meet my friend Liam but I've just received a call. His car has broken down. He can't make it.'

'What a shame.' Eleanor made a sympathetic moue. 'Being stood up is not a nice experience.'

'It's a nuisance but never mind.' Karin smiled and extended her hand. 'I've seen you so often on television, Mrs Saunders. It's a privilege to meet you in real life.'

Her teeth sparkled, white, small and even. Sharp too, she bit his neck last night, not once but many times. A necklace of love, she called it. If his mother knew what was hidden under the collar of his shirt. Jake's palms began to sweat.

'Thank you.' Eleanor gazed speculatively at him. 'Are you going to introduce us, Jake?'

'Em… yes… this is Karin Moylan. She's em… a friend.'

'I'm an old school friend of Nadine's,' Karin cut across his faltering introduction. 'How is she, Jake? I haven't heard from her in ages.'

'She's fine.'

'Why don't you sit down and join us, my dear?' Eleanor said.

'Oh, no, I'd be intruding…' Karin hesitated, toyed with her chunky blue necklace.

'Not at all.' Eleanor gestured towards an empty seat at the next table. 'Bring that chair over, Jake. We're celebrating my birthday.' She gestured towards Louisa, who was waiting at a discreet distance for their conversation to finish. 'Louisa, another menu, please. This young lady will be dining with us.'

'I hope you've had a wonderful day.' Karin pulled the chair closer to the table and accepted the menu.

'It's been a busy day like any other.'

'But now you've a chance to relax with your son. Family is everything, don't you agree? But of course you do. Your party was founded on that core principle. I've always admired your staunchness, Mrs Saunders.'

'Call me Eleanor, my dear. No sense standing on formalities. I've ordered Dover sole on the bone. It's always delicious here. I recommend it.'

'Then that's exactly what I'll have.'

'How do you know Nadine?'

'We were best friends in school. Quite inseparable, actually. But we lost touch over the years. You know the way it is. I was focused on my studies and Nadine...' She glanced down at the menu. 'Nadine was lucky enough to meet Jake.'

'Indeed.'

'I'm sorry you've had a difficult time with your party colleagues,' Karin said when their food was served.

'Are you interested in politics?' Eleanor filleted the sole from the bone with a few deft flicks of her knife.

'I can't pretend to be an expert but I do understand the politics of control and leadership.' Karin attended to her sole with the same precision. 'I don't believe the younger members like Lorna Mason will ever have the strength of character necessary to lead a party like First Affiliation. *You* are the party, Eleanor.'

Jake watched the yachts gliding towards the marina and remained on the sidelines of their conversation. He had never seen his mother engage with Nadine in that way, as if everything Karin said was stimulating, important.

'My treat.' When the meal ended Eleanor whisked out her credit card before Jake could protest. 'It's been a most enjoyable night. I'd like to see some samples of your work, Karin. We're considering updating the image of First Affiliation. Do you have contact details?'

'Of course.' Karin removed a card from her wallet and handed it to her. 'Perhaps we can meet some time and discuss this in more detail so that I can fully understand the aspirations of your party.'

'An excellent idea. I'll be in touch, my dear.'

'I look forward to meeting you again.' She stood up and kissed Eleanor on both cheeks before holding out her hand to Jake. 'Remember me to Nadine.'

Her audacity astonished him but he was forced to admire her tactics. Unlike Nadine, and, indeed, himself, she knew the exact approach that would charm his mother.

'What an interesting woman.' Eleanor picked up the business card and stared at the kingfisher's vivid plumage. 'And so knowledgeable about politics. I'm looking forward to seeing her work.'

After he had dropped Eleanor off at her bungalow he drove to Karin's apartment. He used the key she had given him and entered her bedroom. She was awake and waiting for him. Her certainty that he would come directly to her from Louisa's Loft increased his annoyance. He ignored the folded back duvet and sat down on the edge of the bed.

'Just what did you think you were doing?' he asked.

'Establishing my place in your life,' she replied without hesitation. She lay back against the pillows and stared at him through narrowed eyelids. 'You're forty-three years old. Isn't it time you stopped being afraid of your mother?'

'I'm not afraid… I wanted to talk to her first, prepare her.'

'It's done now. Eleanor likes me, as I knew she would. She hasn't got around to admitting it yet but she's accepted the fact that you and Nadine are finished. This way, she'll believe she instigated our relationship.'

'You're quite the little schemer.'

'I'm a pragmatist, like Eleanor. What's really bothering you? Are you still hoping Nadine will come back to you? She's gone, Jake. But you're here with me… in my bedroom. If that means nothing to you then I suggest you leave right now and close the door behind you.'

Perfume rose from the hollow in her throat, from the bend of her arms as she stretched them above her head. She enjoyed playing games, leading him on then resisting him until she saw something in his face, he never knew what brought about the instant of surrender, the moment he sank into the dark mystery of her desire, so violent and, at other times, so passive and teasing it was like making love to a different woman.

CHAPTER THIRTY-FOUR

Nadine

Stuart lied to me, lured me to Alaska on the pretence that he was a man on a reprieve. Instead, he was on borrowed time and had known that the span of life left to him could be measured in months. Pretence was no longer been possible when we returned to Juneau. Daveth drove us to the hospital where Stuart received a blood transfusion and underwent a series of scans.

'Sinister,' he told me when he was discharged from hospital and we'd settled into the lodge he has rented. 'That's what my oncologist in London called my cancer. I kept imagining it sliding through a dark street in a hoodie. So, I decided to outrun it.' He paused. 'Will you stay with me?' he asked. 'I need someone who won't look away in disgust if things get…' He hesitated, searching for the right words. 'Hard to manage.'

'You'd need a nurse… hospitalisation.'

'In time, maybe. But that won't be necessary until the end. This is my last photographic assignment. I've spoken to my agent. I always hated the thought of a posthumous exhibition but that's what it will be. I've made peace with my death, Nadine. I know my work will be in safe hands.' He smiled, forced me to smile back, which I did to hide my terror.

How does the mind process that kind of information? Probably in stages, in mood swings that veer from wildly optimistic to the darker reaches. Which is better? The slow acceptance of one's death or the instant realisation that it's all over, as Sara must have understood in that instant of collision. No time for terror or regret. No time to put her house in order. I dislike that euphemism, as if the approach of death requires a particularly strenuous bout of spring cleaning.

Stuart's apartment on Canary Wharf is sold and he plans to end his days here. I listen as he tells me what must be done when I return to London with his photographic equipment and photographs, the framer and gallery owners I must contact.

I drive a jeep and learn to negotiate the roads around the lake. Stuart has worked out an itinerary of things we must do, places we must visit. Daveth has returned to sea and the photographs on his blog are of different voyagers leaning over the side of *Eyebright* to stare goggle-eyed at whales and calving icebergs.

Stuart, fiercely independent and proud, is still strong. We sit together on the glass fronted veranda and watch autumn die. Each day brings an added radiance to the forests. The leaves fall suddenly here, a breath and they are gone, says Daveth. Stuart, too, seems possessed by that same radiance. It shines through the grey pallor of his illness as he follows the flight of eagles with his binoculars, photographs a caribou glimpsed between trees, a moose swimming across the lake. Daveth, who lives nearby, calls to see us between cruises. Soon his season will be over and he will build his boats during the winter.

I take my breakfast and my laptop to the veranda this morning. There's an email from Ali. She has a leading role in the next Barnstormer's production. Brian had also emailed. His Willow Passion ceramic boxes have been shortlisted for a prestigious craft award. I'll miss both events. How glibly I promised to be with them, Jake by my side, for all family celebrations. I've already missed the first one. Eleanor's birthday celebration never changes. It's nighttime in Dublin. She's probably back in her bungalow now. I wonder how she and Jake sustained their conversation in Louisa's Loft for the night.

My phone rings. Separate continents are not a barrier to thought transference yet I'm surprised to see Eleanor's name on my screen.

'Thank you for the book,' she says. 'It's kind of you to remember those of us back home.'

I ignore the remark and watch a bird hovering against the grey sky. It's a sullen day in Juneau and the bird is too far away to identify. I suspect it's a sharp-eyed eagle checking out its prey.

'I believe Stuart is unwell again,' she says.

He's dying, I want to shout the words out loud in the hope of lessening their dread.

'He's coping and is still very active,' I reply. 'Did you have a nice meal in Louisa's Loft?'

'The food was excellent, as always. But what used to be a grand occasion has now been reduced to two. At least that's what I thought.' A meaningful pause follows. I know these pauses. They usually proceed a meaningful announcement and Eleanor does not disappoint. 'We were joined by a third party.'

'Oh?'

'Your friend, Karin Moylan.'

'She's *not* – '

'She'd been stood up by her boyfriend so I asked her to join us. She's quite charming… and so knowledgeable about politics.'

'Is there something you want to say to me, Eleanor?'

'I saw the way Jake looked at her. It's only a matter of time, Nadine.'

'Is that what you rang to tell me?'

'I'm not trying to make trouble.'

'Then why are we talking about this?'

'Please listen to me.' Her usual brisk manner is subdued. 'I'm worried about Jake. I can't get him to slow down and think seriously about his future. That awful band, the guitar courses he runs, the sessions he does in that studio. It's all piecemeal work. And tonight he was jittery, on edge all the time.'

'You should be discussing this with him. It's nothing to do with – '

'He's still your husband. Don't you have any feelings for him?'

'Actually, no. I don't want you to ring me again unless we can have a conversation that does *not* include his name.'

'The fact that you're so angry means you *do* have feelings. Your friend – '

'Karin Moylan is not my friend, Eleanor. I left her behind a long time ago. And I've left Jake. I've no intention of interfering in his life. Goodbye.'

I fill my mug with coffee and drink it black. The life I left behind seems alien, petty. Stuart is my only concern. A boat moves through the lake, the water so still it seems to have solidified into glass. The eagle drops to the water, talons razor sharp. The silence is absolute.

Oh, Jake, you poor, deluded fool. I lean my elbows on the table and rest my face in the curve of my arms.

❊ ❊ ❊

Karin Moylan drew my image on a blackboard and I self-destructed. I came home from school that evening and locked myself in the bathroom. Sara was cooking in the kitchen. The sounds were familiar, the radio playing on the window sill, the television rumbling in the dining room. A bird warbled shrilly on a tree outside, a harsh, repetitive note that kept me strong as I removed a blade from the razor my father used for shaving. Sara had bought him an electric razor for his birthday but he'd never taken it out of its box. He preferred the precision of a sharp blade.

I cut lightly into my wrist, watched beads of blood rise to the surface and flow. The sting of pain, the red splash on the white ceramic basin, the sickly-sweet sense of relief, I've never forgotten it.

Afterwards, I vowed it would not happen again. I scoured the basin and stuck a plaster on my arm. Such secrecy and stealth. The broken promises. I wanted to stop and believed I could until the urge overwhelmed me once more.

One evening I cut too deep. I was almost unconscious when Sara's frantic banging on the bathroom door brought me to my senses. I staggered to my feet and turned the key, allowed her to enter into my pain. Eoin was unable to understand why I would deliberately harm myself. It was beyond his ken, he said, and reflected my shame back at me. Self-hatred, it grew like a snow-ball on a steep hillside. Sara did her best to stop my belief that I deserved to be bullied. Nothing made any difference. What if… what if… that same question always lured me back to the blade. The warm trickle of blood, the escape route from guilt.

Stuart talks a lot about Sara. The childhood they shared and the years that followed until she was taken so suddenly from us. I remember the strength of her arms as she struggled to free me from my demons. The voices only I could hear. Unrelenting voices that demanded pain as their reward for silence.

At Stuart's request I drive him to the Shrine of St Theresa on the outskirts of Juneau. The retreat centre is peaceful and quiet. He spends time in a small chapel and we walk together around the circles of stones that create the Merciful Love Labyrinth. He is silent on the journey back to the lodge. Daveth brings armloads of logs from the back of his pickup truck and I build the fires high.

We visit the Mendenhall glacier where ice as turbulent and textured as a flow of lava cuts through the rocky valley. It seems imperishable, indestructible, yet the slow drip of mortality is active here too. There is a skeletal starkness about Stuart's photography. I know it's my imagination but I see limbs writhing within the ice, as if bodies are struggling to be freed from their glistening tombs. Death is here with us, soundless and invisible. I sense it taking a step nearer each day yet we're comfortable in the silence that has settled between us. I buy art materials in Juneau and, while Stuart works on his photography, I sketch the slumbering lake and forests.

CHAPTER THIRTY-FIVE

Jake

He adjusted Brian's bow tie and ran a clothes brush over his son's hired tuxedo. In a few hours' time Brian could become the youngest-ever winner of the R.E. Spencer Ceramics Award. Brian's love affair with clay began at the age of two when Nadine gave him a lump of play dough to distract him while she was feeding the twins. He was six when he told his parents he was going to become a potter. While Ali flounced around in a tiara and princess dress, and the twins raced each other up and down climbing frames, Brian filled the kitchen shelves with lopsided mugs and fantasy creatures with bulging foreheads. Fast forward to what seemed to Jake like only a skip in time and he, along with Eleanor, were Brian's invited guests at tonight's award ceremony where, if Brian was even luckier, he would be chosen from the category winners to win the overall, prestigious R.E. Spencer Craft and Design Award.

'I reckon the goldsmith will get it,' he told Jake before they left Sea Aster. 'His work is awesome. But winning the ceramic category would give my work brilliant exposure.'

The reception room was already crowded when they arrived. A harpist struggled heroically to be heard about the babble of voices and waiters eased through the crowd with trays of champagne and canapés. Eleanor checked out the room at a glance, her political antennae primed for potential contacts.

'Is that Jessica Walls over there?' she asked when Brian was being interviewed by the media. 'I do believe it is. Remarkable woman. All those magazines. I still don't understand why Nadine gave up such an amazing opportunity to build a new career for herself. She won't get that chance again.' She moved towards a small cluster of people and eased skilfully into their circle. Jake never failed to marvel at her ability to infiltrate the most resistant group.

'Isn't this a wonderful opportunity to celebrate such amazing young talent,' he overheard her say. 'You must meet my grandson, Jessica. Unfortunately, Nadine is still in Alaska so I'm here in loco parentis, so to speak. I'm assuming he's going to win but as a doting grandmother I'm allowed to be *totally* biased.'

Polite laughter greeted this remark and Jessica Walls, dramatic in a gold lamé evening gown, accompanied Eleanor across the reception room to where the contestants were being interviewed. Had Eleanor ever expressed such pride in him, Jake wondered. He tried to pinpoint an instant that he could hold up to the light and recognise as a gesture of affection, a memory to cherish. But his recollections of his childhood were cluttered with her busyness. Her constant energy and ambition. Her face on posters, that bland yet determined smile.

'Jake and Eleanor Saunders. I'd never have put the two of you together.' A man who had been speaking to Jessica before Eleanor's interruption nodded at Jake. His thick, brown hair glistened with gel and his aftershave reminded Jake unpleasantly of horse liniment.

'Most people don't.' He smiled ruefully and tried to remember why the man looked familiar.

'Liam Brett's the name,' he said. 'I used to work with your wife. Is she still in Alaska?'

'Yes.'

'She was good. Pity she took off like that. How are things with Shard these days?'

'We're happy.'

'I was at your come-back gig with Karin Moylan. I believe you two know each other from Shard's previous incarnation.'

Jake remembered him now. That night in The Bare Pit, the sinuous dance steps as he moved around Karin, his eyes never leaving her face. Karin only ever referred to him in throwaway remarks that made him sound like a pet dog. But Liam Brett was no one's pet dog and his expression as he eyeballed Jake had the aggression of a rutting stag.

'She's still a dedicated fan.' He reached for another glass of champagne and moved closer to Jake. 'No offence, mate, but her taste in music is something I don't share.'

'None taken, *mate*. Enjoy the night.'

He walked away before Liam could reply. The stoic harpist was still playing, her music lost under the chattering voices. She smiled in appreciation when he moved closer to listen.

The clanging of a bell startled the crowd into a momentary silence. A voice informed them it was time to move into the main hall where dinner was about to be served. The decision of the judges would be announced at the end of the meal.

'There's Karin Moylan.' Eleanor craned her neck and waved across at one of the tables. 'She mentioned she'd be here with the crowd from *Lustrous* tonight.'

He followed her gaze and saw Karin sitting beside Liam Brett, her face turned attentively towards him. As if aware of Jake's gaze she looked over and waved.

'How lovely she looks,' said Eleanor. 'She did a wonderful job on *Lustrous*. Have you seen the new layout?'

'No,' said Jake.

'Are you talking about the woman with the blue necklace?' asked Brian.

'We are,' said Eleanor. 'I'm working with her on the new logo for First Affiliation.'

'She's been to my studio,' Brian said. 'She bought some pieces from the Willow Passion collection.'

'When was that?' Jake tried to hide his shock.

'Last week,' said Brian. 'She's really into my work. Pity she's not on the judging panel.'

Jake had lost his appetite by the time the first course was served. Why had Karin never mentioned visiting his son's pottery? Slí na hAbhann, where the craft centre was located, was not somewhere convenient where customers could drop in on a whim. It would have taken Karin almost five hours to drive there. He wanted to question Brian further but his son was talking animatedly to the young silversmith sitting next to him.

Tension rose as the meal drew to a close. Speeches followed and the competitors sat stiffly to attention as they awaited the judges' decisions. Jake's eyes stung when Brian's name was called and his son walked across the stage to receive the ceramics award. He wanted Nadine to share this night with him but she was on Alaskan time and her day was only beginning.

Brian was right about the overall prize being awarded to the goldsmith but the delicacy of the glaze on the Willow Passion collection received a special commendation from the judging panel.

'Brian, I'm so thrilled for you.' Karin came to their table when the ceremony ended and shook his hand. 'Not that I'm surprised. Your work is beautiful. You must be so proud of your grandson, Eleanor.'

'I'm proud of all my grandchildren but tonight is very special indeed.' Eleanor rubbed her hand affectionately along Brian's beard. 'I'm only sorry his mother isn't here to share this wonderful night with us.'

'I'll send her the video,' Brian said. 'She'd be here if she could. Looking after Great-uncle Stuart is far more important.'

'I suppose you're right.' Eleanor conceded this point. 'Poor unfortunate man. He should be back in London receiving proper medical attention. I've never understood his fascination with ice when all it ever does is *melt*. Now, if you'll excuse me, it's been a long night and I'm off to my bed. I'll be in touch soon, Karin. Goodnight Jake. Congratulations again, Brian.' She blew kisses at them and swept towards the exit.

'Karin, can I buy you a celebratory drink?' Brian glanced enquiringly at her when she slipped into the chair vacated by Eleanor.

'Thank you, Brian. A glass of prosecco would be lovely.'

'What about you, Dad?'

'Nothing for me, thanks.'

'You're sure?'

'Absolutely.' He folded his arms and stared across the table at Karin.

'Nice engineering,' he said when Brian walked towards the bar.

'What do you mean?'

'Brian said you've visited his pottery.'

'Yes, I have. They've quite a nice setup in that craft centre.'

'And you just dropped in purely by chance.'

'No, not by chance. I was meeting a client in Tralee and saw the signpost for Slí na hAbhann. Brian brought me on a tour of the studios. Such talent. Quite remarkable in such an out of the way location.'

'Why didn't you tell me you've been there?'

'Why didn't you tell me about tonight? Were you afraid I'd expect to come with you?'

'It wouldn't have been an appropriate occasion.'

'I agree.'

'So, now you've met my son and my mother. What next?'

'Why are you angry?'

'You're manipulating me.'

'I love you, Jake. Your family are an extension of that love. I want them to accept me on their own terms and if this is the way I do it, why should you object?'

'Here we are.' Brian put the drinks down on the table and clinked glasses with Karin. The cut glass ceramic award in the centre of the table glinted and reminded Jake of ice splintering in sunlight.

Stuart's illness had broken Nadine's resolve not to contact him. He was dying, she said when she rang him last night. Her voice had quavered then strengthened. He would die in Alaska and she would stay with him until the end.

The news shocked him. He had seen the recent photographs that Nadine had taken – Ali always forwarded them to his laptop – and Stuart, muffled in a parka jacket, his padded trousers tucked into mountain boots, looked so fit it was impossible to believe his time was limited. Other photographs charted Nadine's life in Alaska. Ice skating on a lake with Daveth Carew, admiring an ice sculpture with Stuart, standing beside him in front of a small stone church. Each photograph spawned another dozen images in Jake's mind. Why was Daveth Carew in so many of them? Why was he on dry land when he should be on his boat encouraging whales to surface from their icy depths? What right had Jake to feel jealous when he saw a photograph of Daveth and Nadine tucked under rugs on a dog sled ride? And could this heart-sinking sensation be classified as jealousy? He had no idea how he felt about anything anymore.

CHAPTER THIRTY-SIX

He was loading the last amplifier into his van outside The Bare Pit when his phone bleeped. A text from Karin. She was waiting for him in Sea Aster. He sat into the driver seat and read her text again. How had she entered his apartment? The windows and door were securely locked. There was only one answer. She must have taken a spare key from the drawer in the kitchen and had her own copy cut.

Scented candles blazed on the dressing table. A bottle of champagne in a bucket of ice sat on the bedside locker. Karin was sitting up in his bed, pillows plumped behind her, the duvet pulled to her chin. She looked pale in the candlelight, defence-less as he closed the bedroom door. Her expression reminded him of a naughty child who expected to be punished yet the air was musky, vibrating with expectation. He had a sudden urge to shake her and demand his key back. What right had she to break into his apartment and assume everything would be okay with candlelight and champagne?

'What a face.' She shuddered in mock apprehension. The duvet slid from one shoulder as she uncurled her hand and revealed the key. 'You're mad at me again. But I knew Eleanor wouldn't mind if I had my own key cut.'

'But *I* mind – '

'Why? You claim to love me yet you lock your door on me. Are you angry because I took the initiative?'

'Yes. This should be my decision.' The sense of unseen strings pulling on him intensified. He had to keep thinking ahead, to try and anticipate what she would say or do next. Her moods veered from fun-loving and sexy to hurt and petulant. He never knew when an inadvertent remark would cause her eyes to harden, her lip to swell.

'I want to celebrate our relationship, not hide it.' She grasped both his hands and pulled him towards her. 'It's time you took the commitment we made to each other as seriously as I do.'

He filled their glasses with champagne but the feeling that he was participating in a ritual over which he had lost control persisted. She untied the ribbons at the front of her bustier. She stroked her breast, her fingers trailing from the nipple downwards. He responded, as always, a rush of blood, a hardening. Was she like an addiction, he wondered; the longing to consume greater than the satisfaction of consuming? Her lingerie was becoming more provocative. Ribbons strategically placed, heart shaped buttons straining to be opened, alluring slits within folds of lace or brazenly apparent. They drank champagne and made love slowly. Her eyes were pooled in blue but nothing he saw there related to the heat of her body, the promise in her seductive voice. The realisation that she was faking came and went, blunted by the force of his passion.

She fell asleep immediately afterwards. The room was stuffy, the bed too hot. His head ached from the champagne. It had fuelled their lovemaking. What alarmed him more than her possessiveness was the effect it was having on him. He felt as if he was ravaging her with the force of his desire, yet every moan and breathless gasp told him otherwise. He had seen her eyelids flutter and stopped, afraid he was hurting her but she had urged him on. Had the passion he believed they shared been an illusion? He must have misread that unnerving awareness in her eyes. The feeling that he was being observed. Circus tricks. The clown in the ring. No, he refused to believe their relationship was based on such a dangerous lie.

CHAPTER THIRTY-SEVEN

Nadine

I awaken during the night, my senses alert. Stuart is rigid with pain. I administer morphine but it makes no appreciable difference. He is still coherent when he asks me to contact his oncologist in London. He hands the phone to me and I answer the oncologist's questions. Stuart believes this is a glitch but I know by the oncologist's voice that it's the end game. I call an ambulance and fight back panic as I await its arrival. I knew this time would come but I'd hoped he would have another Christmas with me and sometime… way way down the line… I would deal with what's happening now.

Stuart is hospitalised, hooked to tubes and monitors. The ward bleeps, pings and rings with sound: voices, footsteps, flickering television screens. Still resolute, he holds up his mobile and calls out the phone numbers of people I must ring to inform them of his death.

Jake snaps from sleep when I ring him. Over four thousand miles separate us but I can tell he's alone.

'I'll catch a flight,' he says.

'You'll be too late. I'm okay… really. I just wanted you to know. Will you prepare the children?'

'Of course I will. Nadine… is there anyone there to support you?'

'Daveth's on his way. He and Stuart became good friends. He's helped us a lot.'

The pause that follows lengthens. These days they punctuate our brief conversations.

'I'm glad he's there,' Jake finally says and we bid each other a formal goodbye.

Stuart's eyes are closed when Daveth arrives. I'm not sure if he's in a coma or in a morphine induced sleep. Our breathing seems unnaturally loud, an affront to his ragged inhalations.

Three days pass before he releases a final shuddering sigh. The relief of tears, of letting go, is overwhelming. Outside the window seagulls lift into the frozen air and scatter into a drift of snow.

Little evidence of Stuart's presence remains when Daveth drives me back to the lodge. He had arranged for a charity organisation to collect his clothes. Only his medicine gives any indication of the struggle he endured. I feel both grief and relief at his passing, freed from the responsibility of normalising an abnormal situation yet bereft. The space he left behind is too vast to fold over.

I find a letter on the dressing table.

My dear Nadine,

The last fight is the longest but now I'm at peace with myself. We've shared much together these last few months and I'll always be grateful to you for bringing me such comfort. Thank you for all the Christmases we've shared and for making me part of your lovely family. Do you remember what the chaplain said to us when Sara's life support machine was switched off? Her soul was free to fly to God. I'm about to take that flight and am comforted in the belief that she's waiting for me.

I've left you a token of my gratitude. My solicitor will be in touch with you to discuss the details. I hope it makes a difference to the new life you've chosen.

Goodbye my beloved niece.

Stuart

The day is clear but cold when we sail down the Gastineau Channel and scatter Stuart's ashes over the side of *Eyebright*. Daveth reads a passage from the bible and I recite a poem by Emily Dickinson. *Because I could not stop for death. He kindly stopped for me...'*

Unlike Jake, I lack the courage of the atheist or Eleanor's self-assured convictions. I'm an agnostic, clutching at straws, and, so, I imagine Stuart's spirit freed from all earthly yearnings as he floats towards my mother's welcoming arms.

Afterwards, I enter the cabin where I slept alone during those weeks when we were immersed in ice. Daveth comes to me, as I knew he would. I've no sense of guilt that our passion should exist alongside the grey immobility of death. I don't think of Jake or Karin. Nor do I sense Stuart's presence. Nothing dents our pleasure and when it is over we rest in my narrow bunk, which should cause us some discomfort but manages to mould itself effortlessly around us.

CHAPTER THIRTY-EIGHT

Jake

He was dreaming about snow, chasing Nadine through mountainous drifts that slowed his footsteps while she ran on ahead. He had no idea why she was in danger but he had to catch her before it was too late. The snow cracked and they fell together into a white crevasse. He moaned her name as they reached for each other but the snow heaved and she slid from his arms. He awoke with a start, unaware of where he was until he realised Karin was shaking his shoulder.

She lay on her side, her chin propped on her hand.

'What's wrong?' He was filled with the relief of being released from a nightmare, aroused, also, he realised, but that desire was already fading.

'You were talking in your sleep,' she said.

'I never talk in my sleep,' he protested.

'How do you know?'

'Nadine would have told me…' He stopped, pulled back too late. He had upset her again.

'You were dreaming of her.' The bedside lamp, angled directly at him, reminded him of an interrogative spotlight. 'You called me Nadine and then you tried to kiss me. How do you think that makes me feel?'

Did she have a sixth sense? Were her fingers capable of probing his unconscious? They probed everywhere else. He touched her shoulder. Her flesh was warm but unyielding.

'This is ridiculous, Karin. You can't hold me responsible – '

'Can't I?' A surly, almost childish expression crossed her face. Her bottom lip swelled. It's just blubber, he thought. A muscle containing too much fat. The image was vaguely unpleasant. She flung back the duvet and flounced from the bed. 'It's time you realised I'm not a surrogate for Nadine. You're always talking about her. And now you're doing it in your sleep.'

'That's a lie.' He readjusted the lamp and rubbed his eyes, too tired for an argument. 'Do you want me to apologise? Okay, I apologise because my wife's name inadvertently passed my lips when I was in an unconscious state.'

'Were you fucking her in your unconscious state?' She sat in front of the dressing table and brushed her hair with fast, furious strokes. Strands of hair bristled, charged by her anger.

He hated her casual use of the word and its application to Nadine. 'What if I was? Am I to be punished for my dreams now?'

The hairbrush struck his forehead before he could duck. His shock was so great he hardly noticed the pain. She lifted a bottle of perfume, raised her arm to fling it at him. He sprang from the bed and forced it from her fingers.

'What the hell do you think you're doing?' he shouted. 'You wake me up with some crazy accusation than start attacking me. Are you trying to wreck this relationship? If so, full marks. I'm out of here.'

She grabbed his clothes, flung them at him. 'Then go, right now.'

He dressed quickly. His forehead throbbed. He touched it gingerly. A lump was already rising on his temple. He needed to calm down. This was a game and it had been played before. Rows that erupted out of nowhere, tantrums followed by passion on the edge of violence.

He reached the bedroom door and stopped, alerted by her cry. She was slumped at the dressing table, her face buried in her arms.

'Karin… what is it?' He stood behind her and drew her upright until their eyes met in the mirror. The rush of blood to her face had subsided and she was pale, almost ashen.

'Hearing her name like that… all those memories you have. I'm jealous of them.'

'Are they also part of my punishment?' He pressed his fingers into her shoulders, his knuckles braced against her supple flesh. 'I'm with you, not Nadine. How often must I convince you of that?'

'You think I'm a possessive bitch who's demanding far more than you're willing to give,' she continued as if he had not spoken. 'Even when you're fucking me you're thinking of her.'

'Stop saying that.' His fingers pressed harder, kneaded the knobbles of tension under her smooth skin.

'Isn't that why you want to hurt me?'

'I said *stop* – '

'You try to hide it but I know it's there.'

She was waiting for him to overwhelm her, he thought. To drag her back to bed and make love until they were both exhausted. He released the pressure on her shoulders and rubbed his hands together, shocked by the ferocity of his thoughts. The room felt airless. He opened the window. The city was on the move, a slow snail of traffic along the quays but the early morning noises could not reach them. He inhaled and exhaled deeply before turning around.

She had taken a facecloth from the ensuite and soaked it in cold water.

'I'm sorry I lost my temper, Jake.' She stretched upwards and pressed the cloth to his forehead. He winced against its coldness. Her anger seemed to have abated but he was unable to gauge her mood.

'I always seem to be apologising to you.' She smiled, wryly. 'Let me make it up to you tonight. I'll pick up something in the supermarket and call over to Sea Aster after work. What would you like? Fish would be nice for a change.' She glanced at the clock. 'Gosh! Is that the time? I'd better shower. I've an appointment in an hour with a client.'

'I can't see you tonight,' he said. 'You know I always have band practice on Wednesdays.'

'Can't you cancel?'

'No, I can't.'

'Okay. I'll drive over around ten. You should be finished by then.'

Her resentment of Shard had been growing in recent weeks. They were now gigging two nights a week and on Sunday afternoons in Julia's Tavern, a pub fronting the Liffey boardwalk. Then there was band practice on Wednesday nights and Saturday afternoons. All too much, she said.

He listened to the gush of the power shower from the ensuite. Was she waiting for him to join her, as he usually did, the two of them slip-sliding together in the soapy wash? This possibility increased his lethargy. He had sought oblivion in her arms but she no longer deadened his sense of loss. The sounds from the ensuite grew brisker. The clink of jars and bottles, potions and lotions, familiar yet always mysterious. She emerged, wrapped in a white towel, her head turbaned in a smaller one.

She dressed swiftly, each move deliberately choreographed to be noticed.

'I'll ring you later,' she said. 'Make sure to set the burglar alarm before you leave. Don't use *all* your energy at rehearsal.' She fluttered her eyelashes, a teasing promise as she opened the door. 'You'll need some for later.'

After she left, he entered the bathroom, still steamy and scented. He rasped his hand over dark stubble and looked closer. Was there grey among the black, a faint frosting? The longing to hear Nadine's voice rushed over him. Marital tics, phantom pains, he no longer cared.

She would not be returning to Sea Aster. She intended settling in London in the New Year but, until then, she was staying on in Alaska to see the aurora borealis. Stuart was dead. Ashes to ashes, scattered from the deck of Eyebright. Jake imagined her and Daveth Carew, the two of them freed from the spectre of death and all alone in the icy reaches. There was only one place they would go to keep warm and rejoice at being alive.

He turned on the shower. The pressure of the water needled against his skin. The bathroom filled with steam. He closed his eyes and pressed his forehead against the marble tiles. The urge to scream came and went. Finally, unable any longer to endure the pressure of the water he stumbled from the shower. Pain shot through his foot when he stubbed his big toe against the edge of the tray. Blood spurted from the gash. He limped on his heel towards the medicine cabinet. Nothing there except pill bottles, lined neatly in a row. He grabbed toilet tissue and twisted it around the wound then hobbled into the kitchen to search in the presses for bandages. The tissue was soaked with blood by the time he found a box with a red cross on one of the high shelves. After bandaging his foot he stretched upwards to replace the medicine chest. It jammed against something inside the press and he was unable to close the door. He shoved a serving dish to one side and noticed a ceramic box. He drew it forward into the light. The lid curved in two sections. A heart split in two, the Willow Passion glaze unmistakable. He carried it to the breakfast counter and stared at the pale green willow fronds, the hidden lovers.

He laid the two sections of the lid carefully on the counter. The first thing he lifted out was a menu from Lucientes, the tapas bar where Ali worked. Last week Karin had been in London for two days on business. That must be when she dined there. His chest tightened as he imagined his daughter serving patatas bravas or tortilla, unaware, as she must have been, that she was speaking to the woman who spent most nights in her father's bed. He removed a publicity brochure from Silver Ridge University, newspaper features about First Affiliation, a flyer from Brian's pottery. Inside a small plastic bag he found shoelaces from a discarded pair of runners, a lock of his hair, a button from his shirt and a comb that he recognised as his own. At the bottom of the box he found the photographs. The first one had been cut from a magazine called *Families Matter*. The magazine had published an interview with Eleanor prior to her conference. She had allowed the editor to use a family photograph that had been taken shortly before Rosanna's death. Rosanna was in her wheelchair, flanked by himself and Nadine, her four great-grandchildren seated on the floor in front of her. Eleanor stood behind the wheelchair, her hands resting on her mother's thin shoulders. Eight people formed the configuration but it was Eleanor with her imperious sweep of blonde hair and autocratic eyebrows who dominated the group. Nadine was faceless, recognisable only by her clothes, her long hands and red hair. Karin had used a cutting knife with skill and the circle that once featured Nadine's face was as exact as a bullet hole.

The photographs underneath had been taken from Sea Aster. Six photographs, all celebrating different family occasions. Nadine had been defaced with the same precision in each one.

Chilled and sickened by his discovery Jake shoved everything back into the box and replaced it. In the bathroom he removed the sodden tissue from around his foot and flushed it down the toilet. He poured a glass of water and gulped it down, swallowed hard. The pressure in his chest intensified, as if Karin was drawing her nails gently yet insistently over the membrane of his heart. He had to end this relationship before it destroyed him. He left his key to her apartment on the kitchen table and set the alarm code. He took the elevator to the car park and drove away.

CHAPTER THIRTY-NINE

Jake crossed from the barn to his apartment as soon as band practice ended. The few leaves still clinging to the trees were as withered as old skin. He shivered when he entered the apartment but decided against lighting a fire. The leap of flames suggested warmth, intimacy. He turned on the central heating instead and the living-room was warm when Karin arrived. She removed her coat and draped it across the back of a chair, unwound her scarf and flung it on the sofa, kicked off her boots. Within moments she had stamped her personality on the room.

Anger curdled his stomach. His reflection in the window reminded him of an X-ray, a translucent shadow on black glass. Behind him he could see her shaking her hair loose, lifting the collar of her blouse so that it framed her chin.

'What's wrong?' she asked. 'Was it a difficult rehearsal?'

'No worse than usual,' he replied.

She slipped her arms around his waist, rested her head against his back. 'Then why are you so tense?' Her body was no longer visible as she ran the fingers of one hand along his spine. He turned around and held her shoulders, walked her backwards and away from him. She took tiny steps. Why did he always think about her in miniature? How had he been so turned on by those delicate wrists and ankles? Seduced by a fragility that had never existed?

'You told me once I was the most married man you knew,' he said.

'At the time, yes,' she nodded. 'But not now. You've changed.'

'That's the problem, Karin. I haven't.'

She was silent for an instant, absorbing his words. 'Are you dumping me?' she finally asked.

'You can use that word if you like,' he said. 'I'm ending our relationship.'

'Because of this morning?' She sounded puzzled. 'I apologised. I was way out of line – '

'Way out of line doesn't even begin to explain what you've been doing.'

'What do you mean?'

'I found that box after you left.'

'What box?'

'The one you bought from Brian.'

'You were *snooping* in my apartment.' The irises of her eyes darkened, as if a shutter had descended.

'I was looking for bandages – '

'How dare you!'

'I found it by accident but I can't ignore what was inside it.'

'A few mementoes of your life.' She could have been discussing the contents of her fridge. 'What's so awful about that?'

'The fact that *you* don't find it awful. The fact that you don't find it *sickening*.' He released her shoulders and stepped back from her. 'Those photographs of Nadine… I'd no idea your hatred of her was so malign.'

'She's gone from your life, Jake. The same way she went from mine after that summer in Monsheelagh. Defacing her was a symbolic gesture. Ridiculous behaviour, I'm prepared to admit that. I drank too much wine one evening and couldn't handle the memories.'

'What memories?'

'She destroyed my family. Did she ever tell you that?'

'She was fifteen that summer. A child.'

She rolled up the sleeve of her blouse and held the pale underside of her arm towards him. 'Do you remember what you wrote there? I've never forgotten. You drew a heart and wrote *Always Together* inside it.'

'That's not true.'

'Oh, yes, it's true.' Her gaze was unflinching. 'And here's another truth. Nadine doesn't understand love. Not then, not now. You chose her above me but I loved you that summer as fiercely as I love you now. I'm ashamed of what I've done but you keep me at arm's length. All those excuses about not wanting to hurt your family with never a thought about how much that hurts me. So I took what small possessions I found and treasured them. That's what love does, Jake. It fills us with the need to possess and cherish those dearest to us. Don't let something so trivial destroy what we've built together.'

'Trivial?' He was unable to control his fury. 'You deface those photographs of Nadine and you call it trivial. You've taken possession of my life and you call it trivial. You seek out my family – '

She stretched upwards and pressed her fingers against his mouth. 'Shush… shush…' she whispered. 'You can punish me, Jake. I deserve to be beaten… beat me hard… I deserve to be punished… I've been so bad… such a bold, wicked girl… I know you want to punish me…'

'I've no intention of hurting you' His suspicions had turned to cold certainty. Their lovemaking had never been anything other than a performance staged for his benefit.

'Intention is not the same as need,' she said. 'I understand violence. It's unmistakable. But this… what you've been doing is worse. You've been playing with my mind.'

'You can talk about mind games?' He shoved her backwards. 'I used to feel sorry for you. All those whacko boyfriends who messed with your head. Now I just feel sorry for them. Give me back the key to my apartment.'

'Don't do this, Jake.'

'Give it to me,' he shouted.

'You're making a big mistake.' The sleeves of her blouse billowed as she delved into her handbag. An inset of blue on the cuffs, a trim of blue on the collar. He detested the flamboyant touches of colour that had once charmed him. She was not a person, he decided, but an object designed to stand on a plinth and be admired. She handed the key to him and buttoned her coat, wound her scarf around her neck. When she reached the door she turned, as if waiting for him to call her back. No tears this time.

'Nothing can change how I feel about you,' she said. 'Ring me when you can no longer lie alone in that empty bed.'

He stood outside after she had driven away and breathed in the chilly night air. The wind from the estuary was harsh and icy. He had joined the ranks of Cody, Jason, Malcolm, Carl and the others who had been possessed by her. But it was over now. Like a snapped string, a broken spell, a last shuddering sigh.

CHAPTER FORTY

Snow united them all on Christmas Day. An unprecedented snowfall had frozen runways and made many roads impassable. Ali was marooned in London, her flight cancelled. Brian was unable to drive from Dingle and Mallard Cove was impassable for traffic. Eleanor, who had also planned to spend the day with Jake, was unable to reach him and had made alternative plans to dine with her neighbours. Jake would spend the day alone. No need to pretend. To be merry and festive, wear jolly hats and answer daft riddles. He would not have to eat turkey.

Frozen swathes of ice glistened on the estuary as he crunched his way through the snow to feed the huddled, bewildered swans. Back indoors, he fried rashers and sausages, toasted bread, simmered a pot of strong tea. The fire blazed and the hiss of burning logs was the only sound to break the silence. He had stocked up on food before the unseasonably heavy snowfall paralysed the country and could sit it out for at least another week.

By noon his phone was ringing constantly. Ali and Brian first, his friends from Shard and then Eleanor. Everyone seemed convinced that he would deflate with misery by having to spend Christmas Day alone.

He made pancakes for dinner. A stack of them drenched in maple syrup and brandy, delicious with a chilled, white wine. He switched on the television and opened a bottle of whiskey.

Darkness fell early. A flicker at the window distracted him and the outside security light automatically switched on. He opened the door but only the curlicues of bird claws and the deeper indentation of cat paws marred the crystalline whiteness. Nothing to see except his snowbound van and a seagull flying above it. He shook off his uneasiness and returned indoors. The bird had flown too close to the light and triggered it. Nothing to worry about.

Eight o'clock. Still too early to ring Alaska or California. The flow of water was worryingly slow when he turned on the kitchen tap. After eight days of freezing temperatures the possibility of a burst pipe was very real. He switched off his water supply but the tank was in the attic in Nadine's apartment.

The air smelled musty and the oppressive silence of an unoccupied space bore down on him as he crossed the landing. Could it still be called her apartment? It was obvious she was never going to return. Resisting the urge to enter her rooms, he pulled down the wooden staircase and pushed open the attic trap door. His hand tingled with a faint electric charge when he switched on the light. The whole place probably needed rewiring. The sight of the muddle on the floor added to his dejection. Nadine's efforts to clear out the attic had only removed a fraction of what they had taken with them from Bartizan Downs. Sorting through everything would have to be his next project. He stepped over crates of Christmas decorations that he had not bothered opening. He recognised a box of dressing-up clothes from Ali's fantasy childhood world and lifted out a dress dotted with diamantes. She used to wear it to bed at night, along with the matching tiara, which he would remove when she was sleeping. He hunkered down to examine Brian's lopsided early creations. Wisps of memory escaping. They were stored in the frontal lobes of his brain – he had read that somewhere – awaiting the right trigger to free them.

Today they needed no prompting. Nadine must be feeling the same way. Something so strong had to have a magnetic pull. But the time difference... he stepped around two broken computers, a treadmill and exercise bike, broken musical instruments.

He found the stopcock on the tank and closed it off. He inspected all the pipes and the boiler. Everything seemed in order and well insulated. The slow flow must be due to an outside problem. Relieved he reopened the stopcock. He sneezed, dust clogging his nostrils, cobwebs quivering. Nadine's half-finished paintings were stacked under the eaves. This was where she had hoped to establish her studio but the sheer volume of her family's possessions had defeated her.

The twins' trophies clanged sharply when he accidently kicked against a black, plastic sack. They were tarnished, long neglected. He carried the bag from the attic and climbed backwards down the folding stairs. The front door of his apartment had blown open. He had obviously not closed it properly yet his fear that someone was waiting inside was palpable.

He shook off his disquiet. Karin Moylan was gone from his life and he was safe within frozen banks of snow.

He googled how to polish silver and made a paste of baking soda, which he found at the back of a press. The trophies were cleaned and lined up in front of him when the twins rang from Alpine Meadows. Breathless from the rush of snow in their nostrils they wished him a merry Christmas then rushed off to meet their friends on the snowboarding slopes.

At midnight Nadine answered her phone.

'Happy Christmas.' He enunciated each word with the precise concentration of the very drunk.

'Happy Christmas, Jake,' she replied.

'Where are you?' He could hear voices in the background, music, laughter.

'Daveth's house,' she said. 'He invited some friends to Christmas dinner.'

'That's nice.' He batted away the image of Daveth Carew basting the turkey and wearing a ridiculously festive apron. 'I'd better not keep you from your host.'

'I'm okay for the moment. Is the snow bad?'

'It's brought the country to a standstill. I was in the attic earlier checking for burst pipes.'

'Any danger of a leak?'

'No. All sound. I've just polished the twins' trophies. Baking soda and water. You should see the shine.'

'Have you been drinking?'

'A few glasses of wine with the pancakes.'

'You made *pancakes* for dinner.'

'Beats turkey any day.'

'You should go to bed.'

'Nadine… I need to tell you something.'

'What?'

'It's over.'

She remained silent. Only for the background voices, he would believe she had hung up.

'Did you hear me?' His voice was louder than he intended.

She cleared her throat. 'Yes, I heard you.'

'I don't know where to begin… can we talk sometime soon?'

'What's left to talk about?' Her tone brought their conversation to an end. 'I'm sorry, Jake.'

He found his favourite Bruce Springsteen album and placed it carefully on the turntable. Tonight was the time for vinyl and scratching *The River* would be an unforgivable crime. The lyrics released a backwash of nostalgia… down by the river… a girl of seventeen, a boy of nineteen, caught in the spiral of youthful passion. The fire turned to ash, like the ash of their youthful passion, and the room grew cold. Finally, stiffly, Jake rose to his feet. He stepped over the trophies. Whiskey was not a good idea when the frontal lobe was involved, he decided as he collapsed onto his bed. His last image before he fell asleep was of the seagull suspended like a white cross against the black sky.

CHAPTER FORTY-ONE

Nadine

The smells of herbs and spices trail familiar plumes around me as Daveth removes the turkey from the oven. His cousin Nessa, her husband Ryan and their three children have joined us for dinner. I know my way around his house now. Olga's presence is everywhere. She was into crafts, rugs and wall hangings, but she is a gentle ghost and I'm happy here. Daveth has asked me to stay on, to cruise alongside him on *Eyebright* for the next season. I thought about it for a day but I knew, as I suspect he did too, that ours is just a snatched encounter.

Dinner is ready to be served. Each dish is greeted with cheers as it's carried to the table. My presence seems to add an extra bounciness to the atmosphere. They're curious about me, particularly Nessa, who must find it difficult to understand how I can laugh so easily when I'm separated from my family on Christmas Day. Her own three children howl with scorn over the jokes in the crackers, don the funny hats and politely pass the serving dishes around the table. Daveth raises his wine glass in a toast to absent loved ones. We drink and toast Olga, who stares down at us, smiling from a photo on the wall, and remember Stuart in the silence that follows.

When the dishes have been cleared away I sit with Nessa in the room that opens out into a balcony in the summer. It's a small, warm space with well-worn armchairs and crowded bookcases. Nessa lights a cigarette and tells me I'm the first woman Daveth has brought into his house since Olga's death. She looks disappointed when I tell her I'm moving on in the new year. She's easy and kind, and we exchange brief life stories, as strangers do when they know they won't meet again.

'Where are you heading after you leave here?' she asks.

'To Vancouver to visit my friend, Jenny. Then on to California to see my twins.'

I tell her about Brian's pottery. How stressed I was when he dropped out of college but how unimportant it seems now. She's involved in amateur dramatics and interested in hearing about Ali's play. I'll miss the opening night of *The Arboretum Affair*. It's all Ali talks about when she rings. Tina, queen of the sylphs, her first leading role. I thought it was a fairy story but she says it's a bitingly savage satire on capitalism and corruption.

'How long before you return home?' Nessa asks.

'A month. But I'm not going home. I'll settle in London and study art. That's what I intended on doing when I met my ex-husband. He was in a band that was going stratosphere, or so we believed. We were dreamers. That's all we had in common.'

'You stayed together. You reared a family. You need more than a dream to do that.'

'We muddled through and hoped we wouldn't do too much damage in the process.'

I close my eyes against the pull of memory; small faces, laughter, tantrums, hugs, squabbles, the clamber of tiny legs and arms. In a moment I'll weep. Once the tears flow I'll need a mop and bucket.

If only Jake hadn't rung. He sounded so wretchedly drunk. So alone. Why should I care? And that strangled apology. As if regret was going to wipe everything away.

Inside, Daveth is playing with Nessa's children on their Xbox. We made love this morning. His frame is different to Jake's, shorter, heavier, sturdier. Seeing him walking naked to the bathroom always shocks me more than our lovemaking. He's polished mahogany and limber. My body is light, quivering, as if charged with electricity. When I'm with him like this, my blood racing, it's impossible to think of leaving. But our time together has run its course. My mind has already travelled ahead. Only my body remains to be convinced.

On our last night together we sit on the deck of *Eyebright* and watch the dance of the aurora borealis. The sky burns red and the ice is touched by tongues of fire. Daveth hands me a small box wrapped in glitter. I remove a ring, Alaskan gold moulded into a forget-me-not flower with a diamond in the centre. He slips it on the ring finger of my right hand and we make love under the eddying waves of green and strobes of purple, moonflowers exploding. When I leave in the morning the colours are still swirling inside my head. A radiant firmament, brief, intense and over.

CHAPTER FORTY-TWO

Jake

When he first moved into Sea Aster Jake had imagined glimpses of Rosanna. An outline of silver hair if he turned suddenly. A wrinkled hand on the door, her silhouette at the window. Jake did not believe in ghosts, or in an afterlife that allowed them to roam outside his imagination. He had put his experiences down to the shock of losing his house and company, and the ending of his marriage. This feeling had passed but he was now affected by a new sense of invasion. It was different to the gently nudging sensation Rosanna's presence had created but he was unable to pin it down to anything specific.

Small things bothered him. The family photograph that appeared on the window ledge instead of its usual place on the mantelpiece. The cutlery mixed together in the drawer when it was normally aligned in separate sections. The bed neatly made when he came home one night from a gig. He always found an excuse. Coincidences, lack of concentration. Then there was the incident with his Gibson. It should have been sitting on its stand in the breakfast room. Instead, it was propped against the wall. Absent-mindedness or paranoia? How could he prove which was which?

One morning he was unable to find his fleece. It was too tatty to wear outside but perfect for keeping him warm during the cold snap. It wasn't in its usual place on the back of the bedroom door. He searched the wardrobe twice, the laundry basket, the barn, the hot press. He was leaving to keep an appointment with Reedy at the Raison D'être studio when he found it under his black leather jacket, the arms tucked inside the jacket sleeves. This made no sense. He never wore it outside. He pulled it free and carried it to the kitchen. Karin had often worn it in the mornings before she showered. He had smelled her perfume and been surprised at how long it lingered in the fabric. When he returned from the studio he took a bottle of white wine from the fridge. It was almost empty yet he could have sworn he had only taken one glass from it the previous evening. His hand shook as he drained the bottle into the sink. He rang a locksmith and the lock was changed by the next day.

Eleanor called unexpectedly in the afternoon. He was working on his laptop, earphones on. His first indication that she was outside came when his mobile vibrated.

'Please tell me why I can't get into my own house,' she demanded when he opened the door. 'I've been ringing the bell for the past five minutes.'

'Sorry, I forgot to tell you,' he said. 'The lock has been changed.'

She arched her eyebrows. 'Whatever for?'

'The door wasn't secure. I was afraid someone might break in.'

'Like who?' She followed him into the kitchen and sat down at the table.

'How do I know? The house is so isolated. You look upset. Is something wrong?'

'Are you still seeing Karin Moylan?' she asked.

'What makes you think I'm seeing – ?'

'Kindly respect my intelligence, Jake.'

'I was.' Nothing would be gained by lying. He checked the press for the china tea set that once belonged to Rosanna. Eleanor refused to drink from a mug. Mugs belonged on building sites and factory canteens, she said. Little rules, big rules. Jake's childhood had been dominated by them. Hence Shard, rebellion, turbulence, mother-son tension that never abated.

'We're not together anymore,' he said. 'I ended it before Christmas.'

She nodded, as if her suspicions were confirmed. 'I assume you knew she was working on our new logo for First Affiliation?'

'Yes.'

'She's talented, I'll give her that.' Eleanor acknowledged the cup of tea but made no effort to drink it. 'Everyone on the executive committee was very impressed.'

'I'm glad you're satisfied.'

'I was satisfied…initially.'

'Initially? Does that mean you turned her down?'

'I changed my mind.'

'Because of my relationship?'

'My decision had nothing to do with your private life.'

'Then what?'

'Her design was far too aggressive for our image.'

Her answer surprised him. Karin was a skilled designer and would have been anxious to impress his mother.

'What do you mean by "aggressive"?'

She opened her briefcase and handed him a memory key. 'These are the early designs she did for me.'

He slotted the memory key into his laptop and opened the file. Karin's first sketches had been drawn in a naive style, two stick-like parents and four children with intertwining circles releasing a blast of sunshine over them.

'What's so aggressive about that?' he asked.

She took a cardboard file from her briefcase and handed him a sheet of paper. 'Yesterday, I received this in the post from her, along with a letter telling me she wasn't interested in working with me.'

Jake stared at the sketch. It was a similar configuration to her earlier designs but the children's expressions were menacing rather than contented and a dark rim eclipsed the brightness of the circle. The dimming of the light surrounding the family unit had been drawn with such savagery that the paper was scored and torn.

'All I need to know is that she's definitely gone from your life,' Eleanor said.

'Rest assured she is.'

'I'm glad to hear it.' She ripped the paper in two and twisted it tightly. 'Throw that into your rubbish,' she said. 'That woman is disturbed. Keep well away from her.'

'She's upset you a lot. I can see that. I'm sorry.'

She had always seemed indomitable but she was showing signs of aging, lines settling deeper around her mouth, her cheeks hollowing.

'Apart from Karin, is everything all right,' he asked. 'Has there been any further word on the planning permission?'

'No need to worry about that just yet,' she replied. 'You've done a good job keeping the house and grounds maintained. I couldn't have managed without you.'

The unexpected compliment surprised him.

'How is Nadine enjoying Vancouver?' she asked.

'Loving it, I gather.'

'When is she coming home?'

'London will be her home.'

'That's it then.'

'Don't sound so surprised.'

'I'm not surprised. Just sad.' She stood up to leave. 'Family is a precious thing, Jake. Don't ever take it for granted.'

CHAPTER FORTY-THREE

The opening night of *The Arboretum Affair* was an outstanding success. Ali, as Tina, Queen of the Sylphs, led her army of fleet-footed sylphs into battle against a hoard of marauding trolls. Jake had never been interested in mythical creatures when he was a child but this lack of knowledge did not prevent him believing that sylphs wore more than strategically placed leaves when they were flitting between trees. He was so shocked to see Ali naked on stage, or as naked as made no difference, that he lost all sense of the play within the first few minutes. During the interval the woman next to him explained that the misshapen trees represented the threatened universe, the trolls rampaging through the woods were ruthless developers and the sylphs symbolised the transient nature of innocence.

Backstage in her dressing room, after multiple encores, Ali was ecstatic. Up close he realised that the sylphs were covered in flesh-coloured netting woven with a filigree of woodland plants but this did nothing to lessen his shock. He hated Ali's artistic director on sight. This hatred was subjective and based on the fact that Mark Brewer was wearing a tuxedo while his daughter – who used to scream like a barn owl if anyone accidently opened the door of the bathroom while she was occupying it – was dressed in a body stocking.

To his relief, Ali emerged from the theatre fully clothed.

'We're going to Milly's to celebrate.' Christine, her flatmate and one of the sylphs, linked Jake's arm. 'You must come with us.'

'Is that what you want?' he asked Ali.

'Suit yourself, Dad.' She shrugged and walked ahead with her director. Had she sensed Jake's disapproval despite his best efforts to sound enthusiastic about her performance?

In Milly's, a basement nightclub close to the theatre, champagne corks popped as Mark Brewer toasted the success of *The Arboretum Affair.*

'What's wrong, Ali?' He sat beside her. 'Are you angry with me about something?'

'Tell me your honest opinion of the play,' she said.

'You were brilliant, darling.'

'I know that. I'm asking you about Mark's play.'

Unmitigated bilge, he wanted to say but, wisely, kept this opinion to himself. 'It was different… interesting.'

'I *knew* you hated it.'

'I don't hate it. It's just…' He hesitated and rubbed the back of his neck.

'Go on, Dad. Say it.'

'Why can't the sylphs wear tunics or frocks?'

Her fine, dark eyebrows lifted in an arch she had inherited from her grandmother. 'Why not a burka? Would that satisfy you? God! You're so old-fashioned. Your girlfriend was far more complimentary when she came backstage after the preview last night.'

'My *what?*'

'You heard.' She tossed her black hair over her shoulders and glowered at him. 'She apologised because she couldn't come tonight. Apparently, you were hoping to introduce us. How could you have *even* considered bringing her with you tonight of all nights?'

He put the champagne glass down on the table, afraid the slender stem would snap in his hand. 'What else did she say?'

'That I'd beautiful fingers. Expressive, like a musician's.' She turned her hands over and stared at them. 'I know you have to move on, Dad. But I'm not ready to meet Mum's replacement... and certainly not on a special occasion like this. Tell her to stay out of my life.'

'She's not in my life, Ali. She was for a while but not now.'

'Are you telling me she was lying?'

'Yes. She's angry with me. This is her way of hitting back.'

'I don't understand. She was so friendly. Why would she pretend like that?' Ali's forehead puckered, her annoyance giving way to anxiety.

'I've no idea what goes on in her head.'

'She's not some *weird* stalker... is she?'

The music was too loud. Jake was used to volume but this was forcing him to shout about something so personal it hurt his throat. He hugged Ali. How fragile she suddenly seemed.

'Nothing as dramatic as that.' He had to control his rage and reassure her. 'But if she ever contacts you again... I know she won't... but *if* she does you must let me know immediately.'

'Is she the reason Mum went away so suddenly?'

'This is your night, Ali, and not the time or place to talk about it. She'll be back soon...'

He was interrupted by Mark Brewer, who stooped across the table and held out his hand to Ali.

'You'll have to excuse us, Jake,' he said. 'We all want a share of your beautiful daughter tonight. I'd like to introduce Alysia to some friends who flew from New York to be with us for the opening.'

High heels added to Ali's height and she walked with confidence towards the group, aware but indifferent to the fact that she was the centre of attention. Unable to cope with the exuberance of the sylphs and trolls, Jake said his goodbyes and left the nightclub. Mik Abel had offered him his London apartment for the night. Tomorrow he was meeting a tour manager, who was organising Shard's forthcoming UK tour.

He rang Karin. Her voice mail came on, a husky message that teased the caller with a promise of immediate contact.

'I'm reporting you to the police if you dare to go near any member of my family again,' he said.

She was probably listening, smiling as she deleted his message.

It was dark the following night when he emerged from Dublin airport and hailed a taxi to take him to Sea Aster. In the distance, a train, riding high and silently over the viaduct, reflected a seam of gold on the water. Then it was gone and the estuary continued its dark journey towards the sea.

The outside security light switched as he walked towards the entrance to his apartment. He tensed as he was about to unlock the door, puzzled by a repetitive clunking sound that did not belong to the estuary. The wind fanned the smell of dead seaweed over the wall and the overhanging branches poked black fingers into the night. Broken glass crunched underfoot as he hurried towards his van. The front window was shattered, the seats slashed. Deep cuts in the leather, the stuffing sprouting like mottled toadstools. One of the back doors swung in the wind and it was the clunk of steel against steel that had alerted him. He slammed the door and walked around to the side of the van. Someone had dragged keys or a knife along the paintwork, scratching repeatedly through the centre of the distinctive Shard sign.

He checked each room in his apartment as he waited for the guards to arrive. Everything was as he had left it. He opened the fridge, searched for something handy to cook. Fish fingers in the freezer section, kid's food, exactly what he needed. He grilled the fish fingers and carried the plate into the breakfast room. The sky was starless and the curved window flung his reflection back at him, as it did on the night he said goodbye to Karin Moylan.

The squad car arrived. Kids, the guards said. High as kites, probably. Jake was lucky. They offered him cold comfort. Usually, in situations like this, those little thugs went joy-riding in the stolen vehicle until it was time to burn it out.

CHAPTER FORTY-FOUR

Nadine

The lights of London cross-stitch the night in gold as the plane begins a slow descent into Heathrow. My great adventure is over. Ali is waiting in Arrivals. We spot each other in the same instant and, suddenly, I'm ambushed by tears. I feel as if I've been holding them back forever. I don't know why I'm crying or, perhaps, there's so many reasons I'm unable to distinguish one from the other. Ali is in my arms, crying too, as we hug each other. Giddy with excitement she swipes her tears away and I notice the man standing beside her.

'Mum, this is Mark Brewer.' She sings his name, her cheeks glowing. 'Mark, meet my intrepid mother.'

He's tall, dark-haired, sophisticated. He wears crumpled linen with confidence and is probably older than her father. No ring on his finger but he's married. I can always tell. Married men acquire sleekness. Less of the hunter, more of the gatherer, even when, like this one, they are still on the prowl.

'I'm delighted to meet you, Mrs Saunders.' Without asking, he takes my trolley and steers it assertively to the carpark.

'Oh, Mum, you *really* do look fantastic. That *tan*. I thought you were exploring icebergs not sun worshipping.' Ali quickens her pace to catch up with Mark's long stride. 'Your apartment is lovely. I checked it last night to make sure everything was okay.

Mark is going to drop us off there and come back for me when I've heard all the gossip.'

Ali has the key to the two-bed apartment in Chelsea. The rooms are smaller than I imagined when I viewed them online. I've taken the lease for two months and it will serve its purpose while I look for somewhere more permanent.

'I'll be back in an hour,' Mark says after he carries my cases into the bedroom. 'I'll text to let you know I'm outside.'

'It's been a pleasure meeting you, Mrs Saunders.' His use of my surname suggests he's placing an age barrier between us. Does he find it disturbing to know his girlfriend's mother is younger than him? He gives a slight bow in my direction. I almost expect him to click his heels.

'Thank you for collecting me from the airport, Mr Brewer.' I'm equally polite. 'I haven't seen Ali for many months so I'm sure you can appreciate why I want to spend more than an hour with her.'

'Oh, *Mum*.' Ali raises her voice in protest. 'Mark is extremely busy – '

'Then I'll organise a taxi for you or you can stay here for the night.'

'That won't be necessary.' His voice is smooth, assured. 'I've been selfish wanting her all to myself.' He places his hand under Ali's chin and casually kisses her. I know there's nothing casual about it. He's marking his territory, laying down his ground rules. 'Text me when you're ready, Alysia, no matter how late, and I'll pick you up.'

Alysia. When did I last hear that name? Probably at the baptismal font.

'What was all that about, Mum?' She rounds on me as soon as he leaves. 'You sounded so rude.'

'*Rude*. How could you let him dictate to you like that? What's going on between the two of you?'

'Love, that's what's going on.'

'You must be *joking*. He's as old as your father, if not older.'

'Since when has age anything to do with love?'

'He's married, Ali.'

'He's getting a divorce, *just* like you and Dad.' She marches across the room and swishes the curtains closed. 'A *perfect* divorce, *unlike* you and Dad.'

'Are you living with him?'

'Sort of.'

'What exactly does that mean?'

'I'm still living with Christine but we intend on moving in together as soon as possible.' She twitches a fold in the curtain then strokes it back into place. 'I don't appreciate this level of third -degree questioning. You don't know the first thing about Mark yet you're just as judgemental as Dad was. I hope you're not going to start interfering in my life.'

She looks as if she's about to stamp her foot. She was an expert on stamping by the age of two. Instead, she settles for a flurried shake of her head. 'The way Dad went on about *The Arboretum Affair* you'd think I was dancing around a pole instead of acting in an amazing play.'

The euphoria I felt as I disembarked at Heathrow is rapidly beginning to fade. 'I don't want to interfere in your life. And the last thing I want is an argument.'

She shrugs, slightly mollified. 'I don't want to fight either… but Mark is very important to me. I was beginning to lose hope until I joined Barnstormers. You've no idea what it's like out there. All those auditions. It'd be easier swimming with a school of piranhas. Mark's a wonderful director. I've learned more from him since I joined Barnstormers than all my years in drama school. And *The Arboretum Affair* has been so successful. He believes it will run for at least a year.'

'Why aren't you on stage tonight?'

'I changed my night off so that I could meet you.' She snuggles down on the sofa beside me. 'Tell me everything about your trip.'

'It was great to see Jenny again.'

'You said she's met someone. What's he like?'

'His name is Larry. He's her cameraman so they're well matched.' I tell her about this friendly Canadian who has made Jenny happy and how he proved to be an entertaining guide during the time I spent with her.

'And the twins? I'm dying to hear all about them.'

'They're in love with California. I can't see them ever coming back here.'

Samantha filled me in on their life plan before I left. After they graduate they'll run competitively until they stop winning gold. Then they'll study sport psychology and work with the next generation of elite athletes. I listened and marvelled at their confidence. How did they get to be so very certain of everything?

'What else can we be?' Samantha was surprised by my question. 'It's the strength of being a plural.'

I'm still filling Ali in on my hectic Californian holiday when her phone bleeps. She stands up and checks the window.

'It's Mark,' she says. 'He's outside.'

'He won't turn to dust if he has to wait an extra minute.'

She pulls on her jacket and zips it to the neck. 'He's thinking of moving to New York when his divorce comes through.'

'So… what are you saying?'

'He's asked me to go with him.'

'What do you want to do?'

'To be with him wherever he goes.'

I stand on the balcony and watch her running towards his car. The interior light switches on when she opens the passenger door. He leans across to greet her. Everything about him alarms me. If only I could take her in my arms and run with her to a safe place. Lock her in a tower and cut off her long black hair. But Ali has long outgrown my protective shadow. She's a young woman in love and if this man is not to my satisfaction that's my issue, not hers.

CHAPTER FORTY-FIVE

I enrol in The Bonnard Art Institute where I'll attend classes five mornings a week. I plan to rent a studio and paint in the evenings. London is vibrant after the silent grandeur of Alaska. Here, in the midst of clamour and crowds, I'm as anonymous as I was among the ice floes. Everyone is in such a hurry. Why are they rushing? To what? To where? Stuart's ashes float on icy tides and all that remains are memories and the generous legacy he left me.

The rental property market is a battle ground. Sky high prices and a queue of people all with their eyes on the same flat, maisonette, mews or bijou. I stay away from houses with bay windows and try not to think of Karin Moylan each time I pass those warmly-toned Victorian dwellings with their brightly painted doors. But the act of not thinking brings her more vividly to mind. I also ignore the tall white houses with their columned fronts that form such elegant terraces and can only be rented by millionaires. I've no interest in the detached luxurious homes that remind me of Bartizan Downs or the suburban semi's where Jake and I reared our family. One by one I'm shedding layers yet I still don't know where I want to live.

I check out a two-bed flat in Tower Hamlets. The second bedroom has good light and could work as a studio. I can turn it back into a bedroom when Ali or Brian visit. There's a lot of interest, the estate agent warns. She'll let me know when all the viewings are complete. I've three more viewings in the area this evening and an hour to kill before checking out the next one.

The café I enter is full. A woman looks up from the newspaper she's reading and gestures towards the empty seat at her table. Her face is large, dominated by a domed forehead and broad chin. I've almost finished my coffee when she stares at my right shoulder, her gaze suddenly unfocused.

'Cockatoos,' she says. 'Such beautiful birds.' Her eyes have a dark, almost black glitter. 'I can see them on your shoulder.'

I look down at the table. She seems harmless but direct eye contact is probably not a good idea.

'Sorry, love,' she says. 'I scared you. I do it all the time. But I see signs. When that happens I have to speak.'

I risk a glance around the café. Hopefully, help is at hand if she lunges at my throat.

'It's a curse as well as a blessing,' she admits. 'Sometimes it's wiser to ignore what I see but not this time. Your mother's passed but she's very happy and surrounded by cockatoos.'

Of all the birds, why is this stranger talking to me about cockatoos? For years after Sara died I imagined she was still alive. Distance made such an illusion possible. I used to visualise her in her garden with its layers of rock and bush, a flock of cockatoos on the garden fence. She could be on the beach, in the supermarket, barbecuing, relaxing in the hot tub, the swimming pool, the tennis courts… anywhere except buried in a quiet graveyard.

'I've upset you.' Her gaze is focused again, our eyes meeting. 'I'm sorry for intruding on your psychic space.'

'Are you a clairvoyant?' I ask.

I once went to one with Jenny. I was seventeen and feverishly in love with Jake. She told me I'd never marry and was not destined to have a family. A month later I was pregnant. So much for psychic intuition.

'I see myself more as an angel administrator,' this stranger replies.

An angel believer. These I've also met. They talk about floating feathers and the scent of roses perfuming the air and everybody... *everybody*... is happy in this celestial sphere these angel visionaries claim to infiltrate.

'I run the Not Seeing is Believing angel shop on Wharf Alley,' she adds.

'Wharf Alley? Where's that?'

'Have you heard of Container City?'

The name rings a bell. I saw a documentary about it once. 'Is it where shipping containers have been converted into homes?'

'Exactly.' She folds her newspaper and pushes it into an Asda plastic bag filled with groceries. 'Wharf Alley is similar but newer. You should come and see us. We're quite a diverse community.'

She pulls a woolly hat low over her forehead, slips her arms into a bulky anorak. Then she's gone, moving lightly across the café for such a heavy-set woman. She has left her business card on the table. Aurora Kent is her name. Perhaps it's the sound of her name that enchants me. Those Northern lights... that magic... the strength of Daveth's arms... or is it that flock of cockatoos hovering in the ether above me?

CHAPTER FORTY-SIX

Jake

The slapping noise awoke him. Once again, the bedroom shutter in Nadine's apartment had slipped free from its clasp. After breakfast he entered the apartment and secured it. The wood was rotten and needed to be replaced. Another job to add to his 'to do' list. On the landing he paused, suddenly uneasy. Something was different but he was unable to pinpoint it. He was halfway down the stairs when he stopped and returned to the landing. The long handle used for pulling down the attic staircase lay on the floor. The last time he used it was Christmas Day and he had left it leaning against the wall. Christmas had been a blur of loneliness, too much nostalgia and whiskey. How could he know with certainty where he left anything?

He hooked the handle into the trapdoor and pulled down the folding stairs. The naked bulb hanging from the rafters cast an eerie glow over the crates and black plastic sacks. One of Nadine's paintings lay on the floor. The hairs on his neck lifted when he picked it up. A study of fruit in a bowl, the canvas slashed diagonally in three places. He pulled other paintings free, each one destroyed in the same way. His skin was gritty with dust when he climbed down from the attic. He entered the bathroom and ran the cold water over his hands until his skin felt numb.

Nadine listened silently when he rang her. 'They could have been torn by a rat or a bird with sharp talons?' He tried to lessen the impact of what he had told her. 'We've no idea what kind of wildlife is running around up there.'

'How did she get into my apartment?' Her voice had flattened with certainty.

'How do you know it's – '

'Did you give her my key?'

'Of course not.'

'Then she must have taken a copy of the spare I gave you. Has she done anything else?' They had not once referred to Karin by name. 'Has she, Jake?' she demanded when he hesitated.

'Small things, moving stuff in my apartment.' He could not bear to tell her about the family photographs. The blank circles where her head was once visible. The damage to his van. The darkening rim around the image of children and their parents. Speaking such things aloud gave them substance. 'But I wasn't sure until now. Your canvases…that's the first concrete sign. I'd changed the locks on my apartment but I didn't realise she had a copy of your key. I'm reporting her to the police.'

'Do you honestly think they'll believe you?'

'Of course they'll believe – '

'You opened Sea Aster up to her and now her *sick* DNA is all over it.' Nadine ground out the words. 'Burn the paintings. I've no room in my life for contamination.'

The following morning he found a rusting tin barrel in the garden shed and dragged it to the bottom of the garden. The paintings burned easily, combustible materials quickly igniting. Afterwards he showered, the water running black with soot. The smell of flaming oils and chemicals remained in his nostrils for hours afterwards. Did DNA linger forever, he wondered.

Did it build a momentum, create its own venom; a blue aura incapable of being eradicated?

They met in a bar in the Italian Quarter. Karin was perched on a high stool when he arrived, a gin and tonic at her elbow, a pint of Budweiser already drawn for him. Instead of her signature colour she wore a short, black dress with pearls at her neck. Her lips, glossily purple, were darkly outlined.

A group of man entered behind him. Loud and ebullient, they had been to a rugby match and had obviously sipped from their hip flasks throughout the game. Conversation was impossible as they crowded around the bar. Jake lifted both glasses and carried them to a quiet alcove that had just been vacated.

'I was surprised to hear from you,' she said as soon as they were sitting down. 'I thought you never wanted to speak to me again.'

'Why are you stalking me?' He blurted out the accusation, embarrassed at how absurd it sounded but determined not to normalise their meeting.

'Stalking you?' She wrinkled her nose in amusement. 'I follow your band, Jake. I go to hear you sing. Since when has that been defined as "stalking"?'

'Are you denying you attended Ali's play?'

'Of course not. Why shouldn't I go to the West End when I'm in London?'

'Are you denying breaking into Sea Aster and destroying Nadine's paintings?'

'What are you talking about?'

'You know exactly what I mean. You slashed her paintings with a knife.'

She splashed tonic into the gin and drank from the long, slim glass before she spoke again. 'You told me to go, Jake. I gave you back your key. She had a separate key. How on earth could I enter her apartment, much less destroy paintings I never knew existed?'

'I don't believe you. Neither does Nadine. She knew it was you as soon as I told her what happened.'

'Really.' She drank again, crunched ice between her teeth. 'Nadine is the person you should talk to about blades. She's the expert. Are you that unobservant, Jake? How can you live with her for so long and not be aware that she was into self-harm? I use the past tense but it's a nasty addiction. She obviously hasn't outgrown it. Better a canvas than her wrists, I suppose. But blaming me for your wife's destructive actions is inexcusable.'

Nadine's wrists were unscarred that summer in Monsheelagh. Two years later, when they met again, he saw what she had done to herself. Her skin was still rippled but the healing had begun, she said. She told him about the slow erosion of self-confidence. The turning inwards towards self-hatred. She had been bullied, she said, shame written large on her face. How painful it must be to sink a blade into one's flesh, not once but many times, he had thought. He had been bullied for a while when he was twelve but he fought the boy responsible, bleeding his nose and closing one of his eyes. His own injuries were worse, a broken rib and a gash on his forehead where the boy struck him with a stone. They were both suspended for a week. The bullying never occurred again. Physical action was a male response. Girls, it seemed, suffered internally and created toxic wounds that never healed.

Her scars had disappeared or, perhaps, he had simply stopped noticing them. She never named the girl who had bullied her but it was obvious that Karin was responsible. He remembered what she had said the last time they were together. *She made my life hell. But she wasn't responsible for how I dealt with it. That was something I did all by myself.*

'I don't know what motivates you.' He was unable to take his eyes from the plum-coloured stain on the rim of Karin's glass. 'Is your crazy jealousy reserved just for me and Nadine or did you give the same treatment to the other unfortunate guys who walked out on you?'

'No one has ever walked out on me,' she replied. 'No one. As for jealousy… crazy or otherwise. Check the mote in your own eye. What do you think Nadine was doing when she was shacked up in Alaska with the boat guy?'

'If you don't stop – '

'Don't… *don't!*' Her sharp exclamation attracted attention and two women sitting at a nearby table glanced curiously across at them. 'Let me tell you about *don't*. You *don't* accuse me of being possessive when you've wanted to possess me from the first time we met. You *don't* take from me as you've done then shrug me aside like a piece of discarded junk.'

'We took from each other.'

'No.' Her expression hardened. 'You took. I gave.'

'I never asked – '

'You never had to. I knew what you wanted and I gave willingly.'

'What were you, Karin?' he demanded. 'A sacrifice?'

'I knew your mind, Jake. The violence within.' She tapped the side of her head. 'I loved you and so I was willing to indulge your rape fantasies. Who did you want to hurt when we were together? Was it your wife who walked out on you? Your dominatrix mother? Did you want to rip that body stocking from your sluttish daughter? Which of them were you thinking about when you fucked me?'

'*Stop.*' Buffeted by her fury he was filled with a sudden urge to put his hands on her throat, to squeeze until her demanding eyes dulled and closed. 'I refuse to continue this conversation.'

'You started this conversation but I intend to finish it.' She arched her head back and exposed her throat. The air was heavy with her scent. A miasma, cloying his nostrils. 'Go on, do it. I'm inside your mind, Jake. I know you better than you know yourself.'

She was mad, he realised. Not in the sense that he had always imagined madness to be, irrational, erratic, violent, dazed, helpless. This was something different, something controlled and hidden behind a thin veneer of normality.

'You're right, Karin,' he replied. 'That's exactly what I want to do. But, unlike you, I have the self-control to walk away and accept when a relationship like ours is over.'

'It's over when I say so.' She swayed towards him and marked his cheek with the same glossy smear that stained the glass. 'We've said things we'll both regret when we're apart. But we'll forgive each other in time… like all lovers do.' She rubbed the lipstick stain on her finger then licked it. The flick of her tongue, the glisten of saliva, those hot, sultry nights.

'We're not lovers,' he said. 'We never were. Whatever we had between us is finished. Don't come near me or my family again.'

Nothing moved in her face, no twitch or pout, even her eyelashes seemed suspended. She opened her handbag and removed her mobile phone.

'Remember the texts,' she said. 'New York calling. You promised to love me forever.' She held the phone in front of her. The selfie was taken before he realised what she was doing. She snapped her handbag closed and stood up. 'You should never have broken your promise.'

Men turned their heads to watch as her high heels clicked against the marble tiles, an arch of blue visible on the heel and sole of her shoe A Louboutin design, Nadine told him when he asked about that flash of red. He had laughed over what he had seen as a design absurdity but now, as Karin flaunted her signature colour, bile rose in his throat and soured his mouth.

CHAPTER FORTY-SEVEN

Nadine

Thanks to Stuart, I'm a woman with means. Ali and the twins can once again concentrate full time on their careers and Brian, my self-sufficient son… perhaps a new kiln. Our outstanding bank debts can be settled. Freedom, which I so avidly pursued, is mine at last. I can turn in any direction I like and walk towards a new future. But the shadows will come with me. No amount of money can cast a light on them. The only way they can be vanquished is to lose my memory and begin again… shriven.

The configuration of shipping containers – painted in bright, gaudy colours and erected on a once-disused London dockland site – look as if they could topple into the Thames on a high wind. But they are solidly balanced on supports with walkways, balconies, glass-fronted entrances and portholes cut into the steel that serve as windows.

Aurora is working in her angel shop. A week has passed since our meeting in the café but she's not surprised to see me. One of the advantages of being a psychic, I guess. She's a carver of angels, fluttery little creatures with serene expressions and translucent wings. All their accoutrements – blessings, pendants, chimes, crystals, incense and whatever it takes to make the days bearable – adorn the shelves but the angels are her own creation.

Her hands are large and red-rough yet dexterous when it comes to making delicate things. She locks the shop and introduces me to her neighbours. One woman runs a fashion design studio, another makes hats, there's a bearded poet, a sculpture and a silversmith. Most of them have a second container where they live. Before I leave I've arranged to rent one for my studio and a second one for my home.

I return to Aurora's angel shop to tell her we'll be neighbours. Before I realise what she's about to do she takes both my hands in hers. Heat runs along my arms when she touches my wrists with her broad fingers.

'Your mother is still a very strong presence,' she says. 'She asks me to tell you that the blade is blunt. You've healed.'

The blade is blunt... a clever guess. But Aurora's awareness is unsettling. She makes me think of things I'd rather ignore. I imagine Karin on the stairs of Sea Aster, climbing higher into the attic, touching our possessions, rummaging in bags and boxes, building a picture of the lives we discarded when we moved to Sea Aster. What else has she done? Jake hesitated when I asked and fobbed me off. He's not telling me the full truth. Do I want to know it? This is my chance to move on. To rebuild the house of cards that collapsed so savagely around us. My scars barely mar the surface of my skin but they are still capable of cutting open the artery of memory.

Karin Moylan always knew how to cut deep. The gift she gave me for my sixteenth birthday was wrapped in silver foil and emblazoned with red love hearts. A square box sitting on my desk with a tag attached. Impossible to miss when I entered the classroom. *To a kool babe on her 16th birthday. XXXX Annonimus Admiror* was written on the gift tag. The writing was unfamiliar, blocky misspelled letters. I looked across at Alan O'Neill. He'd told Jenny he liked me, had asked her to act as our go-between. His spelling was notorious. Could he have laid it on my desk? An open declaration of intent?

Our history teacher, Miss Gibson, or Gibby, as we called her, should have arrived in the class but there was no sign of her. The box was large and light. It made no sound when I rattled it. One of the girls who'd gathered around my desk asked to see what was inside. I wanted to take it to a private place but I was caught in the hub of their curiosity. Karin sitting two desks away, had removed herself from the speculation.

Quickly, before Gibby arrived, I ripped off the paper and lifted the lid. Another box was inside it, wrapped in a different layer of gilt paper. Then another box, like nesting Russian dolls they emerged from one another, each one neatly wrapped. The girls no longer believed it was a large basket from Bodyshop. Perhaps it was a pendant, earrings, maybe, they giggled, an engagement ring from my anonymous admirer. Alan O'Neill had joined the group. He seemed as curious as the others and my nervousness grew. I willed Gibby to arrive and scatter us. She was always punctual but the classroom door remained closed. The girls cheered each time another box was revealed. The last layer of paper was off, the tiny red box opened.

The blade glistened, silver sharp. A girl snorted with laughter, the sound magnified by the silence of those who stared from the blade to me, a slow realisation dawning. I dropped the box. The blade clinked when it hit the floor. Karin's head was bent, her face hidden. Her nails made a low sawing sound as she slid them along the desk. How could she have known? Long sleeves hid the plasters on my wrists, long socks covered my ankles.

This time I would not run from the classroom. I picked up the blade, placed it back in the red box and left it on my desk. I gathered up the wrapping papers, the discarded boxes, and pushed them into the litter basket. Gibby arrived, rushing late, accompanied by Vonnie Williams. I didn't need to read Vonnie's elated expression to understand why our history teacher had been delayed.

I left the school immediately after the last class ended and ran home through Gracehills Park. Jenny called to my house a short while later. I told my mother to send her away. Neither of them paid any attention to my frantic command. My door was locked but Jenny banged on it until I allowed her in.

'You're the only one who knew.' My pillow was damp with tears. 'I trusted you.'

'You know I wouldn't share spit with that bitch.' She forced me to sit up and face her. 'There's only one way you can deal with this.' She rolled up the sleeve of my blouse. Her breath hissed when she saw the most recent cuts. 'As long as you keep doing this she'll dominate you. Have you the courage to stop? I believe you have. Prove me right.'

Like the drawing on the blackboard, no one was held responsible but Karin's name was whispered along the class grapevine. Students began to ignore her. Vonnie Williams, aware that she might be isolated in the chilliness surrounding Karin, ended their friendship. I felt no pleasure as I watched Karin's growing isolation. I too was isolated, not by silence or by being ignored, but by the skinning of my most intimate secret. The victim and the bully, bound together by the one crime.

CHAPTER FORTY-EIGHT

On Friday I hire a van and drive to Pembroke where I take the ferry to Rosslare. It's a long drive to the Dingle peninsula and I'm anxious to see my son. It's late in the evening when I reach Slí na hAbhann. Brian discovered the craft centre when he was cycling through the peninsula with Peter Brennan two summers ago. That's when he decided to drop out of college and set up his pottery. I don't have a favourite child but Brian stirs something deep and emotional within me. Perhaps it's his single-minded creativity. I had it once when I was very young and, now, I hope to find it again. I park the van and make my way towards the courtyard.

Lights have been switched on in the workshops and studios. They twinkle from windows and speckle the dark depths of the mountain slopes. I hear the rush of the river that inspired the name Slí na hAbhann. It lies below us, a tumbling rush of water heading towards Dingle Bay. Brian is unaware that I've arrived. I watch him through the pottery window. He's glazing something, his attention concentrated on each meticulous stroke. He looks broader, more rugged. My son, the mountainy man. I won't cry, not now. Plenty of time for that later.

The glazing is done and I'm in his arms, swept up on the fervour of seeing him again. I admire his ceramic award and he proudly replaces it on a plinth. He shuts the pottery door and we walk the short distance to his cottage. Its sparseness used to worry me. I'd arrive with cushions and cutlery, lampshades, pictures, crockery, rugs, and bring them home again.

He prepared a casserole. It's been slow cooking for hours, he says, as he removes it from the oven. A wood burning stove warms the room. He opens the wine I brought with me and when we've eaten he shows me the video of the craft award ceremony. This is the full version, instead of the short video I'd seen of him walking to the stage for the presentation.

I see her at a table, a necklace of moonstones at her neck. Her smile is rapturous as she rises, hands high, and claps my son who stands, self-consciously, and holds up the award. She's sitting between Liam Brett and Jimmy French, one of the weaselling *Core* reporters. Jessica is there also, and Gina from Admin. But Karin Moylan is the only face I see.

I watch the video until the end. Brian clears the dishes from the table and then, almost as an afterthought, he says, 'You can expect a call from your friend Karin. She's hoping to link up with you over the weekend.'

The shock of her name on his lips freezes me. He's comfortable imparting this information, no guile or hidden inferences.

'How do you know Karin Moylan?' I ask.

I'm unsure if it's the glow from the stove or the wine or the charm she would have used to flatter and disarm my son but Brian looks decidedly flushed.

'She's been here twice. Bought something each time. She really likes my stuff.'

'When was she here last?'

'A few days ago. She says the two of you go way back.'

'We do. But she's not my friend.'

'Not your friend?' He stops, puzzled. 'Why would she lie about something like that? She knew all about Alaska and you and Dad splitting up. She was delighted when I told her you were coming back for the weekend.'

'She won't be ringing me, Brian. And if she does I'll hang up on her. I don't trust her and I don't want you to have anything more to do with her. Promise me you'll let me know if she comes here again.'

'I don't understand. How am I supposed to stop customers coming into my pottery?'

'She hates me for something that happened a long time ago.'
'Like what?'

'We fought over someone we loved. It hurts too much to go into details but you need to trust me on this one. Don't make her welcome here.'

He's not convinced. Our night together has turned sour. He wants more information than I'm prepared to divulge. How can I tell him the sordid truth? I want to contain my past, not brandish it like a fan that flicks over to reveal… what? No, I can't go there. I never will. Did she love Jake or did she use him as a settlement for a debt I'll never be able to repay? I feel a sudden and unexpected urge to protect him. He's playing with Shard in Donegal this weekend. That's why I've chosen this time to collect what I need from Sea Aster. It's easier this way. The bleakness in his voice when we talk reminds me of Ali's comment. Walking through quicksand. He keeps apologising for lying to me. He needs absolution. To ease the memory of his deceit in my forgiveness.

'I self-harmed when I was a teenager,' I tell Brian. 'I was going through a difficult time and I believed it was the only way I could cope with the pressure.'

It's hard to remember the person I was then. The fear and self-loathing that consumed me. Only for those faint scars, I'd never believe I'd touched such a destructive chord in myself.

'What kind of pressure?' he asks.

'Bullying. There were girls involved. Karin Moylan was one of them. The mind games she played almost destroyed me. Don't let her do the same to you.'

He looks shocked but also understanding when I tell him about the cuttings, the savage and painful path I took. I'll strip my soul if it stops him welcoming her into his life. I watched my children like a hawk during their teenage years for signs of insecurity, of stealth and secret hurts. But they are brash tiger cubs, open and unafraid to pursue their dreams. When I leave in the morning I can tell it's okay. Karin Moylan will no longer be welcome in Slí na hAbhann.

It's late in the afternoon when I reach Sea Aster. Winter has taken its toll on Mallard Cove. The van judders over potholes, the wheels skid on perished seaweed. I drive slowly, nervous in case I get a puncture. It's quiet on the estuary, too cold for the usual Saturday family excursions to feed the swans.

I unlock the front door of apartment 1 with the new key Jake posted to me. He collects my post every day and sends on what's important. The rest is junk mail which he's piled neatly on the hall table. A note from him lies on top. He left a bottle of wine and fresh food in my fridge.

I open windows and allow the breeze from the estuary to flow through the rooms. I heat the soup and make a pasta. The evening passes quickly. I need to pack even less than I thought. Coping in small spaces is habit-forming. My bedroom looks the same as I remember. But appearances are deceptive. Karin Moylan was here. I sense her presence. She trawled through my possessions before she climbed into the attic to destroy my paintings.

Jake has sorted out the clutter. Everything is packed and stacked, each container labelled, and ready to be stored in a warehouse until needed.

I sleep fitfully and awaken, my mind sharp with images of her smile as she flatters Brian, her hands caressing the sensuous glazes on the bowls and ceramic box she bought from him.

When morning arrives, I write a note to thank Jake for the food and wine. An envelope lies in the hall. I didn't notice it last night and post is not delivered on Sundays. My name and the Sea Aster address are printed on the front. There's no postmark. She had been here during the night.

I slide open the flap and draw out a photograph. They are together, her and Jake, staring cheek to cheek into the camera. It's a close-up selfie. Lipstick on Jake's cheek, his lob-sided grimace, as if he's been caught unaware. Her glistening, white smile. When was it taken? I find the answer on the bar receipt she stapled to the photograph.

I load the last of my possessions into the van. Before I leave I tear the photograph into small pieces and replace them in the envelope. I leave it where it belongs, on the hall table with the key and the junk mail. A jigsaw for Jake to solve.

The wind is brisk, the clouds scudding above the estuary. A lone windsurfer, rigid as an exclamation mark, shoots across the water. Canoeists in colourful safety jackets flash their paddles in rhythmic movements as they approach the shore. Alaska stripped the resin from my marriage, separated me from the glue of a shared life. When I drive from Sea Aster I know I'll never return.

Jake rings when I'm on the ferry. I see his name on the screen and turn off my phone. He's a liar who sleeps with the woman who slashed my paintings. Who, even now, all those years later, seeks to sink a blade into my flesh.

'Ring me back, Nadine.' He leaves a message on my answering machine. 'I need to talk to you immediately.' His tone is authoritative, not apologetic as I would have expected. Its urgency alarms me. I lean into the buffeting wind and ring him from the deck. He answers immediately. He's found the photograph, joined to dots, so to speak.

'Why didn't you let me know you received it?' he asks.

'Let you know what? That you lied about not seeing her again?'

'I didn't lie – '

'Are you telling me the camera never lies?'

'Of course the camera lies. It can orchestrate whatever it likes. Anything connected with her, no matter how slight it seems, you must talk to me.'

'She's been to Brian's pottery twice.'

'*Twice.*' His sharpness adds to my fear.

'Did you know?'

'I knew she was there once.'

'Why didn't you tell me?'

'I was trying to keep things under control.' His breath is hard, heavy.

'What else has she done? You must tell me everything, Jake.'

I hear about his discovery in her apartment, the pieces from our lives she assiduously assembled in my son's beautiful ceramic box.

'You've no idea how sorry I am…' he attempts another one of those hopeless apologies.

'That doesn't matter now.'

The ground is shifting, draining my bitterness away. Whatever has gone before is of no importance. Karin Moylan is spreading her spores through our family. Must I wait helplessly until she strikes again or confront her? The ferry churns the water, distancing us.

When I return to Wharf Alley I google her. Kingfisher Graphics. I ring her number and listen to her voice on the answering machine.

Hi there…thank you for calling Kingfisher Graphics. I'm still enjoying the weekend and am unable to talk to you right now.' Her laughter is dark, throaty. I imagine how Jake would have responded, charmed by its contagious inflections. '*Please leave your number and I'll ring you first thing in the morning.*

I hang up without speaking. Soon there will be a reckoning.

CHAPTER FORTY-NINE

Jake

Five musicians standing on a roof. Arms akimbo, folded, plunged in pockets or suggestively clasping a hipster belt. Brooding expressions. It was all there. The five members of Shard staring from the cover of *Core*. Jake bought the magazine in Malahide Village and entered a café. He had been opposed from the beginning to the band featuring in the magazine but Mik Abel had overrode his objections.

'It's free publicity,' he insisted when Jake argued that *Core* was a tabloid rag. 'They're interested in the band's progress. Otherwise they wouldn't have approached us. We can't afford to look a gift horse in the eye.'

'Mouth,' said Jake. 'You don't look a gift horse in the mouth but on this occasion we can.'

'No, we can't,' Mik replied. 'I'll look a gift horse in the arse if it gives the band free exposure. Your personal view of *Core* is not shared by its readership which is massive.'

Last week a photographer had arrived to Sea Aster astride a Harley Davidson and introduced herself as Lucky. She chose the barn as the backdrop location for the photo shoot. The weathered stone walls and deep-set windows would add an un-compromising grimness to the photographs, she believed, but then she changed her mind and ordered them up on the roof.

Jake felt ridiculous as he folded his arms and stared into the camera. He was getting too old for such posturing but Lucky refused to release them until she was satisfied she had achieved the perfect alignment.

Jimmy French, the journalist from *Core*, was a small, wiry man who studied Jake through raddled eyelids and asked a few basic questions about the band. His lack of interest was obvious as he twisted his shoe on the butt of a cigarette and drove away. He left Jake with an unsettling feeling that this was not going to end well.

Lucky's cover shot could not be faulted. The band looked menacing and rebellious, apart from Feral, who could usually brood on command but seemed dreamily preoccupied. He ordered an Americano and opened the magazine. His misgivings rushed to the fore when he turned the pages and saw the ominous headline. His unease turned into dismay as he read through the feature.

Son of Right-Wing Politician Revives Satanic Band

Those who hung out in the Baggot Inn or Toners in the mid-eighties will remember Jake Saunders and his band, Shard. Now reformed, Saunders had taken Shard back on the road again with their new album, Collapsing the Stone. The Shard line-up remains the same apart from one change. Instead of drummer Bad Boy Barry Balfe, who emigrated to Canada, Shard now has a female drummer. With this new addition they can no longer be called a 'boy band', a tag that also conflicts with the aging process of its members.

The younger Shard were often accused of performing Satanic rituals on stage and indoctrinating their young fans into devil worship through brainwashing lyrics. This added to their brief notoriety but the band broke up when Saunders married his then seventeen-year-old pregnant girlfriend.

Saunders is the son of Eleanor Saunders, the leader of First Affiliation. She was unavailable for comment when contacted by this reporter. She also refused to comment on her son's impending divorce. His wife, Nadine Saunders, is currently in London seeking the dissolution of their marriage. Yet she and her soon-to-be ex-husband attended last year's conference where Eleanor Saunders, in her keynote address, presented them as a perfect example of marital harmony. The conference was interrupted by a protest led by gay rights activist, Maggie Doyle, and her wife Feral Childe, drummer with Shard.

Politics and hypocrisy are inseparable. Like love and marriage they go together but an inside source within the party insists that the double standards displayed by the leader of First Affiliation will no longer be tolerated. A vote of confidence in her leadership is expected to be held shortly.

Jake's coffee was cold when he tasted it. His phone rang. It had to be Eleanor. If she had not already read the article she was sure to have heard about it. Shard's hyped publicity, the link between him and Eleanor that would be established, the threat to her position, she had known it would all come true. Sweat broke out on his forehead as he answered the phone but it was Mik Abel calling, apologetic and apoplectic.

'It's too late now.' Jake cut him off in mid-rant. 'I need to go and see my mother… try to explain.'

He was driving along the Howth Road when his phone rang again. This time it had to be Eleanor. He let it ring. Better a face-to-face confrontation than a blow-up over the phone. The ringing stopped then started again. On the third call he pulled into the side of the road and checked his ID screen. The three calls were from an unfamiliar number and added to his anxiety as he rang the caller back.

'Jake, is that you?' The voice was high-pitched, shaky but vaguely familiar.

'Who is this?'

'It's Cora. I'm with Eleanor. We're waiting for the ambulance.'

'What's wrong. Is she – '

'She's going to be fine, Jake. But you need to go directly to the Mater Hospital.'

'I'm nearly at her house. I was coming to see her.'

'Okay… but hurry. I'm expecting the ambulance any minute.'

'What's happened to her?'

'It's just a little turn.' Cora failed miserably to sound unconcerned. His mother must be listening. Jake switched on the ignition and was about to pull into the traffic when he heard the siren. An ambulance raced by on the outside. His heart raced with it as he gave chase.

Eleanor was being carried out on a stretcher when he arrived at the bungalow. On this occasion she made no effort to pull off her oxygen mask. Nor was she shooting impatient orders at the paramedics. Her fine, black eyebrows, those arrogant, intimidating arches, had collapsed in a slack, downwards slide. Her mouth was pulled to one side. Jake had seen enough television advertisements to recognise the signs of a stroke.

In the ambulance he held her hand. She was still conscious but he had no idea of her awareness. Her words were slurred and indecipherable when the female paramedic asked her name.

'You're doing real good, Eleanor.' She adjusted the oxygen mask and took Eleanor's pulse. 'We're nearly at the hospital. There's an expert team waiting to look after you. You'll be in excellent hands.'

At the hospital she was immediately whisked into intensive care. Cora, who had followed in her car, joined Jake in the waiting room and told him what he had already guessed. Eleanor had read the feature in *Core* shortly before Lorna Mason phoned to inform her that a vote of confidence was being organised as soon as possible.

'I drove over to her as soon as I heard.' Cora's cheeks quivered as she pulled her handkerchief from her sleeve and sobbed into it.

'I'm glad you were there.' Jake put his arm around her and waited until she was able to speak again.

'She kept saying the story had legs but she seemed okay after Lorna called. You know Eleanor... she loves a fight. But then she suddenly collapsed. I thought she was going to die right there in front of me.'

'Thanks to you she arrived here on time for them to give her that clot busting drug. It's going to make all the difference to her recovery.' He felt queasy, shivery. 'She's lucky you were there with her.'

'Lorna Mason and her lot have had it in for Eleanor since she changed her mind about Sea Aster. They were just looking for an excuse to attack her.'

'What change of mind?'

'The planning permission.' Cora looked at him in surprise. 'Didn't she tell you?'

'Tell me what?'

'That she changed her mind after it was granted. Oh, dear, I shouldn't have said anything – '

'When did this happen?'

'As soon as you and Nadine moved into Sea Aster. I was the only one she told about your marriage. She kept hoping...' She dabbed her eyes, squeezed her handkerchief into her fist. 'Poor Eleanor. She'll have to resign. What will she do without the party?'

'Let's get her better first. We'll worry about the party later.'

Three tabloid journalists rang. They wanted information on the various angles covered in *Core*, particularly on the Satanic aspects of Shard. Eleanor was right. The story had as many legs as a centipede. He gave them Mik's number. Let him use his publicity skills to kill it.

Cora was running rosary beads through her fingers when he went outside to ring Nadine. Her shock reverberated back at him. 'I'll organise a flight and be with you as soon as I can,' she said. 'Had she been unwell? Were there any signs?'

'I'm responsible.'

'Why... what happened?'

'A stupid magazine feature about the band. All that Satanic nonsense was dragged up again.'

'But why? That's ancient history.'

'We were mentioned, you and I... our marriage break-up and that conference Eleanor organised.'

'Oh, Christ... poor Eleanor.'

'It's typical *Core.*'

A young girl in a wheelchair almost knocked him over as she pushed past him.

'Fuck off outa da way,' she growled, her eyes lost in the fug of drugs.

'Did you say *Core*?' Nadine asked.

'Yes. I *told* Mik – '

'Who wrote it?'

'Jimmy French. I should have followed my gut instinct and refused to have anything to do with it.'

'Stop beating yourself up. *Core* thrives on that kind of sensationalism. Liam Brett is a creep and Jimmy French is cut from the same cloth.'

'Liam Brett? I thought he was the editor of *Lustrous*.'

'He edits both magazines.'

'I see…'

'What is it?' Her voice quickened.

'Nothing.'

'Don't fob me off, Jake. Has *she* anything to do with this?'

'I don't know… it's possible.'

'We'll talk about all that when I see you,' said Nadine. 'Go back to Eleanor. She's all that matters for the time being. I'll be with you as soon as possible.'

'I'll be waiting for you.'

CHAPTER FIFTY

Nadine

Tears roll down Eleanor's cheeks when she sees me. Her mouth moves but she's unable to speak. She's silent for the first time since I've known her. Helpless, silent and scared, my poor, bewildered mother-in-law has suffered an ischemic stroke. Hopefully, there'll be no lasting damage but looking at her lying there it's hard to equate her with the woman she was. I want her back: whole, healthy, bossy and insufferable. She's a warrior and that determination will bring her through. I tell her this as I sit beside her bed. The need for Jake to be on standby in case of a crisis has passed but I'm only allowed a brief time with her. I'm not sure she recognises me or, if she does, how quickly she will forget me when I leave.

He met me at the airport. He was exhausted, older looking, his hair greying. When did that happen? He opened his arms to me. I ran towards him and we hugged like old friends, not lovers, but it was good to feel his familiar embrace. He'd parked the Shard band wagon on the roof of the car park. I noticed the logo. Designed by Feral's wife, he said. It lacks the eye-catching power of the previous one but neither of us make mention of this fact.

'How long will you stay?' he asks when we leave the hospital.

'Until Sunday.'

'I appreciate that.'

We are once again on the bridge, holding our breath in case it cracks beneath us.

We stop to shop in The Pavilions. This is the first time we've shopped together since we moved into Sea Aster. But we're not really together, as our separate shopping trollies signify. We head off in different directions but keep meeting in the same aisles, exchanging strained smiles and making a 'fancy seeing you here' jokes. We queue together at the check-out. I take sneak peeks into his trolley to check if his taste buds have changed. The contents look familiar, the usual staples. Nothing that suggests his appetite has been influenced by her. Karin. My teeth clamp on her name but we never speak it. *She* or *her*, that's our reference point.

When we return to Sea Aster I read the feature in *Core*. I remember Jimmy French. Weasel eyes and fingers stained with nicotine. He was a cypher for this sensationalist piece of journalism, nothing more than that.

Jake makes our evening meal and talks throughout. This loquaciousness is new. It worries me. He never talked for talking's sake, and, now, he skirts around the main subject. He drinks too much wine and it allows him to finally show me the drawings she did for First Affiliation.

When I was seven months pregnant on the twins I went into premature labour. The urge to save them was the most primal emotion I've ever experienced. They were born after an emergency caesarean section and, afterwards, looking at them in their incubators, I was filled with the same joy and unconditional love I experienced when Ali and Brian had been laid in my arms. That same protective love surges over me when I pick up my phone and ring Karin Moylan.

She doesn't seem surprised to hear my voice. Has she been waiting for this moment, knowing we'd face each other sooner or later? She suggests we meet tomorrow and take afternoon tea in the Westbury Hotel. What a novel idea. Business affairs are sorted out over lunch. Affairs of the heart belong to candle-lit dinners but afternoon tea is a civilized ritual and, so, we will behave accordingly. But I'm a lioness whose cubs have been threatened and civility is a luxury I can't afford.

Elegant armchairs are arranged around tables laden with tiered cake stands and plates of finger sandwiches. She's seated when I arrive, her legs crossed, her hands joined and resting on the white tablecloth. Demure is a word that comes to mind until I look into her eyes and see the glitter. It's hatred, disguised under a cataract of guile. But I recognise it, embrace it. The past does not heal. That's the cruellest myth of all. It lies in abeyance until time pulls the trigger on memory. *Three six nine, the goose drank wine...* the words beat a rhythm in my brain. I remember us kneeling on my bed, hands clapping, challenging each other to be the first to miss the beat... our hands moving faster, faster... frantic and furious like the beat of my heart. I resist the urge to run and sit down opposite her in a soft armchair. My neck is damp and the flush that rushes to my face is, I hope, invisible behind the layer of makeup I applied before I left Sea Aster.

'I've already ordered,' she says. 'I hope you don't mind. I've an appointment in an hour.'

As if on cue a waiter arrives with the afternoon tea selection. The clinking of cups and plates makes conversation impossible for the next few moments. Jake has told me about the van. My teeth water as I imagine the gouging she did with her dainty hands. I hear the screech of a knife on metal, the hiss of tyres imploding. Here, in this muted atmosphere where footsteps are silenced on thick carpets and conversations murmur, I want to scream and shatter the illusion that we are having coffee and a catch-up chat about old times.

'How is Eleanor?' she asks when the waiter departs. 'I heard about her stroke on the news.' She pours tea but does not attempt to fill my cup. I do likewise.

'She's making good progress.'

We both choose a sandwich from the selection. The thought of eating makes my stomach churn but I will play this game to its final move.

'I'm relieved to hear it,' she says and sinks her teeth into tuna and sweetcorn.

'I'm sure you *are* relieved,' I reply. 'It would be a heavy burden to carry if you were responsible for her death.'

She finishes the sandwich and dabs her mouth with a white linen napkin.

'Her death?' she says. 'What exactly are you suggesting?' Her head tilts, inquisitively, and her expression implies that what I have to say is of the utmost importance.

'I'm not suggesting anything. I'm stating facts. You gave that information about Jake to Jimmy French, either directly or through Liam Brett. You've had your revenge and Eleanor almost died because of it. Jake has told me everything. This has to stop *now*.'

The bracelet on her wrist slides forward as she takes an éclair from the cake stand. She bites daintily into the pastry, no crumbs or splodges of cream on her lips. She could always eat with style, nothing dribbling on her chin as she nibbled sandwiches oozing with mayonnaise and tomatoes on Monsheelagh Bay.

'I've read that article.' She lays the half-eaten éclair on the plate. 'Did Jimmy French write one word that was untrue? Your mother-in-law believes in perception. No wonder she collapsed when she was forced to confront the truth.'

Her composure is intact, her legs crossed at the ankles. She takes another bite of the éclair, her throat hollowing as she swallows. 'You've just made an appalling accusation with absolutely no foundation. Jake told me you were neurotic and I believed him. Not because he said it, men always blame neuroticism when their wives step out of line, but because I saw it at first hand when you were young. It seems that nothing has changed.'

I'm afraid to reach for a cake in case my hands tremble and, so, I link my fingers and rest them on my lap. 'If you attempt to contact any member of my family again I'll —'

'*Your* family?' For an instant I think she will lose her composure. An image of glass shattering comes to mind but she smiles, as if amused by a joke she's no intention of sharing.

'What about *my* family?' she asks. 'Did you think I'd forgotten?' She places the half-eaten éclair on the side plate. Her teeth have made indents in the soft choux pastry and she now intends to savage me. 'You were responsible for everything that happened on that holiday.'

Jake said she's mad and I believe him. Mad with revenge and imagined lesions.

'How could I possibly have had anything to do with… with…' After all those years I still can't bring myself to speak his name.

'Max,' she says. 'Your lover.' She lifts her handbag from the floor and snaps it open. 'We all have our own versions of the truth, Nadine.' She flings an envelope on the table. It's small, letter-sized, no address. She stands and brushes imaginary crumbs from her skirt. 'Don't ever threaten me again with groundless accusations. A betrayed wife is pathetic but one with a history like yours has even less credibility. Go to the police if you want to make a fool of yourself. I fucked your husband senseless and you could charge me with that. However, last time I checked, adultery was not a criminal offence in the statute books.'

Her words rebound off me. They are visceral and should hurt but all I feel is fear. I open the envelope after she leaves and draw out a photocopied sheet of paper. I see the replication of the original, the dark squiggle of the serrated spiral-bound journal I once used to spill out my heart. I should flitter it, allow it to be swept away with the remnants of bread and half-eaten cakes but I read it, knowing, as I do so, that the contents will bring me face-to-face with my fifteen-year-old self.

Dear Max

This is the first love letter I've ever written. It will never be seen by anyone but me. I'd die, simply die a million deaths if Karin found out or Joan or you... God! That would be so embarrassing. I'm all mixed up and so excited. Like I'm on a swing swooping high and low.

The words blur. I can't read any more. The waiter hesitates then removes Karin's cup and saucer. The stain on the rim of her cup matches the lipstick stain she imprinted on Jake's cheek. She stole my love letters, searched my room in Cowrie Cottage, my clothing, my books, my backpack, searched every corner until she found them pushed deep into the lining of my anorak. What possessed me to write such reckless letters? I try and connect with the teenager I once was. So beguiled and naïve, so utterly self-absorbed, a sylph transiently innocent and dangerous with it. Yes, I've seen Ali's play. A satirical tale of good against evil. The eternal struggle.

She still has the original. I stare out the window and count the pedestrians passing below. I note the clothes they wear, and how a man on crutches, his leg in plaster, stops to light a cigarette. Finally, she appears, striding briskly towards Grafton Street. The wind tosses her scarf, blue, of course, and fluttering like a pennant in the midst of a battle charge.

When all evidence of her presence at the table has been removed I order a fresh pot of tea and continue reading. My handwriting slanted to the right in those days. I tended to add flourishes to the letters at the end of my words, and a small circle, rather than a dot, over my 'I's.

This morning you watched me on Monsheelagh Bay. Just you and me alone on the beach. We saw the dawn rise. I wasn't in love with you then. Just kind of embarrassed and unable to think of things to say. You were sitting on the rocks. I had to walk past you. You were still Karin's father then. The air smelled briny and there was a haze on the sea. I was going to sketch the kittiwakes. I'd seen them from the bedroom window flying against the cliff.

What's this, you said when you saw me. You pretended to be surprised. 'I thought it was a teenage rule never to rise before noon when you're on holidays.'

I told you I always walk early and you said, 'Then walk on, Nadine. It's a beautiful morning. Make the most of it.'

I went far along the strand but I could still see you sitting there when I looked back. Were you watching me too? I didn't understand why that should matter, not then. I sat on the sand. The kittiwakes were going crazy like dive bombers. I did lots of sketches. The haze was gone from the sea and the tide was way out. I pulled off my sandals on the way back and the wet sand squished between my toes. I walked really slow to give you a chance to go back to the cottage if you didn't want to talk to me.

'You must be famished', you said when I reached you. 'How does scrambled eggs and mushrooms sound?

'Delicious', I said. It was true. I was absolutely starving.

'Then let's go'. You jumped down from the rocks and climbed ahead of me up the cliff path.

You were frying mushrooms in butter and I was scrambling the eggs when I fell in love with you. Just like that. God! I never knew that's how it happened. Then Karin came into the kitchen and spoiled everything. She's so small yet its like she fills the place when she's in a mood. Its always... always about her. Being her friend is exhausting! I knew I was in trouble when she looked at the table. You'd only set it for 2. When she saw the sand we'd tracked across the floor her eyes went really narrow. You didn't notice.

'Set another place, Nadine', you said. 'Scrambled eggs for 3 coming up'.

I was going to tell her how I'd only gone to the beach to sketch the birds but you said, 'We saw the dawn together. You could have been with us if you weren't such a lazybones in the mornings'.

You were only teasing her but you've no idea what she's like when she gets into a sulk.

'Look at the mess you made'. She grabbed the brush and started sweeping the sand and stirring all the dust.

You tossed the mushrooms onto a plate and put it on the table. The toast popped and the eggs were ready. But she said she wasn't hungry. Her bottom lip went out the way it does when she's mad. You took the sweeping brush from her and stopped her going back to her bedroom. It was like she was a bird when you lifted her up in the air and carried her over to the table.

'I want to have breakfast with my special girl,' you said. 'So sit down and keep your old man company. I want to know about everything you've been doing since I went away.'

She was really nice at breakfast but she came into my bedroom afterwards and accused me of monopolising you last night and this morning. You'd think I'd planned to meet you deliberately when you were so late coming here.

Were you watching me on the beach? Or were you thinking of Joan and how drunk she was last night. Living with her must be really hard.

I think I'm going crazy. Max.

Is this what love is like?

Nadine XXXXXX

CHAPTER FIFTY-ONE

Jake

Eleanor was moved from the high dependency unit into a private ward. She cried easily and fell asleep in the middle of conversations. All perfectly normal, her specialist assured Jake. Her recovery process was gradual but consistent. Cora was the only member of First Affiliation allowed to visit her. She would move in with Eleanor when she was discharged and look after her. Eleanor's acceptance that she needed care amazed Jake. He waited for the return of her old assertiveness but she remained serene, even when she heard that Lorna Mason had been elected leader of First Affiliation.

Her tears fell when she saw Ali, who had flown home on an overnight trip. Three weeks had passed since her stroke and she was struggling determinedly through the painful rehabilitation sessions. Ali pulled tissues from the box on the bedside locker and gently dabbed her eyes.

'It's my first chance to come and see you, Gran,' she said. 'But Mum's been keeping me up to date on everything.'

'Is she in a…a….*tin*?' Her inability to remember words would improve, Jake had been told.

'A tin?' Ali glanced enquiringly at Jake.

'The shipping container,' he said.

He was unable to banish an image of corrugated steel walls and condensation but Ali assured him Nadine's new home was extremely comfortable.

'It's actually quite a cosy tin,' said Ali and grinned when Eleanor snorted. 'I'll bring you to see it when you're better. You'll have to come to my play, as well. I'll organise the best seat in the theatre for you and Cora.'

Such an event would probably precipitate another stroke, Jake thought, but wisely stayed silent. He would never come to terms with *The Arboretum Affair*. To his amazement the play was still running and had received favourable reviews. Critics could write what they liked about the protest language of movement but it was not their daughter on stage protesting in a body stocking.

'I'm meeting Peter Brennan for a meal,' Ali said when they left the hospital. 'Why not join us? You look like you could do with some cheering up.'

'I'll only be in the way.'

'Oh, for goodness sake, Dad, it's just Peter. It's not a date. He won't mind.'

'You married him once.'

'I was five at the time.' She grinned. 'Grounds for an annulment, don't you think.'

Their wedding had been held in Brennan's garden shed with Brian, wrapped in a bath towel, solemnly performing the ceremony. Afterwards, Ali admitted she had only accepted Peter's proposal so that she could wear her princess dress. Jake wished they were still in love. Boy next door and happy ever after. Jake sighed. He and Nadine had had conversations about Mark Brewer. Initially, Jake thought the idea too preposterous to even consider. But Nadine assured him it was a serious relationship that was bound to break Ali's heart.

A slight shadow of disappointment crossed Peter's face when he saw Jake. Ali was oblivious of it. She ordered chicken masala and ate about three spoonfuls. She drank only iced water. She was probably developing an eating disorder as well as exposing her heart to a man who was going to destroy it, Jake reflected gloomily.

'Sylph-responsibility,' she said. 'It never stops.'

Peter said she must forget all about sylph-responsibility or any other kind of responsibility when they met in London. He was flying over for his friend's birthday party in July and planned to spend a day with Ali.

'Can you believe it? He's celebrating his *twenty-fifth* birthday?' He splayed his hands in amazement and laughed when Jake suggested a Zimmer frame would an appropriate birthday present.

Age and its relentless passage... was he crazy trying to relive his youth through Shard? Was it his love of music or, as Ali believed, a mid-life crisis that had him posturing on a roof? He expressed this thought aloud but, to his surprise, both Ali and Peter disagreed. Peter said *Collapsing the Stone* was one of the strongest musical statements to come out of the recession.

He felt his mood lift. In a fortnight's time he was heading to the UK with Shard on their first tour abroad. The venues were small, mainly clubs and pubs but Mik Abel had promised more high profile venues the next time.

Eleanor was home from hospital and in the care of Cora when Jake drove the band members onto the ferry at Larne. Karin's text arrived as he was about to go on stage in Glasgow. The eagerness with which he once received them had been replaced by dread. Not that there was anything threatening about her texts. Nothing he could hand to the police and claim he was being harassed. He looked out on a mass of indistinguishable faces and was unable to see her anywhere. Another text wishing him luck came before the Carlisle gig. *Break a leg*, she texted before he want on stage in Newcastle. They stopped when he changed his phone number in Leeds.

The days passed in a blur of motorways and fleeting glimpses of cities before driving on to their next destination. London with their final gig. Dee Street on the Kings Road was small – Reedy compared it to a dog kennel with strobes – but it had hidden crannies and long passages at the back of the building that soon filled with young people. Jake heard Irish accents, the new diaspora had turned out in force to hear them. Ali had rung with apologies. Sylph-duty. Jake knew better than to protest or, as she would claim, lay a guilt trip on her.

Nadine arrived about an hour after the gig started. She looked slim and leggy in jeans and ankle boots, her hair more tousled than he remembered, its coppery sheen enhanced by the spotlights. She stopped in front of the stage to acknowledge him then disappeared with a glass of wine into an alcove. The heat in the club was intense. He gulped water and wiped perspiration from his neck, relieved when it was time for a break.

A tray of drinks had been set up at the bar for the band. Still water for Hart and for Feral, who, much to the band's astonishment, had recently announced that she was pregnant. There was also Guinness for Daryl, a shandy for Reedy and a pint of Budweiser for Jake.

'Thanks for the drinks.' He sat beside Nadine and took a long swig of beer. 'I needed that.'

He had a sudden urge to lift the weight of hair from her shoulders and press his lips against her neck. Was she still in touch with Daveth Carew? Her life was a mystery to him and he realised, painfully, that he would never have a chance to unravel it. Why now, he thought, when it was too late for old passions to flare and they had squandered what they once shared.

'Don't thank me,' she said. 'I didn't order it. How's the tour going?'

'Oh, you know… it's a start. The lads are happy enough.'

'Shard sound amazing. It's a really tight sound. I love the harmonies.'

'Thanks.'

'I read about Feral on Facebook.'

'Ah, yes.'

'Any idea how… who?'

'No. Nor have I any intention of asking. All I know is she and Maggie are thrilled.'

'I must congratulate her.' She walked over to Feral, who was talking to Reedy at the bar, and hugged her. Daryl rushed over to greet Nadine and show her the latest video of Jasmine tottering in her mother's high heels. The band break was short. Soon they would be back on stage. By the time Nadine returned to the table they only had time for a brief conversation.

'Have you heard anything from her since you changed your number?' she asked and twisted a tendril of hair around her index finger.

'Nothing.'

Reedy entered the alcove. 'Time to go back on stage, Jake.'

'I'm heading off now.' Nadine also stood. 'I've an early start in the morning.'

'I was hoping you'd stay until the end.' He touched her arm. 'We'll be finished in another hour. We could go somewhere afterwards, have a bite to eat.'

'She's the only thing on our minds. I refuse to give her that space.'

'Talking about her is the last thing I want to do. Please, Nadine, stay.'

'All right.' She shrugged. 'Go on. I'll be here when you finish.'

He was singing 'Fly by Night' when the green and purple lasers slashed into blue. Could he have imagined that glimpse of Karin Moylan within the mass of distorted limbs and lurid faces raised towards the stage? He forgot the words. Daryl shot a sideways glance at him and sang the lead line until Jake recovered. The energy had gone from the song. He could see her clearly now. Her glittery dress sparked off the lasers and gave it the appearance of armour. She danced hard, hands high, her eyes as bold and compelling as he remembered. He looked beyond her to Nadine. She too had seen Karin. Jolted by her anger the dancers parted before her then closed ranks as she headed towards the exit. Karin Moylan had also disappeared. Was she a chameleon, capable of blending into her surroundings, shadowy and insubstantial until she decided to step into the spotlight.

He rang Nadine as soon as he came off stage. Her phone went immediately to message.

The barman had a second tray of drinks waiting on the counter. 'For the band,' he said. 'Left for you with the compliments of a dedicated fan.'

'Get rid of them.' Jake longed to upend the tray, smash the glasses against the wall. He ordered a shot, knocked it back and ordered another. A new band came on stage, three teenagers, younger than the twins. His phone bleeped. A text arrived.

Brilliant performance, Jake. Tell Shard they rocked tonight. Always yours, Karin.

CHAPTER FIFTY-TWO

Nadine

I'd spent the afternoon and evening in the Bonnard library and gone directly to Dee Street. Now I'm standing on Aurora's walkway, glittering with rage. A light is on in her window. She claims she only needs four hours sleep and her light, always the last to go off at night, is like the beacon in Wharf Alley. As usual, she doesn't look surprised to see me, even though it's after midnight.

'Bless you, duck, come in,' she says. 'Sit down and I'll make you a cuppa. Not a good night, then?'

'Not a good night,' I agree. Aurora doesn't need psychic intelligence to gauge my mood.

She clears a choir of angels from an armchair. These hand-carved angels take up all available space. The other kind, the metaphysical ones that hover in the ether are easier to manage, space-wise, that is.

I ask if she saw anyone on my walkway today. It's visible from her angel shop. Blonde and petite, an elfin haircut – the quiff has disappeared. Did anyone answering that description call into her shop to seek the power of an angel? One of the fallen ones, the damned?

Did the letter I found in my post box when I returned arrive by courier or was she here in person, peering through my porthole windows? Same white envelope, no address, no postage stamp. Just my name printed large on the front. Aurora shakes her head. She only had a handful of customers all day and none answer my description.

I bid her goodnight and return home. My container is warm and enclosed but it no longer feels safe. I should tear this letter and scatter it into the fast-flowing Thames. That would be a victory but, instead, I slip it under my pillow. Tomorrow, when I'm calmer I'll read it.

I can't sleep. I'm heading off with my fellow students in the morning. We're leaving before London stirs. Not that the city ever sleeps but before the surge begins. 'Time' is the theme of our latest project and Big Ben is our starting off point. Cameras will click and pencils scrape across sketch pads as the notes of a new day ring out. We've been told that a stack of old coins are balanced on Big Ben's pendulum to keep the minutes ticking. If only it was so simple to balance those moments from our yesterdays? The decisive ones that become weighted down by desire and change everything.

I take the letter from its envelope. I make a pot of tea and wrap myself in a rug. Outside, the wind from the Thames rattles the walkways. Jake rings. I switch off my phone and begin to read.

Dear Max

Today was awful and wonderful. I can't decide if it was more wonderful than awful or the other way round. The awful bit was fighting with Karin. She's still annoyed over Jake. She's a mean, sulky bitch. Like today on the beach when she said I looked like a big red beetroot. When she says things like that I hate her

I'm sorry Max but I do. I hate her because saying it makes it real and thats how I felt until Jake lay down on the rug beside me and asked if I'd go for a walk with him.

I didn't want to go. But I went so you'd see how grown up I am. We walked to the rocks. He brought me into this little cave. It smelled disgusting from all the seaweed but the sand was dry and hard under us. I know thats where he brought Polka Dot Bum and maybe others too. His kisses were rough but not so bad. My face was flushed when we came back. Did you notice? Karin certainly did. She called me a prostitute. Thats one of her worst insults but not as bad as being told I look like a big red beetroot.

I was going to ring my mum and ask her to collect me but Joan started fighting with you about the nomads and going away to the desert. She gets mad for no reason and there's all this tension when we're eating dinner and pretending not to notice how much she's drinking. I was still determined to ring my mum first thing tomorrow and then tonight happened.

I'm glad I woke up when I did. The night was so hot I couldn't go back to sleep. It was midnight and I thought everyone was in bed. I went outside in my pjs and sat on the bench. It was so quiet, no kittiwakes shrieking and only the waves splashing off the rocks. The stars were bright like diamonds. I never see them like that at home.

I heard the garden gate open and slap closed. I figured it was you. Who else would be walking all alone on the beach in the moonlight? You were like a ghost coming out of the dark in your white T-shirt and khaki shorts. I should have run back into the house but I didn't. The bench creaked when you sat beside me.

'It's warm tonight', you said. 'Not even a breath of air on the waves.'

My arm felt tingly against yours. Only two people can sit on the bench and we were sooo close. I was glad it was dark and you couldn't see my face. It was as red as anything. Red as a beetroot! You asked if I'd been going out with Jake for long. Only since the holidays, I said. But we're not going out. Not really.

I told you Karin likes him better and that she thinks I'm trying to take him from her.

You said I mustn't pay attention when she gets angry. She's upset because you're going away again.

She really misses you when you're gone. Loads. She's going to travel with you when she's eighteen and help with your books.

You gave me a hug. I thought my heart would leap out of my chest. You let me go but you kept your arm along the back of the seat. I could have put my head on it if I leaned back. Did you want me to do that? Karin said men send signals. I don't know what they are.

Goodnight Max. I can't wait to see you in the morning. I love you so much.

XXXXXXXXXXXXXXXXX

CHAPTER FIFTY-THREE

Jake

The solid construction of shipping containers amazed him. Wharf Alley was a community of homes, a café and diner, some shops, craft studios, a theatre and an art gallery. A network of steel steps and walkways led to the various doorways and a lift, also constructed from a shipping container, gave access to the higher levels. He rang Nadine's bell. No one answered. He peered in though one of the portholes and saw the corner of a sink, an easel, shelves stacked with paints and bottles of spirits.

'You should have phoned Mum first,' Ali said when he rang. She sounded terse, anxious to end the call.

'She's not picking up. Have you any idea where she might be?'

'I've absolutely no idea.'

'Are you okay?'

'I'm fine.'

'Did you have a row with your boyfriend?'

'*Dad.* I stopped answering those questions ten years ago. Goodbye.'

Jake shoved his phone into his pocket and stood, undecided. He checked his watch. Where could Nadine be at ten o'clock on a Saturday morning? Could anything have happened to her on her way home last night? He gripped the balcony rail. Madness. Karin Moylan was malicious but to imagine her stepping from the shadows with a knife was ludicrous. But she had used one on his van… and also on Nadine's paintings.

A heavily-built women emerged from one of the containers. She had an unfortunate face, her eyes, nose and mouth too closely aligned, an ample chin and forehead. Her long skirt brushed the walkway as she came towards him.

'Can I help you?' she asked.

'I'm looking for Nadine Saunders.'

'Do you mean Nadine Keogh?'

'I guess I do.' His startled laugh rang hollow. 'Any idea where she is?'

'She went out early.'

'On her own?'

The woman pulled the edges of her cardigan over her breasts and narrowed her eyes. 'Is that an appropriate question to ask?'

'I'm her husband.'

'Her husband…' She seemed taken aback. 'I didn't realise…'

'I just want to know if she's okay.'

'She on a project with a group from her college. A mini-bus picked her up. I'm Aurora Kent, a friend of hers.'

'Any idea when she'll be home?' Jake loosened his grip on the railing.

'She left very early so it could be soon. Would you like a cuppa while you're waiting?'

He was surprised by the spaciousness of her container with its insulated walls and wooden floor. Angels stood, lay or stretched on shelves, pensive, meditative expressions, gossamer wings shimmering. The real ones were surrounding him, Aurora claimed, and working hard to heal his troubled aura. He asked if his aura was blue.

'Light brown.' She peered intently at him. 'Are you confused about anything? Discouraged?'

'Isn't everyone?'

Aurora Kent was the kind of woman he would normally avoid like the plague but, two cups of tea later, he almost believed in the existence of her angels.

His phone rang.

'Where the hell are you?' Feral sounded querulous. Morning sickness again. 'We're ready to hit the road.'

'It's not goodbye,' Aurora said when he was leaving. Her handshake was hard, her eyes bright with a hawkish concentration. Despite his protests she insisted on presenting him with an angel.

'Archangel Michael,' she said. 'The Great Protector.'

'I'm afraid I'm a sceptic when it comes to angels,' he admitted.

'That's not an issue for Michael,' she said. 'He doesn't discriminate.'

The little figurine had such a belligerent expression that Jake longed to fling it into the nearest bin. But Aurora's kindness stalled the temptation and he placed it on the dashboard of his van.

Reedy drove them to the ferry. Archangel Michael, sword and shield at the ready, swayed on the dashboard and lulled Jake to sleep. Would Karin be on the ferry, watching from the deck as the coastline receded? Or had she already flown back to Dublin to plan her next tactic to drive him mad?

Samantha skyped the following night, hesitant, tearful, her expression doleful enough to suggest she was falling behind on her personal best.

'How did the tour go, Dad?'

'Good… good. What's wrong?'

'I've done something *really* stupid.' She twirled a hank of hair around her finger. He thought of Nadine, the same nervous habit. Genetic impulses.

'Promise you won't get mad when you hear,' she begged.

'Spit it out, Samantha.'

'*Promise.*'

'Okay, I promise.' He prepared himself for the worst. Banned substance. She had tested positive and was about to be expelled from Silver Ridge. Either that or she was pregnant. She had mentioned a shot putter she was seeing. Jake winced as he imagined a muscle-bound baby with a penchant for spinning in circles.

'I've… em… actually… I've been emailing your girlfriend… only now I find out she's not your girlfriend. Ali says she's a psycho stalker and you hate her guts.' Samantha rushed the final words together and stretched her lips, braced for his reaction.

He drew back from the screen, as if distance could deaden his daughter's voice.

'What were the emails about?'

'Just stuff about Silver Ridge. She wanted information about the athletic scholarship because her friend's son is thinking of coming here.'

'Why didn't you tell me she'd been in touch?'

'Well, it's a bit complicated.' Samantha paused and drew a deep breath. 'The first email she sent to me was a mistake. It was meant for you. She realised what she'd done immediately and sent another asking me to delete it without reading it.'

'And did you?'

'I didn't have time. Not that I would have,' she hurriedly added. 'But I'd seen the photo by then.'

'What photo?'

'The one attached to the email. You and her in a bar. She told me you wanted to keep her a secret until you and Mum were properly divorced. She asked me not to mention anything about it.'

'What personal information did she want?'

'I didn't realise it was personal, Dad. It didn't seem important.'

'Just tell me.'

'Stuff about the gigs you were playing and Mum's new place and your new phone number because she said she'd lost it and needed to get in touch with you when you were on tour.' Samantha twisted her hair even more furiously. 'God! I'm so stupid. I'd no idea she was lying but Ali says… *Dad* – you look like you're going to strangle me.'

'Samantha, leave your hair alone and listen carefully. I'm not angry with you but I will be if you don't send any further email you get from her into spam.' He leaned closer to the screen. '*Spam*… do you understand. And delete her from your address book *immediately*.'

His heart was pounding. Was this how a heart attack started? The feeling of suffocation, the heat across his forehead? The belief that his life was totally outside his control?

'I've done so already.' Samantha was on the verge of tears. 'Dad. I'm *really* sorry. Are you going to be okay? She's not a bunny boiler… *is* she?'

'Nothing as dramatic as that, Samantha. She likes playing games, that's all. She won't bother you again but if, by chance, she does contact you, let me know at once, no matter what time it is. Is that clear? Let me talk to Sam.'

He repeated the same warnings to his monosyllabic son, whose vocabulary gene, Jake suspected, had been hijacked in the womb by his twin.

He switched off Skype and rang Karin. As he expected, her answering machine came on.

'I know what you've been doing to Samantha,' he said. 'Your emails prove you're a dangerous liar who's stalking my family. If you contact her or any one of my children again I'm taking out an injunction against you. This is a warning, not an idle threat.'

She was probably listening, immune to his fury. Her emails to Samantha would have been as innocuously bland as the many texts she had sent to him.

CHAPTER FIFTY-FOUR

Nadine

Ali lives with Christine in a two-bed flat in Islington. Her bedroom is the width of my arms and the kitchen in *Eyebright* is bigger than the galley where she's making lunch. She rang last night and asked to meet me after my art class finished. Christine is out and we're alone. Something is wrong. Shadows under her eyes. Disturbed sleep and she's probably prey to those voices in the small hours that distort whatever rationality she still possesses. I know all about them.

I haven't seen her for a few weeks. She's cancelled on two occasions when we were supposed to meet for coffee. She came to Wharf Alley a few times when I first moved in but not so much anymore. On her last visit, Aurora did an angel reading. Ali was subdued afterwards. Her radiant smile may fool others but not me. When we're together she changes from giddy optimism to tearful admissions that Mark's divorce is not a simple as she first believed. His wife invested money in Barnstormers. She was supportive when her husband was a struggling director. I have a deep sympathy for this faceless woman, whom he is betraying with my daughter. Ali must be patient and understanding; it will all work out in the end. He offers her these reassurances. I can offer a comforting arm but my words of caution are not welcome. She reserves her acting for the stage. I, as her mother, get the full brunt of her emotions.

I sink into a sofa with broken springs and indefinable stains I've no wish to analyse. She seems tense and preoccupied as she sets a low coffee table with fresh bread rolls and cheeses, some cooked chicken and appetising chutneys. I know better than to ask for information. Pull one way and Ali pulls in the other direction. She'll get to the heart of the matter in her own good time. She avoids my eyes and passes the salad bowl, waits until I take what I need before she says, 'I received a letter in the post yesterday.'

'Go on.' I nod at her to continue. Kitten claws scrape against my chest.

'It's something you wrote…' She reaches into the pocket of her jeans. 'Years ago… in your teens.'

The envelope she hands to me has been ripped open. It's printed with her name and address. The letter inside is a photocopy. Saliva floods my mouth and, for an instant, I'm afraid I'll throw up all over this grubby sofa.

'You read it?' I ask.

'Yes, I read it.' She finally meets my gaze. 'I wasn't going to… but once I started I couldn't stop.'

'Do you know if Brian or the twins received the same letter?'

She shakes her head. 'They'd have told me.'

'You're sure?'

'Positive. We're in touch all the time about you and Dad.'

I imagine bewildered and exasperated sessions on Skype and instant messaging. What a worry we are to them. Drama, broken hearts and messiness are the prerogative of a young generation. They should not be expected to deal with the complexities of sundered parents.

'How does that woman know my address?' Ali asks

How indeed… did she stalk my daughter as she travelled from the theatre to her flat? The thought is terrifying. I see my own fear reflected in Ali's eyes and rush to reassure her.

'An address is easy to find if you set your mind to it. Don't worry about her. She's not interested in you. I met her when I was in Dublin. She made it clear I'm her target.' I take the letter from Ali and crumple it in my hand.

'Will you tell me about that summer,' she asks. 'I'd like to know about him.'

Where can I begin? I shake my head. 'Not today, Ali. I'm not ready to talk about him. But I will… I promise. Please don't mention any of this to Jake. He feels responsible for Eleanor's stroke. I don't want him to have to deal with anything else. Promise you'll let me know immediately if another letter arrives.'

'I will.' She nods vehemently.

'And that you'll give it to me… unopened.'

'Are there more?'

'Yes.'

'Oh, Mum.' Ali holds me, a subtle role reversal. I'm glad of her comfort.

I read the letter on the tube as it powers underground then races through the blustery May sunshine. Love letters for my eyes only. Why did I take such a risk? It didn't seem risky at the time but that's the arrogance of youth, its sense of invulnerability. It calmed me down, this physical act, the construction of a fantasy with blocks of words. But, by the following day, my skin was on fire again. My ears attuned to his voice, his laughter, his step, his gaze.

Darling Max

I can't sleep. My back is too hot even for the sheet. But you're okay. Your skin is used to the sun. What were you thinking when we lay together on Table Rock? I still can't believe it, just you and me lying there with the ocean shining around us.

It was Jake who suggested we swim to Table Rock. We've never done that before. Its so far away on the other side of the bay. He really believed he could make it. Barry was the first to turn back, then Karin, Reedy, Hart and Daryl. When Jake decided it was too far he yelled at me to swim back with him. I kept going. I knew I could reach the rock and rest there before heading back. That's what the strong swimmers do. Then the sea got choppy and the rock looked even further away. I was going to turn back when you swam alongside me and suddenly I felt like I could swim to the other side of the world.

You reached the rock first and pulled me up beside you. I couldn't stop panting for ages. We just lay there side by side without talking. Then our breathing became the same and your chest was rising and falling just like mine. The water on your body looked like jewels. Even when I closed my eyes I could see those jewels sparkling under my eyelids.

Well, my lovely mermaid, are you ready for the swim back? you said after a while.

I stood up and so did you. I didn't slip deliberately. It was the rock, all that seaweed. You caught me. I know it was only to steady me but it was like you'd given me an electric shock. The smell of the sea was on your skin and I could feel every part of you, even... well... I'm not really sure if you were... it seems weird to think you were hard, like Jake got when we kissed in the cave. Then you let me go and dived straight into the water.

Karin was furious when we came back. I was dripping wet but she wouldn't even let me dry off.

'Walk,' she said, as if I was a dog and flounced off down the beach in a temper.

'You frightened the life out of my mother,' she said when I caught up with her. 'She was worried sick in case you got drowned and took my father down with you. So was I. Not that you cared'.

When I looked at Joan she just lying there with her sunhat over her face. She hadn't even looked up when we came back. I told Karin to stop getting at me. The only reason she was in a temper was because she hadn't been able to keep up with us. It was the wrong thing to say.

'You think you're so brilliant at everything,' She started shouting at me. 'But you're not. You're just a big, clumsy whale who keeps trying to attract my father's attention all the time'.

I hit her. I'm sorry, Max. Sorry it was your daughter I hit. But not one bit sorry I did it. Oh my God! It was awful afterwards. I was sure she'd hit me back. I wish she had. That would have made us even but she ran back up the cliff path to the cottage and wouldn't come out of her room for ages.

I apologised when she let me in. I told her I was going to ring Mum to collect me. She stopped sulking then and said we should let bygones be bygones and she was sorry she called me a whale. We've made up our row... for now.

I'm not going outside tonight. Her insults stick like glue and I feel like one now. A big, clumsy whale that you all feel sorry for.

I'm so unhappy. I'd definitely go home if it wasn't for you. I can't stop thinking about Table Rock and when I slipped. My skin is shivery every time I move. I'm not sure if it's the sunburn or thinking about how you pulled me into you real close and how I could have kissed you if I'd moved my face just a tiny inch closer.

Goodnight, Max. I love you.

XXXXXXXXXXXXXXXXXXXXXX

The passengers on the tube check their iPhones or stare blankly into space. Some cling to tradition and read neatly folded newspapers. A man speaks loudly on his mobile about the groceries he must pick up from Tesco Express but the years are falling away from me. Curling like onion skins until all I can remember are those heady sun-filled days and star-dazzled nights. How many letters did I write? Four? Five? All of them are in her hands and primed. Where will they explode next?

It's almost a relief when Brian rings. He stammers when he tells me about the letter, uncomfortable and embarrassed by this glimpse into his mother's screwed-up teenage mind. He only read the opening paragraph. That shows a lack of curiosity he must have inherited from his great-uncle Donal. Unlike Ali, he doesn't want to know the back story of my youth. I told him enough when I visited him in Slí na hAbhann. He has a pottery to run and more orders coming in for the Willow Passion collection than he can handle. But Karin Moylan is pushing my buttons one by one, determined to expose me before the eyes of my family.

Brian agrees to scan the letter and email it on to me. Then he will burn it in his kiln. 1400°C should do the trick, he says.

My Darling Max

Tonight we looked at stars. My hands shook when you gave me your binoculars and showed me the path of the Milky Way. You named the constellations. I can only remember a few like Orion and Gemini. But I remember what it was like when you put your hands on either side of my head and pointed my face towards Venus.

'The first star of evening and the wonderful Goddess of Love,' you said. Your breath tickled my ears. A shooting star fell from the sky. You said it happens all the time and that the heavens are always in a state of flux.

We sat on the bench and you told me more about India. How you were almost killed by an elephant and watched a dead man being burnt. I could have stayed there forever listening to you. God! If anyone knew. I feel as guilty as anything writing this. You kissed me. 3!! times. Oh God... oh God... 3 times!!! You opened my mouth with your tongue and it was so different to the way Jake does it. Like I'm dreaming whats happening and there's arrows shooting through me. I wanted so much for us to lie on the ground and keep kissing forever.

It was so dark I couldn't see your face. You told me I was special and beautiful. No one ever said I was beautiful before. Well, Jake did but he said 'weirdly beautiful and thats not a compliment, not as far as I'm concerned. You said it properly and that's when you kissed me for the 3rd time. That one was deeper. A bit scary and it hurt a bit, the way you were holding me so close but I didn't pretend.

I nearly threw up when Karin came out. We'd stopped by then. Thank God we had. If she'd seen... I can't even think about it. She came out in her nightdress, all hot and bothered, even though you showed the stars to her as well. The Big Dog star and the Big Dipper and the rest of the ones we'd looked at together. She said looking at stars was more boring than swimming and we should all go to bed. And we did. I'm going to try and be nicer to her. I'll tell Jake that she likes him. It'll stop him bothering me. I can't stand to think of him ever coming near me again.

I won't sleep tonight. Your lips on mine... oh Max... whats going to happen when I go home? I can't stop thinking and thinking... if only I was ten years, even three years older. Then I'd be grown up enough to know all about signals from men and what they mean.

Yours forever

Nadine

XXXXXXXXXXXXXXXXXXXXXX

CHAPTER FIFTY-FIVE

Jake

Eleanor was relaxed but determined to make a full recovery. It still felt strange, the newness of talking to her without that bristling sense of busyness that always used to surround her. Her bungalow was cosy, a word he would never have attributed to his childhood home. He knew Cora was responsible for the softer lighting and vases of fresh cut flowers, the wholesome meals she prepared for him when he visited.

It was days after her stroke before he remembered Cora's admission about Sea Aster's planning permission. Perhaps, in the confusion of that day, he had misunderstood. Eleanor had never given any indication that she had changed her mind and had always rejected his attempts to pay rent on the basis that he was maintaining the property until the conversion could begin.

She was relaxing in the back garden, a rug over her knees, when he called to see her after the UK tour. Cora carried out a tray of tea and scones then discreetly withdrew.

'Enough about that,' Eleanor said when Jake asked too many questions about her health. 'I wanted to talk to you and Nadine together but she shows no inclination to return home.'

'She is at home – '

'For goodness sake, she's living in a shipping container. That hardly qualifies as a home unless you're an unfortunate immigrant seeking asylum.' It would take more than an ischemic stroke for Eleanor to lose her interruptive skills.

'What do you want to talk to us about?'

'I've come to a decision. I'm gifting Sea Aster to the two of you. A fifty-fifty split.'

'Are you joking?'

'Have you ever known me to have a sense of humour?'

'But… that's very generous – '

'Call it generosity, conscience money, motherly love, whatever,' she said. 'I've been doing a lot of thinking since my stroke.' She began to cry, a sudden loud outburst that startled him.

'It's okay… it's okay.' He patted her hand and glanced helplessly towards the house. 'Will I call Cora?'

She blew her nose vigorously and her voice, although muffled when she spoke again, carried all its old authority. 'Don't bother Cora. A few tears here and there never did anyone any harm. I've already spoken to my solicitor about changing the deeds. He'll be in touch with you in due course.'

'But you can't… what about your plans for First Affiliation?'

'Dead in the water. I don't miss it.' He thought she was going to cry again but her voice hardened. 'That's the extraordinary thing. I thought leaving the party would be akin to an amputation. All my limbs were in place last time I checked. They may not be working as well as I'd like but time and physio will take care of that. I need a second chance, not a second home.'

How could he possibly repay this debt of gratitude? Or even find the appropriate words to thank her.

'Nadine won't come back.'

'She'll still be the mother of my grandchildren, even after your divorce comes through. I don't want any arguments. Sea Aster belongs to both of you. Decide between yourselves how to work that out. Get rid of that ugly wall in the hall and open it up to the light. I want my grandchildren to have a base they can call home when they visit.'

Nadine was equally stunned when he rang her that night.

'Do you think her mind is… you know… *affected*?' she asked.

'She's one hundred per cent lucid,' he reassured her. 'I suspect she was planning to do this even before her stroke.'

'You know I can't possibly live there.'

'The house will be yours as much as mine.'

'I'm sorry, Jake. Sea Aster means nothing to me. She's always going to be there – '

'Only if we let her.'

'You think you can banish her that quickly? I don't. Once the deeds have been gifted to us I'm signing my half over to you. It'll be my property. I can do as I choose with it. Has she been in touch… texts, phone calls… letters?'

'Nothing,' he replied.

'No contact at all?'

'Apart from a message I put on her answering machine when I came back from London. I threatened her with a court injunction if she contacts any of us again.'

'That must have her quivering in her little blue shoes.'

'You don't have to be sarcastic.'

'Do you seriously think she'll pay a blind bit of notice to a threat like that? What solid evidence have you got that will convince a judge she's staking our family.'

She waited for his reply and when none was forthcoming she said, 'What she's doing goes way beyond that fling you had with her. I met her when I came home to see Eleanor. We took afternoon tea together.'

'Afternoon tea?'

'Just because we hate other doesn't mean we can't be civilised.'

'Why didn't you tell me?'

'Because it had nothing to do with you.'

'*Nothing* —'

'She's convinced I'm responsible for her father's death.'

'That's ludicrous. How could you be responsible… ?' He stopped, remember the comment Karin had made about Nadine destroying her family. He had brushed her words aside, believed them to be another example of her heightened sense of drama, her unbounded need for attention. Now, as Nadine cut across his surprise, he tried to pull together the strands of that holiday. To search beneath the sun-trapped days on the beach and the headiness of having two beautiful girls vying for his attention. What else had been going on in Monsheelagh Bay that would have led Karin to make such a brutal accusation?

'Maybe the past would have stayed buried if you hadn't brought her back into our lives,' Nadine's voice had a flattened certainty that chilled him. 'That's that part I find impossible to forgive.'

CHAPTER FIFTY-SIX

Nadine

I can't forgive him… but I wonder if Karin Moylan ever left me. Unfinished business. I pushed those stolen letters to the back of my mind as the years passed but when the memory reared up I'd feel the sudden clutch of panic, knowing they were in her hands. Gradually, the words I wrote were bleached from my mind but not their substance. No, that would never fade.

I tense every time Jake rings. As yet, he hadn't mentioned anything about letters being dropped anonymously through his letterbox but I'm haunted by the knowledge that there's one more out there. That's all I wrote before sanity and the slam of a door closing saved my soul.

The final letter arrives. Samantha rings on behalf of her twin. Sam doesn't have the vocabulary necessary to express extreme embarrassment. She emails a copy. I read it quickly, the last spoonful of medicine gulped down before my stomach turns.

Dear Max

It was a signal. I know it was, even though you were looking at Joan when you said, 'There'll be a shower of meteors tonight. The sky should be magnificent.'

She didn't say anything. I'm not sure she even heard you. It's like she was stoned out of her mind only she wasn't. She wasn't even drunk. She just seemed separated from us by a massive black cloud. I can't figure out how she can look really nice at times and then her face sags like she's wearing some kind of sad skin mask.

Karin said the only stars she wants to see are in the cinema. She's hardly spoken to me since the picnic by the river when we saw the kingfisher. Did she really expect me to lie to you about her age? I still feel your fingers in my hair when you put that feather there. I wish it hadn't blown away. I'd keep it forever. You gave me that same look tonight, kind of sly, like you didn't want them to see and you said, 'Fireworks in the sky. You don't know what you're missing'.

I wasn't going to go out. I wanted to and I didn't. I couldn't decide. I kept going to the window and looking out. I saw you staring up at the sky. The cottage was quiet, like it was holding its breath. But that was me, I guess. I wore my jeans and my jumper, even though it was warm. I was afraid yet not afraid. Is that how drug addicts feel? All fog brained up with wanting and not wanting?

You were right about the meteors. They were like arrows of light in the sky. I could see the Milky Way all stretched out like spilled milk being brushed with a feather. A kingfisher feather. You said I was a poet as well as an artist and I'd be famous one day.

Always remember tonight', you said and kissed my forehead. I closed my eyes and you kissed my eyelids, like you wanted to seal what we'd seen there forever. My knees were shaking so much I was afraid I'd fall.

I was frightened but you told me not to be. You said you wouldn't hurt me and when you kissed my neck it was as if all those meteors were exploding inside my head. You knelt down on the grass in front of me and then I knelt too, even though I knew I shouldn't. I didn't want to think about Joan or Karin or Jake or anyone but you, kneeling there like you were praying in front of me and we kissed like that, I don't know how many times, more than 3 definitely, and then I was lying on the grass. It was damp and ticklish on the back of my neck. I was glad I had my jeans on because they're really difficult to get off but not my jumper... you pulled it over my head and my hair was all tangled in it. That's when I got scared. You were heavy on me and wouldn't listen when I said stop. I couldn't breathe. I kept on thinking of Joan and her sad face and that what we were doing was going to make her even sadder. Not that she would find out. I'd never tell her. Not 'til my dying day. But what if she guessed that you were touching my breasts, my nipples... oh my God... or if Karin knew. She'd kill me absolutely kill me stone dead. All I felt was frightened, like I didn't know you anymore. I wanted you to tell me you loved me but you didn't 'cause you were breathing so fast and kissing me all the time and then we heard the door slam. You said it was the wind. I was glad because it made you pull my jumper back on. Everything was different, even the sky. You shook me and said, 'Jesus Christ, if you say anything...'

Why were you so angry with me? You're the one who hurt me, not the other way round. I was glad the *wind blew the door closed but now I'm scared all over again. What if it wasn't the wind? I wanted to look in at Karin and see if she was awake but I didn't. I heard your bedroom door close. You're in the next room lying beside Joan. Why did I go out tonight? Why does what we did feel awful and exciting at the same time? I hate myself. I really do What would have happened if you'd taken off my jeans? Oh my God... oh my God! How will I face Karin in the morning? I hope it rains tomorrow night and all the meteors have fallen. I'm going to be strong from now on.*

Goodbye Max!!!!!

It's terrifying and cringing, all that innocence… all that womanly guile. Memory is a conjurer. A sleight-of-hand trickster that burnishes bright what was once a tarnished reality. Who was I that summer? What was I thinking? I can remember the longings, all that passion… but I can't feel them. The emotions could belong to someone else, someone I don't know, or don't care to know. But the fear that followed is stamped indelibly on my mind. The search beams on the ocean, the clattering sound of the search helicopter, sirens, engines, voices, the ceaseless crash of the waves against the rocks below Cowrie Cottage… and Karin's grief when Max's body was recovered from the sea. She keened as loudly as Alcyone must have done when she was told that her beloved Ceyx had drowned.

I went with my parents to his funeral. Joan embraced me. She was sober then and has remained so ever since. She never read those letters. If she had done so she would have gazed upon me with the same cold and palpable hatred that radiated from Karin's eyes when she accused me of being responsible for her father's death.

CHAPTER FIFTY-SEVEN

Jake

The wall dividing the hall was gone. Cheap plasterboard disintegrated in clouds of dust when Hart and Reedy helped Jake to bring it down. When the dust eventually cleared, he was able to appreciate the light streaming through the stained glass panels above the front door. The stairs looked wide and elegant as they rose upwards to the empty rooms Nadine had once occupied. She remained adamant about signing her share of Sea Aster over to him but he still believed she could change her mind when she saw the house returned to its original loveliness.

Daryl was interested in setting up a recording studio with him in the barn. Times were tough for financial consultants, he confided to Jake. Too many of his clients were being declared bankrupt. With the way the recession was going that situation was unlikely to improve in the near future. He needed to diversify. They could form a partnership – his financial know-how and Jake's creative talents.

The last band practice had been fractious. Reedy looked more wizened than usual as he lectured Hart over his timing on a chord change and Hart, abandoning, for once, his Zen-like tranquillity, accused Reedy of being a 'know-it-all prick,' which was true, Reedy agreed, since he was the only one in Shard with a lifetime of musical knowledge, disillusionment, disappointment and street cred behind him. Feral's face looked wan under the light. She performed a thunderous tattoo on her drums to silence the argument and announced that all this arguing was creating disharmony in her womb.

Shard's success had taken them by surprise but it was creating its own problems. Jake was afraid the band would not survive in its present format. Reedy would go on, and Feral too. They were born to be musicians but he was unsure about Hart, who was worried about Hartland to Health's falling membership. Touring was a problem for him and Daryl, and Mik Abel was already organising a Shard tour in Germany. Jake, too, was beginning to wonder if there was a sell by date on a dream. A moment when it turned from an achievement into something faintly ridiculous? The memory of the *Core* feature and its consequences refused to fade away.

Tonight Shard had played The Bare Pit again. A good gig, good crowd, good atmosphere. Harmony seemed to have been restored to Feral's womb and to the band. Jake fought off a wave of tiredness as he passed under the motorway bridge straddling the estuary. Years before, when news broke that it was to be built, Rosanna had actively protested against its erection. She was convinced it would destroy the bird sanctuary she loved. Her protests came to no avail but the wildlife now co-existed peacefully with the low rumble of traffic above them.

The sudden wail of a siren reverberated through the van. Two blue lights revolved in the rear-view mirror. Jake pulled sharply into the grass verge as a fire engine swerved past, followed a moment later by a second one. Seabirds fluttered upwards like startled wraiths and the swans, disturbed from their trance-like glide, lifted their heads from under their wings. Two garda cars sped past. Jake's anxiety grew as the blue lights momentarily disappeared around a bend before reappearing. They were going in only one direction.

On Mallard Cove the hedgerows were in full leaf. Branches whipped against the windows as he slowed. The pot holes had not been repaired and seaweed was strewn on the road. The honk of swans, familiar by now and, mostly, unnoticed, seemed to have an added urgency, as did the splash of water washing across the pebbled shoreline. Smoke billowed upwards, caught in the glare of the headlights. He had rounded the next bend before he saw the flames shooting skywards. He skidded to a halt by the edge of the shore and ran across the road. The honk of swans, familiar by now and, mostly, unnoticed, seemed to have an added urgency, as did the splash of water washing across the pebbled shoreline.

When he had identified himself a female guard allowed him through the cordon.

'The fire's confined to the barn,' she said. 'They don't think there's any danger of it spreading any further. No one appears to be in the house and – '

'It's empty,' Jake reassured her.

Firemen in yellow helmets surrounded the barn. Water spiralled upwards from their hoses. The howl of flames as they tried to gain new territory had a terrifying intensity. Jake imagined the old sofa igniting, the Shard posters curling and kindling, the wooden floor crackling, the amplifiers and microphones sparking, melting, everything consumed in the flames. His songs too, his laptop and the notebooks of rough notes he had not copied or recorded. His mind was a blank when he tried to comprehend how much information he had lost and could never retrieve.

The guard urged him to keep back, let the experts deal with it. The flames died quickly. In the scale of a night's work, this fire was easily contained, said one of the firemen as the hoses were wound up. Chemicals, now those were a different story, he added. They never knew what they were going to come up against in that kind of situation.

'I suspect a faulty wire was to blame.' He took off his helmet and rubbed his hand over his bald head, streaked it with soot. 'Either that or you left a heater on.'

Jake shook his head. He was meticulous about checking everything before he locked the barn after rehearsals. The smell of smoke was strong enough to make him gag. When the fire brigade and the squad cars finally left he rang Nadine. Her answering machine came on. The same thing happened when he tried to contact Ali, Brian and the twins. Did anyone pick up anymore, he raged. What was the sense in having a family unit if they were unavailable at times of intense stress?

Hart drove over immediately after he phoned, accompanied by Daryl and Reedy. They surveyed the blackened interior, their expressions growing bleaker as they realised the extent of the damage. They stayed with him for the night, drank beer and talked about the old days. Daryl quoted verbatim *Hot Press* reviews the young Shard had received while a sober and sympathetic Hart did a fry-up for breakfast. Reedy promised to contact a colleague who was an expert on data retrieval. With a bit of luck the songs could be saved from the laptop hard drive.

After they left Jake showered and collapsed into bed. He was unable to sleep yet unable to rise to face the blackened ruins. Ali, waking to his message, rang immediately. She kept crying, as if something precious had been stolen from her, and was too incoherent to be any comfort. Nadine, full of apologies for not getting his message earlier, rang shortly afterwards.

'It's awful, Jake. All your precious songs… it's *awful*. Have you any idea how it started? Could it have been the wires? The electrics always looked a bit shambolic.'

'The wires didn't cause the fire.'

'What are you suggesting?' Her voice dropped, as if she suspected they could be overheard.

'I don't know… I don't *know*…'

'If you believe what I think you believe then you must go to the police immediately.'

'What can I tell them? I've no proof.'

Later, after the loss adjuster had been and gone, Jake imagined the charge he would make. The evidence he would be asked to present if he did report his suspicions to the police. Nadine's slashed paintings, now burned. A piece of pottery, legally purchased and filled with memorabilia of a broken relationship. The sense of an invisible presence in empty rooms, objects that he could have moved in absent-minded moments and displaced. Visits to a theatre and a tapas bar, to nightclubs to hear her favourite band. Those friendly and encouraging texts and emails. A damaged van filed in a garda report as vandalism by persons unknown. What else… oh yes… an unflattering magazine feature about Shard. Eleanor's stroke due to high blood pressure which she had ignored, despite medical advice… and the barn. The loss adjuster had given his verdict. The gas heater had been left on. Indisputable evidence, the path of the flame a clear delineation. The heater had burned on the lowest setting and probably would not have caused any damage except for the close proximity of a wicker bin filled to the brim with sheets of paper. When they ignited the flames licked against the old sofa and its inflammable material had caused an immediate combustion… and then there was the pièce de résistance. Her engagement had appeared last week in *The Irish Times*.

Liam Brett and Karin Moylan are pleased to announce....

Jake saw himself through the eyes of the guard who would file his report. A delusional egotist, caught up in his fantasies about being stalked by a beautiful woman. He would be laughed out of the garda station for making an accusation that had as many holes as a sieve.

CHAPTER FIFTY-EIGHT

Nadine

I keep my fears at bay when I'm painting. It's become my escape. Perhaps it always was, but it's different now. I don't grow disheartened or indifferent as the course becomes more demanding. I don't feel the urge to drop out with half-baked excuses and hide half-finished canvases in crowded attics. The students in Bonnard are young and giddy, happy to miss lectures and still-life classes. The mature students are diligent. Like me, they're aware that time is relative and dangerously swift in its passing.

It's a month since the fire yet the back of my neck tingles when I think of her. Is it over now? The scorching? Have the flames sated her thirst or is she waiting for an appropriate moment to strike again? Was it arson or an accident? Jake sounds shaky when he rings. He's not sleeping well. Night sounds startle him awake. He has a sense of being observed without being able to observe the observer.

I've signed Sea Aster over to him. I could feel the force of Eleanor's decision dragging me down. She meant well but some memories can't be eradicated. I'll always see Karin Moylan in the bay window, sense her imprint on the furniture, in the attic, in Jake's bed, the scorched barn. Why would I need a house with such crushing associations? I want Jake to use the attic as the recording studio. It's perfect for his needs. I can visualise it already: skylights, a spiral staircase, one of the walls knocked down and converted into a picture window with a view over the estuary. He has to put the fire behind him. The insurance company will pay the claim without a quibble. In the cold light of day it's difficult… impossible… to believe she's responsible.

Wharf Alley is busy this morning. Saturday is a popular day for tourists who disembark from the tour boats to explore the art and craft centres. Last week I met Chloe Laker, the curator of the Wharf Alley Art Gallery. She's planning an exhibition for later in the year and has invited me to submit four of my paintings. I showed her my newer work. They're more experimental – we're encouraged at Bonnard to think conceptually – but she picked the four Sea Aster paintings I'd been working on in my spare time. I explained that they are personal and self-indulgent. The portrayal of a life I've left behind. Chloe is adamant. They will fit the theme of emotional alienation the exhibition intends to explore.

At the Wharf Diner, many of the customers are also eating outside. Not Seeing is Believing is doing a brisk trade. Aurora said she gave Jake an angel. I can imagine his expression. He doesn't believe in psychics who see metaphysical spirits in blank spaces.

A taxi pulls up beside the complex and I'm amused, as I always am, when I watch the amazed reaction of strangers, who survey the brightly painted containers. But this young man is not a stranger. My amusement turns to surprise when I recognise Peter Brennan.

'I tried ringing but your phone was off,' he says when he's made his way along the walkway to my balcony. 'When Ali said you were living in a shipping container I thought she was joking. But this place is fantastic.'

I switch on my mobile. Three missed calls, all from Peter. I'm flattered but surprised that he should visit me.

'I'm just about to have my lunch.' I gesture towards the table. 'Would you like some pasta?'

'If it's not any trouble.'

'No trouble at all.' I set an extra place and we eat together, easy as old friends with a history to share.

'How's Madge?' I ask. His mother was known on Oakdale Terrace as a force of nature, always knee-deep in community activities.

'Busy as ever organising everyone,' Peter replies and smiles ruefully.

'And Luke?'

'Dad's retiring soon and looking forward to it.'

'Were they surprised to hear Jake and I had split up?'

'A bit,' he admits.

'Madge used to call us children playing adult games when we first moved in.'

He nodded. 'You and Jake were so young compared to the other parents.'

'That's because we were.'

'All the lads thought you were hot.'

'I find that very flattering, Peter, and quite enlightening. I was under the impression you all wanted to marry Ali.'

'That was before puberty hit. Once the hormones got a grip we had you in our sights.' He laughs then clears his throat. 'I'd planned to spend today with her.' At last he's got to the point of his visit.

'But I can't contact her,' he says. 'She's not answering her phone.'

'She's probably sleeping late after last night's performance.'

'Here's the thing.' Peter walks to the railing and stares across the river. 'I booked a ticket to see *The Arboretum Affair*. I was hoping to surprise her but she wasn't performing.'

'It must have been her night off?'

'I spoke to one of the sylphs afterwards.' He shook his head, his eyes glazing slightly. 'There're something else, those sylphs.'

'And?' I prompt him.

'Christine is her name. She shares with Ali. Anyway, she said Ali left the cast a fortnight ago.'

'That can't be right.' I'm unable to hide my shock as I join him at the railing. 'She would have told me. I'll give her a ring now. See what's going on.'

'You'll need better luck than me. She's not picking up.'

He's right. Ali's phone rings out, even her message machine is inactive.

'I'm sorry you've had a wasted trip, Peter. I've no idea what's going on.'

'Do you have an address for her? I can call around and see what's up.'

I write down her address. 'She may not be there,' I warn him. 'But ring me and let me know if you make contact… or if you don't.'

I fight back my uneasiness and clear away the lunch dishes. It's a month since I've seen Ali. She's cancelled on three occasions when we were supposed to meet. I could understand her cancelling a coffee date but not Stuart's posthumous photography exhibition. We had planned to eat beforehand but she rang just as I was leaving Wharf Alley and said she was coming down with a cold. She sounded croaky and kept blowing her nose, as if to reaffirm how wretched she felt. I was more upset than annoyed. I needed her with me. Seeing Stuart's photographs was going to be an emotional experience and I couldn't understand why she couldn't battle her germs with a packet of Lemsip for one night.

The exhibition was wonderful. I rang Daveth afterwards, unable any longer to put off hearing his voice. He's in Glacier Park at the moment with a group of environmentalists. When the season is over he's coming to Cornwall for his grandmother's hundredth birthday celebration. That's where his roots are. He'd like to spend some time in London, talk about us, our future, if such a possibility exists. He hesitated when he said that and waited for my reaction.

'Yes,' I replied. Yes, oh, yes. Knowing that I would see him again allowed me to admit how much I missed him. His brawny arms, the relaxed slant of his eyelids, his smile, intimate and knowing. I saw us… and the space where we once lay together. Small and closed off from an immeasurable vastness. The smell of oil and brine and, faintly underneath, the scent of the cedar wood soap he always uses. But I can't think of him now. Ali is to the forefront of my mind.

Her emails are breezy and funny, filled with anecdotes about Mark and Christine and other members of Barnstormers. Not once has she hinted that she's unhappy or considering leaving the play. But she's an actress. We paid a fortune to train her to pretend.

Peter rings. He spoke to Christine. Ali is spending the weekend with friends. I know this is untrue and Peter probably knows it too. He's hurt, disappointed that she should treat him so casually. Their arrangement to spend the day together was made some months ago.

Jake is in Germany, the first leg of the German tour, but he answers immediately.

'I rang her before I left for Germany.' He sounds as surprised as I am. 'She never mentioned leaving the play. Not that I'm objecting. I'm relieved she's got sense at last. It was a piece of exploitative – '

'Jake, stop thinking like an outraged father. Being in that play was a big deal for Ali. She wouldn't have left without a good reason. I'll ring you as soon as I get in touch with her. How's the tour going? Any sign…you know?'

'Nothing.'

'Okay. I'll be in touch.'

We're incapable of a normal conversation. Just brief exchanges that break under the burden of an unspoken name.

CHAPTER FIFTY-NINE

On Monday morning I travel by tube to Islington. I'm not sure if it's my anxiety that makes Ali's flat look even more dilapidated than on my previous visit. I ring the bell three times before the front door is opened by a man who looks as if I've dragged him away from tinfoil and a syringe. He stares blankly at me and shakes his head. He's never heard of Ali or Christine. I suspect he may have forgotten his own name. My anxiety since Peter's visit has turned from nagging to acute.

I edge past him and mount the stairs to the flat. At first, there's no reply. I hear movement inside, the scraping of a chair, faint voices. This time I knock more persistently. The peephole in the door bulges like a suspicious eye. I've a feeling I'm being observed before Christine opens the door.

'How nice to see you, Nadine.' Her English is perfect, just enough of an accent to suggest it's not her first language.

'You too, Christine. I'm looking for Ali. Is she in?'

'Alysia is not here.' She steps into the corridor and closes the door behind her. 'I will let her know you called.'

'Please tell me what's going on.' My antennae is on full alert. I sense Ali within, her tense, wary posture. 'I heard she's dropped out of the play. Have you any idea why?'

'She has her reasons.' Christine's expression is as closed as the door behind her. 'It's not for me to discuss her personal life.'

'I'm simply asking if my daughter is okay. I'm worried about her.' I raise my voice in the hope that Ali is listening. 'Ask her to ring me. Also, ask why she didn't meet Peter Brennan as arranged. It's not like her to disappoint her friends. That's why I'm so anxious to talk to her.' I try one last time to pierce Christine's cool Danish composure and there is a shift, a slight puckering between her pale eyebrows.

'Alysia is okay, Nadine. She just needs time alone to sort out her feelings.' She steps back behind the door and closes it. I feel as if it's been slammed in my face.

I fight back the urge to return to the flat and barge into the room. Nothing will be gained by such a confrontation. At least I know Christine is looking after her.

Jake's phone goes to message. He's probably still asleep after last's performance but he rings back shortly afterwards and listens without interruption when I tell him about my visit to the flat.

'Did you talk to her?' he asks.

'Not yet. Christine says she's okay. I suspect it's to do with Mark. He must have ended their relationship.'

This piece of information adds to his relief and his tone lifts immediately. He detests Mark Brewer but I know that's not his real reason. Karin Moylan cleaves to us like a caul.

Ali rings as the day draws to a close. 'I'm in a taxi on my way to you.' Her voice is a shrill whimper, almost unrecognisable. 'Are you at home?'

'Of course. Did Christine tell you I called this morning?'

'Yes,' she sobs and the phone goes dead.

Has Mark Brewer's wife confronted her, revealed that her cheating husband has no intention of getting a divorce? Or perhaps Mark himself administered the cut and she's found it impossible to continue working alongside him. One way or the other, I'm glad. Broken hearts mend, as she'll discover.

I stand on the walkway overlooking the wharf. The breeze from the Thames is cool on my cheeks. A cyclist, wasp-like in Lycra and a helmet, dismounts and carries his bicycle into one of the containers. When the taxi arrives I walk down the steps to greet Ali. Her face is blotched from weeping. She runs past me without speaking. By the time I return to the container, she's coiled on the settee, her face turned to the wall.

'Can I have a tissue?' She snuffles loudly and grabs tissues from the box I pass to her. After blowing her nose she pushes her head deeper into the cushions.

'Turn around and tell me what's going on.' I speak with a calmness I'm far from feeling. Reluctantly, she sits up and faces me. The sheen and swish have disappeared from her hair. It hangs limply over her shoulders and needs a wash. She winces back from my touch.

'Mark has left me,' she says.

'I'm so sorry, Ali.'

'No, you're not.' She glares at me through bloodshot eyes. 'You never liked him. Neither did Dad.' She scrunches the tissues in her hand and pushes my sympathy aside with an impatient toss of her head. 'You were both right, as it happens. Does that make you feel good?'

'No, it doesn't. I hate seeing you so unhappy. But I was afraid for you... the age difference – '

'We were supposed to move in together. We'd even picked out our apartment. He promised... what am I going to do... how am I going to manage...' She bangs her fist against her lip and sobs violently, her thin shoulders shaking.

'You'll manage, Ali. You're strong. You have a whole new future in front of you.' I stop, knowing these are not the words she wants to hear. But they are the only ones that come to mind. 'Why didn't you tell me what was going on? I'd no idea you'd left the play until Peter – '

'I didn't leave the play. I couldn't perform any longer.'

'Why not?' I draw her close and she, weeping more freely, relaxes against me. My hand rests almost intuitively on the hard swell of her stomach. Suddenly, I understand why she's been avoiding me. It seems impossible. It doesn't happen these days. Not to street-wise young women like Ali with their pills and coils and diaphragms.

'Ali… how far along are you?'

'Six and a half months.'

'Oh my God, so long. Why didn't you tell me?' I hold her pale, tear-streaked face between my hands. How had I not noticed? Even now, it's hard to tell, the swell barely noticeable. I was the same when I carried her, slim as a rake until the last two months.

'I don't want it.' She groans aloud. 'I was going to have an abortion. But I couldn't go through with it. I kept thinking I wouldn't exist if you'd aborted me. You should have, you know, you definitely should have aborted me because my life is shit… shit… *shit*… and I wish I'd never been born.'

'You don't mean that – '

'I do… I *do*,' she wails. 'I had the opportunity to get rid of it and I didn't and now it's too late. I'm stuck with it. End of story and I don't want it... I don't want – '

'Ali, stop… stop. You're talking about my grandchild.'

'*Grandchild*. How great does that sound? I bet you want to be a grandmother like you want a hole in the head. And Dad too. Oh, God, what's he going to say?'

'The same as me. This is our first grandchild. I won't have another word said against him or her. Where does Mark feature in all of this?'

'He doesn't want to know.' She grinds out the words. 'I kept thinking he'd change his mind when the baby was born. But, now, he won't even be here. He's been offered this brilliant opportunity to run a theatre in New York and he couldn't care less about me or the baby or anyone except himself.' She dries her eyes but her tears keep falling. 'I hate him and I love him. How is that possible? He dropped me from the cast. He said sylphs don't become pregnant. How can sylphs not become pregnant when they don't exist anywhere except in his *stupid* play?'

She rages on and on. She's exhausted and has probably forgotten what it's like to have a good night's sleep.

'Ali, listen to me. That decision you made, for whatever reason, to keep this baby was a choice between Mark and your child. You chose your baby. Now it's time to start respecting that decision.'

I make tea, toast crumpets, cover her with a duvet, and talk… talk… I'm dragging memories from the deep recesses of another time, recalling my father's fury when he discovered I was pregnant, how his words on that night cut as deep as any blade I ever wielded. This memory strengthens me. I know that Ali has made the right choice.

'I want to go home to Sea Aster,' she says. 'I can't bear to be in London any more. Everything reminds me of him.'

'This is a big city. Mark Brewer shouldn't fill the width of it.'

'But he does, Mum. He's leaving on Wednesday. I've got to get away from here before then. I won't be able to bear it… I *won't*.'

'But your father's in Berlin and the house is locked up. He won't be back for another week.'

This admission brings on another outburst of tears.

'I'll go with you and stay at Sea Aster until he returns.' My mind is made up. 'We'll get through this together. Believe me, when this baby is born you're love it as deeply as I loved you.

And that feeling will never change, no matter what life throws at you.'

Jake's shocked silence when I phone him sweeps aside the last residue of tension between us. He speaks to Ali for a long time. Afterwards, she falls into a deep sleep. I ring him again when our flight has been organised.

'I don't have the new key to Sea Aster. How will I get in?'

'I've organised that,' he says. 'Eleanor has a spare one. Cora has agreed to pick you up at the airport. I wish I could be there to meet you.'

'Don't worry about us. We'll be fine until you get back.'

'Grandparents, eh?' He pauses, as if he's still trying to come to terms with the idea. 'How do you feel about that?'

'Adjusting. How about you?'

'Quite chuffed, to be honest. I just wish it was under happier circumstances.'

Ali is still sleeping, the first time in weeks, I suspect. I think of Daveth. It seemed possible, for a short while, to imagine moving to Alaska with him. Ali would be in New York, I believed. Brian also has plans to travel. He talks about moving to Arizona and opening a pottery in Sedona or, perhaps, somewhere on the South Island of New Zealand. He's inspired by space and magnificent scenery, as Stuart once was, and the twins will settle in California. But Alaska is out of the question now. My place is here with Ali. I'm not going to repeat history and be a grandmother in another continent.

I awaken during the night, our bodies spooned, and I feel something… a patter as strong as the throb of a heart beating hard against my spine.

CHAPTER SIXTY

It's dark by the time we land in Dublin airport. If Cora suspects why Ali is returning so suddenly to Ireland she gives no sign of it when she greets us in arrivals.

'We can take a taxi,' I accept the key from her. 'I don't want to drag you out of your way.'

'It's no trouble at all,' she insists. 'It'll give Eleanor some time on her own. She thinks I fuss too much over her.'

I suspect Cora is the one who needs some free time and this suspicion is confirmed when she drives from the airport. Eleanor's recovery is almost complete. Her dominant personality is coming to the fore again and Cora is looking forward to moving back to her apartment in Clontarf. I wonder about her quiet life and how she became involved with First Affiliation. What drew her to their certainties and intolerance? The need to belong, to be part of something greater than herself? My curiosity dies away as quickly as it came. I'm tired and overwrought, exhausted already from Ali's outbursts, her violent weeping.

The car judders as we approach Sea Aster. Mallard Cove needs resurfacing. The earlier tide overflowed the road and puddles remain in the hollows. A swan ambles towards the car, its wings flapping in the headlights. Cora slows, nervous as water splashes against the tyres.

'It's okay.' I open the window and look down at the road. The wind fans the rank smell of seaweed into the car. 'The water's shallow and the swans are well used to avoiding cars.'

'I was bitten by a swan when I was a child.' Cora sounds uneasy. 'Nasty things. I've never liked them since.'

Ali has fallen asleep in the back seat, her head awkwardly angled against the headrest. The boundary wall of Sea Aster comes into view, the square gatepost visible on the curve. The spreading branches soften the hulking remains of the barn but I'm still shocked at the sight of the blackened walls and collapsed roof.

A car emerges from the gates and swerves onto the road without slowing down. Water aquaplanes from its tyres. To avoid the swan Cora has moved too far over to the wrong side of the road. Headlights clash. She utters a high, frightened shriek and instinctively brakes when she sees the oncoming car. She pulls frantically on the steering wheel and her car waltzes as if the road has turned to ice. A scum of decaying seaweed, strewn under a layer of tidal water. The second car veers past without slowing, dazzling and blinding before it disappears into the engulfing darkness of Mallard Cove.

Cora's wrists are so skinny. I never noticed them before. Frail and skinny as she struggles to control the skid. The gable ends of the barn protrude like ancient pyramids. Above the trees, the moon is a pale shimmer in the black sky. It casts down my mother's face and my terror is reflected in Sara's stricken features. Her awareness in that instant before the collision that there was no going back, accordion pleats imploding and crushing the life from her. She's there now, with me, smiling before she turns away in all her loveliness... and I am suspended between the random nature of existence and the shrouded certainty of death. The screeching night and the shock of steel and stone as the car hits the wall. It overturns in a slow-motion roll before coming to rest. My eyelids flicker. I see the swan scuttling back to the water, its fat bottomed waddle, so ungraceful out of its natural habitat. My eyes close and all is forgotten.

Part Five

CHAPTER SIXTY-ONE

Jake

When Rosanna died, the members of First Affiliation filled the church. They walked respectfully in the rain behind her coffin as she was laid to rest. Today, there were no representatives from First Affiliation. No rain, just bright sunshine as Eleanor headed the small procession making its way towards the open grave. Her grip was talon-tight on Jake's arm and those following slowed their footsteps in acknowledgement of her shuffling walk. She had wept openly throughout the service but, now, she was more in control as she took her place by the edge of Cora's grave.

After the burial, she mingled at the reception with the mourners, Cora's widowed sister and her family, a few friends from Cora's schooldays and from the department in the civil service where she worked until she retired. They were a small group, just two tables drawn together in an alcove of a suburban pub. Eleanor's hand shook, as if affected by a palsy, when the group raised their glasses to toast Cora's memory. Since her friend's death she had shrunk, or so it seemed to Jake, and the effects of her stroke were more pronounced. He too felt shrunken, caved in, bereft.

He drove her home from the pub. The young Nigerian woman who had become her carer took one look at Eleanor's face and gently coaxed her to bed. Jake drove along the Howth Road towards the city centre and found a parking spot close to the hospital.

Ali was sitting on the edge of the bed when he entered the ward. He studied her drooping neck, the fall of her hair. She had been crying again. Her bruises were even darker than yesterday. One eye was completely closed and the other, swollen but partially open, revealed the dark brown slit of her pupil when she looked at him.

'Was it awful?' she asked.

'It was a nice send off.' A platitude but true. 'How are you?'

She made a rueful moue and pulled her hair back. 'What do you think?'

He cupped her face and kissed her swollen lips. 'You heard the doctor. It's only superficial. You'll be surprised how quickly you'll recover.'

'Don't.' She shook her head distractedly. 'I can't bear it if you minimise what happened.'

'I'm not minimising…' Jake stopped, helpless before her grief. 'I don't know what to say, Ali.'

'I know, Dad. Neither do I.' The swelling on her ankle had reduced, he noticed, but her right knee, when it peeked through her dressing gown, was still bandaged. 'Dr Fisher says I can be discharged tomorrow.'

'Tomorrow?' Jake was shocked. 'It's only four days since – '

'I know… but, like you said, my injuries are superficial.' She linked his arm and leaned heavily on him as they walked along the hospital corridor. He had no idea how she had managed to remain conscious enough to ring the help line that sent the emergency services racing to the scene of the accident. Primal instincts stronger than terror. Instincts that allowed her to ignore her injuries and concentrate on the only pain that mattered.

They stopped outside the incubation unit. As always, when Jake looked at his granddaughter with her tubes and patches, and the tiny cap on her head, he was dazed by the strength of his love. Her wrinkled monkey face, the thread veins mapping her tiny frame, her fingers, slivers of bone, sinew and muscle, he loved every part of Sara Saunders with a primal and protective passion.

Tears streamed down Ali's face. 'How can she ever love me?' He had to bend close to hear her. 'I never wanted her and now I can't imagine an instant when I won't want her. Do you think she'll make it, Dad? Do you…do you?' She leaned against him and wailed softly into his neck. 'They won't give me any hope… I don't know what I'll do if – '

'No ifs.' His confidence was brash and overloud in this place of quietness. He wondered how they do it as he watched a male doctor bend over a tadpole baby who could rest easily in the palm of his broad hand.

He said goodbye to his granddaughter and to his daughter, who had been pulled from the wreck of Cora's car in the throes of premature labour.

Apart from an hour here and there, he had not slept since he received that frantic phone call from Eleanor. His limbs felt heavy as he walked towards his car. Once inside, he closed his eyes and rested his head against the headrest. When he awoke a traffic warden was tapping on the window.

'You're over your time, sir.' The warden grinned sympathetically. 'Long night, was it?' He jerked his head towards the maternity hospital.

Jake nodded. 'I dozed off. I haven't slept since… sorry… I'll move on now.' He rubbed his eyes and yawned, straightened his shoulders and indicated into the traffic.

He drove northwards to another hospital where Brian sat at his mother's bedside, waiting for Nadine to open her eyes.

CHAPTER SIXTY-TWO

Door opens. Footsteps. Voices.

'I love you, my darling. I know you can hear me. Listen to me. You're going to get well again. You're going to laugh and dance and sing. I'm waiting for you. This time I'm not letting you go. I want you back in my arms where you've always belonged.'

'Come back to us, Mum. We're all here... and Sara... she's fighting too. You'll make each other strong, I know it.'

'Are my hands too rough, Mum? Can you feel them on your face? What's it like, hiding behind the willows? Come back to us... we're waiting for you.'

'Mum, it's Sam. We've just flown in. Samantha's too choked up to talk. Please wake up and say hello... do something... anything to let us know you can hear us...'

'On the criteria of the Glasgow Coma Scale, her coma is too deep to respond to stimuli. There will be involuntary gestures, spasmodic movements. I'm afraid you can't read anything into them. I'm so sorry – '

'What utter nonsense, Doctor. Ignore him, my dear, and be strong. It's possible to come back from the deep. I should know!'

'It's me, Nadine, your father. I came as soon as I heard. I should have come more often but work... you know how it is... and you never wanted to know Lilian... why must I keep talking, Jake? It's obvious she can't hear a word I'm saying… oh, my poor child… my poor child… what's to become of her?'

'I'm here, Nadine. All the way from Vancouver to sit with you. I know you can hear me so listen up. My wedding is in six months. I want you there. Maid of honour. Understood!'

'Halcyon days, Nadine. Do you remember? Or are your memories lost in the void? What's it like? Dead to the world yet still alive? Is it peaceful or are you haunted by the wrongs you did? Goodbye for now. I'll be back to see you soon.'

Door closes. Silence. Stillness. How long does a dream last?

CHAPTER SIXTY-THREE

Jake – six weeks later

As the weeks passed and Jake waited for a sign from Nadine, no matter how slight, to give him hope, he separated his emotions. He banished pity, grief, rage, helplessness, heartache. Love, he believed, was the key to her recovery. And he loved her, not in the old way with its surety and complacency. Not in the obligatory way of those who 'work' at marriage and are rewarded with companionship that fits like a pair of well-worn shoes. This emotion was so strong he could not name or describe it. It was as raw as a new beginning, as miraculous as a second chance. He had no way of knowing if his love could reach her. He had to depend on memories. On the years they shared when they became what she once called 'a hybrid,' incapable of thinking outside each other's minds. Somewhere in that dark terrain she occupied she must understand that this love would see her through.

Brian drove from Dingle every weekend to be with Nadine. The twins returned to California to finish their semester. Ali's bruises slowly disappeared, although she said she still imagined them when she looked in the mirror. Not that she had much time to gaze at her reflection. When she was not in the maternity hospital with Sara she was with Nadine.

Jenny was strong and resilient when she flew in from Vancouver to be with Nadine but her composure cracked when she saw the utter stillness that trapped her friend. Somehow, she told Jake, even though it sounded arrogant, she had hoped her appearance would signal some change, a flicker of recognition, a nod to the past when they became inseparable. She pushed the sleeve of Nadine's nightgown over her arm and stared at the faint scars that once formed a grid of pain. She rested her cheek against the pulse that still throbbed in Nadine's wrist.

'I'm convinced she can hear us.' On the day before she returned to Vancouver she sat with Jake in the small café attached to Mount Veronica. The clinic specialised in severe brain injury and Nadine had been transferred from the main hospital once her condition stabilised. 'You mustn't lose hope. I want her at my wedding. The two of you, together. You have to think positively, Jake. She's going to come through this.'

'I know... I know.' But what will she be like if she does? This question haunted him but he was terrified to utter it aloud.

'Keep her father as far away from her as possible,' Jenny advised. 'He was always a tactless fool. The sooner he goes back to Australia, the better.'

Eoin Keogh had arrived at Sea Aster with two laden suitcases and no set date for departure. He was no good around illness, he admitted to Jake, especially something as mysterious as the comatose state. When Nadine was a child he brought her to see Snow White. Eoin detested that film, all those tweeting birds and little men... hi ho... hi ho... and that awful glass coffin, the rigidity within.

His unwashed clothes spilled over the laundry basket and Jake constantly tripped over his shoes. A pall of cigarette smoke hung in the air, despite repeated requests that he smoke outside. His initial shock had changed to resigned acceptance of Nadine's fate. He wondered aloud if his first wife's sudden death was not a better option to a living death. Clean-cut, that was how Eoin Keogh liked life. His voice had the carrying resonance Jake remembered. The realisation that he had always detested his father-in-law sharpened his voice when he warned Eoin never to speak such thoughts aloud in Nadine's presence.

The band members buoyed him up but he sensed undercurrent of anxiety as the weeks passed and bookings were cancelled. Anything could happen to Nadine while he was away and unable to reach her bedside, he argued when Mik suggested an overnight concert in Cork. Anxiety had become Jake's natural state. The small ward where Nadine lay had become the centre of his life. All that went on outside – the traffic and hurrying pedestrians, the watchful traffic warden and wasp-headed cyclists – had an urgency that belonged to another time.

'You should find a replacement singer for the band,' he told Mik. 'I can't leave Nadine and you can't keep cancelling bookings.'

'It's not that easy,' Mik protested. 'You're the glue that holds Shard together. If you opt out Feral and Reedy will do the same and that'll be the end of Shard. Daryl and Hart have no interest in keeping the band together when the centre's gone from it. Think on this, Jake, before you make a final decision.'

He had cancelled a tour of the Netherlands at Jake's behest, apart from one overnight booking. The concert in Amsterdam was a prestigious event and one that Shard could not afford to miss, he said when he called to Sea Aster one evening.

Ali came into the kitchen and overheard the conversation. 'Mik's right,' she said when the manager left. 'The band will keep you focused. We need to bring some normality back to our lives. Otherwise, we're going to go crazy and that won't help anyone, Mum least of all. She'd be the first to tell you to go. It's only for one night. Me and Eoin will manage until you get back.'

She had Eleanor's steel, that same gritty determination. Sometimes he heard her at night, the creak on the seventh step as she went downstairs to the breakfast room where the heat of the day still lingered. He followed her once to see if she wanted to talk, and found her curled in one of the armchairs. He thought she was crying but she had been dry-eyed when she assured him she was okay, just sleepless and waiting for morning when she could return to the hospital to watch over her baby. A night away. What could happen in that time? Nothing. This fact added to his grief and to his slow but gradual acceptance that this was their new normality.

He called to see Nadine that afternoon. He talked to her about Sara, still fragile as glass but growing stronger all the time. He played her favourite Van Morrison and Tom Waits discs and, on Jenny's advice, Ice T. It made no difference yet Jake was convinced that somewhere in the inner reaches of her consciousness, sound filtered and stirred memories.

Imelda was on duty. He was on first name terms with the nurses. Apart from Imelda, he enjoyed their company during the hours he spent in the ward but Imelda's voice irritated him, especially the high-pitched intonation she used when she spoke to Nadine.

'How are you, *Nadine*? Looking as lovely as ever, I see.' She straightened the bed cover and asked Jake to lower the music. 'Jake is here, *Nadine*. You're such a lucky girl, all those visitors coming to see you. Her friend Jessica was in again, Jake. And Madge… a very bossy woman but her son's a hunk. I think he has his eye on Ali. What do you think, *Nadine*? Let me see your arm. I need to take some blood. They don't call me Vampira for nothing… ha… ha.'

A band practice was arranged after Jake agreed to do the Amsterdam concert. They met in the basement of the Raison

D'être studios where Shard had been practicing since the fire in the barn and worked on a song Jake had written before the accident. He felt no affinity to the lyrics or the melody yet it came alive as they experimented with it, each member building up the layers of harmony.

When band practice was over they crossed the Ha'penny Bridge and entered Julia's Tavern. The manager leaned over the bar and slapped a sympathetic hand on Jake's shoulder. 'How are you, mate? Silly question… but you know what I mean?'

'It's tough. But I'm managing.'

'Any improvement?'

'Not yet.'

'Jesus, but that's a hard one to fathom.' He poured a measure of whiskey and pressed the glass into Jake's hand. 'Compliments of the house. The slot's still here on Sunday afternoons whenever you're ready to come back.'

Jake downed the whiskey and ordered a double measure, knocked it back with the same ferocity.

'Take your time, man,' said Hart. 'I'm driving you home tonight.'

The Shard van was parked along the quays. Green circles of light dazzled the Liffey as Hart and Reedy supported him over the Ha'penny Bridge. In the passenger seat Jake fumbled with the safety belt until Hart took it from him and fastened it. Street lamps lunged towards him. High towers of spangled glass swayed from side to side. Even when he closed his eyes he could see them. He must have translucent eyelids. He shouted at Hart to stop and opened the door in time to throw up over the kerb. He lay back against the seat, his eyes swimming.

Next morning he was unable to remember leaving the pub or anything about the journey home. His last memory was of tossing back a shot and laughing at something Feral said about

Maggie. Something bitchy about how she never cleaned the kitchen counter after she made a sandwich and how, when Feral complained, she was accused of being a nagging wife. It seemed hilarious, two wives bitching about breadcrumbs, that he laughed himself into a blackout and ended up in bed, his clothes placed neatly over a chair? Who had undressed him? He was too hung-over to feel ashamed. Plenty of time for that later.

He winced with shock when he glimpsed his reflection. His skin looked as if it had been stretched on a rack then suddenly released. When had he last suffered such a hangover? The binge culture had passed him by. He was too busy changing nappies and mixing feed formula when his peers were seeking alcoholic obliteration.

He felt slightly revived after the shower, although his eyes still appeared to have developed cataracts overnight. His notebook was open on the bedside locker. He kept it nearby at night in case an idea for a song came to him, a wisp that would be gone by morning unless he wrote it down. Last night he had written, or tried to write, another song. Some of the lyrics actually made sense. How had he functioned in that unconscious state? He imagined Nadine groping through that same dark void, lost in a tunnel with no light to beckon her onwards.

CHAPTER SIXTY-FOUR

Nurse. The first word comes. Nurse…nurse….nurse….

'Hello, Nurse.'

'Oh, hello there, Jessica. How nice to see you again. How do you think our *Nadine* is looking today?'

'Stronger than the last time I was here. Has there been any change in her condition?'

'Sadly, no. Such a tragedy. It's kind of you to take the time to sit with her. However, strictly speaking, only family are allowed outside visiting hours.'

'I understand. But Nadine is very dear to me. My work hours are so unsociable. I won't stay long. I promise. Do you think she's aware I'm here with her?'

'I'd like to believe so, but I'm afraid we still don't understand the full depths of the unconscious mind. Hearing is the last to go, so we're told. Her family are convinced she can hear them. They tell her everything that's going on in their lives. Such devotion. Isn't that right, *Nadine*?'

'It's been six weeks now, Nurse. How much longer can she go on like this?'

'Who knows? Sometimes her husband plays music. I believe he's in that band… what's it called? Stone or something like that?'

'Shard. They're good. I'm a fan.'

'*Nadine*, I'm going to take your blood pressure then I'll fix your pillows, make you more comfy. Oh dear, blood pressure spiking. I'll need to call the house doctor. Jessica, I'm sorry. I'll have to ask you to leave.'

'I understand, Nurse.'

'Call me Imelda. We believe in an informal atmosphere in Mount Veronica. *Nadine*, your friend is going now but she'll be back again to see you. What's this they say about friends? Old friends are gold, silver new.'

Not Jessica…not Jessica…not Jessica.

CHAPTER SIXTY-FIVE

Jake

The concert sold out. A growing fan base, said Mik, and this was only the beginning. The venue was a deconsecrated church that had been converted into a concert hall. Its hallowed past was still evident in the high, vaulted ceilings and stained glass windows. The audience was hushed when the band came on stage, as if a residue of contemplation and meditation still resided within the walls. They were more interested in listening to the music than dancing to it, and enthusiastically applauded at the end of each number. The familiar adrenaline kicked in and it was possible, briefly, for Jake to lose himself in the moment.

Mindfulness. Hart talked a lot about it. No rehashing the past, whipping it around in a mindless circle. No anticipating the future in that same negative loop.

The strobe lights flashed... red, green, yellow... blue... blue... she was out there somewhere. He could tell. The prickling tension in his spine. But he was unable to see her in the crowd. He was overwrought, he decided. Seeing shadows of a lithe and teasing dervish in the smoky-blue haze.

When the last encore finished he stood by the edge of the stage to sign CD's and autographs. The rush of adrenaline drained away as he approached the bar. Draught pumps, arched as sea horses, shone brightly on the counter. Bottles of spirits lined the mirrored wall behind the bar. He shook his head when Daryl offered to buy him a drink and asked, instead, for a glass of water.

Daryl showed him the latest video of Jasmine in her bath, her hair in a top knot, bubbles on her nose, loud chuckles. She looked so plump and wholesome compared to Sara with her tiny white cap and fingers, still as delicate as stems. Daryl put the phone back into his pocket and stiffened, his gaze focused on the mirrored wall. Jake did not need to look in the same direction to know that Karin was standing behind them. Her dress, it was the one he remembered from Dee Street, clung to her like a sheath, its metallic hues glinting in the brass pumps.

'We have to talk.' She came to his side and spoke softly. 'Can we go somewhere private?'

'We've nothing to say to each other.' He, too, kept his voice low.

'Yes, we do.' She touched his arm. 'If nothing else, I want your forgiveness. Please, Jake, all I need is a few minutes of your time.'

Outside the club a couple who had bought a CD of *Collapsing the Stone* stopped when they recognised him and asked him to sign the cover. Karin leaned against the wall and waited while they questioned him about the band. The overhead lighting pooled around her, honed her profile into the delicate setting of a cameo. For an instant, noticing her unguarded expression, he was startled by the forlorn slope of her mouth.

'I'm genuinely sorry about Nadine's accident,' she said when the couple walked away. 'I don't want to add to your distress – '

'Then why are you here?'

'Liam insists I stop attending your gigs. We're moving to Brisbane soon. Is that far enough away for you?'

'No.' He shook his head. 'Wherever you go, it'll never be far enough.'

'Such anger, Jake. You once loved me with the same fervour.'

'I never loved you.'

'Denying something doesn't make it less real.' Words by rote. He recognised their timbre, how they echoed with control, possession, deceit.

'You mentioned forgiveness,' he snapped. 'Is it a general absolution you require or an itemised one? My van? The barn? Nadine's paintings?' She shook out the pashmina she carried across her arm and draped it around her shoulders, hugged it against her neck. 'I've been seeing a psychologist. It's something I should have done years ago. But if we'd hindsight to guide us we'd never make mistakes.'

'I hope you're finding it helpful.'

'My skin feels raw, as if I'm being eviscerated,' she admitted. 'Is that what you want to hear?'

'My opinion doesn't matter.'

'It matters the world to me,' she replied. 'Women who love too much. I belong to that category. They call it a disorder, a syndrome. What do these so-called experts know about a love that tears the heart out of you? You and I understand that, Jake. The need to possess what belongs to us.'

He should walk away yet something held him there. He was unable to identify it, not curiosity but, perhaps, the fascination he would feel in the presence of a dangerous animal, whose claws, for now, were sheathed.

She paused as Feral, speaking on her mobile, emerged from the club. The drummer flapped her hand at them and moved out of earshot. Streams of neon reflected on the canal and lights spangled the windows of tall, gracious houses. The city flaunted its nightlife in side streets and elegant boulevards but Jake's mind was locked in a small, silent ward.

Karin, too, seemed lost in thought before she spoke again. 'Nadine insisted on meeting me after Eleanor's stroke,' she said. 'Did she tell you that?'

'Yes.'

'She accused me of being responsible for causing it. Is that what you believe?'

'Indirectly… yes.'

'Then you must think I'm monstrous.'

'I think you cause havoc in people's lives but never look behind to see the effect it has on them.'

'My psychologist believes something similar.' Her ring sparkled when she held out her hand. 'A blue diamond.' She studied the brilliant stone. 'They're rare and precious. Liam knew I wanted one and he found the perfect stone.'

'Congratulations.' He turned towards the door. 'I'm needed inside. Good luck in your marriage.'

She moved in front of him and blocked the entrance. 'You couldn't afford to buy the cheapest fake yet I'd give him up tomorrow if we could get back together again.'

'That's never going to happen.'

'You won't be able to cope with Nadine on your own.'

'I'll always be able to cope.'

'I know you better than you know yourself. You need something back from a relationship or else you find a replacement… like you did the instant she set you free. She can't do that now, Jake. She's paid the price – '

'What price are you talking about? Is this another way of hurting her?'

'How can I hurt her when she's a vegetable?'

'What did you call her?'

'She's in a coma with no hope of recovery. Do you have an alternative word?'

He imagined bruises marbling her pale skin and flinched from the desire to inflict them. Had the love she claimed to feel for him ever existed or had it been hammered on the anvil of her hatred for Nadine? He remembered her standing in the bay window that night, the aura of flushed excitement he had mistaken for shock. And the rows, how they flared around Nadine even when she was a continent removed from them. What did it matter now? Nadine was where she wanted her; helpless, speechless, harmless.

'Go back to your fiancée and respect that blue diamond he gave you,' he said. 'Do whatever you want but don't involve me in any part of your future.'

Feral ended her phone call and came towards them. 'God! It's chilly out here. Is everything all right, you two?'

Karin, ignoring the question, stretched upwards on her toes and whispered in his ear. 'She'll always be a vegetable, Jake. I'll be waiting for you when you're ready to let her go.'

The wind from the river feathered her hair as she walked to the edge of the pavement and raised her arm for a taxi.

'I didn't realise you and Karin were seeing each other again.' Curiosity sparked behind the concern in Feral's eyes.

'We're not.'

'I see… well, I don't actually. What's she doing here?'

'She came to say goodbye.' He turned back into the hall. 'You must be tired.'

'More uncomfortable, than tired.' She rested her hands on her stomach. 'Not long now.'

He had never seen that slow swelling on Ali, had never experienced that mounting anticipation as the due date drew nearer.

He ached to be back with Nadine, sharing her silence, yet when he returned to Mount Veronica and she was exactly the same as before he left, he plunged into a rage that left him breathless.

CHAPTER SIXTY-SIX

I moan. No sound. I dream. No waking.

'Look who I met on the corridor. We recognised each other immediately. Memories, eh. That's what'll bring you back to us, my dear, unfortunate child.'

'What a coincidence… imagine bumping into your father like that. I thought he was in Australia but he's here with you, as I am. We're waiting for you to wake up, Nadine. Can you hear us… hear us…'

Worm in ear. Must scratch. Can't. Not Jessica…not Jessica….
Father smacks fist into hand…smack…smack…smack….

'She's getting worse. Look at her eyes. Nothing there but emptiness. Excuse me… I have to go… can't hack it…'

Not Jessica stays. Perfume… can't breathe…

'It's just like old times. You and I alone together sharing secrets. Remember how we giggled ourselves in hiccups over any silly boy who looked at us? Remember the vows we made. Friends forever. Remember what you did to destroy that friendship? Remember, Nadine? Remember?

'I saw you with him. You pretended you were looking at stars but I knew what you were doing. I watched how you flattered him. That sideways smile, brushing against him every chance you got. You didn't even bother pulling the curtains in your bedroom when you were writing those sickening fantasies. I saw everything… do you understand… everything! That day by the river. He called you Alcyone and I knew. You thought you were inviolate. Untouchable. First Jake, than my father. Jake signed my arm that night. He kissed me too. In the little snug in Barney's before he want on stage. Oh, he was a good kisser then… and now.

'We were together in Amsterdam. I freed the wildness in him in ways you never could. A conflagration, that's what it was. Just like the barn. It's the end game, Nadine. You must know that. He wants you dead. He told me so. Dead and buried like my father.

'Did you ever feel a moment's guilt as you trudged through your boring, busy life? Whinging about your marriage and how you never had a chance to decide your future. Did you ever wonder how I managed my broken heart? Drugs dull memory but nothing can destroy the truth. My mind exploded when I saw you at the airport that day. Or did it implode? Implosion crushes, explosion scatters. Can they happen simultaneously?'

'Did you read your letters when I returned them to you? Of course you did. Were you so far removed from reality that you thought my father was in love with you? He would have laughed if he read them… and he would have… if only…if only…the two of us laughing together at your ridiculous fantasies…

'How deep are your depths, now? Fathomless, probably. I want to tell you my secret. But not now. Another time. Eoin is waiting for me. Poor man. He doesn't know what to do with you. His undead daughter. Bye for now. See you soon again.'

Hand on cheek. Cold. Door opens. Door closes. Not Jessica… not Jessica.

CHAPTER SIXTY-SEVEN

Jake

Jake was unable to sleep. His eyes felt hot, gritty. He needed sleeping tablets, something powerful enough to switch off his thoughts. Imelda had spoken to him before he visited Nadine today. Her temperature kept spiking. She had vomited twice during the night. Her movements were becoming more persistent, spasmodic. She needed an increasing supply of oxygen to help her breathe. He could no longer ignore the truth. She was deteriorating, the weight falling from her, the lustre gone from her hair.

Suddenly, his senses alert, he sat up and switched on the light. He heard nothing, saw nothing, felt nothing except the taste of fear in his mouth. Was that how panic attacks began? He sniffed the air, convinced he could smell perfume. Faint, tantalising, as if lightly fanned on currents of air. He was reminded of orchids, not that he knew anything about their scent but he always imagined Karin's perfume originating from the vulva-like centre of some exotic speckled blossom; oily, spicy, intimate. She could not have been inside Sea Aster. It was physically impossible. He ran downstairs, checked the front and backs doors. No sign of entry, not even a scratch on the paintwork. The windows were still locked. He returned to the bedroom and pressed the pillow to his face. Yes, that was the source. It cloyed his nostrils, reminded him of the musky scent he once sought in the curve behind her ear.

He slept fitfully in the spare room for the rest of the night. The smell had vanished when he returned to his own bedroom in the morning. Last night's panic seemed dreamlike as he stripped off the bed linen. Phantosmia. He read about it once. Olfactory hallucinations, usually brought about by an illness. Mental or physical? He was unable to remember. Probably mental, he reflected gloomily as he shoved the sheets into the washing machine.

Eoin was already outside, clearing the barn. He had organised two large rubbish skips and was slowly filling them with the burned-out remains of equipment and furniture. When would he return to his wife? Wry comments about the 'ball and chain' and overheard snatches of phone conversations when he was talking to Lilian convinced Jake it was marital problems rather than his daughter's coma that was keeping Eoin in Ireland. The stale smell of cigarette smoke still hung in the air from last night. He must have been smoking indoors when Jake was at band practice and Ali was with Sara.

He was amazed at his granddaughter's resilience, the strength of her still-tiny kicking feet. She would soon be strong enough to come home from hospital. The thought of her breathing smoke into her delicate lungs enraged him.

He made tea and called Eoin in from the barn. 'You should go back to Lilian,' he said. 'We've no idea how long this will go on.'

'It'd be cruel to leave you at this stage,' Eoin argued. 'I can make myself useful, you know. That attic needs a lot of work if you're serious about turning it into a recording studio. The wiring is shot to hell. I'll make a start on it.'

'Don't touch anything,' Jake held onto his temper, afraid he would go on a rampage if he lost it. Smash… clatter… bang…

it would bring a momentary relief but everything would still be the same afterwards. 'I'll do the attic in my own time. Why not stay with Donal for a while? You've hardly seen him since you arrived.'

'To be honest, Jake, me and the brother were never that close. All those frigging choo-choos would drive a man crazy. The last time he visited me and Lilian he overstayed his welcome by four weeks.'

'How long was he supposed to stay?'

'A month.' Eoin slapped his knee and guffawed. 'Only joking. But seriously, I'll ring Donal soon. There's no rush for the moment. I'm needed here. Are you sure you don't want me to rewire – '

'Absolutely.'

'At least let me move that stack of floorboards from the hall. I don't know how many times I've tripped over them and nearly landed on me arse. You don't want me ending up in hospital with a broken leg.'

Jake shuddered at this possibility. The floorboards for the attic were stacked behind the hall door and had been delivered to Sea Aster before the accident drove everything else from his mind. Eoin was right. They were a hazard.

The floorboards had been moved to the attic when he returned that night from Mount Veronica. A note from Eoin, along with a manila envelope had been left on the kitchen table.

Gone to visit Donal. Found this envelope behind the floorboards. Looks like it's been there for a while. Be back tomorrow.

The envelope was covered in dust and smeared with spider webs. No name or address on the front suggested it was junk mail. He opened it, expecting to find a flyer about a supermarket offer or a special deal from a restaurant. Five smaller envelopes were inside. He opened the first one and removed a letter. The page had yellowed with age and been folded so often the creases were beginning to split. Each envelope contained a similar letter. This was Nadine's writing, a younger, neater hand but still instantly recognisable.

My Darling Max, he read. Shocked, he checked the date. How could she have been writing to Max Moylan that summer… and using such an endearing term? He sat down and began to read.

By the time he finished the five letters he felt like a voyeur, somewhat soiled and guilty. His head pounded, as did his heart. No wonder Nadine had always avoided talking about that summer. How long had the letters been lying in the hall? She must have dropped them by accident when she was clearing out her possessions. By her own admission, she never wanted them to be read by anyone. He would be unable to ask her. The realisation that she might never speak to him again struck him anew and added to his grief.

'What have you got there?' Ali entered the kitchen. Her eyes narrowed when she glanced at the pages scattered on the table. She lifted the first sheet before he could stop her.

'Give that back to me at once.' He tried to snatch it from her but she moved from his reach.

'It's okay, Dad. I know about them.'

'What do you mean?'

'Those letters. I read a copy of one of the originals.'

'When?'

'Before Mum's accident. That woman sent it to my flat.'

'That woman… you mean… why wasn't I told about this?' He gathered the sheets together and shoved them back into their envelopes.

'She stole them from Mum when they were kids on some holiday. Mum made me promise not to say anything. Gran was in hospital and you were feeling bad enough about everything. Brian and the twins were sent copies, as well. It was her way of humiliating Mum. She obviously kept the originals for you.' Ali took the envelope from him. His hands, he noticed, were trembling.

'Did you ever suspect?' she asked.

'No… never.' He remembered Max Moylan on Monsheelagh Strand. The mahogany sheen of his skin as he swam back to shore from Table Rock, Nadine alongside him. Nadine and a man old enough to be her father was as inconceivable as Ali and Mark Brewer had once seemed to him. Strutting Jake Saunders, the singer in the band. An unimportant smudge on Nadine's horizon when he believed he had filled her eyes.

'What happened then is of no relevance to now,' said Ali. 'There's only one way to deal with it.'

He made no effort to stop her when she threw the letters into the sink and struck a match. Nadine's paintings had burned with the same fierce speed. What was he, Jake Saunders, in all this turbulence? A pawn? A stick to beat Nadine? Why had he not tried to save their relationship, assuage the discontent that had made her yearn for freedom… whatever it was that persuaded her to seek a new beginning without him? They could have found another way forward if he had not chosen the dazzling road, the wild blue yonder.

An ultimatum from Lilian forced Eoin Keogh to salvage what was left of his marriage. At the airport he thumped Jake's shoulder then bear-hugged him. He had been crying, the pouches under his eyes more pronounced, his bombastic personality subdued.

'I have to admit I didn't think your marriage would last a year when I first laid eyes on you,' he said. 'But you've shown a different side to your character. My daughter's lucky to have you.'

'I'm lucky to have her. We'll come and visit you and Lilian when she recovers.'

'I'll look forward to the day.' Eoin sounded too hearty to be convincing. 'Keep the faith, man.'

The morning post was lying in the hall when Jake returned from the airport. The Wharf Alley Art Exhibition was opening next month. He had been invited to attend.

Today was special. Sara Saunders was coming home. In Mount Veronica she lay on the pillow beside Nadine. Red hairs tangled in her tiny fist. Ali began to cry, even though she had psyched herself against disappointment, when Nadine's only response was an involuntary eye movement.

CHAPTER SIXTY-EIGHT

Names. Jake…Ali…Brian…Sara…cockatoos…Sara…tiny? Why tiny. Pulls my hair. Tiny fists… Not Jessica comes…

'Do you feel anything? Is your mind a stone or a sponge? When you blink are you warning me to be silent or twitching in the abyss? I believe you blinked a few times today. Are you listening, Nadine? I know you can hear me. Blink once for yes.'

Blink.

Help me… help me… tell them!

'Two for no.'

Blink… blink.

'Jake is going away with me. Brisbane. You'll be dead by then. All it takes is a flick of a switch. Like your mother. Imagine. A flick of a switch and all his troubles are over. He won't let you haunt him the way you haunted me. Do you hear me? Blink, bitch. You can hear me. You killed my father. Can you hear me? You killed him as surely as if your hands pressed him beneath those waves.'

'Ah… there you are, Jessica. Cold out there today, isn't it. I'll have to ask you to leave now. Nadine's neurologist is dropping by to see her.'

'Goodbye Nadine. Don't worry. You're going to be fine. We're all rooting for you.'

Not Jessica… not Jessica… Tell them… tell them… help me…

CHAPTER SIXTY-NINE

Jake

Wharf Alley Gallery, once a cavernous warehouse, was crowded when Jake arrived. He recognised Chloe, the curator, from her profile photograph on her gallery website and made his way towards her. Chloe's professional smile faded when he introduced himself. She led him through the throng to Nadine's paintings. They had been hung with care in a prime space with good lighting. He had expected ices floes, a boat with streams of bunting, gnarled Alaskan faces, Northern lights above snowy mountain peaks.

No mistake, said Chloe when he asked if she had hung the wrong paintings. She had discussed them with Nadine and these were the chosen four. He studied each one. Broadmeadow estuary at dawn; the rim of gold beyond the viaduct splitting night from day. Sea Aster at twilight; swallows swooping, a soft focus painting until he noticed the split in the front wall, the old house riven. She had painted Shard rehearsing in the barn but it was the young Shard, big hair and denim, sullen Eighties cockiness. The final one was harsh and edgy. An easel with a painting displayed on it. A nondescript study of fruit diagonally slashed, a silver blade on the ground. Jake winced, as if the blade had pressed too deeply into his own skin.

People stopped to discuss her paintings. Jake drank tepid wine and listened to comments about texture, form and theme.

'It's good to see you again, Jake.' Aurora rushed through the crowd and greeted him warmly. 'Nadine's paintings are splendid. But sad, too.'

'Sad?'

'She is showing us the split in life that changes everything.'

He knew what she meant. The painting of the band, he decided, was the only one where there was no sign of a sundering. But he was wrong. He saw the dark frame of the barn window and the motif beyond, almost indiscernible. That fall of red hair she could never tame. Nadine and his future, waiting.

'How is Nadine?' Aurora asked.

'She's stable.'

'No sign of an awakening?'

'Not yet, I'm afraid.' Reluctant to continue this discussion he moved on to the next painting.

'Where is Michael?' She lifted a glass of wine from a tray and followed him.

'Michael?'

'Archangel Michael.'

'On my dashboard, keeping me safe.' What a pity his protection had not included Nadine. He stopped the words in time, reluctant to hurt her feelings.

She held out a small gift bag with 'Not Seeing is Believing' emblazoned on the front. 'This is Paschar, the angel of the veil,' she said. 'Our link between the conscious and unconscious. She's my gift to Nadine.'

For an instant Jake cast his doubts aside, banked down his scepticism. 'Will Nadine come back to me?' he asked.

Aurora shook her head. The overhead spotlight revealed her sparse hair and pale pink scalp. 'I don't know, Jake. The angels only bring messages from those who have passed.'

Her glib response infuriated him. As an atheist his view of life and death was unflinching. Death was the end. Those who claimed otherwise were delusional or, worse, exploitative.

Oblivious to his annoyance, or undaunted by it, Aurora explained how she was a conduit for angel messages beyond the grave. He was furious with himself for having sought comfort, in a moment of weakness, from this charlatan. He should have followed his instincts the first time they met and dumped her tacky little angel in the rubbish where it belonged. That was exactly what he intended on doing with the contents of her gift bag.

'The woman says she's not frightened anymore,' she said. 'She's happy now and at peace.'

Startled, he glanced sharply at her. Her broad forehead was puckered with concentration.

'Her name begins with C… Carol… no… do you know someone who's passed called Carol?'

'No, I don't. I'm not into this psychic stuff.'

Aurora shook her head, as if a fly had flown too close to her face.

'Not Carol… Cora. She's handing you a beautiful white feather.'

She cupped his elbow. He was hardly aware of her grip yet he was moving back to stand before the *Dawn Above the Viaduct* painting. She stared at the road Nadine had painted. A squiggle leading to the jetty where he had sat one morning watching the sun rise. Aurora pointed at a lone swan swimming away from the jetty.

'Cora wants you to know she's not afraid of the swan anymore.' The pace of her speech had quickened. Perhaps the wine was going to her head. Jake was unnerved by her vacant stare.

How on earth did she know Cora's name? She must have read about the accident in a newspaper or online.

Unwilling to listen any longer to such vapid nonsense he glanced across the room in the hope that Chloe would intervene and rescue him but the curator had her back to him. In a gallery full of interesting strangers he was stuck with this crazy charlatan.

'She was blinded by the yellow light,' Aurora said. 'Summer was resting on the tide and the air was filled with musk.'

His stomach turned queasily, the tepid wine souring in his mouth. The floor seemed to shift under his feet. He knew the signs. Focus… focus. He stared at the blade in Nadine's painting, small, sharp, deadly. Gradually the dizziness passed, the black spots faded. Was that how angels appeared to Aurora, quivering against the blank canvas of space. He blinked and rubbed his eyes, terrified he was going to cry in this crowded gallery.

'Excuse me. I need to go outside.' He was shaking uncontrollably when he reached the exit. He had to sit down somewhere before his legs gave way. He leaned against the railing until the trembling stopped. Good guesser, that's what psychics were. They read faces like a map — islands of loss, mountains climbed, bewildered pathways — and exploited people's emotions with this knowledge.

A tour boat passed, its windows glittering. Voices drifted from the gallery. An outburst of shrill laughter sounded unpleasantly against his ears. He returned inside and searched for Aurora in the crowd but was unable to see her. The Shard portrait and the sundered house had red dots on them already. He would buy *Dawn Above the Viaduct*. Chloe promised to send it to him as soon as the exhibition ended but he insisted on taking it with him.

On the tube to Heathrow he imagined the unlit road, two sets of headlights clashing. He visualised a car speeding from Sea Aster. The bend beyond the gate that always required a slowing down before taking the right hand turn onto Mallard Cove. Either car just needed to be slightly over the wrong side of the road for an accident to happen. Theory was not the same as fact. Instinct had no place in a court of law, psychic proclamations even less so.

He took out his mobile and checked back over the hundreds of texts he had received since the night of the accident. Eventually, he found the one he wanted. *Berlin Rocks.* Just two words sent from her mobile. A warning. She knew where he was. He had intended on deleting it but the call from Eleanor came and everything that happened before that moment became irrelevant.

The air was filled with musk. Intimate secretions from animals and plants; an alluring fragrance on his pillow. Hallucinatory throwbacks to torrid nights. Why that word? Its echo vibrated from the tracks, screamed in the whistling tunnels… musk… musk… musk.

'You look wrecked,' Ali said when he arrived home. 'How was the exhibition?'

'Four red dots on Nadine's paintings before the night was over,' he said. 'This one is my favourite.'

'It's beautiful.' Ali stood back to admire the painting. 'Where will you hang it?'

'In Nadine's ward.'

'The perfect place.'

'That woman with the angel shop. Did you ever meet her?'

'Once, when I was visiting Mum.'

'What do you make of her?'

'She scared me… no… that's not true. She made me scared of myself… what I was doing. But it was too late by then.'

'Ali, are you okay?'

'I'm fine… fine. Why are you asking about Aurora?'

'I'm not sure… can you remember anything more about the accident?'

'Like what?' She stiffened, raised her shoulders.

'Could another car possibly have been involved?'

'I was asleep when the car skidded.' Her voice shook. 'All I remember is the wall… knowing we were going to hit it. But I can't talk about it, Dad. I just can't.'

Sara, as if sensing her mother's distress, began to cry. She still had the kitten cry of a very young baby but it had a lusty determination that demanded instant attention. Ali took her from the sling and pressed her to her shoulder.

The evenings were shortening. The grass needed cutting. Tomorrow he would work for a while on the attic before driving to Mount Veronica. The wall, having withstood the force of Cora's car, still formed a solid barricade around Sea Aster. The overhanging trees had a late autumnal glow, as if the green leaves leaching into yellow and russet knew their time was limited and bloomed all the brighter because of it.

CHAPTER SEVENTY

Sensations. *Hot. Cold. Sore. Numb. Sting. Tingles. Pressure. Wet. Dry. Shivery. Fear.*

Sounds. *Ping. Hiss. Bleep. Sigh. Sob. Whish. Whirr. Laugh. Whispers.*

Smells. *Flowers. Food. Disinfectant. Perfume…*

'The kingfisher is a beautiful bird. Deadly and aggressive. Not advisable to mess with it. I watched him slide that feather into your hair. I knew then that my suspicions were right. Stargazing when all you saw was him.

'My mother hated his other women. She never stopped drinking long enough to know they meant nothing to him… or maybe she was drinking because she knew she was included in that truth. I should ask her, I suppose. But we've never been into mother-daughter intimacies and, to be honest, I don't care one way or the other.

'When I read your letters I was angry with him. I believed he'd debased himself. I allowed myself to believe your fantastical lies… your mad ravings. You, my best friend. It was intolerable. I heard them fighting that night. I was used to their rows, the names she threw at him… Saumya, Annalyse, Tara, Lynnette. He walked away from her, as he always did. As I wanted to do. Fifteen… eighteen… what was the difference? I wanted to be with him, not her but what was I to make of your lies and insinuations? I followed him. Do you understand? I *followed* him. He was standing on top of the cliff watching the lightening. Better than fireworks, he said. Better than a shower of meteors. I told him about your letters. Do you know what he called you? A stupid child. A fantasist! Do you know what I called him? A liar. Liar! Liar! I pushed him away when he tried to hold me and ran from him. The wind, I hear it still, screaming in from the ocean, and the thunder. How was I to know he'd slip? The mud turning to sludge. The earth breaking away and he was gone. I never knew. I was running… running to Jake… your letters safe in my keep. Jake would have read them that night. Afterwards, when we were alone. But then… but then…

'He's read them now. All of them. He had to know your whorish secrets… what you were like that summer. Lying in that cave with him when all you were thinking about was my father. Imagining him inside you… *slut*. Strange, isn't it, how your letters destroyed my father and now they've destroyed you?

'Was it as quick for you in the end? You and the sylph and the old woman who should have been put off the road years ago. You were not supposed to be there. I won't have blood on my hands… not now… not then.

'I'll be back again. I know I can trust you to keep my secrets safe in your deep, dark well.

Hand on mouth. Tight. Door closes. Quiet…not Jessica… no…Karin…Karin… Shivers on skin. Water in mouth. Stomach cramps. Can't hold back. Imelda must come. Make me clean again… please… please come. I am soiled. I am nothing.

Jake here. Shame… shame…

'Imelda…Imelda! Nadine needs attention.'

No one comes. Holds his eyes on mine… a new word… jewels… jewels… jewels…

'Look at me, Nadine. Don't think of anything else. None of this matters. You are my love… my love.'

He makes me clean. Basin. Sponge. Towel. Napkin. Opens window. Wind good. Air fresh.

Imelda sorry.

'Terrible that you had to do that, Jake. We need two pairs of hands in this job, cutbacks… cutbacks… Are you sure you can manage? I'm run off my feet this evening.'

'Yes. I'll always manage.'

Jewels… jewels…

'This is your painting, Nadine. It's beautiful. I'm going to hang it here so that you can see it. And this angel, Aurora sends it with her love. I'm leaving it here on your bedside locker. Can you see? The angel of the veil, she calls it. Crazy woman, her and her dancing angels.'

Not jewels… tears! Tears falling everywhere.

And another word… love….

Days pass… words come when I don't struggle. Like snowflakes on my tongue… then gone. Then back. Rain falls. Rain stops. Colours. Sky. Rainbow. Jake here. Kisses. Soft lips. Goes. Samantha drew rainbow and Sam too… and Brian… Ali… rainbow pictures on fridge… rainbow on angel wings… on wall. Rainbow on wall. See it. Count it. Red, orange, yellow, green, blue, indigo, violet. Tap fingers. Seven times. Rainbow angel prism. Is promise. Tap… tap… tap… tap… tap… tap… tap…

CHAPTER SEVENTY-ONE

Jake

Imelda had warned him. Nadine was restless, constant eye twitches, her hand jerking towards the metal frame of the bedside locker and banging against it. Jake sat beside her bed and switched on her iPod. Usually, she was calm when she heard her favourite music but not today. Her knuckles were clenched and reddened as she beat against the metal locker. He tried to ignore the sound, hoping she would become exhausted from the repetitive motion. When this failed he placed his hand over hers, willed her to be easy. Her fingers twitched against his palm and he, aware that he was causing her distress, released his grip.

'Guess what? Feral's had a baby boy. Matthew. She's as bad as Daryl with the mobile. Did I tell you about the attic? Remember you said we should have a window overlooking the estuary. The architect says it's possible. Anything's possible, Nadine. Anything.'

Was Eoin right when he claimed that whistling in the wind was as effective as these rambling one-sided conversations? Nadine's breathing was laboured today, a harsh rasp that worried him. Did she need oxygen? Her head jerked sideways towards the bedside locker. Her eyelids fluttered. He had withstood the temptation to throw the tacky little figurine away and, instead, placed it on the locker in the hope that she could see it. What had Aurora called it? Pasket...or something peculiar like that.

'I spent the morning working in the attic,' he continued. 'I never realised there was so much space up there. It'll make a better studio than the barn. Daryl has drawn up an amazing business plan. All he needs to do is convince the bank to lend. We've decided to call it Tōnality Recording Studio. That was your name. Remember when we were trying to come up with one for our company and you said, "What about Tōnality?"'

Nadine tapped once then stopped. Two more taps at a faster tempo. Three beats and the tempo increased. She ended with four rapid beats and her eyes closed as if the convulsive effort of moving her fist had finally tired her out. She opened her eyes after a moment and banged the locker again. Suddenly, alert to the beat of her knuckles, Jake's body tensed. That awareness, her sharp focus, was she demanding his attention? He listened again. It was the same sequence. Could she possibly be communicating with him in his own language? Crotchet, quaver, triplet, semi quaver? In sync with her beat and hardly daring to breathe, he placed the palm of his hand underneath her finger. Her knuckles, he noticed, were grazed and swollen.

'Tap once if you can hear me.'

Tap!

'Are you making music?'

Tap!

'Do you know me?'

Tap!

'Am I Brian?'

Tap... tap!

'Samuel?'

Tap... tap!

'Jake?'

Tap!

'Oh… my darling… my darling…'

Her eyelashes fluttered, not randomly as he had been led to believe but slowly, as if the muscles controlling them were moving to her own internal command. Sunshine spilled through the window and bathed the ward in a white glare. Her eyes once again slid sideways in the direction of the bedside locker. The angel figurine glistened, its shadow elongated against the wall. Her eyes fastened on the wings, glitzy blue sequins. He was attuned to her emotions, his senses alert to every movement she made.

'Are you frightened, Nadine?'

Tap!

'Are you afraid of the nurses… the doctors?'

Tap… tap!

'Of me?'

Tap… tap!

'Blue? Are you afraid of blue?'

Tap!

Her breathing became stressed.

'Karin was here?'

Tap!

'How often has she come. Once… twice…'

Tap… tap! A trickle of perspiration gathered in the hollow of her throat. Her hand was clammy, cold.

'Many times?'

Tap!

Imelda entered. Her smile disappeared when she heard Nadine's breathing.

'She needs oxygen,' she said. ' I'm going to call Dr Coyle immediately.'

'Car.' He spoke directly to Nadine. 'Was there a car leaving Sea Aster on the night of the crash?'

Tap!

'Do you hear me, Jake?' The nurse's voice carried the full weight of her authority. 'Nadine needs attention. You must leave while I attend to her.'

He paced the corridor until Imelda emerged from the ward.

'Nadine is communicating with me.' He spoke quietly, knowing it was important to remain calm for her sake. 'That's why she's hitting the bedside locker. She's been trying to attract my attention.'

'Involuntary spasms. We've explained this to you already. She's bruised her knuckles quite badly. If it continues we'll have to place her hands in gloves to prevent her hurting herself any further.'

He had seen such gloves, soft but obscenely puffed up like those worn by a boxer, used to prevent patients pulling their tubes out.

'Don't you dare touch her.' His chest heaved. 'My wife is conscious, aware, communicating. I want to see her neurologist immediately.'

'I'm sorry, Mr Saunders.' Imelda's tone became formal, her professional mask keeping him at bay. 'Professor Daly is an extremely busy man and according to the Glasgow Coma Scale – '

'Fuck the Glasgow Coma Scale and listen to me.' Composure was no longer an option. 'Does a woman called Karin Moylan visit my wife?'

The nurse shook her head. 'There's no need to be abusive, Mr Saunders.'

'Does she?'

'I don't recall that name. Check at reception. If she's been here she'll have signed the visitor's book. I know you're upset. Believe me, we all want what's best for Nadine.'

He left her talking to the air and took the elevator to the reception desk. The receptionist showed him the list of names from the previous weeks. She had no recollection of anyone called Karin signing in. Jake scanned the signatures. Not so many visitors now, although he noticed that Hart came regularly. He had talked to Jake about working on Nadine's chakras. Positive energy released into the white light of awareness. No sign of Karin's name anywhere. Jessica Walls had been to see her. Quite a few visits, which surprised him. He had not realised she and Nadine were that friendly. She always came outside visiting hours on Wednesday evening when he was at band practice.

He phoned *Lustrous*. Jessica Walls apologised profusely when he introduced himself. Life was so hectic these days. Everyone in the fast lane. Nadine's accident had caused her to pause and consider what all this rushing around was about. She had intended visiting her and would do so as soon as the latest issue of *Lustrous* was put to bed.

CHAPTER SEVENTY-TWO

The carpark in Mount Veronica was hidden behind a screen of trees. Cars came and went but, as yet, there was no sign of Karin's blue Subaru. Jake parked his mother's car – Eleanor had yet to start driving again – under the sheltering branches. He was still stunned by the speed with which Nadine's medical team had swung into action once they realised she was responsive. He imagined her brain, new pathways criss-crossing each other, forming new connections, new functions and, how, when she held his hand, her grip was a little stronger each time.

He remained out of sight behind one of the pillars in the foyer when Karin entered. He could see her clearly, her pert, confident stride as she approached the reception desk and signed the visitor's book.

'Hello, Jessica.' He was beside her before she looked up. A faint gasp, a pause, her hand fluttering upwards as if to touch her cheek then falling to her side, the signs of shock so fleeting as to be imagined.

Maria, the receptionist, closed the visitor's book and watched as they walked silently towards the exit.

'Nadine is fully conscious,' he said when the automatic doors closed behind them and they stood facing each other.

'I'm glad,' she said. 'She must have been in hell.'

'Yes,' he nodded. 'In a hell of your making. If you ever attempt to contact her again I'll kill you with my bare hands.'

'Kill me, Jake? You desired me once and now you want me dead.' A nerve jerked beneath her eye but, otherwise she remained impassive. Perhaps that was her madness. Not to care or be afraid of the consequences of her actions. What barrier had she stepped across to arrive in that space?

'It's not an idle threat, Karin. I love my wife. I'll do what's necessary to protect her.'

'You think she loves you? Fool! The only man she ever loved was my father – '

'This has nothing to do with your father.'

'It has *everything* to do with him.'

'I don't want to know – '

'You needn't worry, Jake. I'm not going to divulge some pathetic incest confession. My father was a charmer, not an abuser. Those other women meant nothing to him. I could cope with them but it was intolerable when she was my best friend. You read her letters. I had to make you understand what it was like for me, knowing what she did with him… I saw them. Do you understand… I *saw* them together.' Her voice quivered suddenly. 'Have you any idea how that affected me?'

'You caused that accident–'

'It was no accident. She drove my father to his death. All those years I've been tormented… I can't forget… can't forgive. I saw them together… so many times. She thought I didn't notice but how could I not see what was going on… she was trying to steal him away from me. Why couldn't she have been satisfied with *you*? She's to blame for everything…'

A sob refused to break. She touched her throat, as if to free the sound then swung away from him and walked towards the car park. He let her go, afraid of what he would do if he touched her. She had driven away by the time he reached Eleanor's car. He pressed his hand against the door and bent over until he was able to breathe normally.

Berlin rocks. An analysis of the cell site would show that the text came from the vicinity of Mallard Cove on the night of the accident. But what could it prove? Shortly after Cora's funeral, he had hammered a small wooden cross into the spot where she died. Every week he laid fresh flowers there. The guards had inspected the trajectory of the skid. The scum of seaweed that turned part of the road into a greasy slick. Only one set of tyres had been visible. Even they had been washed away when another high tide sent the swans swimming with lofty indifference over the accident scene.

A text bleeped on his mobile. He sat in the car and read it.

'I'm in the beat of your heart, Jake,' **Karin** had written. *'Always remember that. I'll be there until the moment it stops.'*

CHAPTER SEVENTY-THREE

Nadine

A month has passed since my awakening. I struggle with memory. My speech is slurred and slow. I take one step, then two before my knees buckle. The following day I'm back at the bars again, one foot following the other. As a case study I'm presented as a triumph over hopelessness. This is what my medical team believe. My neurologist diagnoses selective retrograde amnesia, a rare condition, he says. I detect a tremor of doubt behind his certainty. I'm a medical mystery, a fragmented woman, whom he's trying to put back together. The odds are against my full recovery. I'm given this information gently but firmly. My coma was profound and prolonged. I'm terrified the dark waves will carry me away again. The events that occurred before my accident are lost but I remember the younger years and, also, the memories I formed when I struggled from the blackness.

Jake collects me from Mount Veronica for my forty-second birthday and wheels me over the threshold of Sea Aster. They are all there to greet me, Donal with his patient smile, Eleanor on a walking stick, Brian with clay under his nails and a new pottery collection called Luminosity. Ali has Sara attached to her hip, and the twins, on Skype, are here in spirit if not in person.

Some memories are as bright as diamonds and as enduring. My heart folds over with love when I rock Sara in my arms and think about the random nature of existence. Ali is here in all her dark, moody beauty because of a faulty condom. Brian with his gift for moulding beautiful shapes exists because I forgot to insert my diaphragm one night when Jake and I argued over something long forgotten and made up with a few moments of frenzied sex. Sam and Samantha owe their athletic prowess to a bout of food poisoning that had expelled the last residue of the Pill from my system when I recovered and slid back into Jake's arms. And I'm here again with all of them because he heard and understood the music I played for him. How content they seem, this family we created. Was it always like this? How could it be so if Jake and I had decided to divorce? My brain is a sponge mottled with gaps that memory once filled. My family's patience is infinite as they explain my past. I can retain this new knowledge but I want my own memories, not those chosen by others.

Ali will leave us soon. Her agent contacted her about a new television series to be shot in London Studios. It's a small part but has, I'm told, the potential to be developed. Opportunities have to be snatched when they orbit past and change direction. Like me, Ali has to begin again.

Mark Brewer has tried to contact her but she refuses to take his calls. She's heard on the Barnstormer grapevine that things are not working out as he expected in New York. Every month he lodges money in an account for his daughter. He sends presents. They arrive by courier, a buggy and high chair, dresses in rainbow colours, sparkly shoes and cute hats.

She and Christine plan to move into Wharf Alley and look after Sara between them. Christine is still a sylph. *The Arboretum Affair* continued to attract full houses while I was steeped in darkness. Ali could return to the cast and work under their new director but she wants a fresh start. No negative echoes, she says, yet I see her grief when she believes she's unobserved. I want her to face her loss. Not hide from it as I once did, seeking oblivion in pain.

My mobile phone rings during the meal. The number of my ID screen is unknown. No one speaks when I answer. The silence vibrates with hatred. She's one memory I retain. Is she listening to my family's voices around the table, the clink of dishes being passed from one to the other, the slosh of wine in glasses? The silence stretches. One of us must break it. I've learned patience during those months in Mount Veronica and she is always the first to hang up.

'Wrong number,' I tell them when her phone goes dead. Only Jake pays attention, his expression alert and tense.

'Was I very unhappy?' I ask him when he drives me back to my ward.

'You needed the freedom to make your own choices,' he says.

'And did I?'

'Yes.' Something in his voice prevents me asking further questions.

He will leave me for a few days soon. Shard are building a German fan base. He worries about leaving me but I'm fine. Madge Brennan has taken me on as her pet project and has organised a visitor's rota that includes some of my old neighbours from Oakdale. I'll be well entertained until he returns. The day has taken its toll. My arms are limp, my mind blank. And once again I'm filled with dread in case I fall headlong back into the void.

Jenny rings to wish me a happy birthday. She tells me about a holiday we spent together, trips we took to Whistler, Grouse Mountain, Vancouver Island. Her words form pictures, ski slopes, snow sculptures, a clock that puffs steam like an old-fashioned train. Lakes glinting like shattered crystal. Someone is standing beside me, not Jenny or her friendly Larry, but someone whose name escapes me until Jenny gently nudges me into the past. Daveth... Daveth...

He came to Mount Veronica. I remember his voice. He talked about a green sky but his words made no sense until now. I close my eyes, almost swooning as my body reacts to what my mind cannot grasp. His hands on my hips, lifting me. Shafts of pleasure slanting upwards and I shudder into the hard thrust of his passion, beg him to reach deeper. I recall how we cried out in that dense space and how the sultry tang of our spent passion perfumed the night.

All is silent in Mount Veronica. It's time to sleep. Instead of fighting the waves that threaten to overwhelm me, I sail with them through the glittering floes.

CHAPTER SEVENTY-FOUR

Jake

Ali returned to London. Until she boarded the plane with Sara, he feared she would change her mind. Ali's role in the fantasy series was minor but her agent believed it would create a new sci-fi fan base. When she told Jake the series was based around a race of superwomen with incredible telepathic abilities he immediately thought of body stockings. Men leering. Ali ordered him to get over himself. Some men would leer at a piano leg, she said, and that was their problem. She said it kindly and nodded, as if she understood when he told her that, as her father, he was programmed to worry about her. It was an incurable condition.

He was alone now but he had no time to be lonely. Nadine hoped to be home for Christmas when all the family would be together again. The attic must be finished by then. Once it was floored and rewired, two skylight windows would be installed in the roof. Light would illuminate the shadows beneath the eaves. The walls also needed insulation and plastering. The settlement from the insurance company for the fire would help but the budget was growing alarmingly. The bank managers Daryl approached with his business plan were not interested. Their attitude, once he mentioned monitors, mixing consoles and multi-track recorders, suggested they were dealing with a regressed teenager.

Undaunted, Jake set up a crowd-funding campaign called Attic Action and invited Shard fans to donate small amounts of money to the establishment of Tŏnality Recording Studios. To his amazement there was an immediate response. This was linked to the Shard website. A Facebook page with photographs showed the various stages of progress in the attic. He posted the Before photographs when the crates, boxes and bags still had to be removed and captioned it, *How is it possible to lose everything in your life except clutter?*

The After photograph was captioned, *De-clutter is the new Xanax. Feel much calmer. Finally believe it's possible to make a fresh start.*

The number of Likes and Comments increased, as did the hits on the Shard website. His tweets on Twitter were read and retweeted. He was in the whirl of social media, feeding information on forthcoming gigs, relaying messages to fans, encouraging comments on *Collapsing the Stone*, releasing sound bites of new songs, retro photographs and posters of the young Shard. He rescued an old electric guitar from one of the crates, restrung it and played it for a YouTube video. This was posted under the caption, *Two old friends reunited.* Rosanna had bought it for him for his fourteenth birthday. This present had led to the formation of the original Shard and Jake blogged about it being his favourite guitar.

Before leaving for Berlin he took a final look around the attic and nodded, satisfied. An electrician had already inspected the attic and the rewiring would begin as soon as he returned. He drove to Mount Veronica. Nadine was sleepy by the time he left, exhausted from the rigorous therapies she endured every day.

The band were staying in an apartment owned by the promotor. They played aboard a boat on the Spree and in beer halls, nightclubs and at a Christmas market. Jake searched for a flash of blue among the revellers, an upraised arm. He would recognise that slender curve from a forest of heaving limbs. He thought he glimpsed her once but the women in the shimmery blue top had spiky blonde hair and a sinewy physique that was at variance with Karin's sensuous form.

It was after two in the morning when he went to bed after the last gig. His mobile rang as he was drifting asleep. He banked down his panic when he realised the caller was not phoning from Mount Veronica. He thought of Eleanor. A relapse? Sara, still so tiny? He lived at a constant level of high anxiety.

'I know my bitch fiancée is with you.' Liam Brett was loudly aggressive. 'Tell her to answer her phone so that I can inform her in person that our sham of an engagement is off.'

'Tell her yourself,' Jake replied. 'She's not here.'

'Don't mess with me, Saunders. Put her on the phone.'

'You heard me. She's *not* here.'

'How's that then?' Liam demanded. 'She's been to every fucking gig you ever played. Why should this one be any different?'

'Because you've moved to Brisbane.'

'Brisbane? What the hell – '

'Gold Coast… beach wedding. Fresh start. Don't tell me Karin was lying.'

'Put her on now and I'll talk to her about lying.' The slurred words were followed by a clatter, as if Liam had dropped his phone.

Jake felt an unexpected sympathy for the other man, drunk and at the mercy of his own imagination. They had each experienced that same high octane passion and were now hollowed out. Karin Moylan was like a moth that flew too close to the flame, seeking its heat, not just for her own searing but for those she chose to fly with her.

'Listen, Liam, I don't know what's going on between you and Karin but it's nothing to do with me. I'm in Germany and it's two in the morning – '

'I know where you are. She's not the only one who reads your Facebook page. You've done everything you can to break us up and you've succeeded. You're welcome to her, you pathetic fuck.'

Jake ended the call and stepped outside to the balcony. The city still rocked, the sky flared ruby-red. No sign of blue anywhere.

CHAPTER SEVENTY-FIVE

Outside Dublin airport the queue for taxis moved briskly.

'Mallard Cove?' The taxi driver sighed heavily when he heard Jake's address. 'You could walk there in the time it'll take me to drive you. Have you any idea how long I've been queuing for a decent fare?'

'I haven't a clue.' The man's obvious displeasure provoked an angry response from Jake. 'And I'm too tired to work out the maths.'

They remained silent on the short journey, apart from a low expletive from the driver when the taxi juddered over a pothole on Mallard Cove.

'What happened there?' His truculence was replaced by curiosity when he saw the blackened walls of the barn.

'Arson,' Jake replied. His hands, he realised, were clenched into fists.

He paid the driver and removed his luggage from the boot. At the front door he stopped. Something was wrong. He could not name it or, even, define what he was experiencing but it trembled through him. He seldom used the back entrance since Sea Aster had been made whole again but he quickened his pace and hurried around to the side of the house. His feet crunched on pebbles as he walked towards the parking bay. She had parked her car where she always left it when she came to see him.

He leaned against the wall, his legs weakening, and imagined sliding slowly, spine against stone, to the ground. To coil into a shell of nothingness. He remained upright, breathing deeply as he inserted his key and unlocked the back door. The first thing he saw when he entered the breakfast room was her blue pashmina, neatly folded and draped over the back of a chair. He lifted it to his face. The scent of her perfume still clung to the cashmere. She had made coffee. The cup was cold, scum on the surface. The purple imprint of her lips against the white rim. She had curled on the sofa, as she had done so often in the past, her arms clutching a cushion to her chest or luring him downwards to lie beside her. One of the cushions had been thrown to the ground, the other still bore the indent of her body. Nadine said her comatose state had been like a disjointed dream, like music played off-key, like words that tangled together and made no sense. In her confused recollections she believed her father and Karin had been together in the ward. It was an uncertain memory, one of many that made no sense to her. But, now, it made sense to Jake. That was the only way Karin could have acquired a key, made a copy. How many times had she come here with Eoin? She would have flattered him, stroked his ego… and what else? Jake closed his eyes against the sudden image of them together. But, no, she would have kept him at bay, expressed her reservations about married men. A breed conditioned to lie and cheat.

In his bedroom he straightened the ruffled duvet cover, aligned a pillow that was slightly askew. His legs finally buckled under him and he sank to the bed, unable to move. One of his shirts lay across the bed, the one she had worn on the night she revealed the truth to Nadine. She had left a bottle of perfume on the bedside locker. He opened the top and sniffed, remembering the bed linen he had stripped from his bed, the tantalising scent of her body on the pillow cases.

She had climbed the stairs to what was once Nadine's apartment. Even though nothing was disturbed in the bedroom he knew she had been there. She had opened empty drawers that were once filled with Nadine's clothes, trailed her fingers over shelves that had held her hats and shoes, left fingerprints on the dusty dressing table.

His thoughts slowed as he walked across the landing, his heart lurching painfully with each step he took. The sun shone through the narrow landing window, as if the winter solstice had come early to illuminate a new beginning. Dust mites danced in the glare, a translucent swirl that moved with an even more frenetic energy when he coughed, his throat so dry he found it difficult to swallow.

The folding stairs descended from the open maw of the attic. He set his foot on the first step and listened for a sound from beyond the trapdoor. The air seemed thicker, suspended in the viscid fear seeping from him. Only his harsh breathing broke the stillness. The slats were steep and the frame of the folding stairs shook as he climbed. He hesitated when his hand touched the trapdoor. For an instant longer he could believe his imagination was running amuck. He could believe that everything would be exactly the same as he had left it four days previously when he locked the door to Sea Aster and drove away.

The truth forced him forward. He climbed the final steps and entered the attic. When he called her name his voice had a detached fierceness, as if it belonged to someone else. Only echoes answered him. His eyes, drawn towards the wall on his right side, closed instinctively as the shadows separated. They formed a tableau, frozen, delineated, eternal. He fell to his knees. It was no longer possible to pretend. To imagine another scenario, a love story with a different ending, a tangled thread realigned into a perfect skein. He could mark the pathway of their journey towards this moment in all its fervour and its flaws. Unintended circumstances, inevitable consequences.

She could have been sleeping except for the twist of her body, the rigid tendons on her hand, her grip still on the microphone. He pressed his hands over his eyes but sightlessness would allow no mercy. He must bear witness to what lay before him.

His old electric guitar had been pulled from its stand and lay face downwards beside her. He reached out but drew his hand back before he touched the marbled slab of her cheek. He stepped backwards until the rim of the trapdoor edged his foot. He slipped once on the slats and grazed his shin as he climbed down. The pain hardly registered.

A squad of garda cars arrived quickly. Two guards climbed before him into the attic. The younger of the two, obviously new to the job, put his hand over his mouth. The older guard's voice was clipped with authority when she demanded to know where the fuse box was located. The fuse was removed and the inaudible but deadly hum of live electricity was silenced.

When the investigation was completed and Karin's body had been removed, he stumbled outside. Night had fallen. The gates slid open without a squeak. He hunkered down beside Cora's cross. Tomorrow he would lay fresh flowers beside it. Stars glimmered coldly on the water. Karin's fingernails had been mauve-tipped, a chilling colour that suggested time had passed since her heart became a conduit between two electrical charges. A bruise marbled her forehead, blue and waxen as the feathers of a kingfisher in flight.

CHAPTER SEVENTY-SIX

Nadine

Canoeists cut through the Broadmeadow estuary, paddles zipping towards shore. Their brightly coloured safety jackets remind me of exotic birds sighting land. A swan takes to the air in an ungainly rush, wings spread. Suspended against the sky, its body is as sharp as a woodcut. The main bevy cluster close to shore. I've also heard them called a lamentation. A lamentation of swans seems appropriate.

Three months have passed since Karin Moylan's body was discovered in the attic of Sea Aster. I didn't go to her funeral. Even if I'd been able to walk unaided, it would have been unfitting to bring my hatred to the graveside. Death has not lessened its force or softened her memory. Jake stayed with me in Mount Veronica while the ceremony took place. He looked older, his cheeks caved in, his eyes still reflecting the shock of his discovery and the questioning he underwent from the police about his relationship with 'the deceased.'

Death due to misadventure was the coroner's verdict. Faulty wiring. Case closed.

Did Jake suspect what he would find when he returned from Berlin? This question haunts me in the small hours. I want to shake him awake and ask him. Not only did he know the intimacy of her body but, also, the obsessive nature of her personality, her unbounded desire for revenge. Did this understanding make him culpable? Or did free will determine the course of action open to her? Perhaps, someday, we'll be able to talk about such things… but for now I'm content to hold him when he moans and awakens from his own dreams. I comfort him then, as he comforted me when I was helpless and locked into my own terrors.

Can I forgive her? I hope so. Otherwise, what is the difference between us? If I am to heal fully I must not harbour a festering wound.

Twilight hangs over the estuary. A pewter stillness, the water so smooth it reminds me of ice. Alaska is a dream I lost. I let it go willingly. Daveth still phones every week. He mentions someone occasionally, hesitantly. He will tell me more, I feel, in the months to come. And I'll be happy for him.

The heron stands motionless at the water's edge. Nothing disturbs its concentration, neither the traffic pounding across the motorway bridge, nor the shrill voices of the canoeists as they pull their canoes over the pebbled waterline. Is it the same one I drove past on the night I fled from Jake, trying to banish the image of her as I drove recklessly along this pitted road?

I'm stiff when I rise from the jetty. My feet are still weak. I'll need a walking frame for some time yet. But this evening I ventured out without it. Each week I grow stronger in body. I defy medical predictions, thumb my nose at weighty opinions that decreed my mind would be a broken thing. Hart says all my memories will return if I'm patient and respect the energy of my chakras. He touches the base of my spine and travels upwards, pausing at each chakra until he reaches the crown of my head. Can I feel the energy of his belief, he asks and I nod.

Positive energy pulling me away from the negative. I visualise my memories as a patchwork quilt, ragged edges that I must carefully sew back into place.

Sea Aster is for sale. The new owner will be unafraid of ghosts. Where will we live? A mews or a country cottage? A town house or an apartment overlooking the sea? A shipping container? We'll decide in time. The only decision that matters has already been made.

Jake comes towards me, anxious in case I slip on the uneven surface. He holds me steady when I stumble. I recover my balance and my step is steady as we make our way back to the old house. We close the door behind us. Brian was right. A perfect divorce is an illusion. So, too, is a perfect marriage. It's love that makes it worth the struggle.

LETTER FROM LAURA ELLIOT

Dear Reader

Thank you so much for reading *The Betrayal*. I hope you enjoyed the story. Writing *The Betrayal* was an all-consuming experience. It took longer than I anticipated and, as I worked on the plot, built up my characters, teased out their personalities and issues, it seemed, at times, as if I would never bring all the strands to a conclusion. It's a work of fiction but some of the locations exist. Like the Broadmeadow Estuary, for instance, although Mallard Cove and Sea Aster are figments of my imagination.

I live close to the Broadmeadow Estuary and love walking along its shoreline. I paced it over many hours as I contemplated the lives and loves of my characters and always came home refreshed, ready to sit down at the computer to begin working again.

I have a passion for writing. This passion overcomes the necessity of working in isolation, of turning my back on a sunny day when I have a deadline to meet, of tearing out the heart of a story when it's not working and beginning again.

Writing the words 'The End' and letting a book go on to its next stage is an exhilarating yet difficult experience. Once that happens the book belongs to the reading public. It can be liked or disliked, praised or criticised, discussed or ignored – that is part of its journey - and when some of that reader reaction comes back to me it is always valued. I know then that someone has read my work and I appreciate that they have taken the time to contact me.

I'd love to hear your opinion of *The Betrayal* and hope you will read my other books: *Fragile Lies*, *Stolen Child* and *The Prodigal Sister*. If you'd like to **keep up-to-date with all my latest releases**, just sign up here: www.bookouture.com/laura-elliot

You can also contact me on my website or my author page on Facebook.

Laura

 @elliot_laura

 www.facebook.com/lauraelliotauthor

lauraelliotauthor.com

Printed in Great Britain
by Amazon.co.uk, Ltd.,
Marston Gate.